TRADING DOWN

STEPHEN NORMAN

Disclaimer

This is a work of fiction. Most of it happens inside an investment bank. The cast includes good people, bad people and management consultants. The bank is not any particular bank, and the people are not particular people, and any similarity to any particular bank or individual is entirely coincidental. But still, if you have worked in this bizarre hothouse, I hope you will recognize *us*.

A list of players and
a guide to acronyms and jargon
can be found at the back of the book.

Scene from the Schuster video

21 Nov 2007

[Dubai Police Archives JD-100343/07B]

After breakfast, Robert Schuster and his wife take a taxi to the Dubai Mall, where they part. She has no interest in construction, and he has no interest in shopping. For the next two hours, he walks the hot, dusty lots of downtown Dubai, circling the vast building site where the Burj Khalifa is being built. Bob Schuster loves tall buildings and the Burj is already the tallest building in the world. You can buy postcards at the hotel, but Bob wants a more personal record to take back home.

It is tough to find a good spot. 'Too much other crap,' he mutters, as each site is rejected. Finally, he comes across a walled fountain in front of a large bank. It is the perfect spot. It takes him less than a minute to set up the camera on the marble wall and start filming. You have to be quick with these things. Already he can hear officious shouting from the guards outside the big glass doors.

His first shot shows the forecourt beyond the fountain. A few figures walk across it. One of them is a woman, approaching the bank. She is immaculately dressed in a gold sari, and she is carrying a shopping bag in each hand. They seem heavy. She walks slowly. She could be a wealthy client, except that rich people do not walk in downtown Dubai.

Bob Schuster is not interested in her; he zooms across the road, across the acres of piled earth and discarded steel, to the ground floors of the Burj Khalifa. He provides his own commentary. It is full of technical details about the concrete and the cladding. After admiring the lower floors, the camera swims slowly upwards. One hundred and fifty floors flow by in dizzy procession. On the 150th floor, the construction workers are still laying steel. The building will not be opened for another couple of years, in January 2010.

The camera picks up other voices nearby, shouting. They disturb Bob Schuster's commentary. Irritated, the camera abandons the heights and swings down and left, onto the entrance of the bank, just 50 metres away.

The woman in the sari is now standing in front of the bank. She has put her shopping bags down. A security guard confronts her. He is shouting in

Arabic, pointing, telling her to go away. She turns and looks directly at the camera for a moment. We understand the guard's confusion. She is wearing fancy swimming goggles with holograms of sharks on them. The white teeth of the sharks flash in the sunlight. The camera is transfixed. Bob Schuster is silent.

She rubs her hands inside one of her bags, as if she was washing them, and presses them on the white limestone wall, just beside the main door. The camera zooms in, shows two small, dark handprints. Now the guard is furious and for the first time he lays hands on her, scolding, threatening, pushing her away.

But she's ready for him. She takes a red, plastic can from the bag on the left. It has a spout. Swiftly, she sprays it at him. A thin stream of liquid splashes over his face. He runs inside, clutching his eyes. While he's gone, she kneels down and empties the rest of the can over herself. It takes a while.

One hears Schuster's voice, "Oh my God, oh my God."

Another security guard comes out. He waves his pistol at her. She holds out a small, rectangular object in one hand. He seems frightened of it and backs away. He wants to shoot her but can't bring himself to do it.

Still kneeling, she takes a second can from the other bag and pours it on her body. Now her sari is wet, almost see-through. It clings to her full breasts and buttocks. She bends forward, rests her forehead on the ground. Both security guards are out now, guns drawn. She holds out the plastic lighter again and they back off.

Not far enough. The camera catches the first, tiny spark from the lighter and instantly there is an envelope of flame, twenty feet across. The guard who was splashed catches fire. He runs towards the fountain - and the camera - but he cannot see where he's going. Halfway he falls over and lies writhing. He has made the mistake of breathing in. Pale blue and orange flames caress his face.

Behind him, the figure of the woman can be seen. She could be dancing in a nightclub. Her hands are together, above her head. The sari is gone, the hair ablaze, strangely floating upwards in the flames. One leg on the ground, the other lifted, every part of her is on fire.

We hear Bob Schuster's voice again, shaking, crying. The camera keeps running. Later we see him in a small crowd around the guard with the burned face, trying to help. There is nothing left of the woman in the sari except charred limbs, still smouldering.

Before the movie ends, we hear Bob's voice for the last time.

"No-one knows who she is. They don't know why, they don't know shit."

1

Sana'a, Yemen, 2007

Three weeks earlier - Thursday

Fear stalked Zahra down the narrow streets as she hurried homewards. It was the hour of qat. Every few yards, she had to step around old men, squatting against the walls, wearing old dirty thawbs with their curved Yemeni daggers dangling from the waist. Their cheeks bulged with huge balls of masticated leaves and their eyes, red-rimmed, followed her listlessly as she passed. Young beggars held out their hands, hopeful for bakshish, except for the boy, Asif, who had no hands.

They were familiar, almost friends. She had no fear of them.

Noon prayers had finished half an hour ago, and the souk had been briefly flooded with the faithful going home to eat. Three or four young men had come into the shop. They wore knitted caps and had long, wispy beards. They were zealous and looking for an excuse to be angry.

"Why is she not wearing her niqab?" asked the leader.

Old Abdullah spat. "Am I her father or mother?" he replied. "They are foreigners. They have their own customs."

"The will of Allah knows no borders," said the other, pious and angry at the same time.

One of the boys had started to play with the little mountains of spice, picking up a handful of ground cumin, scattering it in the fenugreek. Old Abdullah shouted and threatened him his ancient thorn bush stick.

The boys were annoying but Zahra was not afraid of them.

No, what had frightened her was the man with the camera. He had appeared from nowhere, dressed in a dirty white thawb with a worn black jacket. But holding a modern camera and taking pictures. Many pictures. Flash-flash-flash. Pointing at her, in her face, like a gun going off. He hadn't said a word, he had invaded the dim, aromatic silence of the spice shop with his electronic weapon and within a minute, he was gone again. She felt violated, exposed, as though the flash had penetrated her garments. What was he doing? As she reached the safety of the street door and started up the long winding stairway, she wondered what she was going to tell her mother. If anything.

It was 2.10pm. Zahra's mother was pleased to see her so early. Jafar's flight would have landed by now, and he always called, right from the baggage hall. Gurjit wanted everything perfect when her husband arrived. Zahra had brought the meat with her, and they started to prepare dinner. Zahra was calm now. She decided to keep quiet about the man with the camera.

Half an hour went by. Every few moments, Gurjit would steal a glance at the clock, and then at her old phone, lying silently on the table. A few weeks ago, Zahra had stolen it. It had been returned, modified. Now whenever Jafar phoned or sent a text, it made a noise like a bullfrog.

2.40pm came and went and the phone refused to croak. Gurjit hid her anxiety. Her daughter would just laugh, and tell her not to be neurotic.

"Excuse me, mother, just a moment..." said Zahra, picking up her phone and checking for messages. Zahra, too, was beginning to get anxious, but she didn't want to worry her mother. Her mother was wonderful, but most of the time she didn't know what day it was, let alone the hour. Time and money, said family lore, those were Dad's jobs. And a good thing too.

She sent him a quick text: *Dad, where are you???*

Then she went next door to check the internet. The family room was light and airy, with a window that looked over Jami' Kabir, the great mosque of Sana'a. It was too light and airy for Ben. Four years ago, when he was barely twelve, he had created Ben's Box, a tiny room within a room. It stood in the corner with walls made from the thick, dark blankets, which he had liberated from his mother. Soon afterwards, Ben and the family's computer had disappeared inside.

Presently, a sign appeared, pinned to the blankets. It said simply 'My name is Ben.' There had never been an explanation. He simply refused to answer to 'Anwar' any more, and the family had gone along with it.

Since then, Ben had spent most of his time in the Box, lit only by the light of the screen, exploring worlds that he could not explain and no-one in the family, not even her father, really understood.

"Get off, get off, Zahra," came Ben's voice.

"I need the computer. Now."

"The internet's down."

"No, it's not, you lying camel."

Zahra was back in the kitchen a few minutes later, triumphant.

"Dad's flight is an hour late. Due in 2.48."

"Oh," said Gurjit, relieved. She hadn't wanted to ask and nowadays she avoided the computer. It was full of unpleasant surprises. She stared at the sink, seeing the disgusting images floating in front of her. Someone in her family had found them, had – what was it called? – *downloaded* them. Had drooled over them. One of the boys, surely. Not Ben, he was too young. Not Ahmed, he never used the computer. But Mahmoud was so pious, so disapproving of almost everything. Surely not Mahmoud?

This speculation led on to a new and unpleasant thought. Gurjit pushed it aside and went to the store cupboard. Black olives, hard goats' cheese and a loaf of bread appeared on the table.

"If your father is going to be late, we shan't eat now. We will eat tonight. Get out the plates, I'll wash some fruit."

But the unpleasant thought would not leave her. Jafar had been behaving oddly. He was due back from Dubai two days ago. Then yesterday. But he said he had meetings. The first time, it was the bank, very urgent. And the next day, with some supplier. But suppose - suppose - he had *met someone*. She was not a fool, Gurjit told herself. Jafar liked women, and women liked him. After Ahmed was born, she had been unwell and stayed in hospital. Jafar had befriended that young nurse. She had wondered a lot about that nurse, but she had never dared to ask him.

And now, all these urgent meetings? He had made a joke the other day about the Lebanese girls in the Dubai travel agency. Weren't Lebanese girls notorious? Perhaps there were no meetings. Perhaps he was carousing with a girl from Beirut. In a hotel room. She had a sudden, vivid image of that hotel room. Such images appeared spontaneously nowadays, ever since she came across those disgusting pictures on the computer.

She told herself not to be stupid.

"Don't just stand there, Zahra, put the food out. Your brothers will be back soon."

Mother and daughter took the food through to the small square table in the family room. The table was covered with an old, white linen cloth. Although clean, it was dappled with faded tea stains and cigarette burns, and every one of them marked a happy occasion. This was where the family gathered when their father came home. Jafar would relax, a cigarette in one hand and a small glass of black tea in the other, and entertain his children with tales filled with his money and the rascals who wanted it. And spices. Jafar Hashemi loved spices and would talk lovingly of them.

"That old Turk, he was a rogue but his rosewater! Mashaa Allah, I would die happy smelling that rosewater, sweet as a virgin's hair with a hint of musk." At these moments, Gurjit would scold him from the kitchen, just a few feet away through the small, open doorway.

"Jafar, that's enough of that!"

Jafar would shake his head at his daughter, and smile, as if to say "what a tyranny we live under," and go on telling his stories of the spice markets. And of aeroplanes. He never seemed to take a flight without some adventure. Engines that failed. Precious bags stolen by customs. Violent storms and lightning strikes.

"And I promised myself, if we reach ground safely, I will give all my children a surprise..." With that, Zahra and her brothers would all start screaming and laughing, knowing that he was about to pull presents from the battered camel skin bag that was his only suitcase. Sometimes these presents would appear magically from his jacket, or even out of his children's ears.

Then he would laugh his big, deep laugh and question his children:

"Have you been good at school today, Zahra? Are you top in Maths? What, no? Then you cannot be my daughter! There must be some mistake! If you were my daughter, you would be top in Maths, and Physics. And Astronomy. We Persians invented Astronomy, you know..."

His teasing concealed a small well of sadness. Jafar Hashemi had hoped for a child who was as clever as he was. It was not until Ben's arrival that his wish was granted. Although Ben was different. The older children used to tease their father about Ben, "Well, you prayed to Allah for a clever kid, father, you should have been more specific."

There were noises outside and Mahmoud and Ahmed walked in, panting slightly from the six flights of steep stone stairs. Mahmoud was Gurjit's eldest son. When Jafar was away, he was the man of the house and she relied on him more and more.

"Sorry we're late, mother," said Ahmed, "we went to Friday prayers."

This was something recent, and disturbing. Jafar was not religious; Ramadan for him was a chance to lose a few pounds – which he rarely did – and he only prayed when his plane was late. But when Mahmoud had started at the Tech, he had caught religion. Not just religion. He had grown a beard and wore a white knitted prayer cap. Now he looked like the young

Yemenis Gurjit saw hanging around the mosques. She felt their contemptuous gaze as she passed, but she refused to wear a burqah like the Yemen women.

"Al-hamdu lillahi rabbil 'alamin," said Mahmoud, "we should always pray."

"I did pray today," said Ahmed.

"Why is that, Ahmed?" said his mother, worried that religion had got to him as well.

"The club finals are in three days. I asked Allah to give me strength, and he did. You wait, I will destroy Grishigar…"

He picked up his older brother by the waist, and tried to throw him to the floor.

"Ahmed! Put me down, you idiot. You are never going to beat Grishigar. How many years has he been the champion?"

"Five. But I have a new strategy."

"He's a baboon," came Ben's voice from inside the Box, "try poisoning his bananas."

"Anyway," said Mahoud, "it took ages to get back from the mosque. Since those foreigners disappeared on Monday, there are police everywhere. Is Father up in the mafraj?"

The mafraj was the room at the top of Yemeni houses given over to the men. Here they would lie, chewing qat in the heat of the day, and let the women get on with the work below. Many women chewed qat as well, mind you, but not with the men.

"He's not home and we won't wait for him," said Gurjit sharply, "now sit down, everyone."

"Ouch! Sounds like Dad's in trouble," said Ahmed.

"Maybe he missed his flight," said Mahmoud, "it wouldn't be the first time. In fact he's getting worse."

For some reason, this appeared to upset his mother even more.

"Something strange happened in the shop today," said Zahra, tactfully changing the subject.

"Go on," said Madmoud.

"Well, these boys came in and started annoying Old Abdullah, and he got his stick out, ready to beat them… He was really mad and I thought there was going to be a fight. But then, suddenly, this man appeared. He started taking pictures with this big camera. Flash! Flash!"

"What of?"

"Different things. The spices. The counters, the store room. Old Mohammed."

This was deceit by omission. For it seemed to Zahra that one object was in every picture. *Herself*. The camera had followed her as she fled around the room.

"Were you wearing your niqab?"

"It's too hot inside that shop, mother."

Gurjit shook her head, exasperated. "She takes it off as soon as she gets through the door," Old Mohammed had once told her, "souk people are talking about it."

Souk people. He meant the locals who lived in the old city and who made the rules. After fifteen years, she and Jafar were still foreigners to the souk people.

"Have you seen this man before?" asked Mahmoud.

Zahra hesitated.

"Yes. He's the driver of the black Mercedes. Sometimes it stops outside."

"How often?"

"Just sometimes." This was another falsehood. Recently the black car had come by almost every afternoon.

"What happens when it stops outside?"

"The window winds down. There's a man inside, wearing these cool silver shades. Looking at me."

"How can you know that, if he's wearing shades?" came Ben's voice.

"Women can always tell,' replied Zahra, with the pride of a new woman.

Zahra was just seventeen, but she always seemed so knowing about men, thought Gurjit. In her own teenage years in India, she had talked to men, gone to school with them, even danced with them. Young, poor Punjabis did not even own sunglasses, but had they *looked* at her? Had they – it was a difficult thought – *desired* her? She had no idea. Gurjit had not taken notice of men, until Jafar had arrived and turned her world upside down.

Gurjit glanced sharply at her daughter. She saw a beautiful young woman, a trifle chubby perhaps, but good bones and her father's laughing eyes. And what was chubby? Yemeni men liked fat women, said souk wisdom, it gave them something to get hold of.

"What was he like, this man in the car?"

"He's fat and ugly. He has a gold tooth. He chews qat, that's all I know."

"What does he wear?"

"A thawb. It was white, but quite dirty. And he had a lot of gold on his fingers."

There was silence. Ben appeared from the Box, driven out by hunger. He looked younger than sixteen. He was pale and thin and his eyes were sunken. As far as Zahra could remember, he had not been outside the house since he got banned from the Tech, almost two months ago. He took a huge piece of cheese and began to eat like a wolf, making little howling noises.

"It sounds like Babu," said Ahmed suddenly, to everyone's surprise.

"Babu? Who is Babu?" asked his mother.

Ahmed was nineteen and a bit simple. He cared mostly about boxing, and wrestling. He was in the provincial wrestling team and dreamed of the Olympics. Of all her children, Ahmed was the one most at home in Sana'a. He had Yemeni friends. His Arabic was old school Arabic of the country, not the modern slang they talked in the Gulf.

"Babu Malik. He's a pimp," said Ben suddenly.

"You don't even know what a pimp is," said Zahra.

"I so do," said Ben, "it's a man who looks after women and sells them for sex…"

"Ben!" said Gurjit, horrified, now she was certain what the word meant. "That's enough!"

"Anyway, how would you know?" asked Zahra.

"Dad told me." There was no arguing with this.

"And Dad told me Babu Malik was 'truly evil'," said Ben.

"Dad says President Saleh is 'misunderstood'," said Zahra, "how do you get to be *truly evil*?"

"I dunno. Once we were coming back from Aden and we got stuck behind this white taxi bus coming out of Taiz…"

"Taxis are yellow, stupid," said Zahra.

"Duh. Not all of them. This one was white with yellow stripes. It was creeping up the hills and Dad said, 'Do you know why it's going so slow? Because it's ashamed.' Then we got to a checkpoint and there was a queue and the white taxi just drove straight up the side and the soldiers ignored it. And Dad started cursing Babu Malik, calling him an evil bastard. But he wouldn't say why."

"So what was inside the taxi?" asked Zahra, who loved mysteries.

"You couldn't tell. The windows were black."

"Well, he's loaded," said Ahmed. "I've seen him down at the gym. When Afsal was in the finals, Babu Malik gave him a thousand riyals and said he could have ten thousand if he won. He had a huge bet on him."

"And did he?"

"Not exactly. The other bloke didn't turn up, did he?"

The family considered this, each drawing their own conclusions.

"He loves betting," said Ahmed. "He's addicted to it. He hangs out with the Army coach and he drinks whisky out of an old apple juice bottle."

There was a disapproving mutter from Mahmoud.

"And he's taking photos of our shop?" said Gurjit, "I don't like it. As soon as your father arrives, Zahra, I want you to tell him the whole story."

But where was Jafar? She started worrying afresh. She picked up some plates and headed for the kitchen. Soon after, the children heard the sound of the TV.

"She is really worried. She's watching the news," said Zahra.

"Uncle Saeed texted me," said Mahmoud. "He hasn't seen Father today. Father had a meeting with the bank and then went straight to the airport."

Zahra went into the kitchen. Her mother was standing, rigid, in front of the TV, watching the national news. Zahra stood beside her. She thought the Yemeni newsreaders looked absurd in their western dress, making jokes and pretending that this was a real country like America or Germany.

It was 1st November, 2007. There was plenty of Yemeni news. There had been a suicide bombing near Aden, and some sailors had been killed. On Tuesday, someone had hijacked a minibus with eight officials from the World Health Organisation. The bodies of two of the foreigners had been found, dumped in a dry wadi forty miles north of Sana'a. Both women, the men were still missing. The army was at the scene. Arrests had been made.

Her mother looked pale.

"They've never killed them," she said, "not in all the years we've lived here. They just kidnap them, collect some money and let them go. They treat them well."

"But this is not the tribesmen, mother. This is AQAP. These are new people, Islamic fanatics."

"AQAP?" said her mother absently.

"Al-Qa'ida in the Arabian Peninsula. A man called al-Wuhayshi is their leader. Everyone's looking for him. And Anwar al-Awlaki."

"I don't know how you know all this, Zahra."

"Online. They put videos on YouTube. Anwar al-Awlaki has a Facebook page."

"I have never heard of Anwar al-Awlaki."

"Oh Mother, you must have. He's an Imam. He lives here but he was born in America. Mahmoud's started watching him. Ben calls him the bin-Laden of the Internet."

"Is that him?" said her mother suddenly. "He looks like a young bin-Laden."

The TV was showing a blurry photo of a young Arab, dressed in white. He had a wispy beard combed to a point under his chin. He was staring out through rimless glasses that made him look like a mole. *A little like Mahmoud*, thought Gurjit to herself.

"No, Mother, that's Abdul al-Omani. He was a bomb maker for AQY, but they caught him. They are going to execute him next Wednesday. In Tahrir Square."

"Oh no, the poor boy. How sickening."

"Ahmed wants to go, all his friends are going."

"Well, he is not going," said her mother. "It's barbaric."

She turned the TV off and looked at the clock. It was 5.15pm. She could feel her heart racing, as though she had just run up the stairs from the street.

"Your father came here because he loved the old city. He loved the old buildings. And the people. Nobody wanted to harm their neighbours. But now, it feels like we are all under attack."

Mahmoud came into the kitchen.

"Mother? I just talked to Uncle Saeed. He says Dad sometimes spends a couple of hours in a hotel by the airport. Before his flight. If you know what I mean." The curls of his beard shook with disapproval.

"No, I don't know what you mean, Mahmoud."

"He drinks whisky, mother. At the hotel. Uncle Saeed says maybe he had one glass too many and missed his flight. It happened once before, he says, just before Ramadan."

"Before Ramadan? No, there was a terrible sandstorm… They couldn't take off…"

"Uncle Saeed says the sandstorm was in the bar of the Dubai International."

"Oh, what a relief that would be," said his mother. Mahmoud looked confused.

Zahra rested her hands on her mother's shoulders and comforted her.

"Let's go into the living room," said her mother suddenly. "At least there's a window."

They stood in silence in front of the big arched opening, watching the square below. The shadows were long and the heat was fading. The city was starting up again and the streets were busy. Beyond the square was Jami' Kabir, the Great Mosque of Sana'a with its twin minarets, and on the right, the gate of Bab al Yaman. Her mother was looking intently at every car, every pedestrian. Hoping.

Zahra's phone rang. She snatched it up. Hope turned to disappointment.

"That was Old Abdullah," she said, "he's at the airport with Ahmed. They've talked to the airline. There's no sign of him anywhere. Or his bag."

Gurjit started to cry, gently. She was no longer worried about Lebanese hussies, she was just afraid.

"You know, I hated that stupid frog noise, but now... I just want it to croak."

The long, rising cry of the muezzin suddenly floated in from the minaret of Jami' Kabir, calling the faithful to Magrib, the prayers at dusk.

"And I hate that noise," said Gurjit.

"What? The muezzin?" replied Zahra, taken aback. "It's just a man, singing."

Her mother had been brought up a Hindu, and had stayed true. She had a small shrine outside her bedroom and every day she made puja, putting fresh fruit in front of the gods. As a child, Zahra had been fascinated by Shiva and Ganesh with his elephant head, and never tired of hearing the old stories. But Gurjit had let her children be brought up as Shia Muslims like their father.

"It's a man singing. This country is all about men. And he's shouting, not singing."

"It's not Chittorgarh, mother. It's not a siege."

"Oh, you have the tact of an elephant, Zahra! Don't remind me of that awful story."

Well, you told it to us, thought Zahra *and it gave me nightmares for weeks afterwards.* Chittorgarh, a great and ancient fortress in Rajasthan, was besieged by the Muslim army of Bahadur Shah. When defeat was inevitable, the defenders lit a huge pyre of firewood and charcoal. While the men went out to die on the battlefield, their women formed a long line.

One by one, they dipped their palms in paint and made a handprint on the wall. Then they walked silently into the flames. Zahra often wondered about those Hindu women. What were they thinking? "This is my only memorial, my fragment of immortality?" Did they hesitate? What did it feel like, to *burn*?

She tried to think of something else. A big white taxi cruised slowly into the square below. It headed for one of the little streets that led to the souk. A cart with a donkey was in the way. The taxi gave a loud blast on its horn. The driver leaned out the window, shouting and waving his American baseball cap. The cart driver yelled back. The donkey, startled, joined in. For a minute, its hoarse braying drowned out the muezzin. It sounded like a strangled giant gasping for air. Then the driver whipped up the donkey, and the taxi squeezed past it. The donkey gave it a kick as it passed. The taxi disappeared into the depths of the souk.

Her mother started to weep. "Oh, Jafar, Jafar, my darling, where are you? Come home, please come home now."

Zahra hugged her mother. "I wonder if Dad got that CD for me?" she said brightly, desperate for something ordinary to talk about.

"What?"

"The new Britney Spears CD."

"Really," said her mother, "what a ridiculous thing to be thinking about."

"I hope he has. I'm sure he has. Dad never lets me down."

In times to come, Zahra would be haunted by these words. Every time she remembered them, she was ashamed. It was the guilt that stalked her, it was the little voice that said *you were spoiled and foolish and Allah has punished you.* And sometimes the little voice went on: *If you had not said those words, it would all have turned out differently.*

2

Hong Kong, 2009

Two years later

It was already raining when he left the hotel. The taxi turned uphill, towards Victoria Peak. The mountain was disappearing into cloud and the tramway had stopped. The buildings all around him were flashing neon signs that meant 'Tropical Storm warning' but Chris Peters didn't notice. His thoughts were back in the office. A tense, tricky day. The first Triple Witching for Portia, only two weeks after the system went live. Big trade volumes, pension funds rebalancing their portfolios, the hedge funds piling in like a pack of dogs, looking for scraps. A lot of stress for the new system and a lot of stress on the Portfolio desk.

And then there was this rumour from London. Chris hadn't heard it himself, one of the traders had told him.

"But Tom's your boss, right? I thought you would know. Don't you IT guys talk to each other? Jesus."

Apparently Cyrus had said something on the morning call. Just a hint. He had asked his management team to keep it to themselves. Hah! Naturally it was all over the planet by lunchtime.

Chris hadn't had time to call anyone in London and now he had no signal. Anyway, Dom would know more, assuming he could get to Dom's party in this weather.

The cab shuddered sideways as a gust of wind struck it, and the rain and the darkness were suddenly upon them. The rain fell in buckets thrown from the side. Chris had never seen anything like it. It was like sitting in a carwash. He looked up. The apartment blocks on the mountainside above were disappearing, wreathed in thick clouds that fled across them. The lights of Central below were dim, the harbor invisible.

The road got steeper as they climbed up the Peak, and the cab's wheels slipped on the corners, where the rainwater was already piling up, splashing onto the concrete roadway in muddy fountains. Chris gazed at the staring eyes of young Lee Mun Fook on the dashboard. Hong Kong taxi driver No. 11049. It looked like a police mugshot. The man actually gripping the wheel and gunning the motor had ancient, leathery skin with deep wrinkles and fingers stained with nicotine. Perhaps he was Lee Mun Fook's dad. Perhaps it was an old photo. Who knew?

After an age, the taxi stopped with a jerk on a patch of worn asphalt. A river of brown water was streaming across it. Lee Mun Fook senior pointed upwards and grunted. Chris looked. They were under a big, apartment block with a curved front wall. The gloomy hulk of the building disappeared upwards into the mist and rain. It made Chris dizzy. It was like the hull of an ocean liner seen from below. He hoped it wouldn't sway. He hated tall buildings, especially in high winds, and Dom's flat was on the twenty-fourth floor.

It was twenty yards to the glass doors. The rain drenched him like a warm shower. He hadn't packed a raincoat and in the four months he'd been here, he hadn't got round to buying one. While he waited for the lift, two girls ran in, waving the ruins of their umbrellas at the concierge and giggling. Western girls dressed for a party. One was tall, with long blonde hair, darkened in streaks by the rain. She was wearing a smart white raincoat. But it was short, and did not quite cover the turquoise silk dress beneath, a weakness that the rain had instantly exploited. The damp silk clung provocatively to her thighs as she crossed the foyer on long, elegant legs. Chris could not take his eyes off them.

"And what's wrong with my face?" she said, stopping in front of him. Chris looked up, embarrassed. There was nothing wrong with her face. A high forehead, long nose, strong chin. Generous lips beneath wide, grey eyes. About his age, low thirties, maybe younger. But her voice put him off. Home Counties. Golf club. Not his type.

Her companion giggled. She was a head shorter, with dark hair that curled in towards her chin and framed a pretty oval face with freckles and a cheerful, perky nose. Pixie-like, thought Chris. She was younger than her companion, late twenties perhaps.

"Olivia, leave the poor man alone, he looks like a drowned rat himself." An Irish lilt.

Chris saw himself reflected in the lift doors. OK, his black Chinese jacket was soaked down one side and dripping water on the floor. True, his jeans had dark patches down the front. But his face was good. An angular jaw, straight nose, dark eyebrows. Closely cropped black hair. The water had run off it. He looked like a US Marine. Nothing rat-like about him.

The lift doors opened.

"Twenty-fourth, please," said Olivia, as though talking to an invisible doorman. Presumably him.

"That's where I'm going," said Chris.

"Not with us, you're not, I don't think we've met," said Olivia. She put a hand across her nose and sniffed loudly.

"Livi, will you stop that sniffing?" said her friend. "Here, you can borrow my hanky." She giggled again. Chris liked her. He suspected they had downed a couple of drinks down in Wan Chai. The lift doors closed.

"You're a geek, aren't you?" said Olivia suddenly.

"Sorry?"

"You're one of Dom's geeky friends."

"I work in IT, yes. And yes, Dom is a good mate."

After that they both ignored him. Dom opened the door, Guinness in hand. He was wearing baggy trousers and a luminous, lime green shirt. Both girls threw their arms round him and kissed him, and he hugged them in return. It didn't seem fair. Dom was a geek as well. He wasn't even a handsome geek, he was a small, dark, ugly lad from Belfast with a pale, freckled complexion and a taste for brightly coloured shirts. And parties.

There were eight or ten people already standing in Dom's living room. The girls disappeared into the bathroom. Dom thrust a can of Murphy's into his hands and nodded sideways.

"Let's go into my bedroom." Dom closed the door and the noise of the party receded.

"Did you hear the news?"

"About Tom resigning?" said Chris. "Yeah, one of the traders told me. Cyrus said something on the morning call."

Tom was their boss. Head of Equity Technology. Tough, competent, unloved.

"It's true. I got a text from him. He's going to Mitturi Bank. He's going to join John Taylor. They were at London Capital together, remember?"

Well, that figured. John Taylor was a maniac who'd joined Mitturi Bank last year. He'd promised the business he could replace the bank's trading systems with a new home-grown mega system called Carbon. In two years. That was classic Taylor snake oil. What was sad, the business believed him. They gave him a big pot of gold and a licence to hire talent – whatever the price. Chris had had a couple of calls himself, but he wasn't interested. He loved his present job.

"So what now?" said Dom after a pause. "What's van Buren going to do?"

Their boss Alexis van Buren was Chief Information Officer of the Global Markets division of SBS, which was a fancy way of saying that he ran IT in the investment bank. Global Markets traded bonds, equities, foreign exchange, commodities and all the derivatives thereof around the world. The bank was big into everything, in fact. Except subprime mortgages, thank God, so it had survived the banking crisis of 2008 without going bust. Derivatives trading was technology heavy, and Global Markets consumed as much computer power and employed as many programmers as the rest of the bank put together. Van Buren was a quiet, unassuming person, considering his responsibilities. Dutch, thorough, slow moving, blunt. John Uzgalis called him 'stubbornly indecisive'. Such impieties were above Chris' pay grade. Van Buren was God.

Chris reflected. He hadn't thought about it until now.

"He's gonna think about it. Then next week, he's going to call you. 'Dom, my man, how would you like to run Equity Tech?'"

"Fuck off, Chris," said Dom, punching him on the shoulder, "van Buren hardly knows me. When did he last come to Hong Kong? Fucking yonks ago."

"Cyrus won't let him think about it too long. Stay close to your Blackberry."

Dom told him to fuck off again. He didn't tell Chris to stay close to his own phone. Which was fair enough. Chris had no desire to climb the management ladder.

"Did you hear about Neil Jenkins?"

"No," said Chris.

"He's been promoted. He's the new head of TIS."

"What? You're kidding me. He's only been here five minutes."

But Dom swore it was true, he had it direct from the horse's mouth. TIS or Technology Infrastructure Services ran all the bank's computers, from the bankers' laptops to the tens of thousands of servers in the datacentres, as well as the storage, network and the phones. Not to mention Information Security, IT purchasing and the help desks. It had an annual budget of over £1 billion and employed 5,000 people.

"Well, he did fix the network," said Dom, "but it's bad news for the iPhone brigade. We'll be the last bank using Blackberries."

Neil Jenkins was famously anti-Apple. iPhones, iPads, Macbooks… they were all toys to him and he refused to let them on the bank's network. His mantra "we won't connect what we can't control," was oft repeated - with admiration by Information Security, with loathing by everyone else.

Chris mulled it over. The rapid ascent of Neil Jenkins was significant to him for personal reasons that he did not share with Dom.

The two girls came out of the bathroom. The dark Irish pixie was half-smiling, a warm, secret look. But it was the other one – Olivia, was it? – who stole his attention. She was just closing her handbag. Her hair was dry now, but she was still sniffing. She moved like a gazelle in her blue silk dress. It had a big bow at the back, half hidden under the cascade of blonde hair. The way she moved, the way she smiled… she was strikingly attractive and she knew it. Chris found her intimidating but he could hardly take his eyes off her.

The Irish girl caught his eye and smiled at him and he dared to go over and say hi. The gazelle ignored him and wandered off, but her friend was happy to chat. Her name was Liz. Yes, from Dublin. Yes, she lived in Hong Kong. What? No, she was a recruiter. IT staff, mostly, that's how she knew Dom. Olivia was a friend, she was just visiting. She worked for a small public relations firm, based in London. Financial PR. Did Chris live in London? Yes. Just here for a few weeks? A holiday? No, work. Must be nice to be paid to travel.

Chris tried to explain. He'd been here four months. So far, he had seen the inside of his hotel, the office, and the underground shopping centre between them. He hadn't left the office before midnight. Except once, when Dom booked dinner and made him go. That was the night he met Annie. He had lived on his nerves and his checklists. He, the Portia team, and his users had watched the dates rushing by. The days got more crowded, the deadlines less possible. And then the HKMA- Who? Sorry, the Hong Kong Monetary Authority - the regulators - had kicked up a fuss at the last minute about Portia. The system was too powerful, they were nervous about the volumes. Except they wouldn't say that directly, they were… inscrutable about it.

But it had all come good in the end. Today was a bit hairy. Today was Triple Witching. "Triple Witching?" asked Liz. No, nothing to do with Halloween. Triple Witching was a day that came around once a quarter, the third Friday of that month. On that day, millions of futures and options contracts expired at the same time – usually during the last hour of trading.

In that hour, investors of all shapes and sizes went into a fever of closing or rolling their positions, creating waves of high volumes and rapid price movements. It was a day when high speed computer systems like Portia could make a lot of money. Or lose it. Today? Today had been good.

Liz was nice and polite but she wasn't really interested. It was hard to talk anyway. Dom and his flatmate Pete were into Irish bands and right now the Pogues were playing full volume on Dom's music system. Chris was relieved when Dom came over, dragging Olivia in one hand and holding an amber glass in the other. The Bushmills bottle on the table was half empty. His freckled face was a little pink, but that was all. Dom had wooden legs.

"Hello, hello. How are you two getting on? My best friends should know each other. Let's go out. Tomorrow. Down to Stanley Market. With Olivia, of course."

Now Chris could look openly at Olivia. He felt his heart thumping.

"Well," said Liz, "that's not going to work."

"And why not?"

"Because Chris is already spoken for, so he is."

"Really?" said Olivia, looking across at Chris with an enigmatic smile. "Here is she? Or is she stuck in England, poor thing? If it is a *she*?"

"Dunno," said Chris, heart thumping, "this is all news to me."

He hoped that Dom was not going to start blabbing about Annie. Dom had seen Chris and Annie sneaking a quick breakfast in the hotel one morning and put two and two together. Anyway, that madness was over. Annie had departed Hong Kong, to sort out some Finance mess in Singapore. She'd left a note in his room, along with a pair of silk knickers, neatly wrapped in tissue paper from the hotel's laundry. "Sweet dreams." She was right there. There were no more midnight assignations. No more fake visits from Room Service and laundry maids. Now the images of her luscious, naked body came to him only in the blessed sleep of which she had deprived him. And he her, to be fair.

"He's married to Portia," said Liz. Chris breathed a sigh of relief.

"Ah, Portia," said Dom, "you're right there. He's hitched up, alright. Mind you, he's a dark horse, is our Chris. You never know, he might be up for a spot of bigamy."

"What are you talking about?" said Olivia, "and who is Portia?"

"Portia isn't a person. Portia is an automated trading system," replied Dom, "and Chris is Dr Frankenstein, its creator."

"How interesting," said Olivia, "and does – er – Portia deliver the goods? I seem to remember Frankenstein's monster caused a few problems. Like killing his bride."

"Chris' software always works," said Dom. "The business folks love it. It's saved their bacon. That's why he's the hero of the hour, and not just in Hong Kong."

"Portia? Strange name for a monster."

"It's an acronym," said Chris. "Portfolio Order Routing with Intelligent Algorithms. It's like a human trader but a lot quicker and smarter. You give it a strategy and it goes into the markets and starts buying and selling things for you."

"Well, I'm sure you'll be very happy together," said Olivia, which killed the conversation. There was a pause.

"Exciting times for you boys, I hear," said Liz, "with your boss disappearing. Opportunity for someone."

"Not me," said Chris, wondering how she knew about Tom. "I've got the best job in the world. I'm a builder, not a manager. Dom's your man."

"For a million quid a year, Chris? I bet you could do a spot of managing," Liz replied.

"A million quid?"

"That's what Mitturi Bank offered your boss to move," said Liz. "That's what I heard."

Chris and Dom looked at each other, wide-eyed.

"Fuck me," said Dom.

"Me too," said Chris. He was a bit hazy about his *comp*, the industry vernacular for what he got paid. What appeared in his bank account was a fraction of the number Tom solemnly gave him once a year. The rest got soaked up in deferred compensation schemes and taxes and stuff. He really didn't pay attention. It paid the bills and the mortgage.

Dom's flatmate, Pete, pitched up, half-hidden behind a pile of sheets and pillows.

"Boys and girls, help yourself to pillows. No one's leaving tonight. Too dangerous. The storm's changed direction, it's coming straight in from the east."

"Well, I'm not listening to this crap all night," said Olivia, taking out her iPod and heading off towards Dom and Pete's Sonos. Before long the Pogues were gone and Beyoncé was belting out Single Ladies. Liz and Olivia were dancing together, and Liz was trying to make Dom dance and he was protesting, waving his bottle. Chris stood on one side, watching Olivia's hips swinging one way and her breasts the other. She and Liz were slapping their hands above their heads and singing along:

If you liked it then you should have put a ring on it,

If you liked it then you should have put a ring on it…

Chris wished he could dance. At that moment Dom's Blackberry lit up.

It didn't have to happen the way that it did. Things could have been different. Dom was holding his Blackberry to one ear. He nodded respectfully and hurried into the bedroom. One minute later, he was out again. He gave his Blackberry to Chris.

"It's Alexis van Buren. For you. You can talk in there."

It was a short call. When Chris came out, Dom and Olivia were looking at him. It felt like the whole room was looking at him.

"Well, go on then." That was Dom. "What did he want?"

"You know. Tom's old job. Equity Technology. He asked me to do it."

"And you said?"

"I said I'd give it a go."

"Fucking awesome," said Dom, giving him a big Bushmills-powered hug, "I'm so happy for you. Fucking fantastic, amazing."

"So Chris is your new boss?" said Olivia, looking directly at him.

"Yes, my best friend is now my boss," replied Dom. "But that won't change a fucking thing, will it, Chris?"

Chris swore that it wouldn't, and Dom said "fucking fantastic" a few more times and then Olivia kissed him on both cheeks and whispered softly in his ear, "Well done you, geeky boy."

"He wants me on the first flight to London," said Chris, just for something to say.

"No flights tomorrow," said Dom, "not with the storm. So let's enjoy tonight."

How did the news get around? Everyone in the room was coming up to congratulate him. Some from the Portia team. He knew them so well. And there were other, familiar faces from the IT floor. He knew what time they arrived to work and what time they left. That was about it.

The building shook as the typhoon reached a new peak. Someone turned the lights down. For a long time, they stood in the dark and watched the rain and the mist blowing past the big windows. Sometimes you could see other objects, leaves and branches and strange objects hurtling by, lit by the glow from the windows downstairs. Once he saw a small tree, cartwheeling down the road, smashing into cars.

Someone put the Doors on, and Jim Morrison's voice filled the room:
Riders on the storm
Into this house we're born
Into this world we're thrown
Like a dog without a bone
An actor out alone…

Am I a storm rider? thought Chris to himself. *Can I really do this job?* He was lightheaded, on two beers. There was a couple dancing in the corner. One of them was a Chinese girl, one of the Portia team here in Hong Kong. As he watched, she and her partner melted together, and then sank to the floor.

Chris' thoughts went back to the phone call from Alexis van Buren. *It's a big step for you, Chris. And a risk for me. But Cyrus thinks the world of you. So does the rest of the business. I think you can do it… what do you think?*

Of course he'd said yes. But could he really? There must be five hundred people in Equity Technology, and his team today was forty-three, mostly in London. Then there was the politics. The geeky derivatives traders looked down on the barrow boys selling shares and bonds. The sales guys were at war with the e-comm team. The Americans didn't like the Europeans. Lots of big egos in the business. All of them wanted more IT than the budget allowed. And his colleagues, people like Dom, could he bring them along with him?

…Girl ya gotta love your man
Take him by the hand
Make him understand
The world on you depends
Our life will never end…

The Doors came to a close. The wind seemed to ease. Pete said that they were in the eye of the typhoon. Someone put on some techno music, very chilled. Chris guessed they had taken MDMA to go with it. The building felt like an ocean liner, passing through the night over black waters. Time stopped. The night rushed by. He talked to different people, watched the storm, drank some vodka.

Later, much later, he went to the bathroom. When he came out, Olivia was standing just outside. She was swaying gently to the beat, arms above her head. Chris thought he had never seen anything so beautiful. She reached out and touched his cheek, as if he was some precious vase. Or a child. She seemed different. Softer.

"Christopher," she whispered. "Look, you're the last man standing." By the light from the bathroom, he could see sleeping bodies everywhere. Dom was asleep, on the floor, an empty bottle of Bushmills beside him. Liz, the Irish girl, was beside him, her arm thrown protectively across his chest.

"I need a man to kiss me. Do you kiss, Geek?" Olivia drew him into her arms. Her breath was slightly smoky, but her lips were soft and their tongues met, explored, parted, came back for more. Chris closed his eyes and felt himself floating in a soft, wet sea.

Wow. Is this real? thought Chris. *Me. With her. The posh princess.*

"Stop, stop," she whispered, after a few more breathless minutes. She fluttered one hand lightly down across his chest, and squeezed the front of his jeans, lightly at first, then firmer. Chris felt himself losing control. She stepped into the bathroom and pulled him in.

"Lock the door." She reached around behind him and turned off the light. Her hair was silvery blue under the dim glow of the emergency lights and their faces were gun metal grey with dark lips. He returned to her mouth, their kisses were harder and deeper. Her soft body was pressed against his. Her breasts were round and soft under his hands, under the silk. She half turned and gathered her hair to one side, guided his hands to the big bow at the nape of her neck, and the silk fell away to her waist. His hands worked out her bra clasp, and suddenly, unbelievably, her breasts were warm and naked in his hands.

He could feel his blood rising, pounding, his jeans tight. She unbuttoned his shirt, and then, more urgently, knelt down and undid his belt and the studs of his jeans and pulled them down. Chris put his hands on her hair and closed his eyes as she took him in her mouth. Just as he thought he could take no more, she was standing again. She reached up under her dress and pulled down her knickers and dropped them on the floor.

She spread her feet apart and Chris bent his knees and after a minute of frantic effort she was resting on his hips. She was guiding him with both hands while his hands and mouth devoured her naked torso. Suddenly he was pushing inside her and their hips moved up and down together.

"Stop," she whispered suddenly, her breath hot in his ear. "I want you ... I need more, harder." They looked around. The bathroom was tiny, the floor was wet and hard and the bath was small.

"I know, I know," she said suddenly. She turned away from him and stood facing the sink. Chris could see her face, reflected in the mirror. She bent a little and grasped the taps, her elbows on the porcelain edge, and shuffled her feet apart.

"Yes," she said, looking at him in the mirror, "yes, do it now, as hard as you can, fuck me now, darling Geek." And he did.

Later, they crept back into the living room, holding hands, and found a space under the long window. Chris found a bedspread and they lay together under it, their heads pillowed on a sofa cushion. From time to time, they kissed and she stroked his face. *I have never felt like this before*, he thought, dizzy with the sudden wonder of it. After a while, the storm returned, stronger, and the window trembled as the wind struck it and the building shuddered to its foundations.

The next kiss was different. Her tongue sought his, her teeth bit his lips gently. She took his hand and guided it down under the sheet, between her naked legs. Her flesh was wet and swelled to his touch and her breath was hot in his ear.

"It's the storm," she whispered. "It's the wind and the rain, it makes me feel like... like I need you inside me. My darling Geek." Her hands moved down his body, aroused him again. After a few minutes, she turned on her side to him and raised her knees to her chest.

"Go on," she whispered. "No-one can see us. Go on."

He obeyed. "I'm all yours," she whispered as he entered her. "All yours, geeky boy, just for tonight. Just for tonight." Outside the storm roared its approval.

I will ride the wind, thought Chris to himself as he felt her sweet, hot gasps coming faster and hotter. She gave a little cry, then another, muffled against his cheek and he could hold back no longer.

Exhausted, they clung together, whispering, touching, wrapped in new intimacy. *Am I in love?* he asked himself in amazement. As he drifted into sleep, the words came again: *I will ride the wind and the storm and I will succeed.*

3

Sana'a, Yemen, 2007

Day One - Friday

Of the long hours and days that followed her father's disappearance, Zahra later remembered only fragments and snatches.

She remembered waking up on the first morning, feeling depressed. And then the wave of fear that came as she remembered. She checked her phone. Nothing, no messages from Dad. She lay listening to the muezzins calling the faithful from their beds:

God is great,
There is no god except God
And Mohammed is his messenger
Hurry to prayer,
Hurry to success
Prayer is better than sleep
God is great...

There were low voices outside. It was Ahmed and Mahmoud, who had been going round the hospitals and the police checkpoints. Their weary footsteps echoed up the stairwell as they continued to their sleeping mats in the mafraj.

She heard her mother going up to the kitchen, as she did every morning, and bringing down some fruit to her shrine, where she put it into the thali tray. Her mother spoke to Ganesh, the god with the elephant head.

"Dear Ganesh, here is my offering. Grant me good fortune, I beg you. Please, please, send Jafar back to me."

She said this many times.

Later, her mother went to the bathroom. Zahra heard running water, and then, distinctly, the harsh croak of a bullfrog.

It took a second to sink in. A text from Dad! Zahra leapt out of bed.

Her mother was standing outside, eagerly peering at her phone. Then she gave a heartfelt cry.

"Ayeeeh, no, no, no."

She ran to the stairs, pushing Zahra away. "Stay in your room, Zahra. Do not come up, do you hear?"

Such was the agony in her voice that Zahra obeyed. She heard her mother's footsteps going up to the mafraj, two floors up and then Mahmoud's voice, asking what was wrong.

Later, she went up halfway, to the kitchen, and made a pot of tea. She tried to take it up to the mafraj, but her mother ordered her back downstairs.

There was a child's shout, and little Yousef came running up from below. Yousef was the youngest son of their neighbour. He had a runny nose and he wore the same filthy T-shirt every day. He lived in the dirt of the street outside and he announced visitors and events of all kinds. Today he was hopping up and down with excitement.

"Policeman! Policeman! In Jeep outside. Come down."

It was true, but she wasn't allowed down. Mahmoud and her mother went with the policeman, leaving Zahra, Ben and Ahmed behind. Zahra crept upstairs to the family room. It was a beautiful morning. The sun had just risen over the mountains to the east of the city. Dust motes danced in the sunbeams and the peeling whitewashed walls were golden. She could hear Ben typing inside the Box. From upstairs, came the sounds of Ahmed punching the old sand bag that hung from the ceiling.

She slipped through the blankets into the Box and sat down on an old crate, next to Ben. Sometimes she would sit here for hours. She would talk and Ben would work, his long fingers dancing like spiders on the keys, his face lit by the glow of the screen.

"You look so weird," she said, not for the first time. He turned towards her. He was wearing her shark goggles again, the ones she got at Sharm-el-Sheikh. He loved them.

"Be quiet," he said. "I'm flying the computer." He made the noise of a jet passing overhead.

"You don't look like a pilot. You look like a fish tank."

"Has Father turned up?" he said, still typing away.

"No. He sent a text, about an hour ago. Mum got really upset. Now she's gone down to the police station with Mahmoud."

"They went to the police?" Expressing disbelief.

"No. A Jeep turned up with a young policeman. He wanted Mahmoud, but Mother insisted on going as well. What's going on? Where's Dad?"

"How should I know? The police came before, remember? Dad hadn't paid his taxes."

That was true.

"Are you still trying to break into the Tech's computer?"

"I've done that."

"Why? What's wrong with our computer?"

"This pile of camel shit?" he replied, kicking the old PC under the table. "Listen, the machine in the e-lab has five hundred processors. *Five hundred*. It can handle ten thousand users at the same time."

"But there's only one of you."

"Ten thousand people will shop on my souk every day. To start with."

"You're building a souk? Like the Old Souk?"

"Yes, a real one. No, not like the Old Souk. I'm building a souk inside the machine. My digital souk will be a hundred times bigger than the dirty old souk."

"Ben, Ben, be realistic. You are sixteen years old."

"Bill Gates was even younger. And he stole time on someone else's computer."

Six months ago, Ben had gone to the Technical University and sat in lectures with Mahmoud. It hadn't worked. He thought the professors were stupid. They couldn't answer his questions. According to Mahmoud, the lecturers hadn't even understood his questions, because Ben spoke bad Arabic and he talked too fast.

Within two weeks, he was banned from the campus but not before he'd learned about the new machine in the e-lab. It was a gift from the University of Helsinki. A gift to Ben, Ben said, because it was unused. Not even one of its hundreds of processors was kept busy by the trivial tasks that the students gave it. He just needed to hack into it.

Mahmoud and her mother appeared up the stairs, looking pale and anxious. Her mother took off her niqab. Underneath, she was still wearing her nightgown.

"Well, children, your father has decided to stay in Dubai a bit longer."

"Why? And why were the police here?" asked Zahra.

"Has Dad forgotten to pay his bribes again?" said Ben, from inside the Box.

"His taxes," said his mother firmly. "Yes. He's going to sort that out as soon as he gets back. So we can all stop worrying."

Zahra looked at her mother and knew she was lying. Later she found her in the kitchen, watching the news on TV, silent tears running down her cheeks. Zahra put out a hand and touched her mother's face.

"Mother, dear, you don't have to lie to me. I know what's happened."

"Really?" said her mother faintly.

"Yes. Dad told me about the girl in the travel agency. Don't worry, he loves you, mother. She may be attractive but he will soon get tired of her. And he doesn't like Dubai."

Her mother's eyes stayed welded to the TV, but fresh tears cascaded down her cheeks. Zahra hugged her. What a strange thing it was, she thought, to be comforting your own mother. All her life it had been the other way around.

But at least the mystery was solved. That evening she sent an email to her penfriend in Cairo:

You ask me where is my father? Mum is quite old now (44) so what do you think?!!! One day when Mum was in the kitchen Dad told me he has a good friend in the Lebanese travel agency in Dubai. I asked him and he said she is very attractive. Maybe the real sandstorm is upstairs at the Airport Hilton!!!!

PS. Also Mother is a Hindu and quite shy while Lebanese women will do anything.

PPS. I had to tell her about the woman in the travel agency because she is worrying so much. I told her that he will soon get tired of her and she started crying again.

4

London

Three years later - Thursday, 14th June 2012

Had his alarm gone off? No. Chris Peters lay still for a moment, confused. Outside the bedroom window, he could hear the birds cheeping, greeting the early summer dawn.

Then the noise again. Familiar and unwanted. He turned on his side and picked up his Blackberry. It was Dave Carstairs, his production support guy.

Fuck. He swore to himself and looked around. Olivia was the other side of the bed, her head buried between two pillows.

"Chris? We've had a bad night on EOS. The risk batch failed."

"Why?"

"Not clear. We had two million trades yesterday. That's a record. After the second failure, we split the batch into two…"

Chris got out of bed, blundering into a chair. He heard Olivia muttering.

"Sorry, EOS problem."

Her reply was unrepeatable and who could blame her? He'd worried about a lot of things when he got promoted three years ago, but he hadn't known about EOS. EOS – or Equity Options System - had chosen the weekend of their wedding to have a nervous breakdown. The crisis had gone on, night after night, haunting their honeymoon like some jealous lover yelling outside the bedroom window.

EOS was a system- Well, no, calling EOS a system was like calling the Tower of London a building. EOS was a sprawling, seething mass of software, millions of lines of code, maintained by a small army of coders. The processes that made up EOS spawned themselves across two thousand computers, a number that grew inexorably. Perhaps there had been a grand design, back in the nineteen eighties, but since then, hundreds of man-years of new functionality had been added. Half were things that the system was not designed to do, but which had suddenly become business critical. No one could predict the consequence of any change, even a small one.

"Two facts about this fucker, Chris. One, it is fundamentally unstable; and two, it is absolutely critical to the equity derivatives business." Those were his friend Dom Macdonald's words three years ago, welcoming Chris as the new head of Equity Technology. Dom had been right.

Chris staggered onto the dimly lit landing and sat down on the top step. Naked and massaging the back of his neck. Trying to think.

"Is it producing the right numbers?"

"Dunno yet. It's running like a dog. Half normal speed. Less. No risk numbers until mid-morning, at the earliest."

Chris swore to himself. This was the second time this week the traders wouldn't have their risk reports when they came in. Cyrus would be unhappy. Tim Hawes in Finance would add it to his charge sheet, the one that said Technology was incompetent and needed new blood. Last week had been awful, a new problem every day, so this was really bad timing.

Chris showered and dressed in a hurry. As he was leaving the house, Olivia called out from upstairs. Something about nine o'clock.

Huh? Dinner at nine o'clock? Were they going out? Or maybe it was a baby-making night?

As Olivia phrased it to her girlfriends, he and Olivia were "trying." Olivia's desire to become a mother was pretty logical. She was thirty-three, he was making good money, she didn't like her new boss… The time was now. But as the months had gone by, she had become anxious. He dreaded the bad news each month, when she would come out of the bathroom weeping. Sex used to be fun. Recreation fuelled by lust. Now it was a diary item.

He shut the front door. He would text her later. He half-jogged to Clapham South and caught a Northern Line train just after 6.30am. He found a seat and started on his overnight mail and his calendar.

He had 37 new emails. Routine, mostly. The trading day was ending in Asia and there was a day's worth of traffic from his guys over there. The EOS incident had been running through the night, starting as blue and escalating to red at about 3am. And there was another red. Chopstix, the Hong Kong order management system, had run out of database locks just as the market opened. There was an email from Peter Elliot, the head trader in Hong Kong, to his boss Cyrus in London, copying most of Equities management:

system probs AGIN this am. Tech guys can't fix. Blackrck put us in penalty box.

Dammit. Blackrock were a big client. And this wasn't the first time Chopstix had run out of database locks. Raul, his new guy there, just didn't seem to be on top of it.

Grimacing, he turned to his calendar. Shit. It was crawling with meetings, starting with meeting his new grads at 8am. He had seven meetings before midday, not all compatible.

PK Ramachandran was in town from Chennai, and needed to see him at 9am. Very Urgent. But at 9am he was supposed to be in some mega Disaster Recovery planning session. He sent a quick note to Dom:

Hi Dom can u cover DR session with Audit for me? 9am Clock Room. Please?

At noon, there was something strange. "Data Security." One hour long. It was marked "secret" and "mandatory." The organizer was Sheila Collins. Sheila ran Information Security for the bank, part of the Neil Jenkins empire. Neil had recruited her from the Royal Navy, where she had spent fifteen years protecting submarines from electronic attack. She was the female counterpart to Neil: red headed, stockily built and bloody-minded. Neil's management team called her Nellie, or The Little Sister.

When he got to the office, Chris went straight to the trading floor, looking for Cyrus, head of the Equity business. The floor was just coming alive. The voices of analysts echoed from the Speakerbus stations on each desk, giving their morning updates. Small groups of traders and sales people huddled across the vast room, firing up their spreadsheets. No sign of Cyrus, either on the floor or in his office.

Crossing the floor, he had a call from Dave Carstairs again.

"Chris? Quick update on EOS: we think it's a database problem. It's table scanning."

"Why?"

"Dunno yet. The dbas have forced the query plan and it seems to be working."

The people who looked after databases were called database administrators or dbas for short.

In the middle of the trading floor, he bumped into Chuck Masters, the chief of Equity Derivatives, hanging out with a couple of his traders. Chuck was not happy about the EOS situation and he was not a man to suffer in silence.

"We think it's a database problem," said Chris once the initial storm had blown over.

Chuck's Aussie accent became more pronounced.

"Mate, it's not a database problem. It's a Chris Peters problem. Right?"

He punched Chris on the shoulder. Not playful, not really.

"You run Equities IT, the buck stops with you."

"Yes, of course," said Chris, unhappily, looking around. Philippe Reynaud, the god of High Frequency Trading was coming over. He and Philippe had got on well four years back, when Chris was his tech guy. Back then, Alchemy was just a dream, a prototype. Chris had been lucky and hired the extraordinary talent of Arshad Zebediah, who became the chief architect of Alchemy. But when Chris moved up and away in the technology world, Philippe changed. He started complaining about the quality of his IT guys. Everything was late. His budget was too small, the software too slow. He wanted an iPhone, not a Blackberry.

Now, looking back on it, Chris realised that Philippe trusted only what he controlled. Everything and everybody else was regarded with deep suspicion. Especially those who had escaped from his estate. Chris had mentioned it to Olivia one evening, hoping for some feminine insight. "Well, he's French, isn't he?" she said simply, and perhaps that was all there was to it.

"Bonjour, Monsieur Peters," said Philippe. "How are things with you?"

"Challenging times."

"Yes, I heard that. Actually from several people. Last year it was Operations but this year it seems to be Technology that is, as you say, challenged. But I told Cyrus, these things are cyclical. Next year it will be Finance that is holding back the business."

Philippe was just teasing him with this drivel, thought Chris, but that didn't make it easier to bear.

His Blackberry rang. It was Holly.

"Where are you? The graduates are waiting!"

Oh hell, the graduates! He was supposed to give them a pep talk at 8am, before they started their training.

"I know, I'm sorry, I'm on the trading floor. I'll go straight there."

He checked his Blackberry while the elevator headed for the sixth floor and the meeting rooms. The Chopstix problem in Hong Kong was ongoing. Cyrus had replied to Peter Elliot's email, copying the whole of Equities management.

Chris what we need to fix this? Miyuki meet pls.10.

Miyuki was Cyrus' desk assistant. She'd been his assistant forever and had an almost psychic understanding of his cryptic pronouncements. She would know whether "10" means 10am, in ten minutes or a ten minute meeting. She knew precisely who was in trouble, who in favour. Cyrus himself was universally abrupt and gave little away.

The doors opened on the silk wallpapers of the sixth floor and he hurried to Room C, the big one. A small army of his new graduate hires was sitting at round tables, big handwritten names in front. Rani came over, looking anxious and holding a briefing note. He scanned it while Rani drip-fed him background.

"Can you talk for fifteen to twenty minutes, up to coffee break? Completely informal."

Chris had a moment of panic. He hated public speaking. Twenty minutes was more than "welcome and thanks for coming."

And now his bloody phone was ringing again.

"Holly?"

"Miyuki called. Cyrus wants you in his management meeting this morning."

"I'm not surprised."

Chopstix down in Hong Kong. And no risk numbers from EOS. Again. A ritual beating from Cyrus was the least he could expect.

Worrying about Cyrus, he did a poor job with the grads. The first question was from a woman called Jane, a UCL grad, "Why is Risk so important?"

Chris started talking about IT risks and disaster recovery, but she cut him short.

"No, I mean, you know, trading risk. I've been working on the desk and every day their risk is late, the traders start throwing their toys out…"

His reply started well enough.

"Look, you all know what a derivative is, right? It's a contract between us and someone else. And that contract has a value, which the system works out using complex mathematics. But that value changes all the time. What makes it go up or down? Lots of things. Interest rates. Exchange rates. Market volatility.

"A trader's risk numbers tell him how sensitive this trade is to particular risks. If interest rates go down, what happens? If the US dollar goes up, what happens? What does he have to worry about? What does he have to hedge?"

He was on the home straight now.

"So, to answer Jane's question, a trader without their risk numbers is blind. Like a pilot with no instruments. Flying in cloud. You would pull your hair out too."

His phone was ringing. An 852 number. Hong Kong. That could only be bad news. He sent it to voicemail. Still, it gave him an excuse to cut things short.

"Folks, I'm sorry but... busy morning. Got to run now."

But Rani was too quick for him.

"One minute for prize giving!" she said. "While Chris is with us."

Chris handed out various tokens and souvenirs while the room clapped and he tried to remember the names of the winners. It seemed to go OK until they got to the Battle of the Bots award. A Bot was a software program, written to strict rules. Bots fought to the death on screen, firing lasers and taking evasive action. Last year, he and John Uzgalis had create a Bot contest, open to all IT staff. It was a great, nerdy exercise, and he and John had led the way by building their own, personal Bots.

Rani picked up the award, a miniature Dalek from Dr Who. She looked across at a young Indian in a check shirt sitting at the back, arms folded. He shook his head, looked down. She hesitated, then came to a decision.

"The winner of the award for the best graduate Bot is... Karthik Singh!"

A few cheers. Karthik stood up.

"But my bot was defeated," he said with dignity. "I cannot accept it." He sat down again. There was an awkward silence.

What the hell? thought Chris. His phone was ringing again. It was Holly, sounding stressed.

"Cyrus wants to see you now."

"OK, OK, just finishing up with the grads, five minutes," he whispered, conscious of the whole room looking at him.

"Miyuki said *now-now*. They are all waiting for you. In the board room," said Holly.

Shit.

"Rani, sorry, I've got to go," he whispered. "What's the problem? Who did win the Battle of the Bots?"

"Shiva the Destroyer. Hassan Choudhary's bot," said Rani. She nodded at the young guy in the check shirt. "That's Hassan over there. But he says he won't accept it. Karthik came second."

Chris remembered Hassan by name. He'd refused to go on a course or something and pissed off his manager in Chennai, P K Ramachandran. Chris couldn't remember the details but right now the obstinate look on the guy's face annoyed him.

"Mr Choudhary, I am told your bot was the winner. Please come and collect your prize." He held it out. No movement. Head down. Arms tightly folded.

Chris felt the red mist rising. He marched over to the young man's table and dumped the Dalek in front of him.

"It's yours. Well done."

Rani chased him down the corridor to the lifts, embarrassed. "He's so obstinate," she said. "And he won by a mile. Dom re-ran the winning bots from last year and he destroyed them as well."

"The grad bots."

"No, all the bots. Including yours. I think John Uzgalis still beat him."

"That's unbelievable." And galling. He saw a tall figure coming out of the meeting room. It looked like Hassan. Striding towards him. The lift arrived and Chris escaped, with relief.

The doors opened onto the trading floor, two floors up. And what the hell? Hassan Choudhary was standing in front of the doors, facing him, still holding the Dalek. It was a bit creepy. The guy must have run up the stairs like lightning.

"Mr Peters, please listen to me. My summer project will finish soon. By the end of June. I will be sent back to Chennai."

He held out the Dalek. "I don't want this. I want to stay in London. I have a strong developer background. I am fluent in Perl and Java…"

He really didn't have time for this.

"Sorry, buddy, I've got to go. Send me an email, OK?"

Stepping round Hassan, Chris crossed the floor, nodding at traders he knew, while he tried to map out the next two hours. He'd see Cyrus & Co now, push PK to 9.30am, fifteen minutes max, then get an update on Chopstix - say 9.45am – then see Dom at 10am to hear about Disaster Recovery. Review EOS batch problems at 10.30am, preparations for Triple Witching at 11am… bingo! His day would be back on track.

In his heart, he knew it was optimistic.

The Equities boardroom was crowded with Cyrus and his business heads, all grim-faced. The trading heads from US and Tokyo were virtually present, on wall screens.

"Chris Peters has just joined us," said Cyrus, talking into the Polycom on the table. "Peter, could you say that again?"

"Chris, do you realise what's going on here?" said an English voice from the Polycom.

It was Pete Elliot, head of trading in Hong Kong. In the old days, a good friend and fun guy who spent every Friday night chasing the girls down at Joe Bananas. They were mostly cabin crew off BA or Qantas flights and came to drink, dance and get chased by guys like Peter. Not today, though.

"I've had the HKMA on the phone, we haven't reported any trades since Chopstix went belly up this afternoon. No end of day reporting either. Your guys are bringing backup tapes into the building, I don't know why but I can see they're worried."

The HKMA had zero tolerance for IT screw-ups that disrupted the Hong Market markets or threatened their reputation.

"Is Raul with you?" said Chris, just for something to say.

"I haven't seen Raul. Jason Soh is here. Jason says Raul has gone to a meeting. Offsite."

The silence that followed spoke volumes. In it, his phone rang, suddenly.

Incoming call from 07921684394 (Olivia)

Not now, not now. Taking phone calls in Cyrus' presence was a major breach of an unwritten etiquette. Even Philippe didn't do it. Why did Olivia pick moments like this to ring? He sent her to Voicemail.

"I'm on the case," he said. "I will be talking to Raul right after this meeting."

"Get on a plane," said Peter Elliott. "Come and see for yourself. Things are not good."

Chris' phone went again, Olivia again. This time Cyrus raised an imperious eyebrow.

"Sorry," said Chris, boiling with shame and anger. He turned his phone off. Thinking, this was the last time, the last time, from now on she could call his fucking office number like everyone else. Which she had always refused to do.

"So, Hong Kong is screwed," said Cyrus, his huge head turned sideways, squinting at him. "Now, let's talk about EOS. What the hell is going on with EOS? Every day, I get EOS hatemail. From all over the planet. My wife knows about EOS, my kids, even my dog knows about EOS."

Chris had never heard Cyrus swear before. He started going through the issues, the volumes, the crazy stuff for the regulators, the new risk models.

"Chris, we know all that," said Cyrus, "I've known EOS longer than you have. It's an old system, it's been bastardized by people like me. It wasn't designed to do what it's doing, I get that. You have to keep it alive and show the US cavalry are on their way."

"We've got a roadmap to replace it…"

"Roadmap? Fuck the roadmap! Give me hope, you know? Deliver something that makes a difference. Now, today, next week. Sometime soon. Chuck Masters, do you agree?"

The king of Equity Derivatives did agree. His agreement lasted several minutes. He repeated his joke.

"Like I told Chris, this is not a database problem, this is a Chris Peters problem."

"OK," said Cyrus, looking round, "anyone else got an issue with Technology? Good grief… one at a time, guys, OK?"

"It's a Triple Witching tomorrow," repeated someone. "If the system can't cope with yesterday's volume, how's it going to cope with two or three times that?"

Chris staggered back to his office 20 minutes later, licking his wounds. Dom MacDonald was sitting at his table, wearing a black silk shirt. What did that mean? Holly charged in, looking stressed.

"P.K. is on the way up. I've got Raul holding. And Olivia called, she wants you to call her urgently."

"Calm down, Holly, I'll talk to Raul now. Then Dom, then P.K. 2 minutes each, then I'll call Olivia, OK? It's probably about dinner this evening."

He waved a hand at Dom, who nodded. Thank God for Dom, always calm.

He picked up the phone.

"So, Raul, is Chopstix sorted?"

Raul started babbling about database restores, which involved throwing away the current database and restoring from an earlier backup. Complicated and risky. As Chris listened, his heart sank. He could feel the adrenalin rushing into his stomach. A database restore was a panic move that might make the situation much worse. It was tempting to get on a call and dive in himself.

He'd gone to the wall to hire Raul from Deutsche Bank. Had he made a mistake?

"Chris, calm down, OK?" said Raul. "Thirty minutes, the system will be back."

Fucking moron, thought Chris angrily to himself as he hung up, *he doesn't even know how bad it is*. He turned to Dom, who was sitting patiently at his table. Chris had brought Dom back from Hong Kong two years ago, and given him a big, global job. It was good to have a friend to talk to, though sometimes he wondered. Dom was so black and white. He didn't do sweet talk or small talk, he just put the facts on the table. Chris had heard mutterings about Dom from the business. Even from Cyrus.

"Hi old buddy, how are you? Give me some good news!"

"Not today."

"Fuck. What's the problem?"

"Audit."

Audit were upset because Global Markets was supposed to simulate the loss of the trading floors and the major datacentres each year and practice recovery. These were weekend drills. But those weekends competed with big software releases or project go-lives and guess which was winning?

"It's just happened again," said Dom, "the Raleigh datacentre practice, two weeks ago. That was the third time it moved. Audit are really pissed off. It's going to be a Major audit point."

"What?! On IT? No way, the business should be getting it."

"They will. We both will. And we've never done disaster recovery in Hamilton… that'll be another Major, any day now." Hamilton was the new datacentre outside New York, Neil Jenkins' pride and joy.

Chris had not had a Major audit point against him in three years. Major audit points went straight to Sir Simon, the Chief Exec. There would be fire drills and conference calls and rivers of shit flowing downhill and life would be miserable until either the problem was remediated (mostly fixed) or a fresh victim emerged.

"Dom, you've got to make the Raleigh test happen."

"That's what you asked me last time, remember? Yeah. We picked a new date. People worked nights, they cancelled holidays, the business was all prepped and for what? Cyrus pulls the plug. Project Miami is 'more critical to the business'."

Chris' phone lit up. Hong Kong. Now there was no mistaking the panic in Raul's voice. Chris cut him short.

"Raul, put Jason Soh on, will you?"

Jason Soh sounded as calm and competent as ever. Chris told him what he wanted doing to restore the stricken system and left him to it. The clock on his wall read 9.53am. Damn, damn, the morning was running on.

"I warned you about Raul," said Dom. "Everyone at Deutsche in Hong Kong knew he was a turkey, but you wouldn't listen."

"Oh stick to the subject, for Chrissake," said Chris, his temper fraying. "We need to fix this audit."

"Impossible," said Dom. "There is no room in the calendar. We can't test Raleigh or Hamilton this side of Christmas. Anyway they're not real tests. A real test would be like a fire drill. No warning, boom! Datacentre down..."

"Don't be ridiculous, imagine the chaos," said Chris. "That would be like a fire drill where you set fire to the building."

Holly opened the door.

"P.K. is here. And you need to call Olivia. You have a meeting upstairs in five minutes."

"Imagine the chaos, Chris," said Dom. "That's exactly it. The chaos would teach us a lesson."

Dom sloped off. Not his usual happy self, somehow.

"P.K.! Welcome to London!"

P.K. Ramachandran came from Tamil Nadu in the south of India. He was short and dark-skinned, with a round, friendly face. He was immaculately dressed as always, in a black jacket with tie. P.K. was an astute politician who had made a career doing banking technology from India. Not easy, because the banks were fickle. Some years, India was all the rage, the next year it would be Moscow or the Philippines. Or bring it all home.

"Listen, P.K., I'm up against it this morning. What's on your mind?"

"Sure, Chris, sure. We have half an hour but let me give you some time back."

Damn right, about twenty-eight minutes, thought Chris to himself.

But in that, he was going to be disappointed.

P.K. begged Chris to be discreet. What he was about to say was top *top* secret.

Two days ago, a young man, a new hire, had been searched leaving the office in Chennai. A memory stick had been found. On the memory stick were the details of 2.4 million clients from the client master database. Retail, commercial, institutional... all of them. Sorry to say. All details, yes. The young man had confessed, an anonymous buyer had paid him one thousand dollars to get the data, another five thousand on delivery.

P.K.'s story was horrible and yet somehow inevitable. It was like watching the incoming tide lapping the foundations of a sandcastle. It had only been a matter of time.

Yes, this data came from a test system in India because, as Chris knew, test systems were loaded with data from the production systems. It was the only way.

"Sheila Collins has a top secret meeting at noon about Data Security, is it about this?"

"How would I know?" replied P.K. disapprovingly, "I am not sufficiently elevated on the totem pole."

Holly put her head round the door.

"Excuse me, Chris, but your next appointment… is on the way up."

Huh? What was she talking about? His next appointment was calling Olivia.

"Not now, Holly." She started to protest. "NOT NOW! Just give us a minute, OK!"

He looked at P.K. who was looking indignant. He had just launched into his protest when there was a disturbance outside. An angry voice, a woman's voice. It was muffled but familiar. Holly knocked on the door again, then opened it immediately.

"Excuse me, Chris, but - er - Olivia's here to see you – she's been in reception almost half an hour, she says she's-"

"And she's not going to wait another bloody second!" said the angry voice.

The door was flung violently open. A tall, well-dressed figure pushed into the tiny office. She was as angry as Chris had ever seen her.

"Where have you been? I've been waiting for you at London Bridge Hospital since nine o'clock. Dr Ireson moved all his appointments just to suit you. I called and I called and I got your snotty little message every time. *And I'll get right back to you.* But you didn't, did you? Why the hell don't you answer your phone?"

The world seemed to be melting down in front of Chris. Dr Ireson. Fertility test results. Damn, damn. It was last week, he'd been in the car, on the way to Heathrow, when Olivia called. Why, *why* hadn't he put it in his calendar? Those calls this morning, why hadn't he guessed? He was dimly aware of P.K. sliding out and Holly closing the door.

"I'm sorry, I'm really sorry, I had-" Oh my God, he couldn't say *forgotten*, that would be even worse.

"You forgot, didn't you? The most important thing in my life. And you forgot. All because of your stupid job. *And* your stupid friends. Why do you have to spend the weekend with them? Don't you see them enough during the week?"

That was his offsite, he remembered guiltily. He'd taken his management team away for the weekend.

"That was ages ago."

"It was three weeks ago."

"It was two months ago. Before Easter. Before our holiday."

"You call that a holiday? Even on the lifts you were too busy checking your Blackberry to talk to me. And the last weekend you were on the phone half the night."

"It was a crisis."

"There's always a crisis. You don't care, Chris, you don't care about having a family or you'd find a way."

Olivia continued ranting and Chris tried unsuccessfully to calm her. He felt as he always did, helpless to explain the complicated bargain that was his job. The intensity that came from trading businesses. The excitement of impossible deadlines. Travels to faraway cities. And the money. It had been alright when they first got married. Sometimes he'd had to work all night but he could make up for it. Dinner at Chez Bruce, followed by an orgy back home, would get things back to normal with his beautiful wife. Their life was almost better for the separation and the stress. Except no baby.

Suddenly Olivia stopped shouting and burst into tears instead. She stood weeping in the middle of his office. Her tears were despairing, not angry. Alarmed, he tried to put his arms around her but she pushed him away.

"Leave me alone, just go away." She was scrabbling for a tissue in her bag.

"Olivia, I'm sorry, I will fix it, I will. Let's make another appointment."

Olivia looked at him defiantly through her tears.

"What's the point? You won't be there."

"I will, I will. I promise."

"Don't promise me, Chris. You never keep your promises."

"I will, I... will this time," he said. She ignored him and picked up her bag. At the doorway she stopped and turned.

"I want a baby, Chris. More than anything. Including you. Don't forget that."

She was gone, slamming the door behind her. After a minute or two, Holly came in, disapproving.

"Holly, don't say anything, OK. I know, I should have told you... I know. But how did she get in?"

"Dom. Dom knows your wife, doesn't he? He met her in reception, and he could see she was upset..."

Dom. Of course, they knew each other. From Hong Kong.

"Well, where's Dom?"

"He's gone. He went to see her out of the building."

Chris called Dom.

"Dom? Where are you? Is Olivia with you? How is she?"

"I'm in Pret. She just left. Not happy."

"I'm coming down. Flat white please."

*

Dom was waiting for him in Pret with a coffee on the table.

"Thanks. And thanks for trying with Olivia."

Dom just looked at him.

"Dom, I know, OK? I really screwed up this time."

"You did and all."

Another silence.

"Got any Bushmills? I think I need it."

Dom shook his head. Unsmiling.

"Dom, old friend, can I ask you something?"

"Sure, Chris."

"You know me. You know her. Today was my fault. I know that. But, nowadays... she's seems angry so often. Even when I don't forget something. You know? I don't know what to do. I love her but it's like... she doesn't believe me."

They sat in silence for a few minutes.

"Chris," said Dom suddenly. "Olivia is a very special lady. If it was me, I'd worship her. Buy her the moon. I'd give her anything she wanted. She'd have to kick me out in the morning, I'd be that loving with her. She would know it. So she would adore me in return."

"Really? And how would you balance all that with working for a bank?"

"This word balance, that's your problem. Stop balancing. Give her everything. Whatever she wants. Let her find the balance."

"She wants a baby."

"Well, aren't you a lucky man? Best get home early tonight."

Chris' phone was going. It was Holly. He was late for something. As he was leaving, Dom grabbed his arm and held it so tightly that it hurt.

"If you lose her, Chris, you're an idiot. But she wouldn't be alone for long, you can be sure of that."

He went back to the office, depressed. He pondered Dom's advice as he walked. It seemed completely impractical but perhaps he was too stupid to understand it. What he did understand for the first time was that Dom was very fond of Olivia. Too fond, maybe. That thought was a little worm that gnawed away in his head.

The rest of the morning rushed by. Dave Carstairs expected triple the normal volumes on Triple Witching tomorrow. In theory, most Equity systems could cope but this was really going to be a problem for EOS. The EOS batch hadn't finished until noon and today's trades were just flowing in. At noon, Chris climbed wearily up the stairs to the Sheila Collins meeting. He'd drunk too much coffee and he had a headache.

His boss Alexis van Buren (AVB) was there already. So was his buddy John Uzgalis, in full flow. He was wearing a black Armani jacket, designer jeans, a black cap and a thin gold chain round his neck. He looked like Chris' vision of a sleazy movie producer. Debt Markets dress code was different from conservative Equities. Chris was in summer chinos and a J Crew check shirt.

"Hey, Alexis, got a new one for you-"

"Please, John, no more of your FoxNews jokes," said AVB, who was a Dutch liberal.

"Barack Obama's on a boat that sinks, who gets saved?"

John looked round the room, winked at Chris and then pulled an imaginary rabbit out of an imaginary hat.

"America!" The room groaned, Sheila and AVB were not amused.

"Now that Chris is here, perhaps we can start?" said Sheila tartly.

The head of Information Security was dressed for combat in a short-sleeved red blouse with a black skirt. She had been thinner when she bought it and her pink blotchy forearms bulged out of the sleeves. Sheila was not fussy about her appearance. Sitting next to her was Shane, who ran the dba group. No sign of their boss, Neil Jenkins.

"Last week," said Sheila, "an IT person employed by this bank attempted to steal a large quantity of sensitive client data... what? No, you don't need to know where from..."

Chennai, India, thought Chris. *This was the memory stick P.K. had told him about.*

"What you should know is that this data came from a test system. Now, how do you guys create data for testing? We all know the answer to that – you copy the live database into your test systems, right?"

Spot on, Sheila. And for damn good reasons.

"Which creates a huge problem. Our IT developers – many of them not even employees of this bank - can see real clients, real trades, real bank accounts. The regulators have woken up to this, and it's got to stop."

There were groans around the room. All of them had known this day was coming.

"Relax guys," said Shane, the king of the dbas, "we've come to offer a solution."

"Anyone heard of ShuffleDB? It's a third party package. What ShuffleDB does is just that, shuffle tables in databases. Let's say you've got a million trades in a system. Every trade has the name of the client on it, right? ShuffleDB can take that million real trades and shuffle the client names across them in your test system. Bingo! You still have a million trades, good for testing, but anonymized."

"Of course, you have to set it up. We've been testing it with some of Dave Trebbiano's people and it works. About four man-weeks effort per system."

It was a pretty neat idea. Even Uzgalis had to admit it.

"So, Sir Simon has asked us to implement ShuffleDB across our top 100 applications by September," continued Shane, hoping he was on a roll.

"Which September, dude?" said Uzgalis. Dangerously casual.

"This September," said Shane. "The next ninety days. DeVries has signed off on the licence-"

But he got no further. There was outrage across the room, led by Trebbiano and Uzgalis.

"Sir Simon has designated this a mandatory project," said Sheila, as if this was the ace of spades, "and the dates have been approved by the board. This is top priority."

"Top priority?" shouted someone. "I have twenty top priority mandatory bloody projects already. Including Dodd-Frank. MiFiD 2. Not to mention Topeka. Maybe Sir Simon could tell me which ones to drop?"

General applause but Chris knew it was all for show.

"The project code is Vegas," said Sheila. That brought a few chuckles. By tradition, major projects in Global Markets were named after US cities. The Mecca of American gambling had not been used before.

"And I need a point person from each of you. Someone senior."

Well, at least that was easy, thought Chris. Dom would be perfect.

Sheila had done well to stay away from the details. Earlier, PK had shared with him two nasty little facts. First, the intercepted memory stick was full. And second, the 2.4 million clients filling it were arranged alphabetically from letters P to T. The implication was clear. These were not the first client records to be stolen. Nor were they intended to be the last. If Sir Simon knew this, he was taking one hell of a risk not disclosing it to the world. Or perhaps someone – like Sheila – had taken the bold decision not to tell him.

He tried calling Olivia several times. No answer. Then in mid-afternoon, he got an email from her, no comment, forwarded from Dr Ireson, London Bridge Hospital. Malcolm Ireson was a man of few words:

Your test results. Self explanatory. Malcolm.

He left work at seven o'clock, leaving his desk untidy. It was raining hard but he found a taxi to Waterloo. There were still a few bunches of flowers left at the late night M&S. He bought them all. Would that make her feel adored?

*

Olivia looked pale and tired. He held out the flowers and started to apologise but she cut him short.

"There's some supper on the table, not that you deserve it."

"Look, I'm really sorry about today."

There was no reply. He tried again.

"That was good news from Dr Ireson, wasn't it? I mean, there's no physical reason why we can't... you know... make a baby."

"You think 'no reason' is better than having a reason? I don't."

She reached for a mug, and knocked over the vase, overloaded with his flowers. It smashed on the floor, spraying water, roses and glass in all directions. She swore, went for the dustpan.

"You keep talking, giving me reasons why I should be happy. I don't want reasons. I don't want flowers."

She looked up from the floor and her beautiful face suddenly crumpled and she started to cry, just like today in the office and Chris felt his heart melting.

"I've had a horrible day at work. It's been a horrible evening, waiting for you. Don't you understand? I just want to know that you love me. That's all. Why is that so hard?"

"But I do. I do, you know I do."

"Do you? You say it but you don't show it. You love that bank."

"But look, I'm always trying... for God's sake, last week I ran out of a meeting with the COO."

"Oh Chris, don't give me logic. Don't you see? I don't want logic, I want love. You're not a bad man. I mean, you are kind to animals and people selling the *Big Issue*. But you have the emotional IQ of... of... an electric toaster. It's like living with a robot."

He tried, he really did. But the more he said, the less she heard. In the end, they both went to bed exhausted. He lay for a while listening to the rain and the wind blowing outside. It didn't seem to have the same aphrodisiac effect on her that it had, back in Hong Kong.

Triple Witching tomorrow, he thought to himself as he drifted off to sleep, *cannot be worse than today.*

Far away across the Atlantic, the massed computers of the Hamilton datacentre hummed peacefully in their chilly halls, while high above, the Fates were smiling as they wove.

5

Sana'a, Yemen, 2007

Day Two - Saturday

Zahra woke up just after midnight. It was hot. The streets below were quiet. She could hear the grinding gears of the night buses setting out for Aden and the horns of impatient truck drivers queuing outside the Bab el Yemen gate.

She wondered where her father was right now. Did the girl from the travel agency have her own apartment? Or were they in a hotel? And then - she tried not to - but she started to think about the pictures she had downloaded from the Internet. Disgusting, wicked pictures. The girl with two men. She thought of the girl, and the two naked men with their big *things* sticking out and her fingers seemed to do the rest. The forbidden pleasure flowered deep inside her and she tried not to make a noise in case her mother heard her, but maybe she did, at the end.

Then she lay still, bathed in sweat, and listened to her heart beating. Just before dawn, it started to rain, a light desert rain that trickled gently off roofs and into gutters. It lulled her to sleep and the call of the muezzin echoed through her dreams.

She woke with a start. She heard a child's voice.

"La-la, la-la. Present. Present."

She sat up. It was little Yousef, the neighbour's son, standing shyly in the doorway. He had never come in this far. He was holding out a small square package. It had ZAHRA scrawled on it in Arabic.

Strange. Dreamlike. Was she still asleep?

"Thank you, Yousef. Thank you, where did this come from?"

"Man. Car."

"And in your other hand? What have you got there? Show me."

He held out a small black box, the sort a jeweller might put a watch in. It was heavy – and tightly wrapped in Scotch tape. It had a label which said MAHMOUD.

"You can go up and give it to Mahmoud." While Yousef clambered happily up the stairs on his new mission, she ran downstairs. There was no-one in the street.

She opened the package. It was the new Britney Spears CD! Brand new, still in its wrapping. She was joyful for a moment. But this was so weird.

Later, her brother Mahmoud examined it gravely and shrugged.

"So? It's a present from Dad. He gave it to someone who flew in last night. He promised you, right?"

"What was in the other package?" she asked. "Was it a watch?"

"I haven't opened it yet."

That's a bit weird, thought Zahra, *why not?*

"Zahra," said her mother, "get dressed and go down to the shop. Take Ben with you, we need the computer."

"Why!?" said Zahra.

"NO!" shouted Ben.

"How dare you!" snapped her mother. "You don't understand anything, you stupid little brats. Why? Because we need to Skype Uncle Saeed in Dubai. Now get out! Get out and don't come back until… until I tell you to."

She rushed out of the room, crying, leaving her two youngest children ashamed and astonished behind her.

*

Half an hour later, Zahra and Ben walked down to the shop, through the Old City. Old Abdullah was already there, setting up. Zahra helped him to shape the great mounds of spice and set them out. Ben lay down under the counter and went to sleep.

Soon after noon prayers, the qat seller came by. Old Abdullah always bought a branch or two. Usually he chewed leaves after his midday meal, but not today. Today he didn't wait.

"Why so early, Abdullah?" asked Zahra.

Old Abdullah just looked at her through old, shrewd eyes. His left cheek was already bulging with qat. Then he spat green saliva on the pavement by her feet. He inspected it, as though it were the entrails of some sacrificed animals.

"Leave. Leave now."

"What do you mean, leave? Leave the shop? Go home?"

His gaze drifted from her, over her shoulder. She turned. The black Mercedes was back, drifting down the narrow street. It stopped a few yards away. The windows stayed up, black in the midday sun. Watchful, menacing.

"Leave Yemen. Go back to your country. Take your mother, your brothers. Go today."

"What about my father? What about him?"

His answer frightened her. She went over and shook Ben awake. She couldn't wait to get home. The black Mercedes had gone, but she kept looking around for it. Suddenly she clutched Ben's arm.

"Look, Ben- past the tourist shop. Who is that? It looks like Ahmed, carrying a bag. No, forget it, he's gone in."

But Ahmed wasn't at home when they got back. He arrived an hour later, carried his old gymbag up to the mafraj, and would not meet her eye.

6

The Hamilton Incident

Friday, 15th June 2012 – a Triple Witching Day

Extract from the KPC investigation:

The new SBS datacentre [Hamilton] is located in a business park near the township of Parsippany, New Jersey, 27 miles west of Manhattan. It is the size of two football pitches and was built primarily to serve the needs of the Global Markets investment bank. It also houses the IBM mainframe computer which hosts SBS's retail and commercial banking platform in the Americas. Hamilton was completed 6 months prior to the incident and incorporates the latest in automation and energy efficiency.

The datacentre space is divided into two halls, named Laurel and Hardy. Appropriately, Laurel is half the size of Hardy.

Responsibility for datacentres is shared. At the lowest level, Property Services provide the buildings, and power and cooling within them. The next level up is Technology Infrastructure Services, or TIS, who provide the bank's network, computers ('servers'), storage, phones and personal computing.

The business applications which run on TIS's hardware are provided by the software engineers or application developers (AppDev). They are not organized into a single group like TIS, but are aligned to the individual businesses they support e.g. Debt Markets Technology.

Hamilton is a 'dark' datacentre. The bank's contractors visit to install and repair equipment as required. The only staff permanently on site are the operators (typically 5) of the TIS Network Operations Centre or NOC. This is in a separate room located within the building. These staff monitor systems processing across SBS's datacentres in the Americas, 24 x 7.

Hamilton datacentre, New Jersey: 11.53 EST, June 15 2012

It was almost midnight. Frank stood in the doorway of the Network Operations Centre (NOC) and sniffed.

"Jesus, you guys been eating chilli again? This place stinks."

"Sweet enough 'til you came in," said Marvin, getting up. His shift was almost over. He landed a couple of punches on Frank's Giants T-shirt. Frank weighed 250 pounds so there was plenty to aim at.

"Frank, did you step on dog shit on the way in?" said young John. "Would you mind checking your shoes? I don't want to smell dog shit all night."

John was new. Night shifts with John could be a pain because he was literal minded and talkative.

"Man, I hate those dogs outside," said Luis. "We've got barbed wire and cameras up the wazoo, what do we need dogs for?"

"'Cos Neil Jenkins wants dogs," said Marvin. "Anyway the smell ain't dog shit, some joker sent us some chocolates, looked good but they smelled like dead rats and they leaked shit on the table. I told Mannie already. Where's Karen? She late again?"

Shift change was at midnight, 5 minutes away.

"She'll be here, don't worry," said Frank. "I'll sign for her."

"Shit, I don't know," said Marvin. "I'm s'posed to give her the key myself, you know? Can't wait around, got my sister stayin'. What's with that girl?"

"She's got a new man, he likes a drink in the evening, that's all."

"Drinking is what you do after work," said Marvin. "This goes on, I'm going to talk to Mannie."

"I'll look after the EPO key, OK?" said Frank. Reluctantly, Marvin unfastened it from his neck and passed it over.

There was only one EPO key and it was the shift leader's badge of office. It never left the building, not even for a minute, and for good reason.

Datacentres are constructed by professional pessimists. Hamilton consumed vast quantities of electrical power, delivered by two independent substations on the New Jersey grid. The cables from those substations entered the building through different routes and led to different transformers. If this mains power should ever fail, the big generator would start up. If that generator faltered, there was a backup, ready to take its place, and a second backup behind that.

And if all these precautions disappointed, a second datacentre – with its own stack of duplication and redundancy - stood 43 miles away in Westchester County, ready to take over if Disaster Recovery ('DR') was invoked. The two datacentres were connected by three independent fibre optic links, so that even a 911-style attack with two planes could not disrupt the flow of data from one to the other.

The EPO key was a suicide pill, a murderous antidote to this litany of failsafes and redundancy. If the building was ablaze, and the massed firetrucks of Parsippany, Whippany and Morristown stood ready to hose it with water, the Emergency Power Off key gave access to a steel cabinet. Inside that cabinet were relays which would shut down the power, killing the generators, the chillers, the lights and every one of the thousands of servers inside, so the water hoses would not electrocute the fire crews. EPO keys were used only once.

"Any problems?" said Frank.

"Not for us," said Marvin. "The EOS batch is late again, Dave Carstairs and the equity boys been on a call for two hours now. Busy day tomorrow, it's Triple Witching. OK, guys, we're outta here, you all have a good night now."

He raised his palm in farewell.

"My children, may the odds be always in your favour."

"Fuck you," said Frank, "and take your shitty pizza boxes with you, OK?"

The new shift – Frank, John and Luis - settled down in front the screens that monitored the Americas network and datacentres. The bank had three Network Operations Centres. The second NOC was in London, and the third in Chennai, India.

"When I started working, guess how many alerts we got a night?" said Frank.

"There were computers then?" said Luis.

"A hundred?" said John earnestly.

"Busy night, mebbe twenty."

"Well," said John, "look at this shit. Every 5 seconds I got a new one."

"Yeah, but it's mostly noise, right? Warnings. Batch jobs running slow. Disks nearly full. It's hard to tell when the real shit happens." He clicked the mouse and consigned twenty alerts to history.

"Weird, here's another heat warning," said John, "I'm sure I just saw one."

"Oh yeah? So did I," said Luis, "what's yours?"

"'ny_dev_swapC34 Controller Board M64 substrate temperature exceeds warranty limit...' Just like the first one."

"Where is it?"

"Er... in Laurel, aisle B, rack 2."

"Mine is Laurel, Aisle C. Next door."

"Hey Frank? Check this out. We've had 3 heat alerts, all in Laurel. Should we call McQuade?"

Frank hesitated. NOC staff were paid to monitor, not to touch. Property Services and their contractor McQuade did power and cooling, and IBM looked after the computers. Neil Jenkins had actually fired the head of the London NOC when he'd tried to fix a server himself. Jenkins hadn't wanted the NOC inside the new datacentre – he wanted it in India – but the Americans had always had one. Paul Carpenter and the spirit of 1776 had defeated Neil Jenkins and his global agenda. So the NOC was built in the Hamilton datacentre, a little room for humans in the midst of vast, dark, chilly halls inhabited by machines.

"McQuade ain't here," said Frank finally, "and last time they took hours to arrive. So, Johnboy, you can go and take a look. Look, don't touch. Take the radio."

John disappeared. A minute later his voice crackled out of the radiophone on the table.

"Frank, I'm in Laurel now. Doesn't feel right, guys, it's... it's warm in here."

Frank and Luis looked at each other. A datacentre is a perverse building, a giant oven inside an even larger refrigerator. Computers consume electricity, and that electricity creates heat, lots of it. But heat is toxic to the computers that created it, and has to be removed by vast chillers, which consume even more power.

Warm was not good. Frank and Luis scrambled for the door and into the little lobby outside. They pushed impatiently through the glass turnstile and joined John on the polished floor of Laurel. The racks of the datacentre stretched into the darkness, lit by the pulsing LEDs from thousands of computers and network cards.

A healthy datacentre is not just cool, it's also noisy. The noise comes from cold air rushing in, and warm air being sucked out.

Laurel was warm and quiet.

"Shit," said Frank, "we got a problem."

He walked down to the first aisle and inspected the grills in the floor. Then he walked back to the other two.

"The CRAC fans aren't running. Could be something tripped. Power's working, so it's probably something stupid. I'm going round to the chiller plant."

The chiller plant: an array of air-conditioning units that sat outside the computer halls. Not so different from the kind of aircon unit outside a suburban house, except in scale. Each chiller weighed 10 tons and was the size of a school bus. Chillers took in warm water and energy and supplied chilled water to the Computer Room Air Conditioning (CRAC) units inside the datacentre itself.

"Should we put out an Incident Report?"

"Let's check it out first."

Frank and Luis hurried back to the little lobby and Frank keyed four digits into a door marked "CHILLER PLANT: Authorised personnel only" and "Danger 1100V."

"Frank, how come you know the code, man?"

"Hasn't changed since the day they put it in."

They arrived in a room built by a giant plumber. The pipes coming from the ceiling were two foot across and controlled by enormous valves. Frank stopped in front of a panel and pointed to the flow diagram on the side, all lit up.

"This tells you what's going on. There's the main pumps, there's six of them. Wait... these three aren't running and these valves are closed. Shit, I've never seen that before. These valves should be open."

"Frank, should we be fooling with this? I mean, it's not our job... we're not s'posed to be here, even."

There was a shout behind them. "Guys, guys, get back here! Quick!"

"I was here when we built this, OK?" said Frank, "I can fix it, no sweat. Go and keep John calm, go on, git."

John was back in the NOC, looking at his screen. "Look at this."

ny_dev832: Substrate temperature exceeds warranty limit: shutting down
ny_dev012: Substrate temperature exceeds warranty limit: shutting down
ny_dev918: Substrate temperature exceeds warranty limit: shutting down
He paged back a dozen pages – the message was just the same.

Luis ran back to Frank in the chiller room.

"Laurel is in meltdown, Frank. All the computers are shutting down. We need to tell somebody quick. For Chrissake, let's call Mannie. And McQuade."

"Luis, just fuck off, OK? Get outta here, I'm gonna fix this. Almost done."

Luis ran back to the NOC. All the phones were ringing. John was on the phone. Luis called Mannie, who was in bed. Mannie was not happy.

"And what did McQuade say?"

"Er, we haven't called them yet. Frank thinks he can fix it."

"Frank? Frank's fooling with the chillers? Oh my God. I'll be there in 10 minutes. Get McQuade right away. Get an incident report out."

Hamilton datacentre: 00:34am, 15 minutes later

Mannie arrived. He was wearing pajamas with a fleece on top and black moccasins on his feet, no socks. When he saw the open door to the chiller plant, he went white. Then he disappeared down it. Luis could hear him screaming at Frank.

They appeared together, Mannie shouting at Frank in Yiddish, punching him on the head, pushing him along. Luis had never seen Mannie mad before.

"And you! Luis! Where is McQuade! And the IR?"

"The Incident Report went out, boss," said Luis, "and McQuade's gonna be here in forty five minutes, mebbe less."

"I'm not your boss, Karen is your boss, and where the hell is she?"

Silence.

"Traffic on the Parkway," said Frank finally.

"At midnight? You're kidding. OK, when did this start?"

"Just past midnight."

"Half an hour ago," said Mannie, "shit, you idiots have wasted half an hour."

"It's just Laurel," said Frank sullenly, "It's something simple. Power's still on. It should be working."

"Mannie, should we call Business Continuity?" This was John, fresh from last week's training class on disaster recovery.

"John, shut the fuck up, OK? We call Business Continuity, we're gonna spend an hour explaining what a chiller is and doing risk assessments. Meanwhile the datacentre gets toasted - and where the hell have you been, young lady?"

The figure in the doorway was a foot shorter than Frank, but weighed about the same. She was dressed in blue jeans with a 48" waist and a check shirt on top. She was breathing heavily.

"Sorry, Mannie, had trouble getting here."

"Heavy traffic in the bar, eh? When this is over we're going to be talking. So, guys, Paul Carpenter saw the IR and he woke up Neil Jenkins in London already. And what was Neil's first question? Yeah, where is McQuade?"

Fearful silence. Paul Carpenter ran TIS in the Americas, and he was a tricky bastard. Political. But he was a pet lamb compared to Neil Jenkins. There were almost 100 datacentres of various sizes in Neil's empire, scattered around the world, but he noticed the smallest transgressions. Which he neither forgave, nor forgot.

"London has opened a call. Karen, dial us in. Put it on speaker."

"Who just joined?" said an English voice.

"Mannie Seibowitz and the Hamilton NOC here," said Mannie, bending over the speaker.

"Thank you, Mannie, can you give us an update at 0545? Right now I'd like to get an update from Business Continuity. Marcie?" said the incident manager with his oh-so-perfect English manners. And his quaint British Summer Time, 5 hours ahead of Eastern Standard.

"Looks like someone called Business Continuity anyways," said Frank.

"Shut the fuck up, Frank" said Mannie viciously, "call McQuade and find out where they are. John, get me the latest temperatures. Luis, how many machines we lost, by business. We got three minutes before we give an update."

Mannie's cellphone lit up.

"Mannie? It's John Uzgalis from London."

"Hi John. Yeah, I'm in Hamilton," said Mannie. "No, it's the Laurel hall. Yeah, only Laurel. Listen, gotta run."

"This is Marcie from Americas Business Continuity," came a voice from the Polycom. "I've called the business heads, especially Asset Management. I've set up an exec call for 1.15am. We need a plan from IT before then."

"Great," said Mannie bitterly, "that's thirty minutes from now. Every computer in Laurel will have fried and the McQuade guys will just be driving in."

Thurleigh Road, South London: a few minutes earlier

Noise. Had his alarm gone off? No. Chris Peters lay still in bed, confused. Outside he could hear a songthrush, greeting the dawn. His brain snapped into work mode. It was Friday. Triple Witching. Had they fixed Chopstix in time? What about the EOS batch?

The noise again. It was his Blackberry, ringing and vibrating at the same time. Bloody hell, must be Dave Carstairs with a production problem. He picked it up and stared at the screen, confused. A call from BUSINESS CONTINUITY – LONDON.

Huh? What?

More noise. The phone in his study was ringing. Then the old phone downstairs. The whole world was ringing and he was suddenly afraid. He pressed the ANSWER button on his Blackberry and it spoke to him:

...THIS IS A MESSAGE FOR CHRIS PETERS. THIS IS NOT A DRILL. THERE HAS BEEN A SIGNIFICANT INCIDENT IN THE HAMILTON DATACENTRE. DIAL INTO YOUR DISASTER RECOVERY BRIDGE IMMEDIATELY. THIS IS NOT A DRILL...

And all the while, the other phones kept ringing, loud enough to wake the dead.

Chris sat naked, hunched over at the top of his stairs, and dialled into the Technology DR bridge. It was chaos. Everyone had a question. No one had answers. The incident manager was struggling to corral the troops.

Chris put the bridge on hold and called John Uzgalis.

"John, what's going on?"

"I called Mannie Seibowicz, he's the TIS guy who runs the NOC in Hamilton," said Uzgalis. "He just arrived on site, looks like a cooling problem in Laurel. Could be worse, Debt Markets got nothing but dev and test kit in Laurel."

"Same for Equities. All the important stuff is in Hardy. Great news. OK, ciao man, gonna put some clothes on."

Chris threw on a pair of old corduroys and a lumberjack shirt. He opened his front door and sat on the steps outside. He wanted the phone on speaker but he didn't want to disturb Olivia. It was a bright morning with scattered clouds. With luck, this incident would be deemed harmless and in half an hour he would be drinking tea with Olivia – swiftly followed by baby making.

As he dialled back into the bridge, the sun slipped behind low clouds and the street darkened, as if to warn him.

Hamilton datacentre: a few minutes later

Mannie was hunched over the Polycom, ready to give his update.

"Well, thank God it is only Laurel," said Luis, glancing at the clock on the wall. It said 00:47. This was a moment he would never forget. He would bore his family with this moment for years to come. But he didn't know that, not quite yet.

"Why nobody cares about Laurel?" said John. "It's full and the Hardy hall's half empty."

"It's not just how many computers," said Luis, "it's what they do. There's only developer and test kit in Laurel. Plus Asset Management - no-one cares about them. Hardy Hall has the mainframe. We lose that, all the US branches will be shut down. Plus Canada, Mexico, Brazil. No banking, no payments, shit, no cash machines. Global Markets won't be trading. On a Triple Witching day. If this was Hardy melting down, we'd be on the front page of the Wall Street Journal tomorrow."

"Mannie? Mannie?" This was John, watching the screens with puppy-like devotion.

"Not now, John, I gotta give my update."

"But look at these messages: 1108 Excess temperature alert. There's six of them, all from different machines."

"So what?" said Mannie, distracted. "We've seen hundreds of them."

"Yes, but these servers are in the other hall. Hardy. The big hall."

"They can't be. Hardy is on different chillers." That was Frank.

"No, John's right," said Luis, "those boxes are in Hardy."

"It's impossible," said Frank, "I'm telling you, there's different chillers for the Hardy Hall, different electrics... ain't no connection."

"Oh shit! There's more of them... look at that," said John. "Those are Windows servers in the same aisle. Houston, we got a problem."

Almost in sync, Mannie's cellphone and the handset on the table started ringing. Then Karen's. It was Paul Carpenter in Manhattan, and the NOC in London, and in Chennai. The whole world was calling, all with the same question: *What the fuck is going on in Aisle E, Hardy Hall, Hamilton Datacentre, NJ 10392?*

Hamilton datacentre: 1.00 am (15 minutes later)

Mannie had no answers. No one had any answers. The vast, failsafe arrays of air conditioning had stopped working in both halls. Even though they were independent and unconnected. There was power. There was cold water in the chillers, but no cold air blasting out to cool the computers. It was as if the CRAC units had gone on strike.

The crisis in Hardy had started later, but seemed determined to catch up. Mannie went out there and felt for himself the hot, humid atmosphere. It was twenty-four degrees and rising. People on the bridge started talking about going to DR, about moving to Westchester. Paul Carpenter encouraged them. He made it sound like moving house.

Mannie knew it wasn't that simple. Going to Disaster Recovery was like jumping off a cliff with a parachute in one hand. DR meant shutting down every application running in Hamilton and firing it up in Westchester – processing a mirror copy of the data. There were hundreds of apps, most of them in the middle of their end-of-day batch processing. Going to DR was like evacuating a town into new homes and factories, transferring the half-built cars and the half-cooked dinners and expecting everything to work. It would take all night to do it and the fallout would last for weeks. And in the case of Hamilton, it was brand new and they had never even practiced it, because the weekend change calendar was so full.

He could tell the AppDev guys felt the same way. He had heard Chris Peters arguing with Carpenter.

"Paul, we must fix the cooling, OK? Believe me, we will be 100% better off than going to DR."

It was 1am. McQuade's engineers claimed to be ten miles away on 287. Two of the day crew from IBM arrived. They rushed into the Hardy Hall to look at the mainframe.

The incident manager was trying to get Mike Tucker and Property Services on the call. No luck yet.

Frank Castagnetto from IBM joined the call, presumably from his home. Castagnetto sounded like a high school science teacher.

"Gentlemen, some facts for you. The temperature in the Hardy Hall is now 28 degrees and rising one degree every five or six minutes. When it reaches 32 degrees, we will shut down the mainframe to protect it. You have 20 minutes, give or take. The bank needs to make some decisions."

"Even if we haven't gone to DR by then?" That was Paul Carpenter. The head of TIS Americas was sitting, naked, in his loft apartment in Tribeca with a speakerphone in front of him. His white cat was stretched out on the sofa beside him. Neil Jenkins had forced him to outsource mainframe support to IBM last year and he had always known it was a mistake. He was filled with sober and righteous anger.

"Yes," said Castagnetto.

"We need more time," said Carpenter, "the electricians will just be arriving."

"Twenty minutes," said Castagnetto, "then we're done. If you are going to DR, you need to decide now. Once we shut down the mainframe, you can't swing it to Westchester."

Carpenter did not reply.

"Okay," said Castagnetto, "then where is Neil Jenkins?"

Mannie didn't remember hearing Neil Jenkins for the last hour. He was drowning. And sweating. He was standing with Frank and the young IBM engineer by the mainframe in the Hardy Hall, watching the temperature rising. Now it was 29 degrees. Already some of the UNIX servers had shut themselves down. It was a total disaster.

He put his hands up to the grill of the nearest CRAC unit. Normally it blew cold air, gloriously chilled, like ice from a glacier. There was air wafting out all right. It was a warm gentle breeze, the same fucking temperature as everything else. A row of green lights twinkled from its status panel. As far as this CRAC unit was concerned, everything was A-OK.

Mannie kicked the CRAC unit several times, until the pain brought tears to his eyes. "Damn you," he shouted. "Damn you! You shitty piece of garbage, why won't you work? Why? What's wrong with you? Give me cold air, damn you!"

He looked at the racks of servers on the nearest aisles, all cooking, all blowing out toxic heat. They were a mixed bag, mostly trading and risk systems for Global Markets. EOS was in the middle of its batch but the other systems were mostly done for the night. The markets opened at 7.30am tomorrow.

Out of the corner of his eye, he saw the temperature gauge move to 30 Celsius. Something snapped in Mannie's head.

"Frank, shut down everything in aisles D and E."

"OK," said Frank, "I'll warn the dbas to get ready ..."

"Frank, I said shut down. Like this."

He moved to the first cabinet. Inside the door frame was a circuit breaker. Flicking up the guard, he tripped the switch. Nothing happened. Dual power supply, he reminded himself grimly, no single points of failure. He found the second breaker and flipped that. The little lights stopped flickering and the fans wound down. It was like killing something.

"Do the rest, Frank. Now."

"Mannie, oh my God, we can't do that."

"We don't do it, it will all be gone in twenty minutes. We need time so some asshole can make a decision. Just do it, Frank. Now."

He ran back to the NOC and found Luis, John and Karen.

"Luis, John, open all the doors. And the roller shutters, starting with the delivery bay. Everything. I want a breeze going through."

"What about the guard dogs?" asked John nervously. "Don't they let them loose at night?"

"Fuck the dogs. Dogs don't produce enough heat to worry about. Run, run, damn you, the mainframe is about to go!"

Hamilton datacentre: 5 minutes later

It was 1.23 am. Marcie Schulman was back on the Tech Bridge, sounding stressed. "The call with the business to decide if we are going to DR is happening now. The business is on but no TIS representation. Neil, are you on? Has anyone heard from Neil Jenkins? Is he on another bridge?"

No-one had heard from Neil. In the silence, Mannie jumped in.

"Guys, this is Mannie Seibowitz in Hamilton. McQuade has arrived."

"What about the mainframe?" asked the incident manager. "IBM's twenty minutes are up."

"We bought time. We shut down a shitload."

"Could you be more precise?"

"Email, the Global Markets trading systems, all the risk servers, sales, you name it. About half the kit in the Hardy Hall."

"Oh my God," said the incident manager, forgetting his lines.

"IBM say the mainframe may last thirty minutes," said Mannie. "Then it's gone for sure."

Hamilton datacentre: ten minutes later

"Hamilton, do you have a McQuade update?" said the incident manager, for the fourth time. Mannie ran down to the Chiller Room and dragged the senior McQuade guy back to the NOC. He was a thin silver haired man in a dirty white T-shirt. His hands and fingernails were stained with silvery grease. He looked like a car mechanic.

"Well?" said Mannie.

"Someone's changed the settings on the chiller controls," the man said. "The pumps were all set to manual. We've changed them back."

"And?" said Mannie, with a murderous glance at Frank.

The mechanic just sat there. Mannie wanted to slap him, wanted to scream.

The man shrugged.

"Made no difference. Power's OK, water temperatures are good, pumps are good, fuses good, everything's good."

He looked up, faintly defiant. "Ain't nothin' wrong with those chillers."

Hope evaporated. Even the incident manager was silent.

"Excuse me, guys, this is Chris Peters. Equity Technology."

Chris was sitting on the front steps of his home on Thurleigh Rd, the dawn sunlight bright on his face. The incident reports said his US trading systems were all down. EOS Americas was down. So were all the US back office systems. In ten years, he had never experienced anything like it. He spoke softly, trying to hide his desperation.

"Guys, all the alarms so far... they are from servers. Individual computers. Right? But the air-conditioning units, the CRACs, they're putting out warm air. They're sucking in warm air. No alarms from them? Why not?"

You could almost hear Mike Tucker from Property trying to figure it out. Mannie could hear someone whispering to Mike in the background.

"Chris, the thermostats for the CRACs are all controlled from the Building Management System in India. Centrally, you know."

"So why aren't the CRACs complaining?" asked Chris Peters. "What's their target air temperature?"

There was a static burst on the line and an Indian voice cut in, a thick South Indian accent.

"This is Murali in Chennai. I can answer that question. The CRAC units should be set to nineteen degrees. But we are checking now..."

There was an agonizing pause.

"Excuse me, please, this is Murali. We have investigated the BMS. Air conditioning in Hamilton is set to sixty-six degrees. I am very sorry indeed for this news…"

"Sixty-six degrees Celsius?" said the incident manager, disbelieving.

"Yes, I am confirming sixty-six Celsius. Hence previous speaker was asking the right question. There are no alarms because CRAC units think hot, hot air is righty-fine. When temperature reaches sixty-seven degrees, then they will turn on!"

"When they will be blowing cold air over a dead world," said Uzgalis, stating the obvious poetically.

"Well, Jesus Christ, Murali, just reset the fucking temperatures, will you!" shouted Mike Tucker.

He had reason to be anxious. Quite apart from the damage to the US economy, if this went down as a Property screw-up, Neil Jenkins would destroy him in the corridors of power.

Murali was back two minutes later and he did not sound happy.

"There is a problem with permissions. Building Management System is not allowing. We change it but then it resets to sixty-six degrees. We have not seen this before."

Back in Hamilton, someone was tapping on Mannie's shoulder. He turned around. It was the young IBM engineer, his face white and sweaty.

"We're up to thirty-three degrees. In E aisle. We're going to bring the mainframe down."

"No, no, stay with it. We've found the problem."

"I can't risk it. It's probably damaged already."

"The bank will take the risk."

"I'd need it in writing."

Mannie looked around. The Disaster Recovery playbook was open on the table. He ripped out a page and scrawled 'IBM must run mainframe until further notice,' on a blank space.

"That's it, buddy. Now run that baby until it turns into a puddle of silicon, OK?"

Mannie was pumped. He was so far out in space, he had no fear of falling back to Earth. He was on his way to some distant planet for good or ill.

Hamilton datacentre: 01:40am Eastern Standard Time

Marcie Schulman was back on the Tech bridge, sounding punchy.

"The executive committee has requested full Disaster Recovery to the backup datacentre in Westchester. IT asked for a twenty minute delay to resolve the situation in Hamilton, which takes us to 2am. The business has instructed IT to execute full DR at 2am. No further excuses or delays."

"Mike, we've got twenty minutes to break into the BMS and turn down the temperature," said John Uzgalis. "Can we help?"

"We're trying," said Mike Tucker. "The system was sold to us by GE, but it was made by Fujitsu. Their industrial controls division in Yokohama. We've got calls out everywhere. No joy so far."

"Who configured it? You must have someone who understands it," said Uzgalis.

"We did. He was a contractor. He's on vacation in Thailand."

"Can we shut it down? Can we unplug it?"

"It's managing eight buildings including the two datacentres in London. And the trading floors. No, we bloody well can't unplug it."

Chris Peters was watching a milkfloat coming up Thurleigh road, Murali's words still ringing in his head: *When temperature reaches sixty-six degrees, they will turn on!*

The idea appeared magically in his brain, fully-fledged, gift-wrapped. Frantically, he searched for Neil Jenkins' private number. The guardian of the bank's infrastructure sounded groggy.

"Neil? It's Chris, listen… how about this? Just listen, will you?"

The noise of the argument carried down the street. The milkman stopped his cart to listen. The young guy sitting on the steps was pleading on the phone. He sounded like he was almost crying.

"Neil, why not? Just ask Mannie to try it. Help us, please. Please, just call him."

Shrugging, the milkman continued on his rounds. He'd seen a lot of strange things in his time, but usually there was a woman involved.

Two minutes later, back in Hamilton, Mannie had a call from a UK number.

"Mannie? This is Chris Peters. Here's an idea. Unusual, but it's your last chance."

Mannie listened with amazement.

Finally he said, "Are you fuckin' crazy? I'm not doing that. Neil would kill me."

"It's Neil's idea, for God's sake!" came the reply, "I'm just the messenger. Neil says get on with it."

What do I have to lose? thought Mannie, yelling for Karen, John and Luis.

"We need hairdryers. Here, as many as possible. In the next ten minutes. Go."

"Just do it," he shouted at their incredulous faces. "There's a CVS drugstore, up by the intersection, it's open twenty-four hours. Buy everything they've got, the bigger the better. Don't think, run!"

Karen was first back. She lived in East Hanover, just a couple of miles away.

"Wow, where did you get these?" said Mannie, looking at a dozen or more hairdryers she'd brought in a plastic basket.

"Well," said Karen, "every year BaByliss comes out with new models and I just buy them."

"OK, work in pairs. Karen, start with the sensors by aisle E. Sixty-six degrees is all we need, don't melt them. Take John's radio with you, I'll tell you how you are doing."

He went back to the NOC and put the Hardy Hall temperature map on screen. The temperature sensor by Aisle E read thirty-five degrees Celsius, but within two minutes it shot up to fifty-five as the air from Karen's hairdryer played over it. He had never been so glad to see a hot spot in a datacentre.

"That's fine, Karen. Now it's sixty-eight, now tape it there."

Mannie found himself holding his breath. A few moments later there were joyful cries from the radio.

"We've got air, freezing air."

During the next fifteen minutes, Karen and her little team of operators installed nineteen hairdryers and four portable electric heaters pointing at the sensors up and down the Hardy Hall. They taped them to cabinet doors, trolleys and pipework. Karen found a neat way of hanging the dryers from the overhead cable racks using duct tape. The IBM and the McQuade guys got the idea when they felt the cold air start up and joined in.

Mannie went over to see for himself. It was hot as hell, but he had to shout over the noise of the fans. The temperature on E Aisle was reading thirty-one and as he watched it dropped to twenty-nine.

Someone tapped him on the shoulder.

"You're wanted on the bridge, we're going to DR in Westchester. Some guy in London has decided."

Shit, he'd forgotten about the rest of the world. He ran back into the NOC. The incident manager was busy reciting a list of timings and actions, swinging the five hundred or so applications across to Westchester.

"Hold it, hold it!" he screamed into the Polycom. "This is Mannie Seibowitz, we're OK here. Neil's plan worked, cooling is back!"

He had to repeat it several times but they got it in the end.

The AppDev guys were almost crying with happiness. Alexis van Buren went off to tell the business. Mannie got a message from Chris Peters:

Great work! I hope they give you a medal.

Van Buren was back five minutes later.

"Guys, we've got a complication with the CFO. Jerome deVries is saying, why not do full DR anyway? Prove it works. Cyrus and the trading heads don't want to take the risk but deVries says if DR doesn't work, that's a SOX issue. As CFO, he's accountable for Sarbanes-Oxley compliance. He's the one who goes to jail, he says."

Mannie knew about Sarbanes-Oxley (SOX). It was one of those lumbering regulatory monsters that emerged from Congress every couple of years and spawned a new generation of bureaucrats, auditors and management consultants.

"What? That's outrageous. He just wants IT to look bad," said someone.

"Chris, John, David, call me on my bridge," said van Buren. The gods of AppDev disappeared, leaving Mannie to industrialise the use of hairdryers while an unknown team of Japanese engineers in Yokohama tried to figure out why their flagship Building Management System had had a nervous breakdown.

Within the ranks of TIS, BaByliss night added another page to the legend of Neil Jenkins. Hairdryers! How cool was that?! Neil Jenkins was an ugly bastard, but man, he was damned smart and ice cold under pressure.

Chris Peters kept his mouth shut. It had been his idea, but he wasn't sure anyone would believe it. He didn't want to look like a glory seeker. His Norwegian ancestry rebelled at that thought. He was happy just to have survived BaByliss night, or so he told himself.

But the event itself haunted him. "It will happen again," he told Dom. "It will. Unless we find out why..." He sent Dom to the postmortem committee. "Torture Fujitsu until they give us some answers."

7

Sana'a, Yemen, 2007

Day Three - Sunday

There was a moment when Ben put it all together.

Zahra went and sat with him in the Box, early on the third day. Their mother was down below, scrubbing the stone stairs, all of them, as if her life depended on it.

"Ben," said Zahra, "things are happening that don't make sense."

"Such as?" said Ben, without taking his eyes off the screen.

"What are our brothers up to? Remember on the way home yesterday? I'm sure I saw Ahmed in the souk. Going into a jewellery store, carrying his gym bag."

"Buying presents?" said Ben.

"Whose birthday? Anyway, later, I had this strange warning from Old Abdullah. He grabbed my arm and he said 'Leave Yemen. Take your brothers and my mother. *Go today*.'"

"And then I said, 'Yes, but what about our father?' and he said, 'If it is the will of Allah, he will be protected.'"

Ben stopped typing.

"I don't like that," he said. "He thinks Dad's in Yemen. And he's in trouble."

"Yes. And then, there's this."

She slid the CD case onto the table.

"Britney Spears?" said Ben. "Who's she?"

"She's my favourite singer, you numskull. This is her latest CD. Dad promised to bring it from Dubai. It was delivered yesterday, by hand. I was pleased. I thought Dad had... But then last night I thought, 'Dad would never have wrapped it in crappy newspaper,' and suddenly I was frightened. If not Dad, who? How did they get it? How did they know where to send it?"

Ben turned slowly to face her. His dark eyes seemed to pierce her, and look through her, at something behind. She noticed for the first time the wisps of hair on his chin, and an adolescent spot.

"Then this morning, Mother isn't wearing our gold bangles."

"Our gold bangles?"

"The ones Dad gave her, you numskull, one after each baby. She never takes them off. Where have they gone? Then just now, I sneaked up to the mafraj and looked in Ahmed's gym bag. It's full of money. Some dollars, mostly Yemeni. Lots of it. How did he get so much money? Do you see? It doesn't make sense."

Suddenly Ben went mad.

"Shit, shit, shit," he said, banging his head on the table. "I've been so stupid. Shit! How did I not see this?" He ducked through the curtains and started ringing the dinner bell like a madman.

*

"You've been lying to us!"

Ben was shouting, holding out Zahra's CD, pointing at his mother and Mahmoud.

"Lying! Dad isn't in Dubai. He didn't miss his flight. He's been taken, right here in Sana'a. Kidnapped. Hasn't he?"

"No!" cried Zahra. It was an unbearable thought. It came with dreadful images of captivity, darkness, and horrible cruelties.

"Yes," said Ben. "And now you are trying to find his ransom money. You've sold your bangles. You skype Uncle Saeed every day, trying to get money out of the bank. So many lies. Do you think we're babies? Tell us the truth. NOW!"

"Alright," said Mahmoud at last. "You remember when the police turned up, that first morning after Father didn't arrive? It was a young guy in a Jeep…"

*

The police driver who had picked them up was young and handsome, with a smooth, almost pink complexion. Perhaps one of his ancestors had taken a Berber woman into his household. He was proud of his old Jeep, too, and thrashed it through the narrow streets. Little Yousef and his urchin friends had run after them, cheering, but soon dropped out, exhausted. In ten minutes, they were inside the police station in the New City. It was gloomy inside with unfinished grey walls. A line of men were sitting on the floor, all silent, waiting. There were two policemen at the desk, drinking tea.

Their driver spoke to them. They looked up, taking in Mahmoud and his mother, her face invisible behind her niqab.

"What is the woman doing here?"

"She is the wife."

The desk sergeant gestured contemptuously towards the queue.

"Wait there."

An hour later, a door at the back opened. A big, corpulent man was standing there, wearing the grey uniform of an inspector. He beckoned them. His office was small and untidy. The walls were decorated with pictures of President Saleh shaking hands with policemen.

"Passports."

"I'm sorry?"

"You are foreigners. Give me your passports."

The inspector's thick fingers flicked expertly through Mahmoud's passport, like an Immigration official.

"You go to Dubai."

"Yes, my father has a business there. He is a spice merchant."

The policeman glanced at his mother's ID card.

"Hashemi. You are the wife of Jafar Hashemi?"

Gurjit nodded, wordlessly. Petrified.

He opened a drawer in his desk and tossed both documents inside.

"Be quiet," he said, over their protests. "Do you know why you are here?"

"No, sir," said Mahmoud. "But… my father has disappeared yesterday and we thought you had news…"

The policeman lit a Pakistani cigarette with a gold lighter and exhaled in a long, steady stream. He was not old. Forty-five, perhaps, but not a picture of health. His fingers and teeth were stained with nicotine and his thick cheeks were pale, almost grey. But his eyes were watchful.

"Do you know who I am?"

"No, sir."

"I am the CID officer responsible for anti-terrorist co-ordination, here in Sana'a."

He smiled cynically.

"Maybe not for much longer. Last week, seven foreigners were taken by al-Qaeda. We turned the city upside down. Yesterday we found the bodies of the women in a ditch outside town."

He paused, said suddenly: "Why did you bring your mother? It was inappropriate."

He hesitated, tapped the ash off his cigarette, took another drag, reached a decision.

"In the afternoon, they kidnapped another foreigner, a Shia, at the airport. His name was Hashemi. Jafar Hashemi. I am sorry, madam..."

"He is not dead," whispered Gurjit. One small hand appeared from her niqab, holding her old phone. "Not yet. They sent me a text from his phone."

She slid off her chair and knelt on the floor, her hands together, imploring.

"You can save him. Please, he is my husband. We can pay, we have money. How much do they want? How much?"

The policeman laid a hand flat across his chest.

"Mother, listen to me, from my heart. This is al-Qaeda. They are islamists, fanatics. Who knows what they want? Not money. Publicity, maybe. Go home, gather your children round you, say Janazzah for your husband. Prepare for life without him."

She did not move. After a long pause, the inspector sighed and stubbed out his cigarette.

"Alright, I will ask. Wait outside."

They waited an hour, then two. Finally they were brought back in.

The inspector looked at their desperate faces.

"I was wrong. Modern jihad is expensive, apparently. The price of your father's head is two million US dollars."

Mahmoud felt as if he had fallen off a building and the ground was rushing up towards him.

"But- but we don't have that kind of money. That's ridiculous. Impossible."

The policeman lit another cigarette, wincing as he inhaled the acrid smoke.

"I don't know why I smoke this camel shit. Even if it was free, I shouldn't smoke it... give Tariq your number. When we find his body, I will call you."

He rang a little bell and the young policeman came in.

"No good. They are leaving, Tariq. Bring me another coffee."

As the young man picked up the dirty cup, the inspector laid one hand gently on his.

"And make it sweeter than the last one, I need to regain my strength this morning."

Their eyes met and the young man smiled. He was still smiling as he held the street door open for them, and he muttered something as they passed.

"What did you say?" said Mahmoud.

"Two million dollars is the starting price. You could make an offer," said Tariq, "it's the custom, here in Yemen. Even al-Qaeda bargains."

Then they were alone in the wide dusty street.

*

"No Jeep. It took us an hour to walk home," said Mahmoud. "On the way, we decided to tell you that Dad was still in Dubai."

"So what has happened?" said Ben. "Did you make an offer?"

"Yes. I offered $400,000. They accepted it."

"How much have we got?" said Ben.

"$2,000 from Mother's jewellery and $3,000 for the truck," replied Mahmoud, opening the old sportsbag.

The inside was stuffed with Yemeni notes, hundreds of them, dirty and crumpled. Zahra remembered her mother's beautiful coral necklace and the four gold bangles and she wanted to cry.

"What about the shop?" said Zahra. "Dad said it was worth a fortune."

"Ahmed and I went round the souk yesterday. No-one offered us a glass of tea. People disappeared when they saw us coming. We were like lepers."

"And that's it? $5,000."

"So far. We've got $300,000 in the bank in Dubai. In a business savings account."

"Wow. What are we waiting for?" said Ben.

"Ben, you can't walk into a bank nowadays and demand sackfuls of cash. They think you are a drug dealer. Or a terrorist. Uncle Saeed is trying to buy gold with it."

"And?"

"They are being very difficult, according to him. Forms. Then more forms. They want Dad's signature on everything. We're trying."

"How long have we got?" said Ben.

"No specific date," said Mahmoud, looking down at the floor.

Liar, thought Zahra. His desperation transmitted itself to her. She felt as though an invisible hand was squeezing her throat.

8

Blackfriars Bridge

Monday, 25th June 2012

Ten days had passed since the disaster of BaByliss night. Chris Peters was on his way to work. The early summer days had given way to a week of rain and hail. The underground was a mess. It took Chris an hour to get to Waterloo Station. He picked up an abandoned, soggy copy of the *Daily Mail* while he waited for a train.

"Who stole our summer?" screamed the headline. Beneath, lurid prose warned of fifty-five mile-per-hour winds and torrential rain in the South of England. "Washout Wimbledon!" cried the Sports page.

The dispirited commuters at Waterloo Station did not need the *Daily Mail* to tell them about the weather. They were already damp. The anodyne female voice over the tannoy merely deepened their misery: "Due to flooding, the Waterloo & City line has been suspended... we apologise..."

Cursing, Chris started looking for a taxi.

Behind him, a short, ugly man with a pockmarked face and ginger beard heard the same announcement, and the despondent mutterings that followed. Neil Jenkins had nothing but contempt for both. He knew how to run a railroad. His profession gave him insight, and with it came zero tolerance for failure. His watch said twenty to nine.

Neil Jenkins was not a walker, but he was not a patient man either, and he needed to get to work. Clutching his old leather briefcase and a cheap umbrella, he headed for York Road, passing the taxi rank. The queue for taxis stretched out of sight, and the taxis stretched exactly nowhere. Halfway down, he stopped.

"Hello Chris! What are you doing here?"

Chris turned in surprise.

"What does it look like?"

"It looks like a line of idiots. There's no bloody taxis."

"Haven't you seen the weather? It's pissing down," said Chris.

"Weather?" said Jenkins, with Northern contempt. "It's a passing shower. Come with me, I'll get you to work in no time."

"No thanks."

"Oh, you're a born loser, you are."

"Why are you always so angry?" said Chris.

"Me? Angry? I'm not angry. Disappointed, more like. You can't choose family, but you can choose your friends. And you've picked Uzgalis."

"He was more help than you were, on BabyLiss night," said Chris.

"Bollocks. You should try my job. You wouldn't last a day."

The Overlord of the bank's infrastructure stared at Chris, and Chris stared back. Neil's eyes were bloodshot behind the thick, steel-rimmed glasses.

"This I will say," Neil said finally, "you deserved more credit than you got. But that was not my doing. And if we had gone to DR, you and Uzgalis, you'd have been right fucked."

Chris watched him go, watched him join the huddled masses waiting to cross York Road. There were angry exchanges as his short, bearded figure elbowed its way to the front.

*

The rain was driving across the road in sheets. After twenty yards Neil's umbrella blew out. One of his shoes leaked. He could feel the water oozing in. Perhaps this was a mistake, but he was not going back. He sheltered under Waterloo Bridge watching the angry waters of the Thames pile up against the piers. When the rain eased, he set out eastwards along the Embankment, holding the tattered remains of his umbrella above his head.

The next squall forced him to take shelter under Blackfriars, where he found himself surrounded by a group of shivering Chinese tourists, dressed in yellow polythene macs.

Their guide was shouting above the wind, pointing out to the river.

"On the morning of June 11, 1982, the body of a man was found hanging from scaffolding, right there, just above the water. His name was Roberto Calvi – you have heard of him – he was called God's Banker. His death is a mystery to this day …"

The tourists were all peeking out into the wind, imagining the bizarre sight of Roberto Calvi, an orange rope around his neck, seven bricks in his jacket and trousers, his feet dangling eighteen inches below the water.

Neil Jenkins was not listening, however. His attention had been strangely drawn to a simple stone plaque, chiseled into the wall above: *1874 H.W.M.*

A horizontal line showed exactly how high the water had reached. It was a good ten feet above him. There was another one above it: *1953 H.W.*

And above that, one more, too high to read clearly. 1928? 1828? It was the highest of all, perhaps twenty feet up. Almost to the roadway of the bridge. On a day like today, with the Thames raging past him, that simple mark was for Neil Jenkins a menace greater than a regiment of dangling corpses.

It was past nine o'clock. He clambered up to the bridge above, and headed for St Paul's. He arrived at the bank at 9.25am. His shoes squelched as he crossed the marble floor and joined the queue for the lifts.

"Hey Neil, been for a swim?"

He looked up. John Uzgalis was standing behind him, with a couple of his guys. One of them decided to take a pop.

"Hey, Neil, the Dark Ages are over, why are we still using these antiques?"

He was holding up his Blackberry.

"Because they work. We won't connect what we can't control," said Neil in his broad Northern accent.

A lift arrived and the crowd surged forward but Neil stayed put.

"Not so fast, gents. I got woken up last night by some idiot in New York. One of your lot, Mr Uzgalis. The mortgages system had run out of disk space. *To his surprise*. It was an emergency, he said. 'Where's your capacity plan?' I asked him. No reply. 'Disk space monitoring, maybe?' No reply. Pillock. I told him to wake you up next time. Have a good day, gentlemen."

Neil Jenkins waved them onto the lift. He thought he heard Uzgalis muttering "dinosaur" as the doors closed. His thoughts went back to the river Thames and the high-water marks under Blackfriars Bridge.

*

"Get Steve Smith in my office ASAP. And Ashok, now."

"Which Ashok?"

"How the hell do I know? Ashok, one of the grads. The young guy who's been modelling bandwidth. The clever Ashok. Does great powerpoint."

"Ashok Kumar," said Mary. Mary had been Neil's PA since he arrived, three years before. She was a mature, calm woman turning fifty. Her memory for names and phone numbers was legendary.

Ashok Kumar arrived a few minutes later. Neil's door was closed, but Neil's voice floated through the walls.

"Don't you understand, Matt? Chris Peters, Uzgalis, even David Trebbiano. Their appetite for disk space is limitless. Whatever you give them, they will consume it. So don't give it to them. Starve them. Let them suffer... then they will learn better habits. That's the right thing for the bank."

"Doing the right thing for the bank" was Neil Jenkins' watchword. He said it even more often than "we won't connect what we can't control". It sounded laudable but it was surprising how much pain it caused. And how many enemies he made pursuing it.

Steve Smith arrived. He was responsible for all datacentres, except in the Americas, which was Paul Carpenter's territory. Smith looked nervously at the noise coming from Neil's door.

"Do you know what this is about?"

Mary shook her head. She did not believe in wasting words, which suited her boss. He was a black box himself. His managers never knew what was cunning, what was instinct and what was stupidity because he explained neither triumph nor disaster.

The door opened and Matt Ford flew out. Neil's parting words echoed across the office.

"Matt, you're not here to make people happy, OK? If they don't like it, tell them to fuck off. Or they can come here and hear it from me. Right, who's next? Come in, gentlemen. Shut the door, Ashok."

No one sat down.

"Right, folks, time for a history lesson. Let's start with you, Steve. What can you tell me about the year 1928?"

Steve Smith opened his mouth, then shut it again. Finally, he decided to take this bizarre question seriously.

"Er, the great depression? No, no, a crash? The stock market crash?"

"That was in 1929, you pillock. And nobody had heard of datacentres in those days. IBM was still making type writers."

"Datacentres?"

"Datacentres, like Drake and Raleigh, which you are supposed to be running and on which this bank utterly depends. Datacentres, that's a clue, Steve, trying to make it easy for you."

There was a long pause.

"Dunno, Neil, you got me there."

Neil nodded, grimly satisfied. He looked down at Mary's paper.

"OK, my friend, I will tell you. In 1928, a lot of snow melted up in the Cotswolds. And where did it go? Down the Thames. At the same time, there was a high tide, and a storm surge in the North Sea, and where did that water go? Yes! Up the Thames. Where they met, the water rose 18 feet. 18 feet! The all-time high. It flooded ten thousand houses in Millbank, it flooded the Underground, Parliament was under water. Can you imagine that?"

He stroked his pointed beard. It had been an angry ginger when he started the job three years ago, but nowadays it was fading to grey. But the anger inside was bright as ever. If anything, Jenkins was less predictable now, his outbursts more violent.

He looked over at Smith and his tone was almost casual. It was a bad sign.

"So, how far is Raleigh above the river, Steve?"

Drake and Raleigh were the bank's two main datacentres in Europe. Drake was new, just three years old, built on high ground west of London. Raleigh was in an old industrial site down in West Ham. Down by the docklands. On a hot summer day, you could smell the effluent from the River Lee as it flowed by, just a mile or two from the Thames.

"I don't know."

"You don't know? How can you not know? It's your bloody job to know. Even I know."

Rajiv and Ashok exchanged glances. This was Neil's little joke. No one else found it funny. Neil's empire covered a hundred datacentres of various sizes in sixty-three countries. His five thousand staff maintained hundreds of thousands of desktops, telephones and computers of all sizes but there was no detail that he could not dive into when he chose. And he did, frequently, picking on some obscure fact and then torturing his staff with their ignorance. It was part of the culture of fear that kept his managers awake at night.

"Neil, I'm sorry, I really haven't investigated floods but... those kinds of floods can't happen again..."

"Oh, really? Why not? The sea is rising, after all. Two feet since 1900, more to come from the Greenland ice."

"Yes, but the Thames Barrier stops flooding... we looked at this a few years ago."

"Oh, the Thames Barrier?" said Jenkins. "I've heard of that. Ashok, are you an expert on the Thames Barrier?"

Ashok shook his head. He was only twenty-four but too smart to pretend. Especially when his boss was in this mood.

"No? Ok, Steve, enlighten us. What is the Thames Barrier?"

"Er, well, it's like a dam. It's these twelve steel plates, across the Thames, down by Greenwich. They are massively strong, each one weighs like three hundred tons. When there's a high tide, they raise them... that's why there haven't been any floods since they build it."

"I see," said Neil. "Sounds like an accident waiting to happen. How many times has it saved us so far? You don't know? All right, who operates it?"

"A government department, I think."

"A government department! That graveyard of IT incompetents. Let's hope it's not the same people as run Waterloo and City Line or I'd be saying, 'Bloody hell, Chaps, let's take the next train to Raleigh and teach our computers to swim.'"

The room was tactfully silent, reminded of their boss's soaking clothes and trying not to look. Word about Neil's journey to work had got around.

"Well, it's worked OK since 1980. Over thirty years," said Steve with foolish defiance.

Neil put his head in his hands, for so long that Ashok wondered if he was ill. Finally, he raised his head and peeked at Steve Smith through his fingers.

"Steve, it makes me ill to hear you. Oh my God... it gives me a headache. Lend me your ears, young Steve, lend your impressionable young brain..."

"Look, the world underprices rare events. Remember that. Eat it, digest it. Get Mrs Smith to tattoo it on your bottom. 'The world underprices rare events.'

"It's human nature, there are books about it. How could the Twin Towers fall down together? Could never happen, why insure against it? Hurricane Katrina, impossible. A Japanese earthquake damages a nuclear power station and then a huge tsunami shuts down the cooling system? Stop, lad. I know what you are going to say – those were all possible. Because those things actually happened, *now* we take them seriously. But before they happened, they were... impossible. Every year the world shuts the stable door on another impossible event."

"Your job, Steve, and my job, is to worry. Never tell me it won't happen because it hasn't. Never. If it can happen, sooner or later it will happen."

"You want to say something? I know. Your tiny mind is an open book to me, Steve, written in big letters. We have finite resources and there's millions of things that can go wrong. Yes? That's why we pay you the big bucks, Steven. Look at the facts, look at the costs, use your noodle. Why are we here?"

"To do the right thing for the bank?"

"Well done, son. Now, go and find out about floods and the Thames Barrier and advise me *what is the right thing for the bank.*

"You can take one of our best brains with you," he added, nodding at Ashok, "I'll give you two weeks. Oh, and one more thing, Steve …"

The exit party stopped in the doorway.

"There are ten gates in the Thames Barrier, not twelve. The main ones weigh over 3,000 tons, not 300. Stick to facts, Steve, don't make them up. It's safer that way."

The three pigmies filed out of Neil's office, leaving the giant to dry.

9

Friday, 30th June 2012

One week later

SBS was regulated by the Financial Services Authority. Compliance with the FSA rules meant that Chris was required to take two uninterrupted weeks of leave, every year. Not just out of the office, but out of contact. No emails, texts, or calls.

Compliance leave was family-friendly but that was a happy accident. The FSA was not concerned with the personal wellbeing of its unruly flock. History had shown that the elaborate deceptions of rogue traders, price fixers and other malefactors required regular, even daily maintenance. Separated from their creator, these constructions might expose themselves through unexpected positions or puzzled calls from clients.

It was a Friday morning and Chris was demob happy. He and Olivia were off to Cyprus in the morning for two weeks of guilt-free sun and sex, courtesy of the FSA. But his to-do list was humungous and he was running late already.

At three o'clock, disaster struck. Two senior members from the HR sorority appeared in his office, unsmiling. One was Rosemary, his HR lady. The other was Rosemary's boss, Carla Bartoli, head of HR. A woman with a hardcore reputation. Gossip said she charmed her victims through dinner and sacked them over dessert, offering them a brandy while she pushed the paperwork over the table. This had to be bad news. Maybe even...? Surely not. He was not that important.

Holly showed them in, looking a little pale. She knew something. She always did.

"We've had a complaint from a front office trader. A senior member of your staff threatened him with physical violence. In the carpark downstairs. We have a zero tolerance policy..."

Chris had a sinking feeling in the pit of his stomach.

There was more to the story of course. The trader was a young American. Yesterday he had put in an order for ten million futures contracts when he meant ten thousand. Sorting out the mess had cost the desk plenty. He said it was a bug in the trading system and his boss had backed him. There had been a bad-tempered meeting with the IT manager responsible for the system, in a little room off the trading floor. The IT guy had rolled up his sleeves with deliberate precision while saying "no" twelve times in succession. Finally he said, "You're not listening to me, you little prick. So let's go down to the car park and I'll explain it another way. OK?"

Whereupon the young trader and his boss had pulled the HR emergency cord and the whole thing got escalated.

It was Dom, of course. You didn't see it often but Dom had a violent temper. He played rugby with the Saracens Club and had been sent off more than once for punching. For a lad from Belfast, that was all part of the fun.

The front office wanted Dom fired. Now. Today. Carla and Rosemary wanted him suspended so they could sack him legally, after a disciplinary. That would take weeks. There would be bad feeling all round. Publicity and gossip. Probably no Cyprus beaches for Chris.

Chris found Dom incarcerated in Rosemary's office, guarded by an HR junior. He took the coffee that Chris had brought, but made no attempt to drink it.

"Listen, Dom, old buddy, just tell him you're sorry, you know? That would help."

But Dom just shook his head. In the end, Chris gave up and left him to stew.

At six o'clock, the storm was still raging. The front office wanted to escalate to Cyrus. Chris tried to ask van Buren for help but he wasn't answering his phone. In desperation, Chris called John Uzgalis. Debt Markets traders were big beasts with big egos, maybe John had some wisdom.

"Sheeyut, it's a pity, Dom's a good guy," Uzgalis said, reflectively, in his slow Kentucky drawl, "and I don't doubt the trader fucked up. But I know these boys. You gotta give 'em some blood. They got to win, in some dimension, or they're gonna be as mean as a bear in a clamtrap."

"So what do you suggest?"

"Simple. Don't sack him, just bury him."

*

It was 7.20pm in Chris' office. The summer sun was dipping slowly behind the ruins of Christchurch Greyfriars. The noise of the rush-hour traffic was slowly dying away.

"Dom, we've got a crisis with Disaster Recovery, as you well know. Especially after Babyliss night. Audit are right on top of us, the business doesn't trust us... I need someone I can rely on, full time. Disaster recovery, business continuity, datacentre testing."

"What about my old job?"

Chris shook his head.

"It's not fair," said Dom, his eyes shining. "I lose my job and that little prick gets away with it? He's a fucking liar, he is. He ordered 10 million, it's there in the logs, clear as a pimple on a baby's-"

"Dom," said Rosemary hastily, "that's not the point. You threatened a colleague. With your fists. You should be leaving the building right now with a black plastic bag in one hand. You could be down in Wood Street."

"Wood Street?"

"Wood Street police station. Waiting to hear if he's going to press charges."

*

Chris and Olivia flew to Cyprus the next morning. But the burning resentment in Dom's eyes seemed to travel with him. Chris drank more than he usually did and slept badly afterwards. He had nightmares. Once he saw endless ranks of servers, smoking and burning in a huge dark building, and the sounds of a thousand telephones ringing. Not ringing, shouting. They were shouting with Dom's voice. THIS IS NOT A DRILL CHRIS THIS IS NOT A DRILL. He woke up sweating in their airconditioned room and reached for Olivia to comfort him.

10

Monday, 16th July 2012

Three weeks later

Chris got back from his holiday and went back to work.

"I'm going to catch up on the crisis," he told Olivia.

"What crisis?"

"I don't know yet."

But the office was calm and after two hours of catch-ups, he went off, unsuspecting, to an Audit meeting.

He texted Holly from the meeting and asked her to get hold of Dom. *Right now.* Dom was waiting in his office, wearing a bright puce shirt with a white collar. Chris waved the audit report in his face.

"What the hell is this? Huh? *In summary… we find 11 SIGNIFICANT issues and 3 MAJOR issues… relating to the IT infrastructure.* Three! We haven't had a MAJOR audit issue for years and now we have three and I don't even know about it?"

"Oh, keep your hair on, Chris," said Dom. "You were on compliance leave with the lovely Olivia. No emails and no phone calls. We had a meeting booked for this morning, sure we did, but you canned it. But don't worry - the negotiation with our friends in audit is still going on."

"It is not bloody 'going on', it has gone! I have just spent two hours in the Audit meeting being roasted. First by Hugh Evans who read out the whole thing, smirking. Then Peter Elliot in Hong Kong decided to chip in. Then Cyrus asked me why IT had so many outages. I don't get it! Nothing's changed, where has this come from?"

"They've just wised up, Chris. BaByliss night scared the business and they don't trust us anymore. Audit are just piling into the gap, egged on by our friend Tim Hawes in Finance."

"It's just bullshit," said Chris, "the Hamilton incident wasn't that bad. It was close but in the end the business impact was contained."

"Contained" was a new buzzword. Yes, a bad thing had happened but "decisive management action had saved the day". Sir Simon had used it to answer a hostile question on the Today programme and it seemed to work. Now everyone used it.

"Get real, Chris. We were ten minutes away from losing Hamilton. The business wanted Plan B. Technology said *wait, wait*. Now they're wondering if there was a plan B."

"Of course there was. We could have gone to full DR. Shut down Hamilton, moved to Westchester. If we needed to."

"There's a new guy called Oleg in audit. Ex-IT. He really knows his stuff. He's got some interesting ideas. He thinks that if we lost Hamilton, we couldn't recover to Westchester. Nor from Drake to Raleigh in London."

"Bullshit. Every year we test it, it works."

"Chris, it's not a real test, you know that. We name the date. We have weeks to prepare and we don't actually turn things off. I think Oleg's got a point. Do you know that no one has actually ever moved from a major datacentre to its backup in 4 hours? Not in our industry? Not with our complexity?"

Chris wanted to scream.

"Of course he's got a point. Everybody knows it would be a tough day, it wouldn't be four hours... I know that. That's why I wanted to stay put on BaByliss night. But we could if we had to. We'd get through it."

"Would we? Suppose it was more than a tough day. Suppose every database was corrupt. Suppose it was... a month?"

"A month? That's ridiculous. Absolutely ridiculous."

Chris turned back to Dom. Dom was looking at him steadily. He was undoing his cuffs and rolling back the sleeves. It was vaguely threatening.

"There is a way, you know," said Dom. "A different way."

"Sure, find another job. Great. Excuse me, I've got to run."

"Let's do a test," said Dom. "A real test. Take down Raleigh. Hard. Prove that we can recover to Drake. We'll learn some hard lessons but the noise will stop."

Chris tried to concentrate, make sense of it. Dom was insane. No one in their right mind would pull the plug on twenty thousand computers running the applications on which the bank depended.

"Chris, think about it. A real pull-the-plug test."

"No, I won't think about it. Not for a millisecond. It's a fucking stupid idea. I will try to forget that you suggested it."

"Why are you scared of it, Chris? Because you know it would be a disaster?"

"Don't be ridiculous, Dom. I'm not going down in history as the idiot who killed the power to a datacentre, OK? Don't mention it again. Ever. That's an order."

Dom looked steadily at him through his small dark eyes, set in his podgy freckled face and Chris realized with dismay that this confrontation was no accident. For some awful, irrational reason his old friend Dom actually believed this madness and was dug in and ready to fight.

Chris changed the subject, softened his tone.

"For God's sake, Dom, there's plenty of shit that already hit the fan. Concentrate on that. Where are we on the Hamilton post-mortem? How did the Building Management System decide that sixty-six degrees was the right temperature for a datacentre?"

For a moment he thought Dom wasn't going to answer but then he nodded, slowly.

"Yes, well, some interesting ideas on that. Fujitsu have tested that unit to destruction and they can't find anything wrong with it. But John Uzgalis has pointed out that sixty-six degrees Fahrenheit is nineteen degrees Centigrade. So maybe someone thought the thermostats were calibrated in Fahrenheit and set them to sixty-six degrees?"

"You are kidding! Even Property couldn't be that stupid. The BMS must keep a log of some kind... when did those thermostats get set to sixty-six?"

"There is a BMS logfile. And Fujitsu have asked us for it. But Property can't find it, says it was never set up. Suspicious, eh? In short, lots of finger pointing and not a lot else."

Dom shrugged and Chris let the subject drop. A moment of inattention that he would soon regret.

"OK, so what's happening with Project Vegas? The project to shuffle test data. I got hammered on that as well. Audit says we don't have a plan. That's your baby as well, remember?"

"Sure it is Chris. And we have a plan."

"Well, send it to me, will you? Listen, Dom, are you on top of this stuff? Or are you just cruising?"

"Oh, I'm trying hard, Chris," said Dom. "I'm right in the middle of it, don't you worry."

Holly poked her head round the door.

"Cyrus wants to see you, Chris."

"When?"

"When? Now, of course."

Dom disappeared, looking pissed off, and Chris went to look for Cyrus on the trading floor. Cyrus had his own megastation with eight screens, four across, two deep, above the desk. He didn't need eight screens, but he was a trader and he couldn't have fewer screens than his guys.

But he wasn't there. Chris found him in his office, gazing intently at a Bloomberg window on his desktop and typing a message. Or an order. The Bloomberg system was part of the glue that bound the professional trading world together. Cyrus was cross-eyed and held his head sideways, looking at the screen as if he couldn't trust it.

When he spoke, it was without preamble, as though they were halfway through a discussion. Cyrus had worked in London for years, but he'd kept the soft Canadian accent from the backwoods where he'd grown up.

"Your new guy in Hong Kong isn't working out."

He went on typing into his Bloomberg. He was the fastest two-or-three-fingered typist Chris had ever seen. Suddenly the door flew open and Philippe Reynaud, head of High Frequency Trading, was standing there, having a Gallic tantrum.

"Cyrus, I'm telling you, you've got to fix this. That's the third time this week. I say never again, you gotta fix it now. That fucking system is a disaster."

Cyrus grunted.

"This is Portia, right?"

Portia was the Portfolio Trading system.

"Yes, Portia. Alchemy's down again, the clients are screaming. I'm telling you, if you don't fix this, I'm out of here, OK? This is unbelievable, this shit."

Cyrus raised an eyebrow at Chris. "Didn't you build Portia, Chris? Way back when? Your baby's a killer, what do you say?"

Portia rarely went wrong. When it did, Chris felt a special sort of guilt. But this time he was just pissed off.

"This has nothing to do with Portia. The Portfolio guys keep tweaking their algorithms which tell Portia what to do. Last week, someone missed out a comma and asked for the price history for every convertible bond in existence. It killed the database."

They all knew which database he was talking about. The tick database was the heart of all high speed electronic trading. The tick database held the second-by-second price history of every product traded on the major financial markets; it was a database that grew bigger by about 150,000 records for each second that the markets were open, and it could retrieve any of this data in microseconds. It was a techno triumph but temperamental. It was shared between several desks, each with their own system, including Portfolio (Portia) and Philippe's High Frequency Trading team (Alchemy). When it died, they all died.

Which had just happened, apparently. Alchemy had pulled its orders from the markets but – according to Philippe – they had lost seventy-five thousand pounds. Peanuts really. Alchemy had a huge public profile but in reality it didn't make a lot and HFT management were mean and vengeful over pennies. Every chance he got, Philippe whined about needing his own database.

"Can't you stop them screwing up?" asked Cyrus.

"Not really," replied Chris. "It's like a chef's knife: you can slice an onion in a second or you can lose a finger. You can't have the speed without the risk. Max and Hamish need to be more careful."

"Careful! Listen, Cyrus," said Philippe, "how many times those Portfolio guys say 'Sorry, never again?' You know? Every week they say that, every week they screw up. They are cowboys. They will never learn. Give me my own database, then they can screw themselves in private."

Philippe calling someone else a cowboy? Chris got a kick out of that.

"His own tick database? Remind me, Chris, what would that cost?" asked Cyrus.

"About two pounds." If you worked on the trading floor, a million pounds was a pound. A million dollars was a dollar. It was cool.

"OK, Philippe, I'm thinking about it," said Cyrus. "Now scram, I'm talking to Chris. Go and make some money. I'll talk to Max and - what's his sidekick called? Hamish? I'll talk to them, OK? Now go."

He propped up his huge, triangular head on one hand and stared at Chris, like a short-sighted bull sizing up a misguided visitor to his pen.

"You're a smart guy, Chris. Good business knowledge, super technical. That's what impressed my management team when the job came up.

"I like that. But that wasn't why I backed you for this job. I backed you because you had delivered stuff. Projects. Rolling out Portia. That was a big deal. Fixing the mess with the regulators in Hong Kong. He's a good organizer, I told Tully, and he gets people on board."

Clearly there was a big "but" coming.

"Also, I liked you. That bunch of egotistical assholes I call my management team liked you. That was two years ago. But now…"

Chris wasn't sure he wanted to hear any more.

"…but now," Cyrus continued, "I'm beginning to wonder. You don't have to win every time in this game, Chris. Shit happens, every trader knows that. But you have to win enough.

"This is a nice, friendly place to work, right? Sure, if you're winning. But when you don't put points on the board, the sharks creep in. They notice you, they start circling. Then one of them dares to take a little bite, gets the blood flowing. The others smell it, they swim in. Pretty soon, you're dead meat. It's dinner time."

Cyrus widened his mouth, showing a row of white, even teeth. It was not a smile.

"Right now, you've got a couple of fins going round you, Chris. You know who I mean?"

Hugh Evans from Audit, no doubt. And Finance. Jerome deVries and his sidekick Tim Hawes.

"Maybe," said Cyrus, "but it's your boss they're after."

"Alexis?"

"Alexis? Is that his name? Alexis Van Buren. The head of IT and I hardly know him, that's not a good sign, is it? He isn't helping you, Chris. He's not a bad guy but he's not strong. You're his insurance. If he thinks it will keep him alive, he will throw you to the sharks."

"And then there's my guys. Any time they can't make money, they get upset. Blaming you is the easy option. The sharks are nibbling, Chris, they're asking if you're up to the job."

Cyrus's dark eyes were fastened on him, brooding.

"*And so am I.* Did we make a mistake? Did we take one of our best delivery guys and give him a big department to run? We do it all the time in the Front Office, we take great traders and promote them. It's a double whammy. We lose a trader and we gain a bozo. A bozo who pisses everyone off and wants more money."

"Anyway, yesterday, there was an emergency meeting of the Exec Committee-"

Cyrus fished a document from the stack on his desk and pushed it over to Chris. Stapled to it was a memo from Sir Simon.

It was stamped *HIGHLY CONFIDENTIAL* and *YOUR EYES ONLY* in red. The document behind was headed in an old-fashioned typeface:

BOARD OF GOVERNORS of the FEDERAL RESERVE SYSTEM, with an address in Washington DC. Chris looked up, uncertain. Surely this was beyond his paygrade?

Cyrus shrugged. "Who cares? It's gonna be on 'Here is the City' by noon. Just read Sir Simon's memo. It's one of his better ones…"

*

The memo was brutally frank. The Fed's examiners had found twenty-three significant deficiencies in the bank's Know Your Client processes. In particular, 52% of client records examined were missing information about the ultimate beneficiary.

The bank was required to check all payments against Office of Foreign Assets Control (OFAC) lists in case they were to people that the US government had proscribed. But not all the systems had OFAC connectivity, so this checking was often manual. The examiners found over a million trades which the bank could not demonstrate had been OFAC checked, with a total value of sixty-three billion dollars. They identified numerous deficiencies in their Suspicious Activity monitoring system, too. The list went on and on.

The examiners concluded that "due to these multiple deficiencies, the bank may have facilitated money laundering, tax evasion, terrorism and other criminal activities." They'd proposed conducting a second, in depth audit, in one hundred and eighty days. If the issues were not fixed, the Feds would impose harsh financial penalties and might suspend the bank's New York banking licence. Indefinitely.

"Which would be a total disaster," said Cyrus. "The US was 27% of our revenues last year. We are a US clearing bank. It's our biggest market. We would not survive."

"All these things are on the Topeka to do list," said Chris happily. Topeka was Somebody Else's Problem.

Cyrus raised his hands. Mere words were not enough.

"Exactly. If Topeka doesn't succeed, we're all fucked. And we need to finish Topeka in the next hundred and eighty days, not two years."

He snorted.

"Wondering what this has to do with you, Chris?"

Chris was fervently hoping that this train-wreck had nothing to do with him.

"So, after this cluster-fuck of an audit, your boss gave a Topeka update. Which is not going well. Even a dumb trader like me can see that. van

Buren has got some guy running the project, guy with a weird English name-"

"Gawain Hughes," interjected Chris. Perhaps there weren't many Welshmen in Canada.

"Gawain. Yeah. 'Is this Gawain guy the best we've got?' asks Sir Simon. Dead silence. None of us ever heard of him. And then CK says, 'Hey, Cyrus, what about your guy? Peters. Didn't he get us out of the shit with the HKMA? How 'bout him? He any good?'"

CK was the head of Debt Markets, and enjoyed occasional point scoring off his rival in Equities.

"Right away, van Buren says no, you've got enough challenges doing your day job."

Chris didn't like the sound of that; not a vote of confidence, really.

"And I said, damn right, no way, I need you here. But the bank is in deep shit, so tell me the answer, Chris. Tell me the truth. Are you our best project manager? Could you deliver Topeka better than this guy Gawain?"

Chris saw the abyss opening in front of him.

"Cyrus, I've done projects. I can do them. But the job I'm doing now, running your IT, that's what I want. I want to succeed at that."

"Well then, I need more action. Fewer incidents, fewer audit points, more stability. For example, there's a Triple Witching day in September. The last one was a disaster, the Americans keep bringing it up. The sharks are circling."

Cyrus bared his teeth briefly to illustrate the danger.

"And take a look at this Topeka train wreck and explain to me why we don't Know Your Customers and all that shit."

Cyrus had said what he wanted. Now he was bored. He turned to his screen and started typing into Bloomberg again. Cyrus ran a business that made more money than Asda but he lived half his waking hours in some inner world inhabited by his risk positions and the next big trade.

Chris went back upstairs, mentally checking that his head was still on.

11

Sana'a, Yemen, 2007

Day Four - Monday

The problem of selling the shop solved itself, the next morning. Mahmoud was out, knocking on closed doors, when a black Mercedes pulled up next to him and the passenger's window went down.

The driver leaned across and beckoned. He was a dark Yemeni with a lined, leathery face, and a red chequered kuffiyeh.

"Get in."

"What? I'm busy."

"Babu Malik asks if you want to sell your shop?"

Mahmoud got in. The car was cold, with white leather seats and a sickly smell of jasmine. The seats were grubby and slightly sticky.

"Don't look round," said a composed voice from the back. "I hear your shop is for sale. I'd like to buy it for thirty thousand."

"The asking price is fifty," said Mahmoud, stunned, trying to gather his wits. The voice behind him seemed amused.

"Want to haggle, do you? Alright. I'd like to buy it for twenty-five thousand."

The driver sniggered with amusement at his master's wit. Mahmoud bit his tongue. Remembered the souk doors shutting in his face. Yemen was screwed anyway, he thought. Perhaps it was a fair price. Perhaps Dad had been optimistic, as usual.

"Shall we call it a deal?" said the voice. "Of course you might do better, but somehow I don't think so. Souk people are so risk averse."

A new worry struck Mahmoud.

"Could you pay in cash?"

"Cash? I couldn't pay you in anything else. Unless you want gold? I love gold. So did my wife. Every year, more gold. When she died, the gold weighed more than she did. Getting it back was my only consolation..."

The driver seemed to find this hilarious. He was giggling like a schoolgirl. Mahmoud realised that he was high on qat. Or hashish.

"What are you sniggering about, Ali?"

"'Allah took back my wife,' is what you actually said, 'but Allah the merciful makes new girls every day.'"

"And so he does," said the voice from the back. "Now shut your mouth. Mahmoud, a lawyer will bring the papers and the money to your shop at 4pm."

Mahmoud went home. With every step, he felt more violated. Where was the justice in this?

"Even Grishigar is worried, that's what everyone is saying," said Ahmed suddenly as the family sat round the table, chewing stale bread and cheese.

"Worried about what?"

"Worried about me. About the fight tomorrow. Babu Malik is offering ten to one on me to win. Imagine that. What an idiot! Ten to one. I mean, with just a million rials, we could get ten million back…"

"Gambling is an abomination," replied Mahmoud. "Do not spit in the face of Allah, Ahmed. His punishment is not ten to one but ten thousand to one."

Mahmoud left the table and Skyped Uncle Saeed in Dubai.

His uncle was steaming.

"Three hours I waited this morning, in different queues. Oh, you need business banking, the first cashier said to me. Then business banking sent me to a desk on the fifth floor. Which was empty. A young man came over and told me to go to another queue, to currency exchange. 'No,' I told him, 'I'm trying to buy gold. I need a letter of credit'. But he insisted. 'No, no, go to foreign currency.'

"When I got to the front, the girl looked puzzled. She looked at our account on her computer, called a colleague. They both looked puzzled. She told me to come back tomorrow because the senior account manager will be in tomorrow. There is a problem on your account. What problem? Just a problem, she kept saying. Is there no one who can deal with this now? No one, only Mr al-Muhairi. I got angry and a manager came over with the security guard."

Mahmoud went to talk to his mother, who was watching TV in the kitchen. Zahra was loitering outside the door and heard every word, as she reported later to Ben.

"Perhaps the bank doesn't have enough money to pay us?" said her mother.

"Ha! No, the banks are full of money. But perhaps Uncle Saeed has already spent it? Dad trusted him to bank the profits every week.

Remember when Dad needed money for a flight and Uncle Saeed said there wasn't enough? Dad was very surprised."

"I never trusted Uncle Saeed," said Gurjit, "he has always been lazy. When your father started the business, Saeed was driving a taxi, did you know that? When the taxi broke down, he didn't have enough money to repair it and he begged your father to take him in. So when we moved here, he dealt with the bank."

"And why did we move to this dump?" asked Mahmoud.

"Your father is a romantic," replied Gurjit. "He fell in love with the Old City, with the tower-houses and the camels and the tribesmen with their daggers. Old Abdullah's father owed him money and offered him the stall in the market instead. But when your father gets back, we're not staying..." She trailed off, then added suddenly, "what time is it on Wednesday?"

"Omani's execution?" replied Mahmoud. "I told you. Three o'clock."

"Two days. Less than two days," said his mother and her voice quavered.

"What execution? What are you talking about?" cried Zahra in alarm, bursting through the door.

"The bomb maker," replied Mahmouod. "Al-Omani. In Tahrir Square."

"What does that have to do with Dad?" said Zahra. "You were talking about Dad."

"Nothing," said Mahmoud. "Nothing at all." Her mother nodded.

How we have learned to lie to each other, thought Zahra.

At four o'clock, Mahmoud went down to the shop to meet the lawyer and sell the shop. The man was there, with the contract and the money. Twenty-five thousand dollars. It felt good, as he stashed it in Ahmed's old kitbag.

But not nearly enough. And they had less than two days. The hours were rushing away. He had a sudden panic.

There were twenty minutes before *isha*, the evening prayers. Mahmoud ran down to the mosque and threw himself onto the hard floor and said *isha* and after that, he prayed on, whispering *wirt*, the night time prayer, not once but eleven times. After that he repeated a prayer of supplication and so he was one of the last to leave.

When he got back, his mother had put supper on the table. She had burned the meat. There were no vegetables, just a spoonful of rice each. Halfway through the meal, Gurjit broke down in tears and rushed out. The children listened to her footsteps going down the stairs. Zahra followed but her mother slammed the door and shouted at her when she tried to open it.

12

Dom's revenge

Thursday, 30th August 2012

Outside Chris' window, the sunshine was bright on the dome of St Paul's but that did not lighten his mood. There were days when things started badly and went downhill from there. Olivia had woken early and wanted to make love, and he hadn't been in the mood. He was thinking about work already, and that pissed her off.

And now here was Holly, barging into his office, holding a pile of papers.

"Alexis wants you to go to the Global Risk meeting this morning. In his place."

"What? No way! That's his job."

Chris would rather go to the dentist. The Global Markets Risk meeting happened monthly. On that day, the investment bank got together in formal session to ponder its risks. Finance always turned it into an IT bitching session. Chris had been once before, when AVB was on holiday. It was a two-hour forced march through a minefield, under sniper fire from Finance.

"Alexis has got a diary conflict," said Holly, heartlessly, "so I've asked Dom to come and brief you on the Disaster Recovery audit points."

She lowered her voice.

"And Rosemary phoned. Again. It's about ROSEBUD. She needs another name this morning."

"Put her off. I haven't decided."

"She's not going to be happy…"

Chris took the stack of papers and sat, brooding. ROSEBUD was a pretty name for a disgusting project. You had to hold your nose even to think about it. Rosemary from HR had come to see him ten days ago, with two management consultants.

"I know you're busy," she said brightly, "so we won't go through the details." She pushed a deck across the table.

"We won't go through the details," was a popular phrase that jarred with Chris. There was something wrong with a world in which the Powerpoint decks got bigger and bigger but the content was somehow irrelevant.

This deck was a skinny 30 pages. *ROSEBUD*. The security classification was *SECRET*, which was unusual. Chris had flicked through the deck and was impressed. It set out the organization of the bank like an army, by level.

"There are fourteen levels between the chairman of the board and the lowest employee? That's amazing."

"It's not unusual in an organization that doesn't have discipline," said Rosemary. Ouch. That wasn't true. But she had enjoyed saying it. He looked across at her. Long legs in black trousers, an expensive silk blouse, ash blonde hair in a tight bun. She was the dominatrix of the back office. All she needed was the whip.

"If every manager had at least seven Direct Reports, we would need 22% fewer managers," said Rosemary.

"Well, I've got eleven Direct Reports," said Chris, "so that's not my problem."

"You've got thirteen," retorted Rosemary. "That's at least three too many. You can't manage more than ten effectively."

"Well, I'm going to die trying."

But he knew he wasn't. It was August. The bonus season was around the corner. Sir Simon had put lipstick on it, but Chris knew this pig for what it was. It was the pre-bonus cull. The real purpose of ROSEBUD was to create a List. The people on the List would become jobless before Christmas, and the survivors would have bigger bonuses.

By the time Rosemary left, he was signed up for two names. One was easy. He gave it to Rosemary on the spot. But the other? He's been agonizing over it for the last ten days.

Chris dragged his attention to the Risk deck. After 150 pages, he felt like a python who has swallowed a goat. Here was an update on Project Vegas, the project to implement ShuffleDB so client information was scrambled before it was loaded into test systems. Most Global Markets systems were now shuffling their test data but the project was amber because (guess what) Equity Technology was late. Damn, damn, why was that? That was Dom's business. He looked at the clock. 10 minutes to go before the meeting.

"Holly," he yelled, "where the hell is Dom?"

"He's not answering his phone."

Fucking typical, thought Chris. Dom had changed since Chris had – reluctantly – demoted him at the end of June. He didn't come to meetings. Or he came and sat in silence. He did what he was told, smiled at jokes. He replied slowly to questions and volunteered little. Chris sensed a molten core of anger and contempt behind the dark eyes. No matter how he tried, Dom would never speak about it.

"You will see him at the meeting."

"What? The Risk meeting? He's not invited, surely?"

"He's down as a presenter," said Holly.

"What? Presenting what? I don't know anything about it."

"Maybe he's up to something," said Holly, "and Rosemary called again. Quite rude. She needs your second name today."

Good PAs saw everything, understood everything, and were very, very discreet. PAs didn't get big bonuses but without them the bank would fall apart.

"What do you want for lunch? Soup or sandwich?"

"Give me a second name for Rosebud."

"That's your job. Smoked salmon or cheese and pickle?"

"You choose, Holly."

There was a curious silence. Chris looked up. She was looking straight at him, her brown eyes unwavering.

"What you need," said Holly, "is loyalty. Loyalty on brown bread, no mayo, no butter. Now scram or you'll be late."

Huh? Loyalty. On brown bread, no butter. What did she mean?

He hurried towards the lifts, feeling sick in his stomach. The answer was obvious. She meant Dom.

That made him angry. No way. Dom was a rare talent. Great business knowledge and deeply technical. He built computers at home and reprogrammed network cards. Yes, OK, Dom was being a sulky pain in the ass right now. Angry, but not disloyal. And the precious talent was still there. Dom could be saved. He could be reprogrammed. Thanks, Holly, but no thanks.

By the lifts, he was ambushed by P.K. Ramachandran, visiting from Chennai.

"Hi, P.K. What's the problem? Lost another memory stick?"

P.K. waggled his head. No, this was a different problem but also very delicate.

The problem concerned a graduate.

This graduate was not fitting in. He was not a bad chap, but he was not a team player. He did not obey orders. He was many times rude to his superiors and upsetting to the other grads. And so, with great reluctance, P.K. intended to put this young man on the Rosebud List. Incidentally this would exceed his quota, which would help Chris globally.

Chris was instantly wary. It was very unusual to fire someone in the grad program, and especially in India where twenty graduates were recruited each year from several thousand applicants.

"What's the matter with him?" asked Chris, feeling his temper rising, "is he useless?"

"Technically, he is brilliant," said P.K., "if a job is taking sixty minutes he does it in thirty. And he learns quickly. Too quickly, he is arrogant and upsetting-"

"-to his colleagues. Yes, you said," replied Chris. "Who is this genius, anyway? Do I know him?"

"His name is Choudhary."

"What, Hassan Choudhary? I met him in June. I helped him get a summer job in TIS. With Tom Hailey and the Market Data team."

"You did indeed. Your munificence was noted," said P.K., "but he is now returning to Chennai and folks are not happy... Sometimes it is better to throw out one rotten apple than to lose the whole basket."

"Rotten apple?" said Chris. He started rubbing his forehead, without being conscious of it. It was a danger sign, not that P.K. could have known it.

"Not so rotten but not fitting into the team,"

"And so you want to fire him?" Chris' anger boiled over. "Listen to me, P.K. We're in the talent game. From what I hear, Hassan Choudhary is the kind of exceptional talent we long to find. He is gold dust. People like him are often difficult. Your job is to manage them. So the answer is no fucking way. Take Choudhary off the list. Now go and do your bloody job. OK?"

He left P.K. in the corridor, looking aggrieved.

That twister Hugh Evans from Audit was waiting outside the room. He was all smiles.

"Hi Chris, just wanted to check Dom's briefed you."

"No, we had – er – a diary problem this morning. But I've read the report."

"And you're OK with it?" said Evans. He sounded surprised.

"Well, I wish things were going better, but I can't complain," said Chris, puzzled in his turn.

They were last into the meeting. Chris looked around. The big room was full of the great and the good of the Global Markets back office. Jerome deVries, the CFO, was sitting at one end, with Tim Hawes next to him. His IT buddies John Uzgalis and David Trebbiano were opposite. And Dom. Dom, sitting at the far end, unsmiling, with a deck in front of him. There was an austere figure next to him, a man with tightly cropped blond hair and a curious pink complexion, almost albino. This must be the auditor Dom mentioned a couple of months back. Oleg. The ex-IT guy who thought that the datacentre recovery plans wouldn't work. What was he doing here? Chris had a premonition that his bad day was about to get a lot worse.

What would deVries and co. say if they knew about Dom's proposal to pull the plug on a datacentre? It gave him goose-bumps just to think about it. But that proved Dom's point, in a way. If disaster recovery worked right, every system would flip over to the other datacentre and there wouldn't be a disaster. In practice, bad things would happen, especially with the older systems. Everyone in IT knew that. Dom thought the bank needed to find out what those bad things were. So it had to be pushed over the cliff. There was a scary logic to it.

DeVries looked around and called for silence. The march through the minefield had begun and Chris forgot Dom. He did his best with the IT section, helped out by John Uzgalis and Dave Trebbiano. And then, just as it was getting ugly, deVries called time. Hoorah!

"We will stop there. We need time for today's special paper, who is presenting it?"

"I am," said Dom. He pushed copies of the deck down the room.

Huh? Chris flicked through it. The final page made his hair stand on end: *In our opinion, the bi-annual drills that the Bank carries out to simulate the loss of a datacentre are inadequate. In reality, the Bank would be unable to switch processing from one datacentre to another within 4 hours. The transition might take several working days, exposing the bank to catastrophic risks...*

Chris looked up in a panic. This was the dirty laundry of the IT department and bloody Dom was giving a guided tour? He was bound to be asked what he thought, what on earth should he say? Yes, it's true?

Massive drains up, FSA investigation. No? Almost worse. Dom would look like a whistle blowing hero to everyone outside IT.

Most decks never got beyond page 2 in big meetings. This one got to the punch line on page 9 without a word being spoken. Chris was still agonizing over his response.

DeVries intervened in his flat Transvaal tones.

"Stop there. I have had my concerns on this topic since the last IT disaster. Perhaps not the last disaster since they occur almost daily. I mean the cooling failure in the US datacentre. Hamilton, is it? I observed some behaviours that night-"

His gaze flickered between Chris and John Uzgalis. Chris tried to look innocent but he knew exactly what deVries was talking about. It was all so unfair. He was the guy who had saved the day, after all.

"-and this paper confirms my suspicions. We need further investigation and frankly it cannot be led by IT."

Dom nodded. He was looking straight at Chris, his eyes shining with stubborn defiance.

The meeting broke up with a lot of excited chatter. Dom disappeared. Someone tapped Chris firmly on the shoulder.

"Maybe you should have fired that boy after all," said John Uzgalis.

13

Monday, 3rd September 2012

John Uzgalis, Chris and David Trebbiano were sitting in Luigi's, just round the corner from the office. Uzgalis was leaning back with one boot on the seat of the banquette opposite.

"What you going do with Dom?" said Trebbiano. "He's a troublemaker."

"Where I come from," said Uzgalis, "we have a boy not right in the head, we just take him into the woods. Don't cost more'n a nickel."

His fingers formed a pistol. He made the sound of a gun going off, and blew imaginary smoke from the barrel.

John enjoyed playing hill-billy. Chris had researched him once, for two minutes. His father taught Electronic Engineering at Arkansas State, and his mother ran a hospital.

"Mind you, he's a smart kid," Uzgalis went on. "I'd be happy to take him, Chris, if you like. New boss, new world. Might suit him."

Meaning, *Maybe the problem isn't Dom, maybe the problem is you, buster.*

"Thank you, I will take care of him," said Chris, steaming.

"Why was deVries taking that meeting anyway?" asked Trebbiano, "instead of the COO?"

"Rumour says John Tully's in trouble," said Uzgalis. "He's been investigated by the Japanese FSA. You remember that Japanese broker we bought a couple of years ago?"

"Yeah. The guys with the retail notes business."

"Exactly. A lot of those notes have turned out to be toxic. The word is we should have known that... but we still bought them."

"But Tully is one of the good guys. He's Mr Clean."

"He was COO for Asia. It was on his watch. He was living in Japan. We've been asked for a truckload of stuff. Market data, emails, dealing records. Neil Jenkins' guys have been digging out tapes in Tokyo... it's a nightmare."

"Poor guy."

"Yeah, well, who knows the future, eh? Maybe deVries is gonna step up. Man, is he a piece of work! Chris, you missed the Investment committee. Neil Jenkins turns up and wants to spend three million quid on a waterproof wall around Raleigh. Because of some floods back in 1928! Tim Hawes says, bullshit, there hasn't been any flooding for fifty years, not since they put in the Thames Barrier."

"What happened?"

"Did you see *Alien vs. Predator*? It was just like that. DeVries told Jenkins he was not funding any more toys for TIS. Jenkins said deVries was like the accountant of the White Star line, who wouldn't spend money on lifeboats for the *Titanic*."

"I think Jenkins has a point," said Trebbiano. "Did you see his picture of that barge, the Sand Piper? It sank in 1996 and dumped three thousand tons of sand on the Thames Barrier. If there had been a big tide that week, London would have been underwater."

"Jenkins is often right but he's so fucking difficult, everybody hates him," said Uzgalis.

"That's always been Neil's problem," said Chris.

"How do you know that?" said Uzgalis, "that boy don't talk about his past."

Chris said nothing.

"You couldn't pay me to do his job," said Trebbiano, who was ambitious and thought about such things.

After the other two left, Chris sat, staring at the floor, thinking about Dom. Remembering Holly's advice. "What you need is loyalty. On brown bread." And then his coach: "Not making decisions, Chris, more damage done by avoiding decisions than taking the wrong one."

Finally, he sent a short text to Rosemary: *put dom macdonald on the Rosebud List.*

And hit the send button. Gone. Decision taken. Problem solved, JFDI. Just Fucking Did It, he thought and he felt great.

His coach might have counselled him on the difference between hard decisions and hasty decisions, but his coach wasn't there.

14

Sana'a, Yemen, 2007

Day Five - Tuesday

The midday meal was a few scraps that Zahra managed to pull together. Stale bread, dry olives, cheese and some desiccated grapes. The dates were gone. Her mother stayed in her room.

Ahmed came down from the mafraj. This was his big day, the day he fought Grishigar. He was edgy and complained of hunger.

"Stop whining," said Mahmoud. "Think of our father. This is not the time."

He was nervous as well. Uncle Saeed had got an appointment for them with a senior manager at the bank, Mr Al-Muhairi. An important man who could snap his fingers and release their money. That's what Uncle Saeed said. Uncle Saeed had given him the number to dial.

Mahmoud kicked Ben off the computer and Skyped the number. A suave young man answered. Mr al-Muhairi was still at lunch. Yes, his uncle, Mr Saeed Hashemi, was here in the room. They were reviewing the case. As before. It was against the bank's policy to hand over such a large sum in cash. Yes, they could buy gold. From a licenced gold broker. That would require a Letter of Credit. Yes, a minimum of three working days. No, from the processing centre in Karachi. Yes, two signatures. Yes, they could add Mahmoud to the signatory list, but that would require two signatures and a board minute. Yes… no… yes… no. No way out. It felt as if some gigantic cat was playing with them, a half dead mouse. Every time escape seemed possible, the cat pounced.

Ahmed was listening over Mahmoud's shoulder, punching the air, getting more confused, more angry. Suddenly he leaned over Mahmoud and started shouting into the mike.

"Listen, donkey prick, give us our money NOW, or I'm coming to get you. I'm going to kick your teeth down your throat and break your fucking neck, no signatures required, OK? Yes, I'm on my way now."

Frantically Mahmoud tried to shush him. It was too late. The meeting was done, the young banker had put the phone down, breathing righteous indignation. Loving every word, in fact.

"Stupid. Always stupid! Yes, you are. Look what you've done! No money now. You've killed our father," shouted Mahmoud. "Get out! I never want to see your stupid face again."

Then Ahmed punched him in the face.

Mahmoud was trying to catch the blood spurting with his fingers while Zahra ran for a towel from the kitchen. Ahmed still had the rage on him. He picked up the family table and smashed it against the wall, then jumped on it. The old terracotta vase with herbs was next. It exploded into a thousand pieces as it hit the wall.

Still shouting, Ahmed disappeared up to the mafraj. Ten minutes later he appeared briefly in the doorway, carrying his new kitbag. It looked heavy and it was almost an hour's walk to the Joint Services Club.

"And I hope that ape Grishigar thrashes you," yelled Mahmoud as his brother went on down the stairs.

Zahra and Mahmoud cleared up as best they could. All this time, Zahra waited patiently for her opportunity. It came an hour later, when Mahmoud went down to the mosque for afternoon prayers.

She sneaked up to the mafraj. She searched through the boys' clothes. No luck. She searched the shelves behind the curtain. Strangely, pushed to the back, was Ahmed's old sportsbag. She took it over to the window and opened it. It was empty, except for the little dark jeweller's box at the bottom. The one little Yousef had delivered. It was still closed but the scotch tape wrapped round it had been sliced open.

She opened the box. Gleaming against the dark velvet was a heavy gold signet ring. She knew the ring, had known it since she was a little girl.

The ring still encircled part of its owner. A single piece, neatly dissected at each joint. Blood had oozed out and formed globules at both ends.

She was nearly sick. But after ten minutes, the little cylinder of dead flesh fascinated and repelled her in equal measure. It was real, it was a part of *him*. Her missing father. She sat on the steps and held the box against her bosom.

After a while, a random thought came to her. She looked at the empty kitbag, puzzled. The random thought bred hideous children. Urgently she texted Mahmoud:

No money in the kitbag? Where is it?

No reply. Mahmoud was down at the mosque. She put the box away and ran like the wind, down the stairs, through the narrow streets.

The old man at the entrance to the mosque tried to keep her out. She ran into the courtyard. Men, dozens of men, were kneeling in tidy rows on their prayer mats, foreheads touching the ground.

"Mahmoud! Mahmoud Hashemi!" she screamed above the murmuring.

Silence. "Mahmoud Hashemi!"

They all looked up, all surprised, some angry. But then the real Mahmoud got up and came running across, just ahead of the boys from the madrassah.

His dismay matched hers.

"What? I haven't touched it today. I added the dollars from the shop last night. It was all there."

"Well who? Not Mother. Not Ben."

They almost shouted it together. "Ahmed!"

"Ten to one, remember? Against Grishigar."

"I haven't got the money for a taxi."

"Nor me. Get the pickup."

"We sold it."

"Then run."

Mahmoud ran. He ran out of the Old City, out onto Al-Zubairah. The horns of startled trucks blared at the intersections. The sun poured down on him. The gutters tripped him. Sweating, panting, he arrived finally at the Joint Service club, an ugly concrete building at the intersection of Al-Zubairah and the Sixty Meter Road. It had been built by the Soviets back in the days that the Russians were still vying for influence in Yemen.

The building was hot inside, but smelt of mildew. There was a crowd in a big hall with a boxing ring in the middle. A fight had just started. Two young men were circling around the ring. One was a huge, young bull with long hair tied in a bun. His eyes were slanted and close-set, giving him an oriental look. *Philippino? Japanese?* He hardly moved, just ambled to face his smaller opponent who was dancing around him, shouting defiance.

Ahmed.

Allah has brought me to see my brother fight Grishigar, thought Mahmoud, and he wondered what it meant. It was too late to change anything. But Ahmed was on fire. He attacked with reckless ferocity. He was cautioned twice for punching. Grishigar looked surprised. At the end of the first bout, Mahmoud could see Grishigar's trainer – an Army sergeant - whispering in his ear and the brute nodding.

In the second bout, Ahmed seemed to tire. And he became more reckless. Grishigar scarcely moved, but squinted at his opponent through narrow eyes, watching his hips and feet. Mahmoud could almost see him calculating. The crowd could see it too and the room became quiet except for the grunts and insults of the wrestlers and the mutterings of the referee.

Ahmed attacked once, twice, looking for a hold and was shaken off. On his third attack, Grishigar moved and twisted with the speed of a scorpion and Ahmed was caught. The crowd started yelling again. Next to Mahmoud, a young soldier was shaking his fists and shouting "kill, kill." Grishigar raised Ahmed over his shoulder and held him there for what seemed an age, struggling. Then he threw him to the canvas with such force that the floor shook. Ahmed did not get up. His eyes were open but he lay, motionless.

"Grishigar, Grishigar!" chanted the crowd as the referee stopped the fight. The young bull acknowledged their cheers as he climbed out of the ring.

"Fuck the foreigners!" shouted the excited young soldier in Mahmoud's ear. After a few minutes, two Army corporals picked up Ahmed and helped him away. Mahmoud pushed his way to the front, shouting. Now he was only a few feet away.

"Ahmed, Ahmed, it's your brother. What have you done? Did you bet the money? Tell me you didn't! Please tell me you didn't!"

Ahmed shook his head and turned away. His face was white with shame. As his minders hurried him off, he turned and gave Mahmoud such a look of abject despair that Mahmoud knew it was true. He was too late. All the money was gone.

15

London, the next day

Tuesday, 4th September 2012

Normally Chris dozed through AVB's management meetings, but today he was covertly texting hearts and kisses to Olivia, celebrating an epic session last night. Holly's text dragged him back to the present.

New COO announced 10 mins ago. You won't like it. Xx

Liz in Sydney had seen it as well. She was sitting in her office, even though it was almost midnight.

"Alexis? Sorry to interrupt - there's a major announcement on the intranet."

Alexis stopped. Liz started reading.

"...want to thank John Tully for his service to the bank... blah blah... very difficult circumstances... blah..."

Uzgalis was right. John Tully was carrying the can for the disastrous Japanese acquisition three years ago.

"...it gives me great pleasure to announce that Jerome deVries will become Chief Operating Officer of Global Markets, effective immediately."

"You knew this was coming, right, AVB?" said Uzgalis.

"No, I did not," replied van Buren stolidly.

Chris thought that AVB really should have known; after all, this was his new boss. And this was bad, bad news that confirmed Finance as Top Tribe and would make Tim Hawes more unbearable than ever.

Everyone started talking at once until Liz broke in:

"Wait, there's more. Now, deVries has announced the new CFO. He doesn't hang around, does he? Who wants to guess?"

"Please, please, don't tell me it's Tim Hawes." That was Trebbiano, who ran – as far as Tim Hawes let him – Risk and Finance IT. There was a chorus of disbelieving murmurs and groans. Liz let them run their course.

"No," she said finally, pleased with the success of her ruse. "The lucky winner of the CFO stakes is not IT's favourite, Tim Hawes. Although he does get a special mention, so they must be trying to keep him sweet. 'Tim

Hawes will continue his invaluable service to Finance and Risk, managing our IT projects.'"

"So who is it?" asked John Uzgalis, above the outrage provoked by this last sentence.

"Pandora Stiegel, presently head of Credit and Capital Risk, will immediately assume the role of CFO of Global Markets…"

"Well, guys, she is damn smart. And she's a hottie," said David Trebbiano.

"Rosemary, will you record that remark on Dave's personnel records?" said Uzgalis. "I believe it violates our most cherished principles."

Bang! Van Buren had slammed his papers on the table. His freckled face was pale with anger.

"This is shit. This is shit."

Chris had never seen van Buren upset before. The Dutchman was always calm and quietly spoken, perhaps too calm. But now he was heading for the door. John Uzgalis was the first to recover.

"Alexis? What about the grads? Shall we stick to last year's numbers?"

"Do what the hell you like. I don't care."

"Boy, van Boring is really upset," said Uzgalis when the door had closed. "Feels like an HR issue to me."

They all looked at Rosemary.

"Sorry, boys, I can't help you."

"Can't or won't?"

Rosemary shook her head, lips tight together, and left the room. Slightly smug.

"That woman was a witch in some previous life," said Uzgalis.

Chris agreed with him but there was no percentage in slagging off HR. They were a sisterhood that patrolled the corridors of power and guarded its secrets. They knew all the juicy little scandals: who was sleeping with their PA, who had a drug problem, who really jumped and who was pushed. They knew what your boss thought of you and not the pap he wrote in your appraisal. And beyond sex and drugs and petty scandal, they knew the biggest and most divisive secret of all: they knew what you got paid. HR sat behind the thrones of kings, and whispered in their ears. They thought they were influential, which was true, and infallible, which was not.

Rosemary was not popular with IT and especially not with the freewheeling guys that ran the trading systems. She stuck to the script and she didn't realize that – heck – they were all underpaid and could get a job for twice the money tomorrow.

"Did Alexis and deVries have history?"

"I have no idea," said Uzgalis, "maybe it's Pandora Stiegel that's upset him."

Smart as they all were, none of them could explain their boss' tantrum. The meeting broke up and the mystery remained.

16

New York

Wednesday, 5th September 2012

"Hyatt Regency at Grand Central," said Chris loudly, getting into a yellow cab at JFK. Even the cab drivers knew Grand Central.

It was eleven o'clock on Wednesday night in New York, 4am Thursday morning in London. Usually Chris came for longer than this, but he had to get back to London and Olivia by Friday night. There was still no sign of a baby and this weekend was prime time.

And here was a late email from Holly.

Carl has arranged for you to give breakfast talk to the US grads. Not just IT, all the grads. 8am in the Honduras room.

Argh. Why had Carl done this? He wasn't prepared. He didn't have a deck. What was he supposed to talk about?

His non-smoking room in the hotel was hot and stuffy and smelt of stale tobacco but he was too tired to complain. He woke up at 4am and powered up his laptop. There were a ton of emails from London. A rare one from Cyrus:

Did u look at topeka yet? What is the problem? C

PS. EOS late again. Give me hope.

Gawain Hughes, the program manager, was in New York this week. He dropped Gawain a quick message, suggesting a catch up.

At 5am, Chris joined a conference call about cuts to his budget. An hour later, a project review with deVries, the new COO. Most of it was spent on Topeka and beating up poor Gawain. At 7am he set off across Manhattan for the office and his breakfast appointment with the US grads, trying frantically to think of things that would interest them. As it turned out, keeping their attention wasn't the problem.

*

"The worst moment of my career? Well, there's plenty to choose from."

He scanned their earnest young faces. If any of them found that amusing, they concealed it well.

"Friday, June 15th this year. That must be right up there. Triple Witching day. I was sitting on the front steps of my house at sunrise, and I thought, we're going to be out of business, especially here in the USA. But in the end, we pulled through."

"Pulled through?" said an angry voice. "Are you kidding? The systems lost the electronic orders so the customers phoned them in. Then the systems came back up and we did the trades twice. We lost $400,000 on one trade. And no email all day."

"In Equities, we didn't have risk all day,' said someone from the back.

"So what's new?" said his companion, and there was a ripple of cynical laughter.

"A friend of mine works in IT, and she said the US systems were working fine, it was a system in London which failed. It's always London, that's what she told me." This last speaker was a young Japanese woman who worked in Operations, Chris remembered her from his last session with the grads in New York.

"The system that failed was the Building Management system," said Chris, appalled by the hornet's nest he had stirred up. "It's run by TIS and actually it's not in London–"

"Chris? May I call you Chris?" said the woman, standing up. "Listen, every time we get an IT screw up, some bozo stands up – I don't mean you, of course – and says we're really sorry, folks. Even more sorry than the last time. By the way, it wasn't our fault. But what they never say - and this is what makes me so angry - they never say *we fixed it, this cannot happen again.* So let me ask you: what happened to the Building Management System and why can't it happen again?"

She was right. So right. Why hadn't Property and Fujitsu got to the bottom of it? This story about sixty-six Fahrenheit being nineteen Centigrade couldn't be true, could it? Incompetents. It was embarrassing. Why hadn't Dom dug into it, like Chris had asked him to?

He stared out of the window, looking for inspiration. They were up on the thirty-sixth floor, with great views down Sixth Avenue. The cars were toys far below, hardly moving. He could feel the building swaying, he was sure of it. The room went quiet, sensing blood.

"It's a good question," he said lamely, "and I don't know the answer. I will find out and get back to you."

Chris checked the time. Almost 9am, time to go. Thank God. He and Carl left the room in deathly silence. It felt like they were running away.

"Yeah, folks are still sore about BaByliss," said Carl on the way downstairs. "In fact, the business asked Paul Carpenter to get an independent report. He engaged KPC. It came out today."

Paul Carpenter ruled TIS in the Americas, and he had done for years. His kingdom included the datacenters. Well, sort of. It was a hierarchy, like the food chain. At the bottom was Property Services who provided the buildings, the power and the cooling. Carpenter ran the network and the computers. The network and the computers consumed the power and the cooling provided by Property. Chris Peters and his colleagues operated the software that ran on Carpenter's computers.

In theory, Paul Carpenter worked for Neil Jenkins, but his roots with the US business went deep. Paul didn't do global and he and Neil were constantly at war. One rumour said Paul would be gone at the end of the year. That would be a tough call if the US business didn't like it.

"What did KPC say?"

"Paul told me it blames human error. One of his technicians."

"I want a copy."

"I tried. Paul told me to get lost. US execs only."

Talk of the devil: later that morning, Chris and Carl were heading down in an elevator and Paul Carpenter got in, talking loudly to a companion. It was a story about someone else's stupidity.

Chris tapped him on the shoulder. Carpenter turned and gave him a fish-eye stare.

"Hey, Paul, the KPC report on the Hamilton outage? Can I get a copy?"

"Sorry bud. US execs only," said Carpenter, winking at his neighbour. *This is how we deal with little pricks from London.*

"Yes, but people want to know..."

Carpenter just turned away and went on with his story. *I hope Neil sacks you soon*, thought Chris viciously.

Then he forgot Carpenter because a woman in the corner of the elevator turned around and looked straight at him, smiling. Dark hair, oval face, green eyes. She was wearing an emerald woollen dress. Nestling innocently above her cleavage was a familiar pendant. A silver fish with sapphire eyes. He felt his heart skip a beat. It was Annie. He hadn't seen her since she moved back from Asia. She was looking well. A new hairstyle, shorter. Sassy, that was the word. The elevator stopped on the next floor and she got out, smiling enigmatically as she waved goodbye.

"You know her?" said Carl as they got out.

"Er, well, I used to. In Hong Kong," said Chris.

"Good friend to have," said Carl, "she's deVries' new business manager."

*

After lunch, Chris took Gawain for a coffee in Frankie's diner, across Sixth Avenue. It was practically the bank's canteen. Gawain was a quiet, tall Welshman with a passion for detail. He spent hours before project meetings, going through milestones and issue logs, checking, and sending hate mails that were famous. His staff called him Tickbox.

"So," said Chris. "Topeka. What's the real story?"

"We're a hundred and six miles from Chicago, out of gas. It's dark and we're wearing sunglasses."

"*Blues Brothers*. That movie has a happy ending."

"Well, Topeka won't."

"Why not?"

Tickbox meditated over his skinny latte.

"Okay. Three things. One: we don't really know what 'done' looks like, because the regulations are so imprecise. Every question to them has to go through Compliance. They don't understand the subject and they're all lawyers anyway. Asking the regulators' lawyers and they are all covering their arses. So the answer is always 'do it the hard way.' Then Ops throw their toys out the pram and round we go."

"OK, that's Number One. What's next?"

"Two: IT changes. We need to make changes to about a hundred systems. A hundred. In six months. Including systems we don't maintain anymore and we don't understand. Not enough people, not enough time. Can't be done."

"I heard Sir Simon is putting fifty million pounds of extra budget on the table. Topeka can do anything, hire anyone – take priority over anything."

"You think more money made it better? Look at these emails. Here's one from Tim Hawes, calling himself the Topeka Program Manager. He's hired a boat load of KPC consultants and he requires my attendance at the Topeka Finance delivery board. No representation from Ops or Risk. Great.

"Sean Miller in Operations is doing exactly the same thing. For Operations. Does he know what Finance is up to? Of course not. And Risk is copying Finance. They're using EWG, not KPC and they're a bit behind. I can't win, Chris. It's an effing nightmare."

"OK, so what's the third thing?"

"That is the third thing. Since Sir Simon chucked money at us, everyone's in charge. Do I care? Fuck no. But you need one design, one strategy. We don't have one. You wait, a month from now, they will all start blaming IT. First me, then you guys."

Gawain gazed moodily into the dregs of his coffee.

"It's not going to work, Chris. There's just too much to do and too little time."

He had deep rings under his eyes. His face was pale. He looked like someone with a Force Nine hangover. Which was impossible, because Gawain never touched alcohol, not even a glass of champagne at a Christmas party.

Chris was deep in thought as he went back to the office. How to explain this to Cyrus? Gawain was bit of an Eeyore, but he was rarely wrong. But Gawain couldn't fix it. He didn't have the authority – or the charisma.

But now that deVries was COO, could *he* make that difference?

*

That night, Chris took Carl and his US team out to dinner. By 9pm, he was back in his hotel room. He woke at 2am. His body clock knew it was 7am in London. He lay awake, breathing the aroma of stale cigarettes and listening to the roar of the fans.

Jesus, it was hot. He found the thermostat. It was set to seventy-seven Fahrenheit. Oh my God, that was... twenty-five Celsius. No wonder he was cooking. He turned it down and opened his laptop.

He had forty-six unread emails but top of the list was one from Anne Steffens.

You were asking Paul Carpenter for this?

Annie xx

PS. Nice to see you again ;¬)

PPS. Please explain this to me in English. Jerome V INTERESTED.

It was the top secret KPC report on the Hamilton disaster. Of course, the COO would get a copy and as Jerome deVries' new business manager, so would she.

He sat and paged through it. His first impressions were positive. The author had the knack of translating technical things into non-technical language. On page 15 he found '*Factors contributing to the incident.*'

Here we go, he thought.

...at some point during the incident, the chiller valves for Laurel were set to manual... we believe that staff from the NOC deliberately overrode the chiller controls during the incident...

Interesting. The chillers were just that. Machines which chilled vast quantities of water. That water was pumped to the CRAC units on the floor which delivered refrigerated air to the computers. TIS staff playing around with the chiller controls? TIS had kept that very quiet.

...and at least one of them (employee T) had working knowledge of the chiller system. We consider that unauthorized access to the chiller controls was a significant factor in the sequence of failures which led to the incident...

Really? What did "significant factor" mean? Did employee T switch off the cooling? Did he cause the disaster or not?

Chris flicked backwards and forwards for ten minutes, but there was nothing else. He stared at the report in disbelief. The truth was, they had no idea what had *actually* happened. They hadn't even mentioned the renegade Building Management System, which had unaccountably set the thermostats to sixty-six degrees.

KPC had listed twenty-seven other actions that should be taken to "remediate the risk". The bank had committed an astonishing one hundred and six million dollars to the remediation program. Boatloads of consulting work required, naturally. It made him angry. How could you fix a problem you didn't understand? It didn't make sense.

He tried sleeping again but it didn't work. He had a headache and his throat was dry. He turned the lamp on and flicked through the report again, recognizing the names of people he'd heard on calls during the night but had never met, mostly TIS people. Mannie Seibowicz, Luis Esposito, someone called Frank, the property guys in India.

The events of the night were coming back to him. The confusion, time running out. People screaming about the mainframe.

Here was something new:

At 2.30am, employee K working in Laurel was overcome by the heat and fainted. Her colleagues carried her to the NOC where she recovered. After that staff took regular breaks in the NOC until the temperature in the data halls returned to normal.

Chris stared at this paragraph for a while. 2.30am was 7.30am in London. At that moment, he had been in a taxi crossing Clapham Common. He didn't remember hearing about someone fainting. There was something odd about this. After a while he realized what it was. Laurel was like an oven *but the NOC was cool*. How could that be? It was just a little room inside the main building. How was it cooled? It raised a dozen questions, none of them really his business.

JFDI: Just Fucking Do It.

At 3.30am he started sending emails. He asked Holly to cancel his flight and rebook him on an overnight, arriving Saturday morning. That should be OK with Olivia. Sort of. Another was to Paul Carpenter, asking permission to visit Hamilton in the morning and talk to the NOC staff. And, finally, he sent some explicit instructions to Property Services in London. God knows if they would listen to him.

Remember to buy a digital thermometer, he said to himself as he tried to get an hour's sleep before his first conference call at 5am. The sun never set on a global organisation.

17

Parsippany, NJ

The next morning (Friday, 7th September 2012)

Chris dozed on the trip out to Parsippany from New York. He had the driver stop at the CVS drugstore just off Highway 10 and bought a little digital thermometer, which he tucked into his laptop bag.

The aisle by the checkout was stacked with boxes of BaByliss curlers, straighteners and hair dryers. Mannie Seibowitz and the NOC staff had raided these very shelves on the night of June 15th. He wondered what the bored looking staff would say if they knew – how would CNN put it? – 'Suburban drugstore saves American banking system.'

They found the datacentre, down a cul-de-sac in the business park. There were no signs, just cameras which watched them approach.

"It looks like Fort Knox," said the driver.

"It may have cost more," said Chris, half seriously. Hamilton had cost half a billion dollars.

You could hardly see the building itself, hidden behind the steel fencing and the mound of the antiblast defences. What you could see was as featureless and forbidding as a prison. It felt like a prison too, as Chris entered the gatehouse and surrendered his passport to Security.

A young TIS guy was waiting for him in a lobby on the other side of the gate. Clean-cut, late twenties, with a US Marines crop. He was wearing a thick check shirt and a white vest underneath. Chris could see why, it was cold in the room.

"Hi, Mr Peters? I'm Luis Esposito," he said, shaking hands. "Mr Carpenter's on his way, be here shortly. We can wait in the NOC."

"Great," replied Chris, hiding his irritation. Carpenter's boys would be cautious in front of the big boss.

The NOC was small, like a family living room. One wall was packed with screens and there were four chairs in front of them, each with an operator. Luis offered him a seat, and Chris explained his interest in BaByliss night.

"Were you here that night, Luis?"

"June 15th? Oh man, was I here! Stayed all the way through, went home the next night. There was me, John – he's a young guy, been with us about three months, Frankie and Karen, she was the shift leader. Only she were late."

"Any of them in today?"

"Nope. John's on vacation. The others are gone."

"Gone?"

"Yeah. You know. Gone gone."

What did that mean? Dead? Quit? Fired?

"Is Mannie coming in today?"

"Mannie? No, he's gone also."

Huh? What the hell was going on? He glanced down at his thermometer. Twenty-one degrees and rising.

The door opened and Paul Carpenter came in, tidily dressed in tan chinos and a Ted Baker check shirt instead of his usual tie. It was his version of Friday dress down. He gave Chris a politician's handshake, firm and reassuring.

"So, Chris, what brings you to our humble abode?"

"Friday June 15th," said Chris, "I'd like to hear what happened that night."

"You were on the calls," said Carpenter. "I remember you. The business was trying to go to full Disaster Recovery and you wanted to wait for McQuade to arrive. That man's scared, I thought, he's doesn't trust his own DR plans."

Carpenter leant across and patted Chris' shoulder with a kind of creepy familiarity.

"Forgive me for being so blunt."

"It wasn't an easy decision," replied Chris, controlling his temper. "We don't know what would have happened, do we?" *Unless crazy Dom MacDonald gets his way and pulls the plug on a datacentre.*

"Well, help me here, Chris," said Carpenter. "What's your interest? We've had internal audit, KPC, the SEC, the Fed all down, crawling around. We've listened and we've cleaned house. It was painful. If we haven't learned our lessons, well, shame on us."

In Paul's world, London was always wrong. And his shop was always perfect. It must have been galling to have US investigators pointing fingers at his staff.

"The KPC report doesn't get to the real issues," said Chris. "It doesn't even mention the Building Management System."

"You've seen the KPC report? How did you get it?"

Chris shrugged. Carpenter looked irritated, then moved on.

"Chris, it hurts, but I accept that report. 100%. Sometimes even the best people let you down … Frank wasn't a bad guy but he screwed up and he had to go."

"Frank is – uh – Employee T in the report?"

"Yes."

"Look, I'm not here to make anyone look bad, OK?" said Chris, "I just want to understand what happened…"

"Ask away, buddy."

How can you help? You were in Manhattan.

"I'd like to talk to Mannie."

"Mannie's a non-person. Legal says we can't talk to him."

"We're in legals with Mannie? I thought he was a hero."

"In TIS Americas, Chris, we value discipline. We need people who do the right thing, no exceptions. Things may be different in Global Markets."

"I'd still like to talk to Mannie."

An angry red flush started from Carpenter's collar and moved up.

"Your limo's outside. Go back to London and get the fuck out of my business, OK? And I'll stay out of yours. Which is quite a mess, from what I hear."

Carpenter started ranting. About London, about Neil Jenkins. The room seemed to heat up as he shouted. Chris took another glance at his thermometer. Wow, the place was starting to cook.

Carpenter suddenly stopped in midflow and leapt out of his chair.

"It's hot in here. Too hot. Damn it. Marvin, what's going on? Call Property. Jesus, why haven't the alarms gone off?"

Chris put his little thermometer on the table.

"It is hot. It's twenty-four degrees. Seventy-five Fahrenheit. It's gone up eight degrees in half an hour. Relax, Paul, only in here, the datacentre rooms are fine."

Carpenter looked at him like a bull confused by the matador's cloak.

"I asked Property to set the thermostats here in the NOC to thirty degrees, for an hour. So the cooling shut down. It heats up quickly, eh? But on June 15th, one of your staff – Karen, I think – was overcome by the heat and they brought her here to *cool down*. Strange, eh? Why didn't the NOC heat up that night? How do you explain that?"

Even the security guys were shocked by Carpenter's language. The abuse followed him as he was hustled out of the building to his car. Chris sank gratefully into the cool leather seats. But what now?

His Blackberry went *zing*! as a new text arrived.

Want to meet Mannie? 10am Howard Johnson. Intersection of 280/287. L.

Thank you Luis! He had half an hour to get there. Perfect.

18

The diner on Interstate 287

Mannie Seibowicz was sitting at a table in the diner, blinking in the sunshine. He was neatly dressed with a white shirt, plain tie and dark pants. He was thinner than Chris remembered, and his eyes were sunken. There was something almost rat-like about him. An anxious rat.

"I just been to see my attorney," he said. "His office is across the street."

"Buying a house?" said Chris.

"I wish. Paul Carpenter is trying to get rid of me. My face doesn't fit anymore, these things happen, you know? But this way ain't right."

"What way?"

"I got a letter a month ago, from a big law firm in the City. It said the bank was dismissing me for gross negligence. Gross negligence, me? I work for the bank twelve years, you know, every night those twelve years my wife says I'm married to that damn bank and she's sick of it."

"If I sign the letter, they pay ten thousand dollars, ex-gratia. That's it, full and final. I've got two daughters in high school, a new house, the bills come in every month... it's frightening. I can't afford an attorney, but I need one. My congregation wants to help but everybody's struggling. Anyway, what can I do for you, Mr Peters?"

"Hum. Mannie, I have seen the KPC report. I'm surprised. It doesn't mention that the BMS went crazy. It doesn't mention hairdryers. It blames one of your guys – Frank, is it? – for playing around with the chillers. What's the story?"

"How would I know?" said Mannie. "I haven't seen it. But it doesn't surprise me. See, Fujitsu came back. They can't find anything wrong with the BMS. They can't explain how it started chasing sixty-six degrees. They can't say whether it can happen again. Paul Carpenter doesn't like that. The business was angry, he needs a victim. He decided it's gonna be Frank. And me."

"But KPC..."

"Mr Carpenter briefed KPC thoroughly. When they came to see me, all they wanted to talk about was Frank. Sure, Frank was fooling around with the chillers, like an idiot. Maybe he slowed the recovery – but he didn't start it. Listen, I told them, the first time this happened, Frank wasn't even in the country."

"What do you mean, the first time?"

"The week before. June 8th. No warning, servers overheating in Aisle F, Hardy Hall. Same deal, CRAC units were just blowing out warm air. And Frank was on vacation in Puerto Rico."

"I never heard about this."

"It only lasted thirty minutes. Then suddenly – *poof* – everything's fine again. We told Property Services but they couldn't find anything wrong. Doesn't make sense, does it?"

Oh yes it does, thought Chris, *it makes perfect sense*. He stayed for another half hour, his thoughts in turmoil, trying to listen while Mannie told his story.

Finally, he got up, in a hurry now. Mannie looked up, his desperation evident as his worries flooded back.

"I'll do my best for you, Mannie. I will talk to Neil, see if he can help."

Chris hurried back to the City. His driver wanted to chat but Chris ignored him. Paul Carpenter's angry red face kept coming back to him. What a ruthless bastard. Four staff were on duty that night and he had fired three of them. Frank had broken the rules to try and fix the chillers, now he was the scapegoat. Mannie, also disobeying orders, had had the courage to switch off a thousand servers.

And what had Carpenter done? Fuck all. He had sat in his Soho loft apartment and ducked the hard decisions. But the official report thanked Carpenter for saving the bank and Mannie was being pushed onto the breadline. Was Carpenter covering his ass or did he have something bigger to hide? Either way he was pure poison, no wonder Neil Jenkins didn't trust him.

When he got back to the office in mid-town, he found a quiet cubicle on the technology floor and logged in. Property Services had sent him Fujitsu's manual for the BMS. He spent an hour going through it. The more he read, the more certain he was. The more certain he was, the more incredible it became. What was he going to do? He called John Uzgalis. It was 7.30pm in London.

Uzgalis was on the A4, heading out to Bath for the weekend. Chris could hear his English wife in the background, shushing two boisterous kids.

"Am I on speaker?" *Click.*

"Not now. What's on your mind, boy?"

Chris told him. Uzgalis was silent for a long minute.

"This is some kind of weird Limey joke, right?"

"No. It's all true, I swear."

"Then we need to escalate immediately to Alexis. And Neil."

"Neil Jenkins?"

"Yeah. He runs Information Security, right? Stay there, I'll call you back."

Uzgalis rang back ten minutes later.

"OK. Our boss is unavailable, as usual. So is Neil Jenkins. So we're going to deVries."

The new COO? Chris didn't like that. Way, way above his pay grade.

"Ready? Here we go. I'm patching him in."

DeVries answered immediately, but in a low voice.

"Your timing is shit, guys. I'm in a meeting."

At 7.30pm on a Friday night?

"Chris believes we have had a major cyber attack," said Uzgalis.

"Neil Jenkins tells me we have hundreds of attacks a day."

"Those are external," said Chris. "This is an attack from within."

DeVries' voice was suddenly full volume. He must have left his meeting.

"Ok, speak. I don't have all night, guys."

"You remember the cooling failure in the Hamilton datacentre?"

"How could I forget it? That was the night I discovered IT didn't have a DR plan. It was you two clowns who led the resistance, as I remember... and you were saved by some kludge from Neil Jenkins using hairdryers."

"Did anyone tell you what went wrong?" said Chris, hastily.

"Human error. Someone shut down the air conditioning. Tim explained it to me."

"No, that's a myth. There was nothing wrong with the chillers. They just weren't doing any chilling because the thermostats of the BMS – that's the Building Management System that controls it – had been set to sixty-six degrees instead of nineteen. No cooling needed, so the BMS shut down the chillers."

"Fujitsu make the BMS. They can't reproduce the problem. US management hired KPC to investigate. Their report blames a technician called Frank who has been fired. Today, I discovered that he had nothing to do with it."

"So?"

"The BMS is remotely programmable. I believe someone wrote a program that deliberately reset the thermostats. This was sabotage."

"That's a big statement, boy. What evidence have you got for that?"

"The KPC report says during the crisis, staff went to the NOC to cool down. The NOC in the middle of the datacentre. It's cooled by the same chillers, but with its own thermostats. Why didn't it heat up as well? There are eighty-six thermostats in the building. Numbers Twelve and Sixteen are in the NOC, the rest are in the Halls. What kind of accident sets eighty-four sensors to sixty-six degrees and misses out Twelve and Sixteen?"

"Why would someone want to miss them out?"

"Because the NOC heats up incredibly quickly. This morning I got Property Services to set those two thermostats to thirty degrees. The NOC reached twenty-four degrees in twenty minutes. Whoever did this knew about the NOC and they didn't want the alarm raised too soon. They wanted maximum damage."

"And the second thing?"

"Today I met Frank's boss, Mannie. He told me that one week earlier a single aisle – aisle F – heated up. It lasted half an hour and then mysteriously fixed itself. Never explained."

"Why is that significant?"

"It was a test. Just one aisle, thirty minutes. Our attacker was checking that his program worked."

"Then, why wait? If it worked, wouldn't they want to press the button right away?"

"They were waiting for Triple Witching. Volumes are so high on Triple Witching, even a small incident can have a big effect. We had most of the night to recover in June, and it was still a really bad day."

There was a longer pause.

"Meet me in the office tomorrow morning. Both of you. 10am. Good-night."

Saturday morning, thought Chris. *Olivia's gonna kill me.*

Uzgalis rang.

"Chris, are you sure about this? This is going to be a major shit storm."

"What do you mean? The Audit committee?"

"That's the least of it. Hamilton is an American datacentre. So we have to tell the Fed about it. Those guys have been having wet dreams about terrorist attacks on banks since 911. And here it is, a US datacentre attacked from Asia. Prime time on FoxNews."

"Asia? What do you mean, Asia?"

"The BMS is managed from India, right? Man, there could be drone strikes on Delhi."

"For God's sake, John, the BMS is on our network. You could access it from anywhere on the planet. All you need is the password."

"You're no fun. Have a good flight, see you tomorrow."

19

Sana'a, Yemen, 2007

Day Six - Wednesday

"Finally, I met al-Muhairi this morning," said Uncle Saeed. "And he told me the truth. Our account is frozen. He doesn't know why, he says it comes from London."

"But, but… what can we do?" asked Mahmoud. There were so many things to be angry about, he didn't know where to start.

"We can open an account with another bank. Then they will transfer the money. They would be happy to get rid of us. I am starting now with Citi, they are across the street. And Barclays. Don't worry."

"But they said today is the last day. When al-Omani dies, they will kill Father. An eye for an eye."

"They won't do anything if the money is coming. Give them the cash you have, that will help."

Mahmoud had to explain how Ahmed had gambled away every penny.

"Even the money from the shop?" Saeed was incredulous.

"Yes. Even that."

"Well, borrow some. And get a message to them, say it's coming. Two days, three days. Call the policeman."

Mahmoud didn't need to call the Fat Policeman, because only a few minutes later, little Yousef appeared and announced a policeman downstairs.

Tariq's jeep smelt of hot canvas and dust. At first, they headed west on Al-Zubayri, and Mahmoud thought they were going back to the police station. But when they crossed the A1, Tariq turned off and pulled up in front of the Sheba Hotel.

Tahrir Square was only two hundred yards away. Mahmoud could see that the scaffold was already up, ready for the execution of al-Omani. The floor was made of simple plywood, covered in red felt. A dozen soldiers surrounded it, fingering their automatic weapons and looking self-important. The crowds were ten or twenty deep around it already, with an hour to go.

"Go in," said Tariq, "he will meet you at the bar."

Mahmoud had been inside the Sheba only once before and he didn't like it. It was very expensive and it served alcohol. It was popular with Western businessmen. His father came here, but not often.

"Once," his father told him, "I saw this big white taxi arrive and two women got out, wrapped head to toe in black burqas. They walked unsteadily, like women in high heels. The doorman showed them straight to the lifts." His father had winked. Mahmoud was disbelieving and disgusted in equal measure.

The guards outside the building looked hard at him as he walked in. They looked at his long, brown thawb and the old sandals slapping on the marble. They saw his beard and cheap skullcap, and they wondered whether to stop him. They wondered whether he had plastic explosives underneath. But they did not move. It was hot. If it was Allah's will, they would die. If not, not. Inshah Allah.

He found the bar and sat down. The barman came over, but Mahmoud waved him away. Even a glass of water in this place would make him unclean.

The big policeman suddenly appeared and sat down. His face was flushed and sweat ran down his cheeks. The barman brought him a coffee, and a little shot glass with clear liquid, then departed in silence. The inspector mopped his face with a paper napkin.

"Drink?" said the policeman.

"No," said Mahmoud.

"You may wish you had," replied the other, pouring the shot into his coffee and downing it in two gulps. He glanced towards the bar. The barman brought him another shot and another coffee.

"This hotel is under my protection. Even the marines from the American Embassy drink here."

He looked around the deserted bar and sighed.

"But it is getting harder. Every week I look at this nice glass and this nice carpet and I thank Allah, and I say to him, 'Another week, please give me another week.' And so far, it has worked, alhamdulillah. Do you understand?"

"No," said Mahmoud, in a panic now. "Stop talking. What about my father? Time is running out, there's only half an hour left, what is going to happen when-?"

"Relax, my friend, someone is coming," said the fat policeman. "Nothing is going to happen, I promise you, nothing, until we have talked. You have the money, yes?"

"No, not all of it."

"But you have some? Then it's OK."

How to say, I have five hundred dollars I borrowed from little Yousef's father? Damn, damn Ahmed.

But the policeman didn't want specifics. He wanted to talk.

"We are the beggars of the Arab world. We produce three billion dollars a year and we spend that much on qat, do you know that? Nobody cares about us, we have no oil. Still, we could have been poor but happy."

"But not anymore. You know why? Because after Anwar al-Awlaki came back here, the Americans and the crazy guys decided that Yemen was a good place to fight a war. Anwar al-Awlaki used to be a scholar of the Prophet. But he has become the Pied Piper of jihad. He uses Facebook and YouTube and his sermons are broadcast all over the internet. Have you seen them?"

Mahmoud shook his head. This was all mad.

"The Americans didn't like that, so we locked him up. It only made things worse. The extremists are coming, like flies to rotten meat. From Afghanistan. From Pakistan, from Iraq. Every day there are more jihadists running around this country. We put them in jail but the little bastards don't stay there, do they?"

"Last year, twenty-three of the crazies escaped from jail, right here in Sana'a. What do you think? By jumping over the wall? In a helicopter? No. They dug a tunnel to the mosque next door! It came out in the women's toilets. Ha-ha. They were reborn in the women's block. The prison service tried to keep *that* off CNN. Anyway, now the country is swarming with crazies and they all want jihad. They hate Americans. They hate the Saudi. They even hate women."

He took another sip from his shot glass and gazed out placidly at the guards and two Chinese businessmen coming into the lobby. Behind them was a big man, a Yemeni, wearing blue jeans and a black T-shirt.

"Here comes the Debt Collector now. Be careful. He is a difficult man."

20

JFK Terminal 7

Friday, 7th September 2012

The BA lounge at Terminal 7 was packed with business people heading home for the weekend. Chris bagged the last table in the corner, just ahead of two IT guys he recognized from Citibank. With relief, he plugged in his Blackberry and started on his emails.

"Take a break, for God's sake. It's Friday night."

Annie Steffens stood in front of him. Friday was dress down day. She was wearing expensively faded blue jeans and a white top with African animals printed on it. She was holding two tumblers filled with ice and amber liquid.

"Well, hello again," said Chris, "and congratulations on your new job."

"Dunno about that. I've only been in the job twenty-four hours and he's run me ragged already."

"Hard to control deVries from New York, I imagine."

"That's why I'm moving to London, young Christopher. Tonight. Now take your techie shit off that chair, and I will reward you with this."

Chris sniffed the amber liquid suspiciously.

"What's this? Bourbon?"

"It's not just bourbon, it's Woodfords Reserve," she replied, sitting down. "BA has Woodfords Reserve sitting behind the bar! I am never flying American Airlines again."

"It's good," said Chris cautiously. He looked over at Annie. She was an extrovert. She worked in Finance but she had friends everywhere. She loved parties. She was smart enough to climb the management tree but she had no ambition. Politics seemed to flow by her; she understood it but she was not interested in taking sides. She was attractive and she had many admirers. Annie was not promiscuous but she was occasionally, unpredictably, generous with her charms. Waves of testosterone followed her progress across the trading floors.

Right now, she was torturing a paper napkin.

"Shit, how can I drink bourbon without a cigarette, you know?"

"Give it up. Try acid drops like your boss."

"Talking of bosses, how's van Buren? Is he still sulking about Pandora Stiegel becoming CFO."

Chris shrugged. "Yeah, really strange. He stormed out of our management meeting."

"And you don't know why? Everyone knows."

"Well I don't."

Annie took a reflective sip of Woodfords.

"Really, really? Amazing. OK, well – in brief – Pandora got divorced last year. Her husband works at Credit Suisse and they never saw each other blah blah. Marriage, eh, what's the point? Last March, the Top 100 dogs in Global Markets went off to a strategy weekend in some swanky hotel. First night is the icebreaker dinner, mystery partner etc. Guess who Pandora gets?"

"AVB?"

"That's right, Alexis. They had a few drinks. Pandora tells Alexis about her ex and the divorce. Come bedtime, Alexis invites himself to her room for a last drink. Stupid woman, she didn't think. Naturally he makes a pass at her. I mean, what man wouldn't? Office party, attractive tipsy woman in a bedroom... it's a winning ticket."

Annie took another sip of her Woodford and looked at him over the glass, one eyebrow raised.

"There was no bedroom," said Chris.

"Don't I know it?" replied Annie. "Twice that skirt has been to the cleaners and still they can't get the stains off it. Worse than English grass."

Chris tried to avert his gaze from the smooth curves of her breasts and the tantalizing hint of the darker points – oh, once so familiar! – just visible through the zebras and the lions. She smiled, a little secret smile, and put the glass down.

"'Whoops,' Pandora realized, 'this is not the nightcap I had in mind.' But, Alexis being Dutch and very drunk, there's a bit of a tussle. One of them knocks over a wine glass, sprinkling red wine and glass all over the room. Forget sex, the Dutch and the Dane are on their knees, trying to get the stains out of the carpet."

Annie laughed so heartily that the Citibank guys looked over in surprise.

"Enter Room one-oh-three, next door. Good old Room one-oh-three calls reception. He says he's heard a woman screaming. Hotel security rushes round, and knocks on the door. Eventually Alexis opens the door a crack and says 'everything's fine,' as best he can after six hours of boozing with the Top 100. But he won't open the door any further and security notices he has blood on his fingers. Oh my God. Next thing you know, the lobby is full of policemen."

"Pandora who is a compulsive truth-teller says 'he tried to kiss me,' and the policewoman hears sexual assault and attempted rape. Poor Alexis is taken off for questioning and Pandora is invited to provide..."

Annie leaned over and whispered in his ear.

"I can't believe you!" Chris shook his head.

"It's all true. Trust me. The next day the Top 100 suddenly became the Top 97. Sir Simon went down to see the local police personally. Ha! Jerome says he turned up in a black 'S' class Merc with his driver and parked in the space marked 'CID.' Not a good start. But they managed to hush it up."

"So, what happened? Why was AVB so angry when she became CFO?"

"My child," said Annie, taking another generous sip of Woodfords, "that's where the farce becomes a tragedy."

"Back in the office, Alexis went to apologise. Good idea. Except he lost his Dutch temper and started saying it was all her fault. She threw him out of her office and she told HR. OMG, now he's harassing her at work, it's more serious. Allegations of sexual harassment require investigation, by an independent referee."

Chris could imagine. It explained a lot of AVB's behaviour recently. He'd been silent in some meetings and mysteriously absent from others. Poor guy, what a nightmare.

"Who was the referee?"

"Jerome."

The new COO, who had just appointed Pandora his successor as CFO. A clear endorsement. A snub to AVB. No wonder he was upset. No wonder he couldn't face deVries as his boss.

"That's enough gossip for one flight," said Annie. "How's your love life these days?"

"Er. Well, I got married. Two, no three years ago."

Whoops. That reminded him. He had forgotten to call Olivia and tell her he wouldn't be back until the morning.

"Pity," said Annie. "Well, that's my flight. Buy me a drink some time. We can talk about anything except effing Topeka." She leaned over and brushed his cheek with her lips. Then she was gone, leaving behind the scent of her hair, mixed with bourbon. The two guys from Citi stopped to admire the view as she picked her way elegantly between mounds of suitcases and laptop bags.

Olivia answered on the second ring and cut short his explanations.

"I know, Chris. Holly called me six hours ago. I'll stay in bed until you arrive: Dr Ireson says we need lots of time, not to rush things."

Well, that was going to be tricky. He didn't mention the emergency meeting deVries had called for ten o'clock. Chicken.

21

London

Saturday, 8th September 2012

Chris slept for three hours and woke somewhere over the Irish sea.

The flight landed late, so it was almost nine when the car dropped him at home. He went upstairs and into the darkened bedroom. There was an Olivia-shaped hump under the duvet. Pulling off his clothes, he slid in beside her. He took a last look at his Blackberry. 9.07. He had twenty minutes, max. Assuming the Northern Line was working. Hastily he set an alarm. 9.25. He should tell her now.

She turned and gave him a warm, wet kiss. She had that dreamy look in her eyes. Sometimes she had erotic dreams and woke aroused like this. She took his Blackberry and buried it under the pillow. Then she placed his hand gently on the smooth curve of her navel. Moving it in a circle full of promising destinations.

Ten minutes later, he was lost. Olivia was kneeling over him, her long thighs astride his head on the pillows. In the dim light, the curves of her naked form were an aphrodisiac that drove the blood to his loins and all other thoughts from his head.

She stopped for a moment, recognized the danger.

"Don't come, darling, don't come..." she whispered and then a moment later, "yes, yes, like that, go on..."

He had forgotten where he was, forgotten the time. They were just two naked bodies, wrapped together in lust. It was almost like their first time, back in Hong Kong, when they were strangers coupling amid the fury of rain and wind.

And then the bloody Blackberry went off. His forebrain took back the controls. Despite her protests, Chris knew what he had to do. At first, she resisted his assault. Her protests had turned to something else, cries and moans that inflamed him, drove him deeper. He came quickly, exploded in spasms so intense they were almost painful.

"Wow," she whispered, unsatisfied but not unhappy – not yet – "what got into you?"

It would have been okay if they'd stayed in bed. Talked. Bathed in the scents of sex and sperm. And coffee. But he couldn't. He leapt out of the bed and started throwing on his clothes. He had to confess where he was going. Her anger was instant and frightening.

It was Saturday and the Northern line trains were further apart. Chris sat and waited, suffused with anxiety and guilt. He was ashamed. But the forebrain disagreed. Yes, it was a bit hasty. But wasn't passion better than clinical? Surely Dr Ireson would have approved, had he been there?

His bladder was full and he had a pain in his groin, and a headache. And now he was going to be late for this meeting. *I've done it again*, he thought, *I've tried to please everyone and fucked it up*.

Chris was ten minutes late. DeVries gave him the death stare.

The little glass office was crowded. He had expected John Uzgalis, and Sheila Collins from Information Security. But here also was Mike Tucker from Property, looking seedy and hungover, and his own boss, Alexis. And Oleg, the albino auditor who was Dom's partner in crime.

"Folks, thanks for coming in at short notice," said deVries. "Who can forget June 15th? Eh? Not me. I was woken up by a talking computer. The same wretched machine that wants me to sue my bank for mis-selling PPI. But not that morning. That morning our North American datacentre was about to melt down. We were saved by some miracle conjured by Mr Jenkins and his men."

"So what went wrong? A brand new datacentre. Half a billion US, I am still crying over the bill. The place was literally bombproof. Everything duplicated. We have two Coke machines, even. We commissioned an independent report from KPC. Two months of work, ninety-two pages, it probably cost us half a million. And was the cause? Let me quote from page thirteen: 'a sequence of manual interventions!' By a technician in TIS.

"We fired the guy, job done, back to work, yes? But one of our senior technologists has a different theory. Mr Peters, over to you. Don't take too long, your boss is wanted back on the golf course."

"Golf is not my game," replied Alexis stiffly.

"Yes, I remember you missed the golf match at the Top 100," replied deVries. Bastard, thought Chris, presumably Alexis had been down at the police station trying to avoid a rape charge and deVries knew it.

Chris wanted this meeting over. He needed to get home. Take Olivia out to lunch. His account of the attack on Hamilton was brief and to the point.

But it didn't seem as slam-dunk convincing as it had the day before, on another continent. Even to him.

"Questions?" asked deVries when he'd finished.

"Yes," said Uzgalis, instantly. "Mike, I'm curious. How could someone get access to the BMS system? Would they not need a password?"

"Well, that's a good question, John ..." said Mike Tucker, looking uncomfortable.

"Let me guess," said Uzgalis, "the password was *secret?*"

"No," replied Sheila, pretending to be helpful, "I believe it was *changeme.*"

Chris struggled not to laugh hysterically.

"OK, OK," said Mike Tucker, "but listen, we've got a forty-two-point plan to fix it-"

Mike Tucker was a weak manager but he had charm. That's how he had survived seven years running Property. No one with real prospects wanted his job anyway.

Oleg the auditor took off his glasses and rubbed his eyes as though tired. He was older than Chris had realized. Mid-forties. Maybe older.

"Your forty-two-point plan is irrelevant."

Silence. The auditor looked slowly round the room.

"Mike, I'm sure you're working hard mending the holes in that fence. But if Chris is right, the fox is already inside the farmyard. *He's one of us chickens.* His next attack could be completely different. Completely. We can't guess. Forget the fences, we must find this treacherous fox and shoot him."

Which – at last, as far as Chris was concerned – started an excited discussion about how the log files from the BMS might provide clues. Chris, John, Sheila and even Alexis all joined in.

"Enough!" shouted deVries. "It's like kindergarten at break time. Where is the discipline? No wonder nothing gets done in Technology. OK, you all seem to think there is something to investigate. Let me be clear: such investigation is a job for Information Security. No-one else, unless Sheila asks for your help."

"Especially you, Chris. You need to focus on your day job. No more Sherlock Holmes, is that clear?"

He wasn't satisfied until Chris had said yes, not once, but twice.

"Should we tell the regulators?" asked Uzgalis hopefully. "After all, this is an American datacentre."

"Premature. Next?"

"Should we tell Mackenna?" This was Sheila. Chris had never heard of Mackenna.

"Mackenna? Yes, definitely. Any questions? No? I wish you all a pleasant weekend."

Chris hurried home. He ran all the way back from Clapham South tube, but he was too late. The house was empty and there was an angry note on the kitchen table:

Gone lunch at Wilsons. Back sometime. PS. Ironing basket full.

22

London

The weekend passed. Chris did the ironing. He felt sick with shame. When Olivia got back, she was still steaming and he couldn't blame her. If only she conceived, everything would be alright again.

He couldn't sleep on Saturday night. He lay awake and stewed. Not just about Olivia and fatherhood. He couldn't stop thinking about Hamilton. His theory was fantastic. It was science fiction come true. Like Stuxnet. How come the NOC stayed cool? It had to be deliberate.

On Sunday morning, he tried talking to Olivia about it. She was not impressed.

"Lots of people don't like that bank. It could be me."

At 4am on Monday morning, sleepless with frustration, he emailed Murali in Chennai, directly asking for a copy of the BMS logfile for June 15th. Not really in hope, more interested to see what their excuse was. After all, Dom had been badgering them all summer without success. He copied Mike Tucker, who was Murali's boss. Mike knew he wasn't supposed to be doing this but Chris had known Mike a long time.

23

London

Murali's reply arrived at 6am on Tuesday morning. Chris felt steam coming out of his ears as he read it. Yes, the BMS did keep a record of its activities, but only for one week. Each week's activity overwrote the previous week. And so, most regrettably, he was unable to help Chris with his request. Chris typed an angry reply:

Yes but TIS must have been backed up that system during that week! THE FILE WILL BE IN THAT BACKUP TAPE. HAVE YOU ASKED TIS?

Silence. Idiots. Why the hell hadn't Dom dug into this? He asked Holly for an urgent meeting with Neil Jenkins. Maybe Neil could get him that backup tape.

He dressed quickly and got into the office just after 7.30am. His desk phone was showing a missed call and the message light was flashing.

It was from a Bruce Mackenna, needing to speak to Chris Peters urgently. He left a mobile number.

Mackenna? The mystery man Sheila mentioned on Saturday. Chris shrugged and went down to the trading floor. He was chatting to the Structuring desk when his Blackberry rang.

"This is Bruce Mackenna."

A strong Scots accent. Precise, confident and disapproving.

"I will be in your office at 8.30. Please be there."

Click. *Who does this guy think he is*? He texted Holly.

bruce mackenna?

The reply was swift: *Core Internal Security ;~(*

At 8.30am he was back on the eighth floor.

"Holly, can you get me an emergency meeting with Neil Jenkins? Tell him it's about a backup tape."

"OK," said Holly, looking anxious. "A man called Mackenna is in your office. He's very rude. He said he's going to call Simon and complain about you."

She dropped her voice. "I think he means Sir Simon. He's a bit of a snob."

Chris glanced discreetly at the big man sitting in his office, studying a notebook. He was late forties, maybe fifty. A pale face with large overlapping freckles and fading ginger hair. He was wearing a brown tweed suit and a regimental tie that clashed. He did not look like a banker. He looked like a prosperous farmer or a provincial accountant, come to the big city for the day.

"Hello, I'm Chris Peters. I'm-"

Mackenna regarded him steadily. "I know who you are. You're late."

"Yes, I'm sorry. Difficult morning."

"Don't waste your breath on excuses," said Mackenna in his broad Glaswegian. "Those moments are gone and nothing will bring them back."

Bloody hell, this guy was ugly.

"And speaking frankly, Mr Peters, you are not quite what I expected."

Chris caught a glimpse of himself in the glass of his office door. Thirty-six years old, but he'd always looked, well, a bit baby faced. Short dark hair, thin, sharp nosed. He often wore jeans in the office, but today he was wearing blue chinos and a striped Italian shirt that Olivia had bought him. He wasn't sure he liked it. A gigolo's shirt, really. What was Mackenna expecting? Pinstripes?

"Well, here I am."

"Indeed. I should be grateful for that."

Mackenna regarded him for another long moment.

"I heard a strange story about an American datacentre. I'm told it comes from you. I'd like to hear it from the horse's mouth, if you will excuse the metaphor."

"Ah. Excuse me, Mr Mackenna, but who are you? I've never heard of you."

"That pleases me. I work behind the scenes. I don't have a fancy title like yours. But I can do something you can't, Mr Peters. I can pick up that phone any time, and call Simon. Or Teddy. And they will take my call, day or night."

Simon must be Sir Simon, thought Chris, and Teddy is Edward Feugel. If Mackenna had that kind of access to the Chief Exec or the Chairman of the bank, he was someone to fear.

"Yes, but... ok... what do you actually do?"

"I keep out the wolves out," said Mackenna cryptically. "Now tell me about this datacentre."

Chris told him. Mackenna sat and listened. There was a curious intensity about him. He took no notes.

"So," he said when Chris had finished, "it reminds me of those Iranian centrifuges that got toasted."

"Stuxnet," said Chris, impressed.

"Aye. Stuxnet, that was it," said Mackenna. He brooded for a minute or two.

"So in practice, Christopher, how do you go about resetting eighty-four thermostats? That's a lot of typing…"

"You wouldn't do it manually. Fujitsu supply sample scripts and instructions on how to program the BMS remotely. You would write a program to do it."

"And where would we find this program?"

"I don't know. Sitting on a computer somewhere inside this bank."

"I see. A kind of bomb factory. Interesting. How could we find it?"

"According to Fujitsu, the BMS keeps a record, a logfile of what it does. That logfile will record who told it to do what, when. Property need to pony up that logfile. Simple. Except that they can't. Or won't, who knows?"

Mackenna brooded some more.

"You are articulate, Mr Peters," he said finally, "and you tell a good story. Though it lacks the final proof. You need to find this bomb factory."

His gaze was suddenly piercing, under his bushy eyebrows.

"Tell me, Christopher, do you have a car?"

Bizarre question.

"What? No. I don't drive. Why?"

"Where were you at 2am, last Wednesday, a week ago?"

Chris felt threatened. He suddenly couldn't remember. "Wait. Yes! I was halfway across the Atlantic. On a flight to New York. Why do you ask?"

"Would you ask your young lady to come in, please?"

Thank God for Holly. She gave Mackenna the same answers, and left a minute later, looking indignant. Mackenna unlocked his briefcase and took out an A4 manila envelope.

"What I am about to show you is for your ears, not your mouth, understood? Not to be discussed, not here, not at home. Is that clear?"

"It's a secret."

"Secret! Don't use that word in this bank. Do you remember Project Cinnamon?"

"I think so. A new bond issue. Something went wrong with it."

"You could say that," said Mackenna. "The bank planned to raise eight billion, mostly from our Arab and Chinese friends."

"And it didn't happen?"

"It did not," said Mackenna, grimly satisfied. "It was a very public debacle."

Chris had a faint recollection of the headlines. Some rumour about the collapse of the bank's card business.

"Well, Cinnamon was secret. Highly secret and for good reason. In this bank, we put confidences on email. Email! There are no secrets in this bank. We are as leaky as a bucket wi' nae bottom." He leaned forward. "Do you know why? No? Because in this bank, a secret is something we tell to just *one special friend*."

Chris smiled to show he'd got the joke. Mackenna opened his manila envelope and extracted a sheaf of photographs.

"You will be familiar with the bank's datacentre in East London?"

"You mean Raleigh? Down in West Ham?"

Raleigh was the datacentre that Neil wanted to build a waterproof wall around. Familiar was not a word Chris would use. Raleigh was a huge, expensive shed on an old industrial estate near the Olympic Village. He had been there only once in the flesh, but most of his European systems were hosted there. Neil Jenkins and the TIS guys had 25,000 computers in the building and the numbers kept going up.

"These images were recorded on J camera at Raleigh, a week ago. Just after midnight, while you were halfway to New York. J camera covers Three Mill Lane, which runs down one side of the site."

"See this gentleman walking up the lane? Here he is, standing beside the perimeter fence, looking up. And now? Where is he?! Gone! But not quite, look here – you can see his outline on the far side of the fence. Athletic, isn't he? Straight over the fence. Now he's disappeared into the grounds of the datacentre. Twenty minutes later, he's back again. Got his phone out, taking pictures of this dark seam across the road."

Chris studied the pictures. A short male figure. Wearing dark trousers and an anorak with a hood. And a scarf. Definitely didn't want to be identified.

"What's below that seam in the road?"

"The fibre ducts. Leading to the datacentre."

"No! Really? As obvious as that?"

Fibre ducts carried the optical fibres that connected the datacentre to the rest of the bank's network. They were information superhighways, the industrial version of the domestic broadband connection.

"Oh yes. There are two ducts coming out of the building. They are buried in a shallow trench with a steel cover. They are not armoured, a small digger could destroy them in five minutes. With a big one, like this one, it would take you seconds."

He pointed to the gaunt angle of a mechanical arm that could be seen on the far side of the fence.

"What's that?" asked Chris.

Mackenna shrugged.

"TIS are doing some building work. But come back to our friend here. Where did he park? We contacted our neighbours and we struck lucky. These images are from CCTV in the BestFoods warehouse. About three hundred yards away."

Chris studied the pictures. The same man. Dark trousers, dark top. The face concealed by a scarf and cap. The car was visible, from the side. Something nondescript. A Toyota? A Ford? Light coloured, hatch back. There was a pale oval sticker on the rear window with indistinct markings inside it.

"The car is a Ford Focus," said Mackenna. "Three years old, a UK model. We were unlucky not to get the registration. If that's a standard paint job, the colour is Moondust metallic, a kind of silver."

"And the white sticker in the window?"

"The sticker is a worry. We've enlarged it, here. A crescent shape, and inside, a large star. The experts tell me it's probably red or orange. A red crescent, Mr Peters, with a star inside. What does that tell you?"

Chris shrugged, which irritated Mackenna. "Don't be stupid, Mr Peters. It's an Islamic symbol. That's a worrying prospect, especially when you combine it with this ..."

Mackenna passed over the last two photos.

In the first, the intruder was bending over, picking something off the ground.

"As he approached Raleigh, he remembered that he was wearing a pass on his belt. He took it off, and then dropped it. We were lucky – we have a frame showing the card, we've enhanced it."

He passed it over. Mackenna took out his ID card and placed it on the table.

"See that smudge there?"

"It could be our logo…"

"It is our logo. He works for this bank. Christopher, show me your ID, please."

Chris felt vaguely threatened as he put his pass on the table.

"See here. I'm a Core Function, Christopher. I have a solid bar on my pass. You boys in Global Markets, your passes are special, so we can keep an eye on you. You have two bars. Commercial banking has three."

"Now, look at the picture. See? Two bars."

Mackenna fastened an accusing eye on him.

"Someone employed in Global Markets is planning an attack on Raleigh. But who is he, eh? Some banker who didn't like his bonus? He knows about fibre ducts. He clips his pass to his belt…"

Chris thought about it. Bankers did not wear their passes on their belt.

"He's TIS. One of Neil's guys. They run the datacentres, they know about fibre channels."

"Nice try, young man, but no cigar. TIS is a Core Function. They have a solid bar on their pass, like me."

Mackenna's gaze hardened.

"Global Markets IT, Chris. Someone in van Buren's organization. Maybe he works for you. Ring any bells?"

"No," said Chris. "I mean it could be a lot of people." His hands trembled as he handed back the photos.

"So," said Mackenna, "if our friend got a digger and dug up the fibre, what would be the effect? I asked van Buren. He said there would be an outage but not significant because the other datacentre - Drake - would, as it were, take up the load."

Alexis was a politician.

"Well, no data would be lost," said Chris. "Data in Raleigh is copied in real time to Drake through those ducts. You would have all the data in Drake, up to the instant that the fibre was cut. But after that, Raleigh would be invisible. Like a bomb went off in it."

"So?"

"So, we would have to bring up every system in Drake to continue processing that data. There would be a lot of disruption, especially to trading. In theory, we could get back in business in four hours."

Mackenna sniffed, like a bloodhound on a new scent.

"In theory? Really? And what about in practice?"

Oh God, what had he started? The last thing he needed was Mackenna listening to Dom and his crazy ideas and then calling his buddies Sir Simon and Teddy Feugel.

"In practice also. It all works. We test it every year." *Sort of.* "Mr Mackenna, this can't be a coincidence, can it? This proves I'm right. Someone tried to destroy Hamilton. Now he's trying again."

"Maybe. Your Hamilton theory is all technology and speculation. I canna' get my teeth into it. But I need your help. We need to find this man before 21st September."

Chris must have looked confused.

"Your Hamilton incident was on the June Triple Witching, was it not? The next Triple Witching is on Sept 21st. A week on Friday. Perhaps this laddie plans to come back with a digger that morning. Wouldn't that spoil your day?"

Too bloody right. Cyrus was going to fire him if Triple Witching didn't "go well." An outcome that was radically incompatible with the destruction of Raleigh.

"How are you going to find him?" asked Chris.

"I'm not sure. Mostly I deal with criminals. Kidnapping in Columbia. Armed robbery in Russia. This fellow is different."

"Why don't you go public? Put the pictures on the intranet? Someone will recognize him, or the car."

Mackenna shuddered. "Go public? It would be in the *Evening Standard* by nightfall. Sir Simon would never hear of it, he still remembers the Cinnamon debacle. And whoever our friend is, we would warn him."

"Well, that's what I would do."

"It's a non-starter. Have some better ideas. Until you do, we shall tackle this the hard way. Go through IT, name by name. Physical attributes. What kind of car do you drive? Where were you that night? I started with you. I will interview the prime suspects myself."

Holly put her head round the door. "Chris, Neil Jenkins can see you, if you go right now."

Excellent. Mackenna repacked his photos and stood up.

"Who knows about this?" asked Chris.

"Apart from my staff? Just Neil Jenkins. Neil is urgently reviewing the defences of our datacentres."

Holly was hovering.

"Dom called. His flight lands at noon. He wants some time with you this afternoon."

"Flight? From where?"

"He's in Belfast, of course. Haven't you talked to him?"

He had no time for the treacherous Dom. *I'm right, I'm right. If I can get that logfile, I'll show them.*

"No, I haven't had time. Put him in for tomorrow."

He hurried down to see Neil.

*

"Sorry, have I kept you waiting?" said Neil. "Just had to straighten out a vendor. Come in, come in." He seemed almost jovial.

"So, what's this? You want an emergency restore of a backup tape? That's not like you, Chris. It's usually Uzgalis and his mob. I thought your guys were better organized. What system is it?"

"The BMS system in India. I want the disk backup from June 15th."

There was a long pause. Neil raked his fingers across his stubble.

"Well, well. You're after the log files."

"I think it's important. Especially after I had a visit from someone called Mackenna this morning."

"Did you now? Mr McKiller himself. Well, you're out of luck. That system's got nowt to do with me."

"It's in one of your datacentres-"

"It's not in one of my datacentres. I have no bloody idea where Group Property keep it, probably in a cupboard under the stairs. Anyway, your new COO has directly ordered you to stop playing the detective. Anything else? No? Then I won't keep you."

Neil turned his back on Chris, started going through his inbox.

Chris wanted to punch him.

"There is something else, actually. Something personal."

"I hope it's not money for your next marathon, I don't do those."

"No, it's about our Dad."

Neil stopped typing. After a while he said, "Your dad, you mean. He was no father to me, not after you were born, any road. Why, is he dead?"

"No. He's been ill, though."

"Thank you telling me. I haven't missed him for thirty years and I shan't start now."

"He wants to see you."

"Well, I don't want to see him. Tell him I bear no grudges. I shan't be dancing on his grave."

Neil went back to his typing, banging the keys. Chris felt the red mist rising.

"That's rich, coming from you, Neil. He was your dad. He did everything for you and you treated him like shit."

"Get lost, Charlie. I'm busy."

"Don't call me Charlie," said Chris, "and why are you such a dick? I never did anything to you."

Neil went on banging the keyboard, shaking his head angrily from side to side. He would not speak, and in the end Chris left him to it.

*

"What the hell is his problem?" said Olivia that evening. "After our wedding, he came up to me and he said 'Hello, I'm Neil, I'm Chris' ugly brother. Don't worry, you won't be seeing much of me,' and then they left. He and that tarty Essex wife of his, they got into their big car and drove off. She was pregnant with Harry."

Pregnancy. Quick, change the subject, thought Chris.

"There are some things that I've never told you about Neil."

"Well, go on," said Olivia. "Every family has a few skeletons."

"I barely remember him as a child. He is eleven years older than me. He was like a grown up. According to Dad, he was happy until our mother died. After that he started getting into trouble. Drinking. Playing truant. Stealing. The school tried. He was clever, they thought he could get a scholarship to Cambridge. In Maths. Their first ever."

"I thought he got one but he didn't go?"

"That's the family legend. But the truth is, he just didn't turn up to the exams. Dad told me that, last Christmas. And then…"

"Yes?"

"And then, the day he finally disappeared… I dimly remember it. There was this blue van outside. I remember a hand coming out of it and helping Neil get in. He had a little suitcase. He had flaming red hair in those days."

"That's when he ran away to sea?"

"That was another lie that Dad made up. He wasn't going to sea. He was going to prison. Borstal. And after, I don't know. He wound up in Australia a few years later, I know that."

"Wow," said Olivia. "You know, that explains a lot."

"It doesn't explain why he is so angry with me. I hardly know him."

"Maybe when you were born, he felt neglected? Jealousy can be very powerful."

"Well, maybe. But it was only six months and then she died."

"Enough dwelling on the past," said Olivia. "C'mon, let's go upstairs. I'll give you some new memories. Dr Ireson says regular sex is better than watching a thermometer."

"When are you going to do the next test?" said Chris as he followed her up, watching her long legs disappearing into her tight, grey skirt.

"Tomorrow."

Fool. He shouldn't have asked. Her mood changed, stress returned. She went to the bathroom and he glanced at his Blackberry. There was an email from Mike Tucker:

Just heard from Fujitsu. They have reproduced Hamilton problem with BMS. They say it was an accident. Details tomorrow. Mike

Bloody hell. Impossible. He felt his stomach churn. It was impossible. The NOC had stayed cool! How could that be an accident? It couldn't. It just couldn't. Distracted, he and Olivia made love, and afterwards Chris lay awake, feeling the earth spinning under him, dizzy with all the questions going round and round.

Not for the first time, he wondered if his life was someone else's soap opera. Box-set galactic entertainment for alien viewers. Every week was a new episode, every day a new drama. You couldn't make it up.

24

Sana'a, Yemen, 2007

Day Six - Wednesday

The man they called the Debt Collector was not handsome. He was big, with a flat nose, and big, rubbery ears that stuck out below his chequered kuffiyeh. His face was pockmarked from some ancient disease, and his left cheek misshapen from chewing qat. Still, he was wearing expensive jeans and the barman stepped forward hopefully, offering whisky.

"Go fuck yourself," replied the Debt Collector. "Go check your stock."

He sat down, staring at Mahmoud.

"Salam alaykum," said the fat policeman without warmth, touching his chest.

"Salam alaykum," said the other, his eyes still fixed on Mahmoud.

"You can trust this man," said the inspector. Mahmoud got the impression that the policeman neither liked nor trusted him.

The man tossed his head sideways. Dismissal.

The policeman got up hastily. "Good luck, young Mahmoud," he said. He sounded sincere, almost regretful. But pleased to be leaving.

The man took out his phone and placed it carefully on the table. He looked steadily at Mahmoud, then down again at the phone, as if it had some hidden meaning. The little device seemed to expand in front of Mahmoud.

"I don't see the money."

Mahmoud started to explain about Ahmed and his gambling losses.

"I know about that," said the other, which made no sense. "Where is the rest?"

"In the bank, we need to open a new account. I need another day, maybe two... we have three hundred thousand. And I have this."

He took out the five $100 bills and laid them on the table. The man glanced at them.

There was shouting outside, from the Square. By now, the condemned man would be kneeling, facing Mecca. The Imam was asking the families of the bombmaker's victims if they would offer clemency to the condemned.

There was a great sigh from the crowd. No clemency. Now the guards would strip al-Omani and the doctor would paint a circle on his back, behind the heart.

"He killed twenty-three people," said the Debt Collector. "What did he expect?"

"Do you know him? al-Omani?" said Mahmoud.

"How would I know him? He's a fucking terrorist," replied the other. He pushed the $500 back across the table. He picked up his phone and pressed a key, looking intently at Mahmoud while he waited for someone to answer.

"Who are you calling?" asked Mahmoud in sudden alarm.

The other drew his finger across his throat.

"I am the Debt Collector. I have failed. Now I am calling the Butcher. Don't worry, he is not a cruel man. Your father will die quickly."

"Stop, stop," cried Mahmoud. "Stop, I beg you, just one more day, you will have the money."

"You had six days and you came here with this shit. What did you expect?"

Mahmoud fell on his knees, begging, crying. Pleading that he had nothing, that they had sold everything.

"Not quite," said the other. "You are underestimating your assets."

He was pulling black and white photographs from a brown envelope, laying them neatly on the table. Snap, snap.

Mahmoud stared at them. Nothing made sense. He recognized the scales, the spice jars on the shelves, Old Abdullah shaking his fist and in every one, his sister Zahra. Without her niqab, her beautiful brown hair flung to one side or another as she danced to escape the flash. And then he remembered. The man with the camera, the black Mercedes waiting outside.

"This is my favourite," said the man. Zahra was half turned, hiding her face but you could see her eyes, peeking at the camera between her fingers.

"See? She is half a whore already. Babu Malik is obsessed with her."

"What does Babu Malik have to do with it? The fat policeman told us al Qaeda had taken my father..."

"And you believed that disgusting catamite? He was just playing with you."

"But he's a policeman. How does he know Babu Malik?"

"He's family. He married Babu's sister. No children yet."

It was then, slowly and with infinite sadness, that Mahmoud understood everything.

"So it was all a lie? The terrorists? Al Qaeda? The ransom money?"

"Terrorism? It's just business. Babu Malik wants your shop. He wants your dollars. Most of all, he wants your tarty sister. So if you want to see your father again, make sure he gets what he wants."

In the silence that followed, they heard the shots from Tahrir Square. First one, then five or six more. Sometimes if the doctor was inexperienced and marked the wrong place, the first shot would miss the heart and the victim would flop around until the executioner got it right.

25

London and the news from Fujitsu

Thursday, 13th September 2012

8.15am. Chris was writing a tricky email to Cyrus when Dom appeared in the doorway. Chris sighed inwardly. But Dom was on the List. Dom was a condemned man, though he didn't know it. There were courtesies to be observed.

"Hi, Dom, come in. Where were you yesterday? We missed you."

"You knew I couldn't make it, right? I've been in Belfast. My Dad was ill. I left you voicemails."

"Ah, no, I missed them. That's weird, isn't it? My father's not well either. Must be something going around, eh? How is he?"

"He died on Saturday morning."

After that, there wasn't much to say that didn't sound insincere. He said it anyway. Dom was going back for the funeral next Tuesday.

"It was a year, to the day."

"Really? A year since your mother… I didn't know, I'm so sorry."

"My mother? What? No, my mother's fine, she lives in Florida with my stepfather."

"Sorry… so it was a year to the day since…?"

"Since he was diagnosed with leukaemia. They made him quit his job. He never really got over it. He loved his work."

"What did he do?"

"He ran our Wealth business in the UAE."

"That's right, he's one of us, I'd forgotten."

He thought Dom was going to punch him.

"You don't remember much, do you? You actually met him. Three years ago in Hong Kong. We went to dinner in Wanchai. You were too busy screwing Annie Steffens and sucking up to the business."

Now he remembered. MacDonald senior was a real banker, a silver fox with charm and immaculate manners.

"You don't care, Chris, do you? You pretend to but actually it's just me, me, me. I've shared my life with you, but you don't give anything back. I used to think you were different from the other creeps around here but now I realize you're just a better actor."

Which was bullshit but he had no time to argue. Holly was knocking on the door urgently, not waiting for an answer.

"Jerome deVries has called a special meeting. Right now, in his office."

He left Dom to stew in his own bitterness. On the way, he remembered Mike Tucker's email from last night and had a sudden premonition.

deVries' office had the same crowd as Saturday morning. John Uzgalis, AVB, Sheila Collins, Mike Tucker from Property. Mackenna was there as well, sitting in one corner. DeVries appeared and banged a stack of papers on the table.

"Gentlemen, there is new manure in the stable, I thought we should all hear it. Mike?"

"We've had some news from Fujitsu," said Mike. "An engineer called Sedohara has found a race condition in which the memory of the Building Management system becomes corrupted... look at page two. 'The system will behave unpredictably... the behaviour reported from the American datacentre Hamilton appears consistent with this condition.'"

Silence. Everyone turning the pages, heads down. Embarrassed for Chris, waiting for him to start grovelling.

"I totally disagree," said Chris, hot blood rushing to his head. "We didn't see unpredictability. Quite the contrary. No buildings in London overheated. The NOC stayed cool, the halls got hot-"

"Enough, Christopher," said deVries. "Gentlemen, I cannot judge this and I'm late for a meeting. You are the IT leaders of the bank. Tell me. Do we have a terrorist? Or just a hardware problem?"

"Please listen to me," said Chris desperately. "A tiny room in the middle of the Hamilton datacentre stayed cool – this is not explained by Fujitsu's 'race condition.' A week earlier, a single aisle overheated, this is not explained either. There was nothing random or unpredictable about it."

deVries' glance swept round the rest of them like a flamethrower.

"I don't think there's enough evidence to judge," said Uzgalis.

"Try again," said deVries. "Who agrees with Chris? This is important." This silence lasted a minute.

"Alright. We have wasted enough time on this," said deVries with finality. "Get back to your day jobs. Especially you, Chris. Not another word on this nonsense."

He got home at 9.30pm, depressed and irritable. Olivia was strangely quiet. She had opened a bottle of wine that was already halfway down.

"Hi, babe, how was your day?"

"Why are you being horrible to Dom?"

Whoops. What did she know?

"What? I'm not. What are you talking about?"

"He called me. Poor Diarmid has died. You didn't even know he was ill."

"Diarmid? Oh, yes, Dom's Dad. Very sad. Did you know him?"

"Of course I know him. I've known him since Dom and I were in college. He used to take us out on the river. He was such a nice man."

Chris had forgotten that Dom and Olivia went so far back.

"I'm going to his funeral next week. At least one of us can show that they care."

Her grey-blue eyes were puffy and bloodshot. She had been crying and her make-up had run.

"What have you got against Dom? He says you won't talk to him."

"You've got this all wrong. I'm trying to help him but he's destroying himself. First he threatened to punch a young trader. And now he's wandering around promoting crazy ideas."

"Are his ideas crazy, Christopher, or do they just make you look bad? You and your friend Uzgalis. What if he's right? What if your disaster recovery plans don't work?"

"You have no idea what you're talking about."

"Dom does. You always said he was brilliant. You said he was one in a million."

"I never said that."

And so it went on. The bottle was empty. Chris opened another bottle. If this was going to be a wake for Dom's father, Diarmid MacDonald, well, so be it. Should he tell her that Dom was about to get fired? Not tonight. He wasn't that stupid.

"Dom says you're in trouble at work."

"I've been telling you that for weeks."

"He says Philippe Reynaud and the other trading heads went to Cyrus the other day and asked him to get rid of you."

"First I've heard of it."

"And Uzgalis badmouths you behind your back. Apparently, you've got some theory about a saboteur and no one believes you."

"It's not a theory, it's a fact. And I'm going to prove it."

"Uzgalis doesn't believe it. He's going round telling everyone you're nuts."

"For God's sake, Olivia, leave it. I don't need this at home. Why can't you just be nice for a change?"

"Me? Me be nice? How dare you! I'm trying. I try all the time which is more than you do-"

It was the first real row of their marriage. They finished the wine but not the fight. So they piled into a small bottle of cheap brandy. At half past two, half drunk, half poisoned, they stumbled up to bed.

26

London, the next day

Friday, 14th September 2012

That day, the wheels fell off.

Chris felt like a zombie all morning. His head hurt, he could still smell the brandy on his breath. His inbox filled up with stuff that needed more brain cells than he had available. And he was angry, steamingly angry. With Olivia. With Mike Tucker. John Uzgalis. Even Fujitsu.

About 11 o'clock, he gave up pretending to work and went down to the basement, home of Property Services. He found Mike Tucker in his office talking to a couple of his guys.

"Morning, Mike. Not a social call. Where is the BMS logfile from 15th June?"

Mike's guys discovered that they had meetings elsewhere.

Mike looked belligerent.

"I thought Murali told you already. It gets overwritten every week. Deleted."

"But the machine is backed up?"

"Oh yes, to tape. Full backup weekly."

"So the logs from June 15th should now be on tape. Where is the tape? Do you have it?"

"Yes and no."

"Start with the yes."

"We have it. But we can't find it."

He sighed.

"Alright, come with me and see for yourself."

*

Chris looked around the little room in horror. There were racks along one wall, containing a medley of ancient computers. Piles of printer paper, cables and old manuals were strewn across the floor. A McDonalds carton was hiding in one corner. There were power extension bars all over the place, including one that was hanging – *hanging* – from a plug on the wall.

An old PC monitor was perched on an office stool with a keyboard balanced on top.

There were tapes everywhere. They overflowed a canvas trolley. They were piled on a table, next to an old tape reader. There were cupboards full of tapes on the wall.

"When TIS moved away from tape backups in the datacentres, they had thousands of tapes going free. My guys took them and we've been using them ever since."

He pointed to the canvas bucket. "The June 15th backup is somewhere in there. My guys have been through it. They can't find it. Not that it matters now."

"What do you mean, not that it matters now?"

"Now that Fujitsu have reproduced the problem, who cares about the log file? It was an accident."

Chris was temporarily speechless. Then the anger and the hangover took charge.

"Fuck you, Mike. I look like a complete dick because of your fucking incompetence. I will find this tape myself. Send down whoever created this pile of shit. I will wait."

One of Mike's guys came along. He was willing but clueless. He and Chris stacked up the tapes and started feeding them into the tape reader one after the other. His phone was ringing. It was Holly.

"No. I'm out for the rest of the day."

"You can't do that. You've got meetings."

"Tell them I'm ill."

"Where are you?"

"I'm in the basement. Get hold of Dave Carstairs and send him down."

"Oh my god, what is this place?" said Dave when he arrived, "this is a disaster."

"It's Group Property's private datacentre. They say that TIS charges too much so they steal old kit and use it."

"So, er, what…?"

"What are we doing here? See the machine in the corner? That's the famous Building Management System, which is currently controlling the heating and lighting across most of our major buildings."

David Carstairs' job was production support. Keeping things running. Preventing problems. Given the realities of investment banking, his life was one of daily disappointment but this didn't stop him striving for perfection. Which was why he was turning white, right now.

"We'll tell TIS about it on Monday morning, OK? Right now, I need your help to find this backup tape. It could be any one of these nine hundred. They stopped relabelling them after a few months. When they ran out of labels."

"OK, let's get a tape hopper."

"They don't work, not with these tapes. They're too old. We just have to load them one by one and read the catalog. Quicker with two of us."

Dave had some good ideas for speeding the process up, so in the next hour, they checked seventy-three tapes. Of which about eight were illegible and the rest were negative.

At noon, Dave had to go to a meeting. A few minutes later, Chris looked up to find John Uzgalis standing in the doorway. In Friday dress down, cowboy boots, blue jeans with a big leather belt and a check shirt.

"Please, *please*, don't tell me this is what I think it is."

"Get stuffed, John. And yes it is. Somewhere in this hopper is the backup tape that will prove I'm right." Silence. He looked up at Uzgalis.

"I hear you've been saying bad things about me, John."

"Kid, your behaviour is saying bad things about you. Jesus, if deVries walked in now... holy Moses, you'd be history. C'mon, give it up. Come upstairs with me."

But Chris wouldn't budge and Uzgalis left, still shaking his head.

It was slow going without Dave's help. He was thirsty and his hangover was back, Force 10. Dave returned about 3pm.

"Chris, I need to leave at six o'clock tonight, is that OK? It's our anniversary. But I could come in tomorrow. Finish it then?"

Chris accepted, with a sinking heart. He was supposed to be playing golf with Olivia tomorrow. This was going to be big trouble. It was as if the fates had singled him out.

Dave left at 6pm, and Chris continued on his own, slowly. Taking the top tape of the pile, putting it in the deck. Run to the console, run the "check catalog" script. Wait for result. If the file wasn't on the tape, it read, "File not found."

Which it did, over and over again.

"You could have warned me, before you grassed to Neil." Now it was Mike Tucker in the doorway.

"I haven't talked to Neil."

"Well, someone has. Neil Jenkins is sending in a SWAT team tomorrow to take over this room."

Shit. After Neil's people took over, Chris would be locked out for sure.

At 6.40pm, he was hesitating over a small stack of tapes. His brain hurt. The pile seemed to shimmer in front of him. He thought he had checked this lot already. But now he wasn't sure. He could have cried with frustration.

Holly was texting him. Olivia had called. Urgent. Go home now. With a heavy heart, he abandoned the tapes and headed for Waterloo.

*

When he opened his front door, he heard voices. Strange. The door to the living room opened and out came Olivia's sister, Sarah, holding a packet of Silk Cut.

"I'll be right back... oh, hello, it's the geek." She looked at him like a guest who's arrived on the wrong night.

"So, which continent have you come from?"

"None. I've been in the office today."

Sarah worked for Lambeth Council. She refused to understand his job. She pretended he worked on an IT helpdesk and liked to ask him how many calls he'd had today. What was she doing here? She kissed him on both cheeks and disappeared out of the front door, lighting up a fag as she went.

He put his head into the living room. Brian was sitting in an armchair, drink in one hand.

"Hello, Chris," said Brian. "Would you like a drink? Silly really, after all it's your house. But we brought a bottle of Bubbly. It's over there."

There was no sign of Olivia. He went upstairs. He knocked on the bathroom door.

"Go away," said a muffled voice. He pleaded with her to come out but she wouldn't. He could tell she had been crying. And then he remembered. Today was Friday. Pregnancy test day. And he wasn't here.

She came down ten minutes later. Her eyes were red and puffy.

"I'm sorry," he said, trying to hug her but she stepped round him.

"You're late. Brian and Sarah dropped by and I invited them to dinner."

"Oh, great." He was always happy to see Brian. He was a good bloke who never seemed to realize that his wife was a Bitch on Wheels.

"How are the numbers looking?" asked Chris, sitting down. It was his standard opening with Brian, who worked at the Office of National Statistics and always had some interesting fact to talk about.

"Olivia, darling, could you pour me another glass?" said Sarah. She moved over towards the drinks tray in the corner. Chris caught a fragment of their conversation.

"...you shouldn't be."

"Just a half, darling."

"You shouldn't be smoking, either."

"They're so light, almost nothing. But I know you're right."

Chris was preoccupied. He was thinking about the BMS logfile and trying to keep up with Brian's statistics, so he did not read much into this conversation. The penny dropped with him later, when Olivia insisted on opening another bottle of champagne. As he glanced from the radiant Bitch on Wheels to the unhappy face of her barren but beautiful sister, he was suddenly overwhelmed with pity. And guilt.

But the worst was yet to come.

"Just one bottle," said Olivia to her sister. "Chris and I tee-off at 7.30 tomorrow."

The moment he had been dreading all day had arrived. There was a sudden silence.

"Yes," said Olivia, "with Mark and Emily. Club foursomes."

"I think Chris had forgotten," said Sarah, delighted. "Look at his face."

JFDI, you promised, said a little voice. *Just make a decision.*

"I hadn't forgotten, Sarah. But I can't do it. I've got to go into work tomorrow morning. I've just got to. I'm sorry, I've got no choice."

The wretched, hollow words echoed around the room. Sarah managed to look shocked and satisfied at the same time.

Olivia brought the champagne bottle down on the drinks tray with a crash that made them all jump. Shards of broken glass flew in all directions.

"You horrible, pompous man. 'I'm sorry, I've got no choice.' Of course you've got a choice, you just made it. Go on then! Fuck off! Go to work. Go now, why not? I don't want to see you. I hope they do sack you. Then you'll have no wife and no job."

Then her face crumpled up and she ran from the room. They heard her feet on the stairs and a door slamming. Chris felt as though a part of him had just died.

*

"Olivia, please open the door?"

Half an hour had passed. Brian and Sarah had left. Even Sarah had seemed subdued. The bathroom door opened and Olivia came out, holding her iPhone.

She looked different, calmer.

"It's fine, Chris. I've found a substitute. You can go to work."

She brushed aside his grovelling, she wasn't interested. They went to bed as though the other wasn't there. Anger was replaced by formal courtesy. Chris would have preferred a good row instead of this icy composure. He wasn't sure what was going on.

After she had switched off the light, he lay awake. He started again, obsessing about that file. He had to find it. It could save him. At home and at work.

Friday night wore on. There were sirens in the distance. Two women had an argument with a cab driver just outside. Olivia went to the bathroom, stubbed her toe on the way back, swore.

At 4am he got up, threw on a few clothes and called a minicab. If Olivia heard him, she did not stir.

27

London

Saturday, 15th September 2011

Chris passed the front desk at 5am. His friend Kevin was on duty. Kevin came from Kenya and his English was so-so, but his memory was legendary. He knew the name of every person in the bank, and had a smile for all of them.

Chris began working again, methodically, making his way through the big bucket of tapes. 6am came, then 7am. Eight o'clock and he heard people outside. At ten to nine, someone rattled the door.

"I'll get the key," said a voice. Then silence. Time was running out. As soon as the TIS squad got in, he would be hurried away. And Neil would get to hear about it.

He was moving mechanically now, tape in, run script, tape out. He almost missed it, he'd actually taken the tape out before he saw the blessed message

"One file found."

He replaced the precious tape with trembling fingers. It was true, the internal disk of the BMS had been backed up on Sat 16th June at 2am, to this very tape.

After a little trial and error, he managed to unpack the backup and restore the precious file he was looking for. Then he copied it to ldn_dev_1024, otherwise known as Tonto, where he had an account. Most Front Office developers had accounts on Tonto, or its companion, LoneRanger. Many years ago – longer than anyone now working in IT could remember – Tonto must have been an actual computer, a real box that sat under a desk. But now Tonto and his pal were virtual machines, hosted in the rows of big servers that sat in Drake and Raleigh, all part of the Neil Jenkins drive to efficiency.

His skin felt tight. Yesterday's headache had returned with interest, a steady throbbing behind his temples. But he didn't care. He was on fire. He abandoned the little room and hurried upstairs, stopping only to get some water on the way. He texted David and told him not to come in. Then finally, shaking with anticipation, he could log onto Tonto from the privacy of his office. It was 9.30am.

His triumph did not last long. The logfile was garbage. Lots of random circles, squiggles, 8 bit characters. He was afraid it was encrypted. Or corrupted.

He slumped in his chair, his chin resting on one hand while he paged through it.

It was gobbledegook, but there were recognizable timestamps. He organized the garbage so each timestamp started a new line. OK. Many of them were followed by the familiar IP addresses of the bank's computers. Better. That must be the IP address of the device sending an instruction to the BMS. Or receiving it.

But everything in between was incomprehensible. After a while, he realized why. It was Kanji. It was designed to be read by Fujitsu engineers, no one else. He downloaded an editor that claimed to support Japanese and displayed the file. It looked more orderly in Japanese script but it was meaningless to him.

Still, there were patterns.

After a while, he became absorbed in them. Hacking, winnowing, sorting. Guessing. Time flew by.

The Building Management System logged 100,000 messages during BaByliss night. Ninety per cent of them started with the same three characters, and most of the rest with a different set of three characters. He reckoned the 90,000 were messages coming in from sensors around the buildings that the BMS controlled. Temperature readings, humidity, status reports. And the others – about 9,000 – must be instructions going out: open that valve, turn on the fan, start the aircon... maybe.

It was the incoming messages that interested him the most. He sorted them by the devices that sent them. Some seemed to report at regular intervals, like sentries doing their rounds. Probably thermostats reporting in, not suspicious. He filtered them out. And then he took what was left, and chopped out everything except the hour around midnight.

He didn't hear anything, or notice the silent figure standing in the doorway – until it spoke.

"Morning, Chris. Been here all night?"

Chris looked up with a start. It was John Uzgalis, wearing a Killers T-shirt, faded designer jeans and his snakeskin boots. And a single gold earring with a diamond in his left ear. He could have been a roadie or one of the warm up band, except that real roadies didn't have that kind of money.

"John! What are you doing here?"

"Big release this weekend. New risk models, Dodd-Frank workarounds, capital reporting. Good stuff delivered by Debt Markets IT. And you?"

"Just catching up with a few things."

Uzgalis stepped across and looked over Chris' shoulder.

"Japanese lessons? No, wait... you sneaky bitch. You found the logfile!"

He was silent for a minute or two, studying the screen.

"This is an unhealthy obsession, Chris. DeVries ordered you to stay out of it."

"I looked like a dick on Thursday, John. When you didn't back me up. But I am right about Hamilton and I will prove it. And also, a certain Bruce Mackenna has asked for my help."

John spat out his gum into Chris' wastepaper bin. Then he grabbed a chair, spun it round and sat like he was riding a horse, facing Chris across his desk.

"You don't know about him, do you?"

"Yes I do. Bruce Mackenna. Internal Security. Sounds like Billy Connolly, looks like a farmer come to see his bank manager."

Uzgalis leaned forward with sudden intensity.

"Listen to me, Chris. Before you get hurt. There's nothing comical about Mackenna. Interesting career. Started out in your Paratroop Regiment with Sir Simon. Way back when you Brits were oppressing the Irish."

"Spare me the guilt trip, John, I wasn't even born."

"Just listen, will you? When he left the army, he disappeared. He said he'd been in Oman, with the SAS. Then in Yemen, freelancing. Then he had an interesting contract with Military Intelligence back in Belfast. He was an interrogator. He did stuff that makes Guantanamo look like a holiday camp. They kicked him out in the end."

"He went too far?"

"Two Ulster Unionists were found dead in the trunk of a car. Suspected informers."

"You can't be serious. He killed them? What? How do you know all this?"

"Buy Rosemary a drink one day. HR knows everything. And to answer your first question: they weren't just dead. Someone had ripped their tongues out. Yeah. And to answer your next question, did they die first? I don't know. Rosemary didn't know either.

"So listen to your old hill-billy friend, OK? Don't get caught between deVries and Mackenna. They don't get on and the one you piss off will chop you into little pieces. Stay out of it. What do you Brits say? 'Keep your head below the parapet.'"

Chris nodded, shocked. But after Uzgalis had gone, he went back to the search. After all, this would help Mackenna and deVries would never know.

He started searching the logfile for a burst of messages into the BMS. Probably just before midnight on June 15th.

And he found a computer with the IP address 174.0.59.119.

Well, well. 174.0.59.119 had sent in three hundred messages in less than a second, at 11.47pm, Eastern Standard Time. And the messages were very similar, most of them, and short. He counted them. Yes, exactly one for each thermostat in the Hamilton datacentre. And 174.0.59.119 had not sent any other messages – none – during the rest of the day.

He beat the desk with his fists and shouted for joy. Yes, *yes*. This was it. Hardcore forensics. To anyone with a half a brain, this was as good as a bloodstained axe and a trail of gore.

But where did the trail lead? This was the IP address of a computer, but IP addresses were as temporary as cloakroom tickets. Every time a computer reconnected to the network it got a new IP address. What he needed was the real name, the physical name of this computer. Somewhere on the bank's network there had to be a record of which IP addresses were given out when. At a particular moment back in June.

An hour later, he wasn't so sure. There was lots of chat on the web about it but nothing conclusive.

He sent an IM to his friend Tom Hailey, who ran Networks and Market Data. He stressed the urgency and offered liquid rewards. He knew one of Tom's architects and asked him. He sent the question to his own top techies, including Dom. Dom was great with these kinds of problems.

Then he packaged up the hundred and sixty messages and sent them to Sedohara, the Fujitsu engineer who had found the race condition. He needed those messages officially translated to English, to silence the doubting Thomases. Surely even deVries would believe him when he saw one hundred and sixty messages saying "Hamilton thermostat one hundred and twenty-three please set yourself to sixty-six degrees."

Fantastic! Triumph over adversity. It was 10.30am. Olivia would be on the golf course. He decided to reward himself with an hour of bot programming. The Bot Wars started in a week's time and right now, his bot didn't do anything, just sat on the board and waited to be killed. It didn't even have a name. He needed to show his troops that he could still cut the mustard. Mustard, good name. He reread the rules of the competition and started coding.

OMG, it was suddenly half past one. Unbelievable. Why did he never learn? The golf must have finished hours ago. He called Olivia. He got voicemail. He packed up and headed home in a hurry.

But when he got home to Thurleigh Rd, the house was empty. She must still be on the golf course. Strange. He hung around for half an hour, expecting her back. He sent her a text, no reply. Finally, he gave up and made himself a sandwich, washing it down with a can of beer. By then it was gone three o'clock. Still no sign of her. He decided to go for a run.

He circled Clapham Common, and then cut down Broomwood Rd and then did a lap of Wandsworth Common. As he came down Bellevue, he saw her. She was standing on the pavement, waving goodbye to someone driving off. The car came past him, the driver staring ahead, eyes fixed on the lights at Trinity Road. Chris had a moment of confusion, then shock. The car slowed for the lights. He started after it, running up the road. The lights changed and the car disappeared, heading down towards Earlsfield.

He jogged back and waved at Olivia.

"Hello, where did you come from? I thought you were still at work. It being a Saturday," she said, giving him a cold peck on the cheek. But she didn't seem so angry.

"The Common. I went for a run," replied Chris absently, glancing up the road. "Who was that? In the car? He looked just like Dom MacDonald."

"That was Dom. Since you couldn't come, I invited him to play instead. We played together in college. And then he bought me lunch. What's the matter, Chris, you look like you've seen a ghost."

It was weird. She seemed to have forgotten the huge row they had last night. She asked him how his morning had been.

"I found it," he said. "I found the file that shows I'm right. I need it translated from Japanese, but the proof is there." She seemed vaguely pleased.

"Chris, I want you to talk to Dom," she said later. "He needs your support. He's grieving for his father and he's very unhappy."

Chris didn't say much in reply. It was all too confusing. Eventually they went to bed. She was wearing an old favourite, a short silk nightie. She had taken it on their honeymoon and it was so successful that he christened it Aphrodite.

But no love potion tonight. He said he couldn't explain, but he just wasn't in the mood.

*

Olivia cuddled up to him in the early dawn of Sunday morning and he hugged her, grateful. But he was distracted and anxious. They got up soon after nine o'clock and had breakfast.

"Is Dom still living down in Richmond?" he asked abruptly.

"Why do you ask?" she replied, suddenly alert.

"No reason. Just realized I haven't been there for ages."

"Yes, he's still in Richmond. We should go and see him. He's grieving for his father, but he's also hurt. He thinks you've gone all high and mighty."

Chris did not reply. After breakfast, he went for another run. He was away so long that Olivia gave up and ate lunch without him. When he got back, he disappeared into his study and stayed there for several hours. Then he went to bed early, saying he was tired after his run.

28

London

Monday, 17th September 2012 - Anxiety

Chris woke at 2am, and lay staring at the ceiling, his stomach churning. At 4am he got up and went into the office. Kevin was still on nights and greeted him like an old friend – which he was, really – and so did the cleaners. The trading floor was almost empty, except for a couple of guys on the Emerging Markets desk, trading with Russia and Kazakhstan, whose timezones were four hours ahead.

He tried to use the time wisely but he got nothing done, except opening a few emails. His brain was running round and round the same track like some mechanical greyhound, going nowhere. By the time Holly got in, his headache was back, big time.

"Holly, have you got any Nurofen?"

"Maybe. Have you and Olivia been partying?"

"No."

"That man Mackenna has called twice. I told him you had meetings and he said he didn't care. He's on his way."

He knows something, thought Chris to himself and felt the adrenalin pumping into his stomach.

Mackenna marched in two minutes later. "Mike Tucker tells me you have searched his tape repository. What did you find?"

Chris had a moment of silent panic. Mackenna looked at his pale face with contempt.

"So you did find something? What was it?"

"I found a file. But it was in Japanese. I've asked Fujitsu for a translation."

"Japanese translation? I can get that in ten minutes."

"Er, not just a translation. I need a technical explanation. It just looks like gobbledegook, here, let me show you."

Mackenna regarded him steadily. Suspiciously. "That would not be a good use of my time. Tell Fujitsu you need it today. By 1pm. Or Sir Simon will be on the phone. Got it?"

"OK. Er... how is the police work going?"

"Slowly and badly," said Mackenna, and he stormed out.

I have sowed the wind and reaped the whirlwind, thought Chris to himself.

He worked on through his mailbox, resting his head on one hand, hoping the Nurofen would kick in. *It can't be true*, he kept saying to himself and then, *But it is true.* Which led on to, *What should I do?* And so on, back to the beginning.

At ten o'clock he went off to AVB's management meeting. He was distant and distracted.

29

London

Tuesday, 18th September 2012 - Counting heads

He hardly slept on Monday night. He got up early again and left the house quietly, before Olivia woke up. The US regulators had started a new IT audit and were demanding documents on every topic. He was deep in it when Holly put her head round the door.

"Mackenna called. He'll be here at 10 o'clock. He was almost chatty. I think he likes you."

Mackenna stormed in on schedule. There was no sign of affection.

"I'm expecting to hear from Fujitsu this morning," said Chris, defensively.

"Better late than never but that's not why I am here." He tossed the CCTV pictures of the mystery visitor outside Raleigh onto the table.

"Remember him? The man planning an attack on a major datacentre? We know what he looks like. We know where he works. We have a picture of his bloody car. He should be locked up in five minutes. But no, not here, it seems. Not in this bank and especially not in the wretched IT department. Or departments, I should say."

He sat down heavily and looked at Chris accusingly.

"Do you know how many of you clever techies there are in this bank?"

"No, not really."

"You are not alone."

He picked out a tatty sheet of paper and started reading.

"Van Buren – Global Markets IT – permanent staff: 2,451. Retail and Business Banking, including TIS – permanent staff – 4,200. Most of whom seem to work for Neil Jenkins."

"OK."

"Wait, wait. Is this it, I ask? Oh no, she says. Don't you want the contractors as well? Oh yes, I say, let's round up the whole herd. Another 3,000 names, on six spreadsheets. UK only, mind. So we start to process that and I ask the lady again – and by this time I am losing the will to live – 'is this it? All the IT people?'

"'Yes,' she says, 'except for managed service and outsourced.' Well, how many of those? Do you know what she said? 'Oh, no, that's the point. We don't count those.' She doesn't even have a list of them." He turned his gaze directly on Chris. "We have been at work for a week. We have identified sixty-three potential suspects in Global Markets, and another hundred in TIS. One hundred and sixty-three in total. So far we've interviewed ten. And we haven't started on the contractors!

"I've got three people working on this. At this rate, it will take years. Today is Tuesday. Triple Witching is on Friday. We've got three days. I've changed my mind. I want to go public. Discreetly public. I want these CCTV pictures posted on the intranet."

"Ah, I see. But I thought Sir Simon-"

"Sir Simon has given permission. We'll keep it simple. An act of vandalism was committed outside the bank's offices. This man may have witnessed it, can you identify him?"

"Yes, very good. Clever."

"You don't seem so enthusiastic. It was your suggestion as I remember. I want this up today. I need someone technical to get that done."

"Sure, no problem. So, er, what happens when we catch him?" Chris tried to sound casual but his voice sounded odd. Strained.

"What happens? What do you want, a medal? You go back to your day job."

"No, I mean what happens to him?"

"After I've finished questioning him – which may take some time – we will hand him over to the police."

"Will he go to jail?"

"Yes, in the UK. But eventually he – or they – will be extradited to the USA."

"The USA? Really?"

"Really. For a start, the Americans don't like cybercrime. They really don't like people who threaten the US banking system and they are absolutely paranoid about homeland security. This guy ticks all the boxes. Trust me, they will throw the key into the Hudson River."

"Long jail time?"

"Remember Gary McKinnon? The young Scots lad who hacked the Pentagon's computers? He was a minor, he had Asperger's and they wanted to give him seventy years. Our boy is going to die behind bars in a Federal penitentiary."

He stuck his finger in Chris' chest.

"And you're in trouble, young Peters. Do you know why?"

Chris distinctly felt his heart jump.

"What? No. Why?"

"Because this is one of your people. You or your friends Uzgalis and Trebbiano. Clever, deeply technical, understands software and hardware … you've got as many of those people as Neil Jenkins. Maybe more."

Chris said nothing, trying to control his trembling.

"It's the car that's going to do it," Mackenna went on, "very distinctive, with the sickle and star in the back window."

He stopped in the doorway. "What kind of car do you have, Chris?"

"I don't own a car. I told you that a week ago."

"I know you did. But my nose is twitching, see? Can't control it. No? Well, you know how to find me. Don't leave it too long."

He marched off.

Brushing past Holly, Chris almost ran to the bathroom. He retched over the basin, but nothing came up. He sat on the toilet seat and rested his head in his hands. What he knew could not be unknown.

He knew, with absolute certainty, that Dom MacDonald owned the pale Ford Focus in the photos. He knew what the CCTV did not show, that the oval sticker in the back window had 'Saracens Rugby Club,' written across the bottom. He had inspected it himself, after running six miles to Richmond on Sunday morning. He knew that Dom MacDonald had sponsored the Indian grads who had worked on the BMS system as their summer project and therefore would understand the stupendous powers invested in that system. And finally, and most damning of all, he knew that Dom and his father had good reason to hate the bank. They were loyal and the bank had trampled on their lives and livelihoods. And Dom's father had died, a year after losing the job he loved.

Dom was clever and cunning and had to be stopped.

And yet – could he send him to rot in an American penitentiary, and to die there, perhaps after fifty years? Was that fair?

He looked at himself in the mirror by the basins and saw someone he hardly recognized. A pale-faced man with dark rings under his eyes. No wonder Mackenna was suspicious. He felt dizzy. He held onto the taps until the world stopped spinning.

Holly was standing out in the corridor, holding a stack of papers.

"You're late for Alexis' management meeting."

"Holly, stop bossing me, for God's sake. So I'm late! What the fuck do I care?"

Shocked, Holly turned and went back to her desk.

30

First step to recovery

Chris walked into Alexis' meeting room and wished he hadn't. Jerome deVries was sitting at the head of the table, and next to him was Tim Hawes. No sign of Alexis.

Chris poured himself a coffee, trying to stay calm. When he turned round, deVries was giving him the death stare.

"I'm sorry I'm late."

"Your tardiness record is 100%," said deVries. "The surprise will be when you turn up on time."

He pulled out a paper from the stack in front of him.

"I was just saying to your punctual colleagues that IT is like a restaurant, where the meal is always late and the bill is double what you expected. Just this morning, I get this request... from you, Mr Trebbiano. Seven thousand blade servers for Market Risk. Ten million pounds. Very urgent."

Trebbiano nodded, staying cool, like this was no big deal.

"But each year, the servers get twice as fast, is that right?"

"Every eighteen months," said Trebbiano.

"OK. Eighteen months. So every eighteen months we should need half as many computers to do the same job. Makes sense, right? Double the speed, half the computers. Nice job, we're all happy. Except with you boys in charge, every eighteen months we need *twice as many* computers. Each one going twice as fast. Two times two is four, yes? So every eighteen months, we quadruple our computing power. Do I have four times the office space? Or the people? Do I have four times the revenues to pay for it? No. Only the fucking computers breed like rabbits."

The "boys" said nothing. It felt career-limiting to object and in any case there was no easy answer. The industry was in an arms race and compute power was – what? Like the fuel that drove the tanks and powered the rockets. Half the demand was driven by the regulators, whose appetite for complex risk models seemed inexhaustible, and the other half by electronic trading in all its forms.

"And," ranted deVries, "all those computers fill up the datacentres. Do you know that Hamilton cost more than this building? And it's half full already. The cost of technology is unbearable. And you guys don't care. As long as you get your toys, you're happy.

"You are all going to change, starting today. The first step to recovery is to accept what you are. And what are you? You are shit."

The Witwatersrand accent was strong and flat.

Dead silence. Odd phrase, thought Chris, but somehow familiar. *First step to recovery is to accept what you are.*

"If you can't change, I will change you. When I started with Finance, it was the same. Bullshit everywhere. Crap numbers. Late numbers. Everyone blaming everyone else. But we changed things, didn't we, Tim? And now Finance is a happy place and everyone knows what their job is."

Tim Hawes nodded and smiled enthusiastically.

"Do any of you have questions? According to our Leadership Excellence framework, high performing teams are curious and have many questions..."

There was a frightened silence.

"Well, perhaps as we become high performing, we will have more questions," said deVries finally.

"Where is Alexis?" asked Uzgalis.

"Van Buren has resigned. So now we have a vacancy. You three are the most senior on the team. My inbox is full of people who want me to get rid of you as well."

"And then what?" asked David Trebbiano.

"And replace you with better people. Better people from other departments... or better people from outside."

"You mean outsource?"

"Yes. Companies like Accenture and IBM do IT for a living. It is their core competence. Our core competence is sales and trading. See where I'm going with this?"

DeVries laughed at the dismay on their faces.

"Well, guys, don't worry, that is a big bad decision and we aren't going to take it today. But someone has to be in charge of IT. One person. Send me your recommendation. Or come and see me. I don't bite. OK? To be fair to you, I was thinking of Neil Jenkins. Or Tim Hawes. But feel free to disagree."

The door closed behind him.

"Sheeyit," drawled Uzgalis in his best hill-billy, "that man scares the crap out of me."

There was a long pause.

"Well," said Trebbiano, "who wants to run IT?"

Apparently none of them did. In the end, they agreed to sleep on it.

*

Chris walked slowly back downstairs, his worries about Dom temporarily suppressed by this new development.

Did he want David or John as his boss? No. Still, David or John would be a thousand times better than his brother Neil, or Tim Hawes. Neil knew nothing about the business. Tim Hawes hated all IT people.

Should he bid to become CIO? Ok, he was the youngest and least experienced. But just rolling over and saying "not me," was that a good idea? Did that demonstrate lack of ambition that might hurt him one day?

Holly brought him a mid-morning coffee from Pret. "Mr Mackenna called. He said he's waiting for a name from you. Technical help."

"Bloody man. Tell him I'm working on it."

Oh shit. His worries about Dom came flooding back. His hands shook as he drank the coffee. He knew what he should do, but he shrank from it. Exposing Dom would be like a bomb exploding in his life, starting today. The consequences, the escalation, the regulators, even the police, he could imagine them all.

Twice he picked up the phone and put it down again. He felt trapped like a man on the roof of a burning building. If he jumped, he died. If he stayed, he died. Time was running out. Perhaps he could go back home and start today over again. Not come to work, take Olivia out to lunch, take a holiday. But Mackenna would find him.

In the end he made a decision. He had to get Dom out of here.

He made the call from his Blackberry. Mobile calls were not recorded, at least not yet. It was an amber issue on the bank's audit report and the FSA were constantly moaning about it.

"Rosemary? It's Chris. Rosemary, can we accelerate the Rosebud exits? Why not this week? Well, then, kick the lawyers. Which? The two from my management team. Yes, Dom, for example. Having them hanging around, it's not good for morale, you know."

He ended the call. His palms were cold yet sweaty. He could see Holly looking at him through the glass of his office. She was looking hard at him. Reproachful? Suspicious?

No, he was imagining it. But he could not deny his guilt. He had just conspired to pervert the course of justice. He had crossed a line and left his footprints on both sides. He didn't really believe it – did he? – but he could spend the rest of his life in an American jail.

Ping! He had an IM from Tom in Networks: *Re your reverse IP address query. Not easy. Is it urgent?*

He texted back: *No. Forget it, thx Chris.*

And in the same spirit he sent an email to the unseen Sedohara at Fujitsu: *English translation of the BMS logfile not needed. Pls ignore my request.*

He needed to bury the damning evidence from the BMS logfile. It proved sabotage and even Sheila Collins' dopey hounds would be right on it. The trail might lead them to Dom.

Holly interrupted his thoughts.

"Mr Mackenna called again. He will call every five minutes until you get him some technical help. He says."

Damn. Damn. Mackenna was like a bulldog.

"Yes, OK. Get hold of Jason Crisp, you know, works for George. Tell him to call Mackenna."

"Are you sure? At the last inter-ranking, George said he was useless. And also..." she dropped her voice, "*He's on the List.*"

"Holly, just do it, will you? And Holly, about Dom? Until he leaves, keep him busy. Out of the office. He is not to meet Mackenna. OK?"

Holly sniffed. She wasn't upset about Dom. She was upset because something was up and her boss wasn't sharing.

"OK," she said grudgingly. "Also someone called Dirk Pascalides wants to come and see you this afternoon."

"Who's he?"

"Compliance. He says he must see you today. What's the matter?"

"I'm OK." *It's just that I am sick with fear.* "Find out what he wants."

"I tried. He said it was confidential."

After that, Chris couldn't concentrate. Compliance were the secret police. They watched the rest of the bank and kept themselves to themselves. Most of them were pleasantly ineffectual, confused by the complexity of the machine they tried to control. But there was a hard core, and Chris had seen them at work before. It started with a few easy questions. It ended when people left the building suddenly and didn't come back.

He went to a couple of meetings and barely heard a word. When he spoke himself, it was a stranger's voice. His hands shook and he was so pale that Holly decided he had flu and sent him home.

"Mr Pascalides can wait until tomorrow," she said and that was one consolation.

*

By the time he got home, he had a splitting headache. He took too many Nurofen and sat on the sofa and tried not to worry. About Pascalides. About Dom. About Triple Witching on Friday.

Olivia was late home from work, which was unusual. It wasn't book club night. She seemed quiet. She microwaved a quiche from the freezer and he made a salad.

"I had a drink with Dom tonight," she said. "He says you are behaving strangely. Your management team can't work it out. He asked me if you had something on your mind. I told you you were looking for something, a missing logfile, is that it? I said you had found it but you were waiting for a Japanese translation. He wants to help."

Oh shit. Now Dom knew the hounds were on his trail. There was no way he could tell her. He said it wasn't so important after all. He didn't need Dom's help. She looked disappointed. Suspicious.

They went to bed. His head was still pounding. He was exhausted but he couldn't sleep. He lay listening to the soft sound of her breathing and the late night traffic.

At 1am, he got up. In the bathroom cupboard, he found some old SleepGels. He took one. Two hours later, he was still lying awake, listening to the early morning traffic.

Dom. What had got into him? It was surreal. Dom was trying to bring down a datacentre, had almost succeeded. He must be mad to protect him. If the authorities ever found out that he knew and had kept quiet, it was jail. Jail in America. Then this man Pascalides. What did he want? It must be some innocent query. If Pascalides thought he was trying to protect a criminal, he would turn up in force, wouldn't he? Or would he? Maybe not. The cardinal rule of compliance investigations was *do nothing that would tip off the suspect.* Was he a suspect?

He fell asleep at some point and his dreams exhausted him.

31

Sana'a, Yemen, 2007

Evening of Day Six - Wednesday

Mahmoud had raged in the bar of the Sheba hotel. He had walked away, leaving the Debt Collector at the table. But each time the man lifted his phone, to sign his father's death warrant, it pulled him back. The debt collector was the angler, and Mahmoud was the fish. Slowly but steadily, he was being reeled in.

His objections became weaker and weaker, ending with, "But how could I tell her?"

"You don't have to. Just give me her number."

He prayed earnestly for forgiveness, as he walked back from the Sheba, amidst the stream of voyeurs, chatting happily as they returned from the execution. But then he asked himself what else he could have done.

He felt awful when he saw Zahra. And more awful when he saw the text arrive on her phone. He watched her face as she read, watched her distress as she hurried to the privacy of her bedroom. He felt like a voyeur himself.

He waited. She didn't come out. He went down and knocked on her door. Her face was pale and tear-stained in the crack of the door.

She was wearing one of her mother's saris. Red and gold.

"This is what they want," she said. "I am to be an Indian princess."

"I'll come with you," he said. "I will look after you."

"No," she said bitterly. "You can't do what I have to do."

After a long moment, she closed the door and locked it.

He went back upstairs and prayed to Allah but there was no answer. Around midnight, he thought he heard an engine down below. He leaned out of the window but whatever it was, had gone already.

32

London: Compliance comes to call

Wednesday, 19th September 2012

The next morning, Chris had an email from Mackenna.

"Global Markets would be more secure if a planned or even an unplanned event caused the loss of a primary datacentre because the physical and cultural remediation after such a crisis would drive more realistic risk management."

Unplanned event! Who is D Macdonald? He works for you. Please ask your lady to track him down. URGENT B Mackenna

Chris recognized the quote. It was from Dom's paper on datacentre recovery. Shit.

"Mr Pascalides will be here at 9.30," said Holly primly, "and you look awful."

He called Rosemary's desk on his mobile but got her voicemail. He left a message, asking for an urgent call back. Then he tried her mobile. Same thing, same message.

At 9.27, he heard Holly greeting someone outside, a man. A glimpse of white shirt and a broad yellow tie. Must be Pascalides from Compliance. He was trapped in his office.

Just then Rosemary returned his call. It was on his landline and recorded but he was beyond caring.

"Rosemary, hi. How's it going? I mean, with Dom?"

"Chris, I haven't heard back from legal. Dom's a senior guy… realistically, an exit this week is unlikely."

"Rosemary, not just this week. I want him gone today. Tomorrow latest."

"Chris, there are a hundred and thirty-seven permies on the Rosebud List. We're swamped. I think we should let Dom flow through the process with everyone else?"

Chris could see Holly through the window, tapping her watch. Pascalides was waiting. He wanted to scream.

"Rosemary, no, no. I want him out of here, ASAP. It's a security issue, OK? The guy has all kinds of access…"

He'd played the ace of spades. Security. Access controls. Rosemary folded. He put the phone down, sweating. Job done, although he'd left an audit trail that glowed in the dark.

Dirk Pascalides was in his thirties, with a pink baby face. He smiled a lot.

"Chris, thanks for seeing me. Look, the FSA have read the KPC report on the Hamilton incident. Now they've got some questions about our DR plans. Neil Jenkins and I drafted some answers, just wanted to check the IT heads were comfortable…"

Chris could have jumped for joy. Pascalides didn't know about Dom, wasn't here to show him out of the building. Maybe, just maybe, he could keep the plates spinning for another day.

33

London

His phone rang early the next morning.

"Hi, Mr Mackenna, how's it going!? Are those photos on the intranet?"

"They are not. Your man Jason Crisp promises noon today. He promised the same thing yesterday. In my opinion he is a halfwit. But that's not why I am calling you. I'm calling you about this fellow, Dominic MacDonald-"

Chris' heart skipped a beat. Or two.

"-yes, Dominic MacDonald. A man with some interesting views. Does he speak Arabic, would you know?"

"Arabic? His father lives- lived in the Middle East for a long time. But Dom? Arabic? No, I don't think so."

What the hell did Arabic have to do with anything?

"Mind, I would ask him myself, but I canna get hold of him. Nor can your young lady. Now why is that?"

Because she's obeying orders, thought Chris. "I have no idea, let me look into it."

Mackenna rang off, morose and suspicious.

At that moment, a Change Request from Jason Crisp popped into Chris' mailbox. It sought his approval to post Mackenna's images on the intranet.

The photos and an eight second video were attached. He felt the adrenalin surge as he looked at them, especially the footage of the dark figure walking up Three Mill Lane. It was Dom. It really was. This was a bomb with a short fuse. Dom had friends. He played rugby for Global Markets. And golf. One of his teammates would recognize the car from the stickers. The whispering would start. The journalists at *Here is the City* would get an anonymous email. They would love it: *Did Bank Employee plan to cripple SBS?*

There would be a panic in the executive offices, and the firestorm would spread downwards, gathering heat. Mackenna would take Dom away and then the police would be called. He was Dom's boss; he would never survive it.

But he couldn't just ignore this request. After a short hesitation, he selected *REQUEST DENIED* and a pathetic comment *Are these the best images?* He downloaded a copy of the images onto his iPad.

Then he called Rosemary.

"Yes, Chris, I know I said today. But I can't get any numbers from Payroll. What exactly is the urgency here, Chris? This is all quite irregular."

"Just get it done, Rosemary, there is a real problem here. Let's shoot for 2pm, OK?"

"No promises, Chris."

*

"At one o'clock, you've got the Infrastructure Investment committee," said Holly. "And John Uzgalis called to make sure you were going. He said it was a surprise."

"I don't need surprises, Holly."

That was two hours ago. No word from Rosemary – bad news – and no angry phone calls from Mackenna – good news. Neither knew it, but they were racing each other, and the prize was Dom.

Now Chris was upstairs in the Debt Markets boardroom, wondering what Uzgalis had meant by a surprise. The meeting was almost over. Tim Hawes was in the chair, Uzgalis on his right, close together as if they were buddies. Odd.

Neil had turned up in person, which was unusual. Chris was shocked by the sight of him. His brother seemed to have aged five years in the last week. His beard was straggly and there were flecks of pure white amongst the fading ginger. Still, he defended his projects and his money with angry determination.

"Any other business?" said Hawes. People started gathering their papers.

It was 2.20pm. No word from Rosemary, it was not looking good. His phone rang. It was Mackenna. Shit. He sent him to voicemail and turned the phone off. He was going to play this game to the last card.

He'd missed something. Uzgalis had just said something that froze the room.

"What did you say?" That was Neil facing him, eyes glaring.

"You heard me," replied Uzgalis, "I said, where did you get the money to build this?" He tossed a pile of photos onto the centre of the table.

"See, one of my guys was down at Raleigh last week and notices this big digger, right by the entrance. Huh? Digger? So I send one of my spies down there. He comes back scratching his head. Hey, John, looks like someone is putting up a big wall, right round the datacentre. A big waterproof wall."

Neil glanced at the photos. The colour faded from his face, leaving an angry red patch on either cheek.

"Now, last meeting, there was a lot of wild talk. Some people accusing other people of being like the beancounters of the *Titanic*. Remember that? But in the end, we decided not to spend money on flood defences for Raleigh. Do I need to check the minutes?"

Long pause.

"You know what I think? I think you started that wall before that meeting. We said no, so you went back and said to your guys, finish that fucking wall quick before those dumbos in Global Markets figure it out. Am I right? Dude?"

In the shocked silence, the door opened and Holly put her head round. She beckoned frantically to Chris.

"Rosemary's trying to get hold of you. 2.30pm in your office."

"What? Why?"

Her lips mouthed the answer: "Dom."

Dom. Allelujah.

Rosemary was sitting in his office, with a large white envelope in front of her.

Holly followed him in. "I've called him, he's on his way," she said, "and I've warned Security." She looked stressed.

"Right," said Rosemary, "Chris, remember, no explanations, no debate. Just say the words and leave the rest to me."

Dom arrived. When he saw Rosemary and the white envelope, he turned pale under his freckles, and turned, as if to flee back to the safety of the lifts.

"Have a seat, Dom," said Rosemary firmly.

"I heard you wanted to see me," he said. "I thought we were going to talk."

Chris tried to think of something to say, but no words came, only guilt. His voice echoed in his eardrums, as if someone else talking.

Restructuring. Role no longer required. Your employment is at risk. You will not be required to come in to work… you will be escorted from here to your desk… clear your personal possessions… do you understand?

Dom turned deathly white. Rosemary took over, opening the white envelope, making sure all the legal niceties were taken care of.

When he had gone, Rosemary turned to Chris.

"If I was you, I wouldn't hang around in dark alleys for a while."

"You're joking."

"I don't think you've told me everything, Chris," she said briskly, putting Dom's pass and Blackberry into an envelope, "so it's difficult to judge. But he's from Belfast and those people don't forgive a wrong, not in a hundred years. I know, OK?"

Holly was back.

"Mr Mackenna is on his way here... he doesn't sound very happy."

Mackenna didn't frighten him anymore. He was committed. He felt the same burning desire that he did on projects. Get to the end, get it done.

"Holly, I want a call with my management team at six. All of them, OK? Including Sydney and Hong Kong. I'm going downstairs, tell Mackenna to hold on."

He watched Dom escorted from the building, carrying a bulging dustbin bag and his laptop. Then he hurried upstairs. In the lift, his Blackberry went *ping*! It was a text from Infosec: *Confirming removal D MacDonald's network access.*

Even better. He went back upstairs, and ran straight into trouble.

He hadn't seen Mackenna really angry before. His face was puce and little flecks of foam clung to the corners of his mouth.

"For three days now, I have been trying to get those pictures on the intranet. I have had nothing but excuses. Your man Jason Crisp is an idiot. And now, when every last bureaucrat has been satisfied, I am told that you – you personally – have not approved it. Did you reject this change? One word. Well? Yes or no?"

"Yes, but wait-"

"No buts. Inexcusable. And this fellow MacDonald, where is he? I have been trying to contact him for two days without success – is that your doing as well? Yes? Let me tell you, young man, you are finished. Finished. I will talk to Sir Simon personally-"

"Just listen a minute, please," said Chris desperately. "You don't need to put those photos on the intranet. The man you are looking for. The one caught on the CCTV outside Raleigh is Dom MacDonald. I have seen that car myself, with him driving it."

"What? Where is MacDonald, I need to talk to him immediately!"

"He has left the bank."

"What do you mean? Where is he? Get me-"

"He is no longer employed by the bank, he has no access of any kind. He has gone."

The Celtic rant continued for some time, especially when Mackenna realized how narrowly he had missed his prey.

"Look," said Chris, "do you want this in the papers? A trial, headlines, extradition, the American regulators busting our chops? Or just dealt with? Sorted."

There was only one answer to this but it took Mackenna another twenty minutes to simmer down.

Holly appeared. "Excuse me, Chris, Cyrus wants to see you urgently."

Chris leapt up but Mackenna wasn't having it.

"Stay there, young man. I'm not finished with you."

He waved Holly. Now he was standing, looking down on Chris.

"I trusted you. But you did not trust me. You have known about MacDonald all week, but you did not tell me. You asked me what would happen to the culprit, already knowing who he was. You assigned an idiot to work with me. You lied to me. You have not treated me with respect-"

Chris looked up. The sudden change in Mackenna's face was shocking and frightening. He looked as if he was having a fit. The corners of his mouth were flecked with foamy saliva. His eyes were wide open and staring down at him.

And then the unbelievable happened. His right hand shot down and grabbed Chris by the crotch. And squeezed. The pain was sudden and intense. Chris cried out and writhed in his chair but Mackenna's fingers were like steel rods. And now his other hand was wrapped around Chris' throat. He couldn't scream, he couldn't breathe. Pure panic took over. *Oh my God, he's going to kill me.* Mackenna's red face was six inches from his own.

"Never again, do you understand? Never. Or I will kill you." He left, leaving Chris doubled up in his chair. It was five minutes before he could stand and another five before he felt well enough to walk.

Cyrus was in his office at the edge of the trading floor. There was a new picture stuck on the door, a child's sketch of a monster man with a mop of black hair and staring eyes, and the legend, *DAD AT WORK.*

"So, Chris, today is September 20th. What does that mean to you?"

"It means Triple Witching tomorrow."

"So? Am I gonna spend Monday on my knees to our clients?"

"We are as ready as we can be. All the new hardware is in. The big performance fixes are done."

"Good. By the way, our new COO has been busting my chops about you."

"DeVries?"

"Yeah. Since Sir Simon put him on Topeka, he's been a pain in the butt. He says you are obsessed with some fantasy about sabotage inside the bank. I told him you were more sensible than that."

"Thanks, Cyrus. I was worried about something but it's OK, it's all sorted now."

Now that Dom has gone.

Cyrus looked puzzled, like he thought of digging deeper before deciding life was too short.

"Remember, Chris, deVries is important but he's not the business. I am the business. Tell your guys, tomorrow had better go well. And why are you limping?"

Chris hobbled back upstairs to his conference call. His team were all on, even Australia and Hong Kong. Holly, Carl and Dave Carstairs joined him in his office. Carl was over from the US on some management training course.

"We're all here," said Carl, "except for Dom."

"Yes," said Chris, "Dom is item one on the agenda."

He told them about Dom. Not Dom the mutineer, not Dom the saboteur, but Dom the victim of Rosebud and the pre-bonus cull.

None of them seemed surprised. Carl said, "Good guy, Dom, but he fell off the back somewhere," and Dave Carstairs nodded. They didn't want to talk about Dom, they wanted to talk about deVries as COO and what it meant for Technology. He let the speculation run on, relieved.

"OK, guys, enough. I have a personal message for you from Cyrus: 'Tomorrow had better go well.' To which I add: if you screw up tomorrow, you will join Dom, OK? That was the deal."

There was a short silence but they all bounced back. They sounded confident, even Raul in Hong Kong. After a few minutes, Chris wrapped it up.

"OK, London folks, see you down at the Pepys in ten."

"Tonight's Tahiti night," Dave Carstairs explained to Carl, "third Thursday of the month. We get together for a few beers."

Down at the Pepys, one of Dave's guys was ready with a tray laden with beer.

"Sorry it took a while," he said, "Neil Jenkins and a bunch of TIS guys are hogging the bar. Looks like they've been there a while."

Chris looked over. His older brother was sitting alone at a table. He had a glass of Scotch in one hand, and two empty glasses on the table.

Chris went over.

"Well, look who's here. Mr Christopher Peters. Nice of you to come down and say hello to us hardware monkeys."

"I thought you'd given up Scotch."

"I drink what I like, thank you. Tonight I like the amber nectar. Where is your little buddy?"

"Who?"

"Uzgalis. Little bastard he is. You can tell him that from me."

"Are you talking about the flood defences?"

"I certainly am. He's a bloody troublemaker, that's what he is. It's my fuckin' budget. I try to do the right thing for the bank, as you well know. But I will not have people telling me how to do my job. Especially Yanks. Job's hard enough without back seat drivers from Global Markets."

Chris could see his point.

"Have you seen our father? I sent you the details."

Neil banged his glass down and clapped his hands over his ears.

"For fucks sake... he's not my father. My father was Owen Jenkins and he's dead. And no, I have no plans to see *your* father. So sod off, will you?"

"OK. It's Triple Witching tomorrow. Remember the last one? I'd stay off the Scotch. Just friendly advice."

"Let me give you some friendly advice, Charlie. Keep your guys away from the datacentres. Here, America, Asia, anywhere. There are men with guns. Trespassers will be shot. I mean it. Okay?"

Chris bumped into a couple of Neil's guys, Tom Hailey and Steve Smith, by the bar. They were paying attention to a short, good looking young woman with dark hair and an olive complexion. She was wearing a tight silk blouse with a lot on display.

"Chris! Come here," said Tom. "This is Anita, she wants to meet you."

"Well, the famous Chris Peters," said Anita, "at last! I call Holly every month, trying to get in your diary. I send you emails every week. And still you haven't bought anything, you bad man." She poked a finger in his chest, leaning forward a little, showing a lot of cleavage. "What am I talking about? Talent, Chris. Talent. Tom here has three of my staff, Tom, are you happy with them?"

"They are the best, Anita."

She glanced over Chris' shoulder, suddenly distracted. "Oh, excuse me, don't run away... I'll be back."

She eased past him and disappeared into the crowd.

"She does have some good people but it's the after sales service you remember," said Tom.

"She sells contractors?"

"Yup, mostly TIS people, dbas, sysadmins, network people. She knows everybody. Even him."

Chris looked round. He could see Neil sitting, hands still cradling his glass. Anita had an arm round him, her hair shrouding his face, maybe whispering into his ear. He was shaking his head angrily. Whatever she was selling, Neil wasn't buying. But there was something tender in her pose that surprised him.

"Hi, Mr Peters," said a young female voice behind him.

"Well... hi Jane... and all, what brings you here?"

"We've been learning about networking. We've come to practice on you," said the girl, indicating four or five of this year's grads who were deploying themselves around him, looking keen. Standing behind her – shy, maybe? – was Hassan Choudhary, the difficult one whom P.K. had wanted to put on the List.

"Excellent. Well, practice away," said Chris. The grads looked at each other, unsure what to say next.

"Your bot Mustard was really amazing," said Jane, who seemed to be the ringleader. "How do you find the time to program a bot and do your day job?"

"Why? How did he do?" said Chris. He'd forgotten about the Bot Wars. He hadn't had time to see Mustard fight, he'd just despatched the code to David Carstairs and asked him to run it.

"He beat Shiva the Destroyer," said one of the others, "but he lost to the Narita Ninja."

Shiva was the Chennai bot, Hassan's brainchild. Chris glanced over at him, pleased with Mustard's victory but wondering how Hassan felt about it. The young man stared back at him, unblinking. Chris got a sudden sense that Hassan minded about his bot losing, minded very much.

Jane changed the subject, tactfully. She would go far.

"Who is that man sitting over there?"

"That's Neil Jenkins. Head of TIS. And that's most of his management team with him."

"Boy, let's hope there isn't a datacentre problem tonight," said Jane.

Chris had a beer with the grads, and then they disappeared. Tom Hailey reappeared.

"Don't lose that one," he said.

"Which one?"

"The tall Indian, Hassan. He's phenomenal. He knows more about market data after ten weeks than most of my guys. I'd like to offer him a permanent job."

"Get stuffed," said Chris, "go find your own grads."

It was almost ten o'clock.

"Guys, it's bedtime, big day tomorrow," he said to the diehard core of his management team.

"It'll be OK," said one of them, "we can handle it."

Outside, he almost bumped into Anita. She was leaning against the wall, smoking, and talking to a young man standing in front of her. It was Hassan Choudhary. Maybe Tom Hailey wasn't the only one trying to hire him.

"Anita," he said, "Hassan is one of my best and brightest grads. If you poach him, I will be seriously pissed off, OK?"

"Chris, would I do that, now that we've met?" she replied. "Can I call you tomorrow? Have lunch with me."

"It's Triple Witching tomorrow," said Chris, "I'm busy."

"She's too old for you," he said to Hassan as he passed. Hassan did not reply, just looked at him with the same steady gaze. Chris wondered why he'd said it.

It was after eleven when he got home. He checked his Blackberry as he crept into the bedroom beside the sleeping Olivia. The EOS batch was running to schedule. The trading platforms in Far East markets were all up and working.

Dom was gone. Whatever stupid, dangerous stunt he had planned, he couldn't get into a building, he couldn't get into the network. TIS management might be off their faces but Neil had surrounded the datacentres with armed guards. There were times when it was good to have a humourless Geordie control freak in charge.

His own team had spent six weeks preparing; they were ready for whatever madness Triple Witching could throw at them.

He set his alarm clock for six, feeling good. Suddenly he remembered that he hadn't told Olivia about Dom leaving. Whoops. That was going to be a difficult conversation. *Tomorrow evening, mustn't put it off,* he said to himself as he drifted off to sleep.

34

Sana'a, Yemen, 2007

Day Seven - Thursday

Zahra shut the street door firmly behind her.

The van was sitting silently in the alley. It was white, with yellow taxi stripes. It had no windows at the back but the sliding side door was open. It was like the one that Ben had described, that he had followed in the mountains near Taiz. Maybe it was the one that she had seen by the shop, a few days ago.

In the gloom, she could just see the driver's pale face looking out at her. He made no sign, just watched and waited.

Beyond the open door, the interior was black. Through that door, a new life was waiting for her. Gathering her sari, she climbed in, groping for a seat. Behind her, the door slammed shut, and there was a sound of a bolt being drawn. She saw the driver getting back into the cab. There was a wire mesh screen between them. Now she saw that he had a companion in the passenger's seat. She could see their kuffiyehs outlined against the faint lights of the buildings. In between them, the barrel of a gun, pointing upwards.

The taxi set off, gently. It stank, a pungent smell, like the smell of goats. And something else, something sweet and cloying, like cheap perfume. Zahra looked round. The back of the taxi had no seats, just wooden benches down each side, bolted onto a dirty metal floor. It had iron rings crudely welded on to it, and piles of chains attached to them. There were rusty holes in the floor – she could see the roadway flowing away beneath.

"What's that smell?" she dared to say, after a few minutes.

"Animals," said the driver.

"Women," said his companion, and they both laughed.

They drove out through the Bab-al-Yemen gate and turned left, keeping the walls of the old city on their left. After a few minutes, they turned through an old gate, into the eastern slums. Even the most intrepid tourists never came here.

The taxi stopped in a small dark space between high, silent walls. The side door opened and the driver got out and beckoned Zahra to follow. The companion vanished ahead into the gloom. They passed a tea house with lamps and Zahra could see the dark shapes of men huddled around tables. Later on, there was a mosque with a single bulb illuminating the entrance. Then the passages became narrower, so narrow that her shoulders rubbed the walls on each side, and there were no lights, no people.

She could hear something, though. Shouting, getting louder. A man's voice, asking a question over and over. And then a scream. It could be a woman, or an old man. Or even a child. It went on and on. Her guide paused, muttered something and went on. The noise stopped. There were houses all around them, but no sound came from them and no lights went on.

Finally, they knocked on a wooden door fortified with iron studs. It was opened by an old man wearing a threadbare jacket. He had a full, straggly beard turning white, and his face was scarred and pockmarked. His left cheek bulged from a lifetime of qat. He was leaning on a polished wooden staff cut from a thorn bush, like old Abdullah's. He beckoned them inside.

They passed into a small courtyard with an open fire burning in the middle. There were six or seven men around the fire, the tips of their cigarettes glowing in the dark. Judging by their white robes, beards and dark leathery faces, they were tribesmen from out of town. One had a rifle across his knees, and there were other weapons stacked against a square metal table.

The door closed behind them. Zahra heard the bolts being drawn, and then the tap-tap of the doorkeeper's stick as he followed them in.

The men were amused when they saw her, standing like a newly arrived bride at an Indian wedding. The old man grasped her roughly by the shoulder. His grip felt like a bird of prey perched there, digging its talons into her flesh.

"Come," he said. "Babu is waiting for you." He led her round the fire. On the ground by the fire she saw a human ear, a bizarre sight. It lay, facing upwards, as if the earth was listening to the sky. The old man flicked it away with his stick, muttering.

"Do you know who I am?" he said. His Arabic was strange. Not from Sana'a. Zahra shook her head.

"I am Khalid Malik. I am Babu's father."

"I want to see my father," she said.

"Not here. Later." He stopped, thought for a moment.

"Here, come." He dragged her off to one side. On this side of the courtyard, there was a steel door. It looked new. The old man shuffled up to it, and rolled it to one side. Behind were vertical bars, like a prison. Khalid Malik pushed her forward.

"Look, look," he said reverently, as one showing off a treasure chest, "people."

Zahra blinked. It was a small room, behind the bars, pitch black. And then, dimly, she saw the eyes, dozens of them, all watching her. They were low to the floor. He could imagine the unseen bodies sitting, squatting in silent terror. And then the stench hit her and she turned away, bewildered.

"Who are they?"

Khalid Malik shrugged. "African peoples from across the Red Sea. Somalia, Ethiopia. Going to Europe." He smiled his little showman's smile. "These ones have no money. They stay. Some work, some die."

Slaves. Zahra had heard stories of such things but never seen them.

"Come," said the old man again. "Hurry, Babu is waiting."

She resisted. He turned, and his eyes pierced her.

"What do you want, little princess? Make Babu happy or join black peoples?"

35

Triple Witching Day

Friday, 21st September 2012

Chris woke early and got up.

The Northern line was doing well and he got a seat. He read his iPad. Wired had an article about the politics at Google between the Chrome guys and the Androids. He wondered – as he did most days – why he didn't jump ship and join a West Coast tech company. These guys had *fun*. Then he remembered his mortgage.

He decided to walk from Bank to the office. The autumn sun was just up and throwing long shadows down Poultry. The old Midland Bank building ahead of him looked golden in the morning light. The air was chilly but invigorating.

He went straight to the trading floor. The TV screens were showing Bloomberg TV and an anorexic blonde in a tight black skirt was talking above the caption *Triple Witching Tips*. Did Bloomberg only recruit skinny women or did the hunger to sell more terminals drive out other appetites? Chris didn't know, but Bloomberg women were always razor thin. They ordered rocket salad with parmesan in expensive restaurants and left the parmesan on the side. Mind you, they could drink, and they did. He watched this one for a minute or two.

"Hey, Chris. Systems gonna stay up today?"

It was cowboy Hamish on the Portfolio desk. Hamish was short and dark and wore Oakley sunglasses perched on his thick, wavy hair like a hairband. Hamish used to work in IT but the desk liked him so much they'd hired him direct to look after Portia and now he part-traded, part-coded.

"Yeah, unless you do something stupid."

Which was a significant possibility given Hamish's record. It was Hamish and his cowboy ways that had crashed the tick database more than once, and pissed off Philippe Reynaud and the HFT team. They were neighbours on the trading floor but barely on speaking terms.

"There's rumours coming out of the US about a rate rise. You guys ready for that?"

"Market data's running on ten Gigs now," replied Chris.

Market data. Ticks. The world's exchanges were in principle hardly changed from the marketplace of ancient Pompeii. Merchants posted prices at which they would buy and sell their wares. When someone offered that price, the deal was done and the goods despatched. Except that in today's markets, every merchant was watching the prices posted by every other merchant – across hundreds of thousands of shares and bonds – and changing their own prices as often as their technology allowed. Every price change was called a tick. At the turn of the millennium, there were five thousand ticks every second across the world's markets. Which sounded a lot in those days. Today, that number was two hundred thousand a second, thanks to the automated trading engines.

Hamish was a regular guy. If you planted a palm tree behind him and scattered a few buckets of sand on the floor, he could be a windsurf instructor. But his toys were processing and – even more astonishing – storing two hundred thousand ticks a second in the tick database. And deciding, in a few millionths of a second, what they wanted to bid for and sending that message back. Tick.

The new ten Gig network could handle a million ticks a second, and deliver them to every server in the building, and that was ten times faster than the old one. The network had been rolled out by TIS folks, working shifts and weekends, in a race against time. But probably in another two years, the new network would be the old one, and struggling to cope.

But not today. Chris was quietly confident that today he had the tools in place to cope with the triple witching hour. He could gift-wrap a million trades and send them to David Trebbiano's systems in the back office, no sweat.

"Hey, have you seen this?"

Hamish was pointing at one of the windows on one of his six screens. It was a picture of a rev counter. Not revving high at the moment, the needle jerking like an engine ticking over. The dial went up to two million revs a second, so this was an unusual engine.

"Yeah, what's that?"

"It's a gadget I got from one of Philippe's guys, Pauline. Philippe told her to give it to me so we can all see when shit happens."

On the trading floor, everyone was a guy. Even the girls.

"Shit happens meaning one of your toys has run amok and brought down the High Frequency Desk?"

Hamish pretended to look hurt.

"OK, so what is it telling me?"

"The dial comes straight off the RMDS servers – it's telling you how many ticks a second they are processing."

RMDS or the Reuters Market Data Distribution System was a highly specialized infrastructure whose sole job was to distribute prices – ticks – from the markets to the many humans and computers within the bank that needed them. And conversely to take prices created by the bank's traders and their computers, and feed them onto the markets.

"Hmm… you're getting five thousand ticks a second, before London opens. Mostly the other European markets?"

"Seventeen of them. But we're just ticking over, right now. When the LSE and LIFFE open in a couple of minutes, it'll go straight up to 50,000 a second. Or higher." The London markets were huge, bigger than the rest of Europe put together.

"And what's that? You monitoring Philippe's heart rate?"

To the right of the big dial was a green window with six lines flowing across it, each line blipping upwards every second or so. They had labels but Chris couldn't read them.

"Kind of. That's our markets heartbeat monitor. Every second we send a dummy order to each market and see how long it takes to get a reply back. The higher the blip, the longer the delay. We don't like big blips. The top line is LIFFE, the London Futures market, and right below it, this little guy is the NASDAQ."

"How come the NASDAQ blips are smaller than LIFFE? New York is a hundred times further away, it should take longer to get there and back, surely?"

"It doesn't have to go across the Atlantic and back, remember. Our computers in New York are sitting in NASDAQ's own datacentre."

The rev counter was suddenly swinging. From five thousand up to fifteen or twenty, then bouncing around.

"Look at that. London's open," said Hamish.

"How high does it get?" asked Chris.

"When the American markets are open and before Europe closes, we get about two hundred and fifty thousand ticks a second. That's the record. We hit that three months ago, last Triple Witching in fact. Effing nightmare that was."

Hamish took a call from a client.

"SBS. Yeah, speaking…"

A sudden movement on the screens caught Chris' eye. The rev counter was in new territory, almost vertical and climbing: 260, 400, 500K. And on the heart rate monitor, one of the markets had blipped up and not come down. It was flat at the top of its range. Dead. Huh?

One by one the other lines blipped up and flat-lined as well. It looked like a death in a hospital drama. Chris tapped Hamish on the shoulder and pointed at the screen. Hamish did a double take, almost dropped the phone.

"Cheryl – great, listen, got to run. Bye."

"Half a million ticks a second? Holy cow, what's going on?"

Hamish started typing like a madman. After thirty seconds, he banged the keyboard in frustration.

"The servers are maxed out. Nothing's getting through. Fuck! We are out of the markets."

"Hamish! What the hell have you done?"

That was Philippe's sidekick, Eric, yelling from the HFT desk.

"Nothing, we're not trading," Hamish yelled back.

"Well, something's broken. All our prices are stale. And the LSE opened two minutes ago."

Suddenly the green lines dropped back again, all together, and started beating.

"We're back," said Eric. "Val, call the TIS guys. We just had a network problem."

Radiating innocence, Hamish ambled down to the HFT desk. Chris followed him, seething. This was not a good start to his big day.

"Can't be a network problem, Eric," said Hamish, "did you see the dial? We were getting half a million ticks a second. Something insane is happening in the market."

Eric looked skeptical.

"I don't see news. I don't see prices going crazy. Nothing."

He hit a key on his dealer board, a specialized phone system that connected him to other market professionals. He was answered immediately.

"Goldman. John Tullane."

"Hi John, it's Eric, SBS. Say, have you guys just seen a big spike? Massive order volumes? No? So nuthin' unusual, right?"

He hung up and looked accusingly at Hamish.

Tom Hailey called. As head of Market Data, the RMDS infrastructure that moved prices between the world's exchanges and the bank's computers was his baby.

"Hey, what's going on up there? At 8.02, RMDS processed twenty million ticks in sixty seconds, which is about sixteen million more than usual."

"I just called Goldman Sachs. They don't see anything," said Eric.

"The sixteen million didn't come from the markets. They came from us," said Tom.

"Huh? One of our systems is putting out more messages than the rest of the world put together?" said Eric.

"Yes. And it started when the London markets opened. So, what do you think, guys?"

They all knew what he meant. One of the bank's trading systems, working the open on the London market, had gone berserk.

"Tom, which system are these messages coming from?" asked Chris.

"Don't know. Yet. But my guess, gents, is that it's one of you two. This is a very powerful machine." He rang off.

Eric and Hamish eyed each other with mutual suspicion.

"If you're behind this, Hamish, I will personally track your servers down in Raleigh and set fire to them."

Half an hour later, Eric's desk phone rang again. It was Tom. Eric put him on speaker.

"We found out where these messages are coming from."

"It's Alchemy, isn't it?" said Hamish. "I knew it."

"In your dreams, cowboy," said Eric.

"It's both of you. But not just you – these messages are coming from everywhere. There are literally hundreds of different sources, maybe thousands, all pumping out their piece of the sixteen million. All inside the bank."

"What sort of message?"

"We don't know yet. I've got John Templeton from Reuters support here. John?"

A nervous voice floated out of the speaker, sounding like a school teacher.

"Yes, er, hi all. Well, as a first step, we recommend that all servers should be running RMDS nine and patch level up to level sixty-seven. Our investigation shows a number of servers – about one hundred and thirty – with missing patches-"

Chris felt his blood pressure rising.

"We're short on time here, John. Does one of these patches fix our problem?"

"Well, we are trying to get hold of Engineering in California to advise-"

"Why can't you get hold of Engineering in California?" Unconsciously, Chris started to rub his forehead.

"Well, eight hours behind, it's early there – it's 1am and those guys get to work about 7.30am – but there's a guy called Tvi on overnight and we are trying to raise him ..."

Chris lost it.

"John, listen to me. This is Triple Witching. Do you have any fucking idea how critical this is? If we're down and some hedge fund computer figures it out, we could lose millions in seconds. Stop pissing about, get the lead engineers on this call, NOW."

"Well, ah, Chris, of course but the problem has not re-occurred since eight o'clock and everything is running normally, so ..."

"Are you stupid? It hasn't happened again because the markets haven't been busy. But it bloody well will when New York opens. John, listen to me. Wake them up, get the people who engineered this stuff on this call in ten minutes ..."

Chris was shouting. He knew he was way out there but it seemed to work. Miraculously, deeply techie people appeared who spoke in deeply techie terms to Tom's guys.

Chris left them to it and went onto the floor. Hamish and the portfolio desk were feverishly busy processing a basket trade for a big client.

"First big order from Fireman's," he said, "we've been working on them for months. Years."

Fireman's Fund was just that – the fund that held the pension savings of America's firemen. Portia started to drip feed the client's positions into the market. It was a big, complex basket.

"How many stocks in that one?" asked Chris.

"About eight hundred," replied Hamish.

"Relax," said Hamish, sensing his tension, "on busy days, we trade a dozen baskets that size, all at the same time. This is nothing."

Chris looked down at the little rev counter. It was fine, somewhere around 100K. Suddenly it kicked up to 120K, 125K. No, no, no, what was going on?

"Oh my God, they finally did it," said someone, looking over his shoulder. Chris turned to the TV.

BREAKING NEWS: Israeli commandos storm Iranian nuclear fuel processing center. Many dead in Natanz attack."

Chris could see the markets around the world exploding as the news spread. Hamish's tick counter hit 180K and then swept steadily upwards to 500K. The market heart beats died on Hamish's window, one after the other. There was commotion and angry voices across the trading floor. SBS was out of the markets just as the markets were going crazy.

Chris ran across to where Miyuki was sitting, serenely efficient.

"Miyuki, we have a crisis. I need a room."

"Cyrus is out," she replied, "you can use his office."

Chris invited Eric and Hamish to join him and they dialled into the technical bridge from the Polycom on Cyrus' table. The bridge was a virtual meeting room monitored by a TIS incident manager 24 hours a day. There were a bunch of people already on the call and the incident manager was calling for calm.

The door opened and John Uzgalis came in. Behind him was a gaggle of traders, operations people, even a woman from HR. None of them were invited exactly but during crises, people huddled round anyone who might know more than they did.

The Incident Manager called for business updates.

It was one disaster after another. Every trading desk depended on data from the markets and none of them were getting it. Every London business was out of the markets.

"Hi, it's Tom Hailey here. I have news." His voice sounded strained.

"Who's this charlie?" asked one of the traders. He was an Equities cash trader of the old school, born within earshot of Bow Bells and always good value.

"He works for Neil Jenkins in TIS. He runs Market Data," replied Chris.

"Huge volumes of market data messages are flooding the network. Half a million messages a second, it's unreal," said Tom.

"There's an effing war starting in the Middle East," said the trader, "there's a lot of nervous people out there."

"The Iranian situation is not the immediate problem-" said Tom.

"Too right, mate. You come down to the bleedin' desk, I'll show you the immediate problem."

"What I mean is, the turbulence on the markets isn't the problem. We can handle it. What causing the problem is the messages coming from our own systems. In the last twenty minutes, we have analysed those messages."

And like the best whodunnits, it was so obvious when you knew the answer.

"Half of them say 'the message number I just got is not the number I was expecting, please send again.' The rest are more specific, like 'Message corrupted.' But all of them ask for messages to be sent again."

"We think it's the tail end of a vicious circle. Somebody – some process – is generating a burst of messages. So many that some of the other systems can't keep up. So they ask for those messages to be sent again. But sending them again loads the system even more. Now even more servers can't keep up – inside a second, the system is flooded and everybody's screaming, 'I missed that! Give it to me again!'"

"Mate, sounds like a great party," said the cash trader.

"I get the idea," said someone else, "but how does it start? Who is sending this burst of message that creates the panic?"

"Pass. Still working on that. But whoever it is kicks off when the outside world gets busy, like at the London open."

"Why would it ever stop or die down?"

"According to Reuters, there's a limit to the number of resends that a computer asks for. After that, it just gives up. When enough servers give up, the storm dies down. For a while."

"It's going to happen again, isn't it?" said Uzgalis. Tom did not reply.

The door opened and Philippe Reynaud walked in. He was thin, tanned, wearing expensive jeans and a white shirt. He stepped inside the room and looked around. He spotted Chris.

"Chris, who is in charge of this disaster?"

"Tom Hailey. Market Data," said Chris, pointing to the Polycom.

Philippe raised his voice at the device.

"This is Philippe Reynaud. Do you know who I am?"

"Yes, Philippe," replied Tom, who knew him well, "you run High Frequency Trading for Equities."

"Yes. But as Cyrus is out today, I am deputizing for him. This situation is completely unacceptable. This is a very important day for our clients. Do you understand? I need your assurance that this situation will not re-occur. When will you have a plan?"

There was no answer to this impossible question.

"Look, everyone, this bridge is a technical bridge," chipped in the incident manager bravely, "if you're not technical, please drop off now. We will publish status updates on the Global Markets home page."

No-one moved in Cyrus' office. There were no beeps of people dropping off around the world. By now, there were probably a hundred people listening. A hundred souls with just one thought: screw that! This is the very place to be. I am drinking from the fountain of truth that those selfish techies try to keep to themselves.

"You," said Philippe into the phone. "Tom Hailey. I want you here. Now. In Cyrus' office. I will return here at 1pm to hear your plan." He left the room, confident that he had seized the initiative.

"Hi, Tim Hawes here," said a voice. "I'm wondering if we should tell the FSA officially about this outage? Jerome had a catch-up with them last week and they were very concerned about our IT problems."

You little bastard, thought Chris.

"We are having intermittent system problems. Every bank has such problems somewhere, every day," said Philippe, to general relief. No trading head wanted to go near the FSA if they could avoid it.

"Whoa, whoa, guys, hold on," said someone, looking outside. The whole trading floor was standing up, looking at the TV. Chris caught the headline.

Iranian government regains control of nuclear plant at Natanz... 'many' Israeli special forces dead.

"Bad news, Tom, get up here quick," said Chris, into the Polycom.

He was right. The markets boiled. Within a minute the rev counter on Hamish's screen was back in the red and the heartbeats had stopped. There were people screaming on the trading floor and the noise on the bridge swamped the Incident Manager's pleas for calm.

Tom and his two guys rushed in, looking stressed. One of them was young Hassan Choudhary, the IT grad with attitude. Chris acknowledged him and got a nod back. They sat down at Cyrus' desk and logged on.

Chris' Blackberry started vibrating with an incoming call. It was the switchboard. Huh? He ignored it.

Tom Hailey was trying to say something above the babble.

"Listen, listen, guys! We have discovered something new. Hassan?"

Chris' phone rang again. It was Reception on the ground floor. What? What did reception want? He sent it to voicemail.

Almost immediately it rang again.

'Incoming call from 07921684394 (Olivia)'

Argh. Just like last week. But no appointment with Dr Ireson today. He just didn't have time to talk to her now. Immediately she called again. Bloody hell, what was so urgent? He sent her to voicemail again.

Hassan Choudhary was standing up, talking. His hands were shaking. He spoke softly but clearly.

"We have investigated the last outage. When the problem starts, many computers are asking for data again. For the first time. But we found two computers that have already asked for resends by then. They are saying 'this is the fourth time I have asked you to send this data.'"

"Does everyone get that?" said Tom. "We've found two servers which are weaker than the others. We looked them up on the Resource Database."

The room was suddenly quiet.

"They are not servers. They're laptops."

"Laptops? Who uses laptops for trading, for Chrissake? No one," said a trader.

"You are correct. According to TIS records, these laptops are in the recycle store."

The recycle store was a graveyard for unwanted kit that could be reused. In theory.

"How old are these machines?" asked Chris.

"One is five years, the other even older."

"What does age have to do with it?" said the woman from HR, instantly suspicious.

"I get it," said John Uzgalis. "You think these guys are the trigger. They sign up to all this market data and when it gets busy, they can't keep up, right? Because they're slower."

Hassan nodded. Philippe was on the attack.

"But what incredible stupidity to allow these machines to subscribe for market data. How could you do that?"

"We didn't," said Tom.

"Well, who did? I want names."

"We don't know," said Tom, "these machines are supposed to be in storage."

"Well, where are they?"

"We don't know. We are going to disable their network IDs. We don't know where they are but we can stop them connecting. They will be off the network in two minutes."

Philippe was reassured. He switched effortlessly from panic to blame game.

"I will inform Cyrus that the crisis is under control. It is seven minutes to one. We should meet again at 1.15 to discuss the causes of this disaster."

Tom swallowed. His forehead gleamed with tiny beads of sweat. He was wrestling with the temptation to let Philippe go off happy. Chris knew that would be a mistake.

"Tom, taking these two machines off the network – will it fix the problem?"

Philippe stopped abruptly in the doorway.

"We don't know," said Tom, "in my personal opinion, probably not."

"What?" said Philippe, "but you said these machines were the trigger."

"I did. But there may be other machines. The logfiles aren't complete. Maybe there are other, even slower machines that had already checked out. Or faster ones that took a bit longer."

Philippe wiped his forehead. He was a sharp guy and he instantly grasped the abyss of complexity opening up in front of him.

"1.15pm," he said, "next update. In this office."

Someone handed Chris a handwritten note. It said simply: *your wife is in reception.*

What the hell was this? He raced down the stairs.

"She was here for half an hour," said the receptionist, faintly disapproving, "and she left two minutes ago. We were trying to reach you all over the building."

Chris tried calling her. It rang twice and then went to voicemail. Bad sign. Arrgh. Why now, why today?

No time to speculate. He pushed Olivia to the back of his mind. He needed to concentrate. He went back to the trading floor. The two laptops had been taken off the network.

The next two hours went by in a flash. Everything stayed up. Perhaps disabling those two machines had made a difference. Tom and his guys detected another ancient laptop and took that off as well. But they had no idea how many others might be out there.

Perhaps, perhaps they would make it through the day. Every minute that passed was another win, but the last thirty minutes in London would be the next test. Still, you could see hope creeping across the trading floor.

Then, soon after three o'clock, the Israelis released footage of the raid on Natanz. Troops landing from helicopters, eerily dressed in white overalls with gas masks. The pundits started to talk about radiation and the dangers of attacking a nuclear installation. It was a new angle and new experts appeared on the screens. That was a shock to the markets and at 3.16pm, market data failed again across the trading floor.

Chris was standing in Debt Markets, talking to John Uzgalis when it happened.

"Shit, shit, shit," said Uzgalis, listening to the howls of fury raging around them. Out of the corner of his eye, Chris saw a trader pick up his keyboard and smash it on the desk. Sam Tassone, king of Commodities, appeared like a raging bull.

"John, what the fuck is this?" said Tassone. "We just got hit on uranium, the guys tried to pull our prices and they can't even do that."

"It's a market data storm according to TIS," said Uzgalis. "We've got some slow consumers out there who can't keep up with the prices. They keep asking for resends and those resends are killing the network."

"Consumers? You mean housewives on the network? Oh my God."

Real comedian, Tassone, even in a crisis.

Chris' Blackberry rang. It was Carl in New York.

"Chris, Alchemy is down here. Also Mack and Tuxedo. We're getting hosed from London, like a million updates a second. Our prices on the NASDAQ are frozen right now."

Shit, the disaster had crossed the Atlantic. Chris had a moment of pure panic. The bank was a market maker on the NASDAQ and had an obligation to make prices in certain stocks. In the three years that Chris had been running the shop, they had never failed.

Chris tried to think straight. It was hideously complicated. What prices came from London? What could be disconnected? What else would break?

He hurried back to Cyrus' office, followed by John Uzgalis and Sam Tassone. Tom was there, hunched over the Polycom. Hassan was in the corner, using Cyrus' screen. The room was packed and stank of sweat and stress. Chris had to push to get in.

Philippe was in front, screaming at Tom.

"I don't know when it will stop," Tom was saying. "This one's going on longer than before."

"You don't know! Unacceptable! The slow laptops, have you found them?"

"We've detected three. They are off the network. We've checked the recycle store. There are another fifteen laptops missing."

"Fifteen? Oh my God. Surely you can find fifteen laptops?"

"The network is global. They could be anywhere in the world."

"Don't you understand? We cannot trade. No one. This is a catastrophe. There are twenty-four minutes to the London close. You must find them."

"We've got a search party looking for them. All my staff, and most of the helpdesk. We are searching every building in London."

At that moment, there was a loud, American voice from the Polycom.

"This is Harvey in New York, we are out of the markets here. I confirm, we are out of the NASDAQ, we are out of the NYSE, the CME. Everywhere. The SEC called me two minutes ago. They want to know what the fuck is going on. We've got clients on the phone screaming. We're dying here. What are we doing, guys?"

Tom was silent, staring wordlessly at the PolyCom. Now the sweat was running down his cheeks and there were dark patches on his shirt. He was desperate, and everyone could smell it.

"We're going to keep looking. Our best technical guys are talking with Reuters, trying to figure it out..."

"That's it? Hope?" said Tassone. "That is not a strategy."

"Mr Hailey? Mr Hailey? Excuse me. I have an idea."

It was the young Indian, Hassan. Tom didn't hear him, didn't move.

"Hassan, what is it? Make it quick," said Chris.

"Reuters says that when a machine loses a packet, it asks ten times for another one. Then it gives up. When everyone gives up, the storm stops."

"Yes, so?" said Tom. He brushed an arm across his forehead and looked absently at the damp patch on his sleeve.

"If we make every machine give up, not after ten times, but after the first time. The storm won't happen. Or it will be very short."

Chris wondered why he hadn't thought of this before.

"Yes," said Tom slightly wearily, "but we don't know where these laptops are."

"We don't know where they are but we can broadcast a message to all of them with new instructions. I have checked RMDS manual. It is possible."

Tom came to life like a toy robot with new batteries.

"Yes! Yes! Is Reuters on? Do you agree? Well find out, damn you. Hassan, write the script and let me know when it's ready."

Chris left Cyrus' office an hour later. He felt limp. He was hungry and thirsty. To his surprise, Cyrus was back, out on the floor. He was sitting, his huge head turning from side to side, scanning his screens, reading emails and messages on Bloomberg.

"So?" he said, not looking up.

"It worked."

"Too late, Chris. We missed it. The most volatile day since 9/11. A huge opportunity. Our biggest customers are pissed off. It's a total disaster in New York. Philippe is giving me hell. And we're on *Here is the City*, which we need like a hole in the head. Have you read this?"

He pointed at his screen.

Hubble Bubble, Trading Trouble hits Major Bank. SBS is having more snafus with its computer systems... customers have been unable to place orders electronically all day. And today is Triple Witching... blah, blah... SBS could not be contacted for comment...

"Cyrus, this was something completely new."

"It's always something new. What is it, Chris, why can't you make the technology work? Why do we have these accidents?"

"Maybe it wasn't an accident."

"What? Is this what Jerome was talking about? I thought you had more sense. No, not another word – some idiot put old laptops on the network, I get that. It was an accident. Find out who did it and fire them."

"OK. It was probably one of Tom Hailey's people."

"I don't care if it was fucking Martians. You are my technology provider. The technology was not provided. Bring me some heads on platters. When you've done that, we can talk about your future. This was not the sunny day I requested."

Chris turned to leave but Cyrus wasn't finished.

"Oh, another thing. Philippe says you should hire some guy called Hassan."

"I did hire him. He's one of our grads."

"Well, put him somewhere where he can do some good. Give me hope."

Chris went back into Cyrus' office and beckoned to Hassan. He came out, looking nervous.

"Would you like to stay in London permanently? You can join my strategy team. Or High Frequency Trading, take your pick. Or what would you like?"

Hassan's answer was so astonishing that Chris thought he had misunderstood.

"Information Security? Are you sure? You would prefer InfoSec to a trading team?"

"I think so. Information Security is an interesting area."

He seemed determined and Chris wasn't going to push it. On the other hand, his influence over Sheila Collins was limited, to say the least.

It was after 7pm. Chris felt drained by stress and depressed by Cyrus' threats. He headed for home. Halfway there, he remembered Olivia's visit to work. Why had she come? And then it came back to him. He had offered lunch. Trying to make peace after last weekend. He had kept her waiting in reception for half an hour and then she had stormed out. Oh shit. She would still be boiling. He was too tired to be apprehensive.

36

Trouble at home

"Why have you sacked Dom?"

She was in the kitchen. Her eyes were angry. And slightly red rimmed. Had she been crying?

"Ah. Yes. I meant to tell you. I've been worrying about it. Look, there was a List. I had to lose two managers, I had no choice."

"Yes you did, and you chose Dom. After everything he's done for you. What a mean, vindictive man you are – just because he dared to tell the truth. He explained it to me. He's not trying to destroy anything. He just wants the bank to do a real test. Which would be good for it. And you won't let him because you're scared. You're the problem, Chris, not him."

"Oh yeah? Total bullshit. His father got cancer, then he was laid off. Then he died. Dom blames us. He hates us. He came up with a clever way to cook Hamilton but it didn't quite work so now-"

"Oh, don't be ridiculous. Dom would never do anything like that."

"Will you shut up and listen to me! If the Americans discover that he attacked Hamilton, they will extradite him to the United States. As a terrorist. They will lock him up for the rest of his life. Don't you get it? I'm trying to save him."

"Save him? By marching him out of the building? You know what I think? You're just jealous. You can't bear me having lunch with another man."

"Don't be stupid. You can have lunch with him every bloody day for all I care."

"What? How dare you talk to me like that! And why is that stupid? Why aren't you jealous, Christopher? You should be."

They were both so angry that Chris slept in the spare room, something that had never happened before.

*

The bed was comforting, solid. The rest of his world was disintegrating. He woke at 4am and lay awake for hours, trying to make sense of it.

Olivia had been thinking overnight as well. She was icily polite in the morning.

"So, what was this crisis yesterday, Chris? What was so important that you couldn't even get down to reception to apologise?"

It was unexpected. But welcome. Gratefully he explained about Triple Witching and the nightmare of the market data meltdown.

"Some old laptops did that?" said Olivia. "Really? That doesn't sound right."

"I know. But it can happen. It happened once before, a couple of years ago. So TIS improved the security to stop people doing it accidentally."

"So? You mean it wasn't an accident?" she asked, suddenly casual.

"No. Anyone with the technical skills to connect old laptops to the markets would know how incredibly dangerous it was. No, this was planned. A time bomb set for Triple Witching day. Like the first one."

"But Dom wasn't there yesterday, was he?" she said, triumphant. "You sacked him the day before!"

Various permutations of this thought had kept Chris awake half the night so his answer was immediate.

"He didn't have to be there. Once those laptops were on the network, it was a disaster waiting to happen."

They faced each other, Chris defiant. Her grey eyes widened and the colour rose in her cheeks.

"You think you're so clever, don't you? But you're wrong. You'll be so sorry one day."

She stomped off to do the shopping, slamming the door behind her.

All right, I will prove it to you, thought Chris, his stomach churning, *I don't care if they fire me. Dom can take his chances.*

He grabbed his pass and his Oyster card and headed into work, seething with anger.

He restarted his investigation into the mysterious computer that had shut down the cooling in Hamilton. He asked Sedohara at Fujitsu to come back with English translations of the BMS log files. Mega urgent. He again asked Tom Hailey and his Networks gurus which computer had the IP address 174.0.59.119 when Hamilton started to cook. He started researching the internet, looking for wisdom on reverse IP lookups.

Nothing. Nada. Three hours later, he was tearing his hair out, literally, when John Uzgalis walked in. Black Armani T-shirt, black leather boots, no diamond studs today. Chris was pleased to see him. John was like Dom, lots of deep technical knowledge.

"John! What a surprise. What are you doing here?"

"Dude, I'm not 'the surprise'. Debt Markets never sleeps. What are you doing here? Still looking for logfiles?"

Gratefully, Chris explained his problem.

"An IP address from three months ago? Chris, forget it, no one cares. If you want to play detective, find out who put those laptops on the network. The business is baying for blood."

"John, that wasn't an accident. Hamilton wasn't an accident. Both on Triple Witching days. There's someone behind this."

"You are obsessed. And paranoid, Chris. You should see a doctor."

"John, I know who did this. And I'm going to prove it."

"You're on a road to hell, my friend. Get off at the next intersection."

He disappeared back into Debt Markets land. Chris resumed his search. Ten minutes later, Tom Hailey called with some new ideas.

Each of which had a flaw.

"That won't work," Chris was saying, "not as far back as June ..."

Chris felt a sudden hand on his shoulder. He dropped the phone, and jumped out of his chair. Jerome deVries was standing behind him. Unshaven. Baggy black trousers, dirty white shirt, open necked. Coffee in one hand.

"So, it's true. What are you doing here, Christopher?"

"Er. Just work. A network problem."

"A network problem that happened back in June? Jesus, you are one obstinate pig-headed Boer. What do I have to do to make you listen? Hit you over the head?"

After deVries had gone, Chris picked up his phone from the carpet. Tom had rung off but there was a text from him.

OMG was that devries? Whoops!!! I will ask Neil J. about your problem.

Well, that was a good idea in theory. His brother Neil used to run Networks, before he got promoted. He had personally driven the design of the new network, and he had masterminded a long and risky project to clean up the hotchpotch of networks the bank had acquired as it swallowed smaller banks.

But no way was Neil going to help him with this.

Outside his window, he could see two men, climbing up the dome of St Pauls, holding ropes. It looked lonely and dangerous. He would happily have swapped places.

On a whim, he decided to work on Mustard, his bot, before he went home. He rationed himself to half an hour, working on an offensive strategy. It got pretty interesting. At the end of half an hour, he had a new idea, a really good one, for surprising attackers with a wall of fire when they least expected it. When he had coded it, he tested it, pitting two copies of Mustard against each other. That showed up some weaknesses in the defensive strategy. Which had to be fixed! Just another half an hour, he promised himself. Just a few minutes more.

It was suddenly half past four. Unbelievable. Worse than last week. Why did he never learn?

He hurried home. Olivia had gone to see her sister. There was no baby making activity that weekend. On Sunday, he went up to Bedford to see his Dad. Just to escape, really.

37

Sana'a, Yemen, 2007

Day Seven – Thursday

It was night time, but Gurjit had forgotten how to sleep. She lay on her back, looking at the dim light coming in from the window. The Old City was quiet, with an occasional taxi cruising the narrow streets, lights off.

In the early hours, a car stopped down below, she could hear its fanbelt wheezing. Then the sound of a door rolling shut. She got up to look. It was turning the corner out of the square, but she saw it clearly.

*

Mahmoud woke early and lay agonizing over the bargain he had made with the devil. What should he have done? He wondered where Zahra was now and what had happened to her.

There were no Jihadists in this plot. There never were. There was just a predatory gangster called Babu Malik. By kidnapping his father, Babu Malik had acquired the shop for a song and Zahra for free. Perhaps Babu Malik had persuaded Ahmed to bet foolishly on himself. The Fat Policeman might be in charge of anti-terrorism – or not – but he was Babu's brother-in-law. This was Yemen, family first.

Ruin. Babu Malik has ruined the Hashemi family, he thought. I will kill him. Then he cursed himself for a fool. His father was still a hostage. What he needed to do now was save his father, at any cost.

Where was Zahra?

He tip-toed downstairs in the early dawn light. He passed his mother's door. Zahra's door was ajar. Her bed was empty. He turned and nearly jumped out of skin. His mother was standing like a ghost in front of him, wearing her nightshift.

"Mother, I …" He could not confess.

"Come," she said calmly, "I know. She's gone."

She led him over to her little shrine. The Hindu gods smiled out from their frames. Ganesh for luck, Rama the selfless and the smooth round phallus that was Shiva the Destroyer.

"Look," said his mother.

And then he saw it. Above the images of the gods, there were two new marks on the wall. Two small dark palm prints. The bowl of turmeric powder was half empty with powder scattered messily on the floor.

He knew the story. Like the women of Chittorgarh, his sister had walked out into the unknown, leaving behind this small memorial to her courage.

He had a sudden premonition.

"I will never see her again."

"What?" said his mother. "What did you say?"

Had he said it out loud? He must be going mad. He hadn't slept for three days, not really. He felt feverish. He had a sudden crushing sense of loss.

They huddled in the kitchen. Ben, Ahmed, Mahmoud and Gurjit. Gurjit blew on last night's embers, trying to make a fire.

About noon, Mahmoud skyped Uncle Saeed to see what fresh obstacle the bank had thrown in their way. He had no hope, but he felt strangely calm. He felt the end was near.

38

London: trouble with laptops

Monday, 24th September 2012

On Monday morning, Chris' headache was back, just nagging. And it was raining. He was scuttling up Cheapside, trying to stay dry, when Holly rang.

"When you get in, go straight to the trading floor. Cyrus wants to see you."

Ominous.

Then Tom Hailey rang, from a train. He sounded nervous.

"Chris, did you see... email... We found the laptops. About midnight? I'm sorry, this... got escalated... quicker..."

"Tom, you're breaking up. What got escalated?"

But Tom had gone into a tunnel, or something.

Philippe Reynaud was in Cyrus' office, waving his arms around, and the solid figure of Sheila Collins was sitting at the table.

Cyrus looked pissed off.

"Have a seat, Chris. What I am hearing from..."

He hesitated, maybe trying to remember if this was Sheila or Susan. Cyrus didn't have a lot to do with Information Security as a rule.

"...our colleagues in Information Security concerns me greatly. If even half of this is true, your guys need a kick up the pants..."

"Cyrus," said Philippe smoothly, "we cannot only blame Technology. No doubt the business has lessons to learn as well..."

Pure Teflon. Brilliant. Cyrus was not in the mood for it.

"Whomever did this, I want them out of this building today. Even if it's Arshad. And, Chris, you need to fix this- this total lack of discipline."

"Hang on," said Chris, "you are all ahead of me. All I've been told is that the slow machines have been found. And that was three minutes ago."

"Gentlemen, would it be helpful if I shared a few facts?" said Collins, with a faint emphasis on the last word. She did not wait for an answer.

"Over this weekend, a TIS search party found eighteen old laptops in a comms room on Eleven. The Finance floor."

"OK," said Chris, "what do that have to do with me?"

"They are physically stacked in the comms room as part of a larger group of sixty machines. Many have stickers put there by some comedian. For example, 'TIS Free Zone' or another, 'Equities HFT test machine - TOUCH ME AND DIE.'"

"Oh."

"These machines have been set up to subscribe to market data. When the markets get busy, the laptops can't keep up – with the disastrous results we saw on Friday. The other machines – the rest of the sixty – are not laptops. They seem to be developer desktops smuggled upstairs when a developer got a new desktop. They are more powerful. And most of them are not connected to the markets."

"The network logs show that this test environment was started two years ago and it's grown over time. But the laptops only appeared in the last two weeks. We can't find any requests to install these computers. None. This is an unofficial test environment created without consulting TIS. Which is a major breach of policy."

"But not the only one. Following an incident two years ago, TIS introduced new controls. Connecting a machine to the markets requires access to a highly privileged account."

"Good," said Cyrus, "and who has the password to that account?"

"Who?" said Sheila. She squinted at an A3 printout in front of her and then looked at Cyrus, as if mystified, through her thick-rimmed glasses. Chris thought she was enjoying herself.

"Yes, who has the password? Is it more than one person?"

"It is one hundred and seventy-three people," said Sheila, "including six people who left the bank two years ago."

There was a shocked silence.

"Half them are TIS people, which I would expect. But of the remaining eighty, fifty are in IT. They work for Chris. A gentleman called Arshad Zebediah is on the list, for example."

"This is unbelievable," said Philippe, shaking his head.

"I was surprised by some of the names," Sheila went on, "for example, there are two members of your management team, Chris."

"Really," said Chris, "who?"

"David Carstairs and Dominic MacDonald. Can you explain that? You must have signed off on it."

"I have no idea," said Chris. "This is all news to me." *Dom again.
Always Dom.*

He knew he sounded weak and defensive. But who wouldn't? He could be unemployed by lunchtime.

But Sheila Collins was not finished.

"You said, Philippe, that the business also had lessons to learn. I agree. In some ways, the business side is more troubling than the IT side. There are about thirty front office people on the list. I am not familiar with the chain of command in your organization, Philippe-"

Ha! Chain of command, thought Chris. If you worked in High Frequency Trading, you worked for Philippe. Period.

"-but they are all your people. And you are on the list yourself. Is this something you have requested? If so, when and why?"

Cyrus turned his huge head slowly from Philippe to Chris and back.

"You two. You are an embarrassment. You have put our business back two years. Get out before I fire you. And don't come back until you have cleaned up this mess."

Chris got up, hesitated. Swallowed hard. Sat down again. Cyrus raised one disbelieving eyebrow.

"Cyrus, look. It looks like we screwed up, yes, but... I think someone put those laptops there deliberately. I know Hamilton was deliberate, it could be the same guy."

"Are you trying to cover your incompetence with this fantasy? Bring me the head of the idiot who did this. Then prove to me that it can't happen again. Now fuck off, I need to call some clients and beg forgiveness."

Chris went back to his office, humiliated and seething with anger. In the lift, his phone rang.

It was his brother Neil, sarcasm dial on max.

"Do you know Tom Hailey? Runs Networks and Market Data? Three hundred and fifty million quid budget, six hundred staff? Oh, you do? Well, he's just sent me an IP address and he wants to know which computer had this address three months ago. I said to him, fuck knows, and he says it came from you... aren't you in enough trouble with the laptops? Why are you wasting his time?"

"Neil, listen, please. I know who attacked Hamilton but I can't prove it. No one believes me. DeVries,, Cyrus, John Uzgalis... even Olivia's got involved. I need to find this box. I'm trying to save my job."

"Well, I tell you what, Charlie. You save my job, and I'll save yours. Tell your friend Uzgalis to lay off me. Until then, go fuck yourself."

Great. Chris spent the rest of the day grilling his guys. They all denied stealing laptops and Chris believed them. He didn't think it was the traders either. It had to be Dom's leaving present.

At seven o'clock, he sneaked upstairs to Eleven. Most doors in the building had electronic locks. The electronic locks recorded who went through them. And most corridors had CCTV cameras.

He found the room easily. Sod it. The door lock was broken. He pushed it open. The laptops were gone. He looked around for clues. What was he expecting? There were a few old cables, and a yellow plastic label. He picked it up.

"This is a Finance floor, you know," said a soft voice from the doorway, "other departments by invitation only. So who invited you?"

Chris jumped. It was Annie Steffens. No Friday dress down today. She was wearing a curve-hugging charcoal marl dress. With a double string of pearls that discreetly kissed her cleavage.

"Are you looking for your missing laptops? I saw TIS taking them away. Have you found out who did it?"

"My guys all deny it. Arshad think it's one of the traders."

"Would they know how? I mean they're traders."

"You'd be amazed. There are more geeks on the floor every year. Especially in High Frequency. Did you ever meet Boris Luchenko? He was a derivs trader. He built his own computer and tried to bring it to work. I was hoping the records from the door lock would tell us something, but it's broken. But there's a camera in the corridor."

"Did they keep hamsters here?" said Annie. "Don't you think it smells funny? Like something died here."

Chris shrugged.

"I'm going home," said Annie suddenly. "I've been here all weekend."

"All weekend? Holy cow, why?"

"Topeka. Remember Topeka? The project to save the bank from the American regulators?! You're about to get summoned to a meeting on Wednesday. Massive drains up. Poor Gawain been working all weekend on the reports. Anyone who's late is going to get a public flogging from Jerome. I hope you're on top of your stuff."

Chris was guilty and alarmed. He wasn't "on top of his stuff". He was too busy firefighting in his day job and looking for terrorists.

"How about a drink before I crash?" said Annie.

Why not? It would be nice to have a friendly face to talk to.

"OK. Just a quick one. Meet you in the Pepys. In 10?"

He hurried downstairs and sent an email to the Building Manager, asking for CCTV images from the camera outside the little comms room. Then he texted Olivia and said he would be home late.

He found a corner in the Pepys. Annie appeared a few minutes later with his beer and her Bourbon.

"Sorry this took a while," she said, "the TIS folks are hogging the bar. That Lebanese Jezebel has just bought a round of drinks for the boys and disappeared with Neil Jenkins."

"Annie, I don't know what you're talking about."

"Freelance recruiter. Lebanese, maybe? Short, dark hair. Don't know her name, pretty face, big tits. She sells IT contractors, especially to TIS."

"Oh, yes. I met her last week. Um, she's called Anita. She invited me to lunch."

"I bet she did. Well, it's not lunchtime, you can stay right here. She's busy in some dark alley with Neil Jenkins…"

That seemed unlikely. Neil was a stickler for loyalty and he was married to Sally. And they had a young son, Harry, who must be two by now.

"You look tired," said Chris.

"That's because I am. When Jerome was CFO, he worked six days a week. Now he's COO and he's taken on Topeka, he's working 24/7. Sometimes I get Sundays off. By Sunday night I wish I hadn't because my inbox is full of his totally unreasonable demands. And he calls me, any time. Day or night."

"I don't get it," said Chris, "he's new to the job. Why doesn't he say, 'Oh my god, lads, Topeka is a disaster and John Tully was an idiot.' Then he could slip the milestones, and take his chances with the regulators?"

Annie pretended to swoon.

"Honestly, Chris, you shouldn't be allowed out without your nanny. How do you think he became COO? Do you think Sir Simon likes him? Or the business? No way. He got the job because he promised the board he would deliver Topeka and save the bank."

"But what made him think he could do that?"

"He's a gambler."

"Come on. He was the CFO. He's an accountant."

"Maybe, but he's a gambler. He looked at his hand. He had two decent cards. One, he thought he could drive Topeka harder than John Tully."

"That wouldn't be difficult."

"Yes. But now, Jerome has realised that bullying the Topeka team won't be enough, so he's going to play his trump."

"Which is?"

"KPC. Tim loves those guys, and he kept whispering in Jerome's ear, get them in, spend the money, make them accountable. So Jerome went to the board and got a blank cheque, signed by Sir Simon. Tomorrow Praveen's coming in – he's the senior partner – and we're going to cut a deal."

"I get it," said Chris, "but that won't fix anything."

"Why not? I have a forty page deck from KPC on what's wrong with Topeka and how they would fix it."

"Forty pages? Bullshit. It's bloody obvious what's wrong with Topeka. I could write it on the back of that beer mat."

Annie passed over the beer mat. Then a pen.

"OK, smart guy. Show me. I need nicotine. Back in five."

And she was. She looked briefly at his scrawl, then tucked it away in her handbag.

"Hmm… juvenile writing, but legible. Thanks. So, how are you enjoying life in this new world?"

"Challenging."

She made a picture frame with her fingers and looked at him through it.

"Am I looking at the next head of IT?"

"Probably not."

"Fine," said Annie, "but don't blame me if you wind up with Tim Hawes. Jerome is planning a re-org, that I do know. He's cooking it up with that witch from HR."

"Rosemary?"

"That's the one. They don't invite me but Tim spends his waking hours running in and out of Jerome's office."

Shit. Shit. He, John and David really needed to agree their candidate. He glanced at his Blackberry. It was after eight. Time to go home. Olivia would have been home for hours.

He stood up and so did Annie. She kissed him on the cheek and then, before he realized, brushed his lips with hers. The faint musk of her scent took him back to tangled bedsheets and sex before dawn in the Shangri-la. Once she came down to his room wearing only a towel and let it drop as he opened the door. Her silver fish pendant was the only witness to the orgy that followed.

He left the Pepys in a hurry, trying to control his arousal at the memory. On the way to Bank, he texted Holly and asked her to fix a breakfast meeting with Uzgalis and Trebbiano.

*

Olivia arrived home just after he did.

"Hi, darling, you're late tonight," he said.

She gave him a cold peck on the cheek. "I met up with a friend."

What did that mean? What friend? It was an imprecision that annoyed him. Olivia wasn't about to tell him.

"And what have you been up to?" she retaliated. "Apart from sacking your best friend. Oh no, that was last week. You smell of beer."

"Er, yes, I went for a drink after work."

"On a Monday? Who with?"

"Oh, er, just John and David," he lied. "Trying to decide who is going to be the next CIO."

Ridiculous, why did he lie? What was wrong with going for a drink with Annie?

"Uzgalis wants it," said Olivia, "he's got the lean and hungry look."

"I'm not sure I want to work for John."

"Well, then you'd better get your bid in pronto."

"We've got a breakfast meeting tomorrow to discuss it." Which was true.

Supper was pizza. They ate in silence.

"So?" she said suddenly, "did you find the laptops?"

"Ah. Yes." He explained about the HFT team and their bootleg test environment.

Olivia thought this was hilarious.

"Oh dear. So it was you who brought down the trading floors? That's not going to help your promotion chances."

"Not if it's Dom and I can prove it."

"Which it's not."

"We are going to find out. There's a CCTV camera outside the room where the laptops were stashed. I've asked the building manager for the CCTV footage. Tomorrow, they told me."

He couldn't wait to see what Property came up with. He could hardly sleep from thinking about it. That would wipe that snide smile off her face.

39

London

Tuesday, 25th September 2012

He woke early and left the house quietly, before Olivia woke up. He felt pleasantly calm until he looked at his inbox.

What the hell was this? The building manager had asked Mike Tucker's permission to hand over the CCTV footage and Mike Tucker – *bastard* – had told deVries and deVries was not happy:

Request denied. What are you playing at? Leave internal security to the experts.

Focus on your day job.

PS. THIS IS YOUR LAST WARNING.

And he had copied Cyrus as well.

Depressed, Chris arrived at Luigi's. He found John and David in deep conversation. They stopped abruptly when they saw him.

"OK, boys," said Uzgalis, "who wants Tim Hawes or Neil Jenkins as their boss?"

Puking noises all round.

"So, it's one of us three, right?"

"One of you two because I don't want the job," said Trebbiano.

Longer pause.

"Shit, I don't mind working for you, Chris," said John. "No problem with you in that slot."

"It shouldn't be about 'what we mind'," said Trebbiano. "It's about the best person for the job. Who's got the experience, who's got the business relationships…"

"What are you saying, David?" said Chris. John Uzgalis was four years older than him and had been in the industry all his working life.

"I'm not saying anything, Chris, just listing the criteria."

It was obvious that David and John had done a deal. At that moment, his phone rang. It was Dave Carstairs, calling about EOS. The batch was still running, still slow. No ETA, no diagnosis. No risk for the desks.

The other two were looking at him. "Batch still in trouble?" said John, "is it something Karthik can help with? His guys are really good on performance tuning."

Meaning: *how can you step up when your own house is in trouble?*

Holly was waiting for him back in the office.

"The Scotsman called. He will be here in five minutes. He sounded happy."

Mackenna bounced into his office without knocking and sat down, rubbing his hands together.

"Well, a little bird showed me an email from your new COO. To yourself. Mr deVries doesn't beat about the bush, is he?"

"About the CCTV on Eleven? Ends with, 'THIS IS YOUR LAST WARNING'?"

"That's the one. You're making quite a name for yourself, Christopher. Even Sir Simon has heard of you. And not in a good way. 'Incompetent IT combined with paranoid delusions,' gives you the flavour. Don't let that bother you, lad, he thinks most of Global Markets should be in an asylum."

"Mr. Mackenna, am I crazy? No one believes me. They don't even want to ask the question."

"Well, to be fair to your colleagues, they don't know about your friend MacDonald and his midnight excursions, do they? And your theory about the Building Management system is a bit airy-fairy. But cheer up, lad, I have good news for you."

"Really? Am I going to wake up soon?"

"Don't be foolish. No. Your almost suicidal attempts to help this bank have impressed me. I have decided to confide in you."

"Thank you, Mr. Mackenna, but I don't see-"

"You don't need to thank me, just listen. I also talked to Group Property about that CCTV camera outside the comms room. Yes, lad, I made the same request that got you into trouble – but me, they could not refuse.

"Well, well, a little surprise there. That camera's not very well. Somebody sprayed it with silver paint, two weeks back. You can't see anything through it. Property noticed it but had no spares. Your request revealed their incompetence. So Mike Tucker shopped you to deVries instead.

"So. The disaster with the laptops was not caused by stupidity. It was deliberate. It was cunning. It was on a Triple Witching day. Yes, I think we have a serial villain at work."

Mackenna pulled at his bushy eyebrows.

"Who carries out the digital attacks we read about? The viruses and worms? Denial of service attacks? Data hacking? Answer: criminals, foreign governments and unhappy teenagers. Not the terror groups. They prefer more physical means: bombs, bullets and knives. Aircraft when they get a chance.

"But it can't go on. Today's terrorists are becoming computer-literate. It's only a matter of time before al-Qaeda runs classes on SSL vulnerabilities instead of bomb-making. And recruits the criminals and the unhappy teenagers. You don't need weapons and explosives to be a digital terrorist, you just need knowledge and the right job."

Mackenna must know more about computers than he let on, thought Chris, trying to conceal his surprise.

"For years we have worried about this scenario. Medium probability, huge impact. Bombs threatens one building or one aircraft. Bad, but limited. A digital terrorist *with the right access* could destroy a bank like ours. Or bring a whole city to its knees. Knock out air traffic control in Europe. There is no end to the chaos and destruction you can create when you control the computers. But somehow it hasn't happened, at least until now."

"Wait," said Chris, "we're talking about Dom, right? What does Dom have to do with terrorism?"

"We shall see. This theory about your friend MacDonald does not quite work. Yes, he's angry. Yes, he's bitter. But murder? I doubt it."

"Murder? What? No one's been killed."

"You are not in possession of all the facts."

Mackenna got out an iPad from his briefcase. He turned it on with one expert flick and shoved it across the table. It showed a confusing webpage. It looked like an Arab newspaper in hell. A lot of red ink, photos of angry clerics and weapons.

"This is the home page of Al-Hamidya, a website in the dark web. It's a kind of Islamic protest wall. All kinds of violent stuff gets exposed here. Threats. Messages. Requests for weapons or information. Mostly in Arabic."

"Three years ago, a fatwah – an Islamic judgement – was posted on al-Hamidya by an Imam called Anwar al-Awlaki. Not long before his death. This bank – he ruled – was guilty of numerous crimes. Usurious money lending. Doing business with Zionists. Bringing death and dishonour to Muslims. The death of one man was not sufficient, he said."

"Death? Whose death?" said Chris.

"We had no idea, at the time. Al-Awlaki said that the bank itself, SBS, should be destroyed. Which caused trouble in the Gulf. There were demonstrations outside our offices in Abu Dhabi and an arson attack in Kuwait."

"Who is al-Awlaki?" asked Chris. He had a feeling he had heard the name before.

"An infamous Imam. A skilled propagandist," said Mackenna. "He was killed not long ago by a Predator missile. His death caused quite a stir, especially in the US."

"But thousands of people have been killed by drones."

"Aye," said Mackenna, dead-pan, "but he was an American citizen. That makes it murder."

"Then it went quiet, for two years. Until three months ago. On 14th June – yes, the day before Triple Witching – someone calling himself Anwar al-Parsani posted this picture on al-Hamidya. Anwar the Persian. It's not his real name, of course, it's a kunya or street name. Very fashionable in terrorist circles."

The image was of a man, hanging upside down, his head perhaps three foot off the floor. His back was to the camera. His torso was naked and his hands were tied behind his back with zip ties. His body looked fat and flabby in the dim light. He seemed to be underground. There was a square concrete pillar behind him, and another behind that. The man had short, dark hair, with a bald patch.

Chris looked up, shocked. "What does it say?" he said, pointing to the caption underneath. It was in Arabic.

"It's a quote from al-Awlaki's fatwah. It says 'One death is not enough. The bank itself must be destroyed'. Allahu akbar. God is great."

"Oh my God. Who is the man?"

"We thought it was a stock photo, a scene from a movie - you can see the bank's logo on his back, clearly photoshopped. And nothing happened in the weeks following, so–"

"Nothing happened? Except Hamilton melted down! That night, in fact."

"Yes, but we were told that was an accident. We get a hundred threats a week. We moved on. Until last Friday – the next Triple Witching day – *this* was posted on the Al-Hamidya website. Looks like the same man, hanging upside down, now from the front. He has been beaten. Broken jaw, teeth, nose. He's lost some blood, which is that dark pool beneath him. And again the quote, 'One death is not enough.' And you know what happened the next day with the laptops."

"Oh my God," said Chris, shaken. "So did this really happen? Who is this man?"

"Yes, we think this is a real killing in progress. We don't know who he is. It looks like a building site, you can see a wheelbarrow there, and some builder's tools. Somewhere in the Middle East, about five years ago."

"How do you know that?"

"Look at these strange marks, on the pillar behind him? Handwritten in chalk?"

He turned the iPad round. "Now look at them upside down. What do you see?"

"Arabic?" said Chris.

"It is Arabic. Two dates, about a fortnight apart. November 10th and November 21st, 2007, on our calendar. Builders sometimes chalk the date of a concrete pour on the wall, to show when it reaches full strength. The building was still unfinished when this picture was taken, so we're looking late 2007, 2008."

"So, Chris, was your friend MacDonald so angry back in 2007? His father lived in the Gulf, yes, but does Dom speak Arabic? Where does he fit into this puzzle? Has he been recruited by someone else?"

Chris remembered how Dom had threatened the young futures trader. Dom liked a good scrap. But not this, surely? He could not answer Mackenna's questions.

He went home on the Tube, packed in like a sardine and he saw only the fat man, suspended by his ankles in some cellar. Helpless. How long did one stay conscious, upside down? On Clapham Common, he googled the question and the results disgusted him. Yes, you could stay conscious long enough to be slowly beaten to death.

40

Sana'a, Yemen, 2007

Day Seven - Thursday

Mahmoud had finally caught up with Uncle Saeed. He had been out all day.

"I hired my neighbour to drive me. We've visited eleven banks today, trying to open an account."

"Why? What's the problem?"

"As soon as I produce my passport, and they see I'm an Iranian, they smile politely and call the next guy in the queue. No-one wants our business, not even with $300,000. They are all scared of the Americans."

Mahmoud sighed. The cat had caught the mouse again.

"And then," said Saeed, "I had this idea. I went into an Iranian bank! Bank Melli has a branch down by the Palm. And they were pleased to see me, we spoke Parsee, we drank tea while we did the paperwork. So civilized. The account will be open tomorrow. Then we can transfer the money into it. And Bank Melli says we can take it out in cash, or a letter of credit, no problem."

Mahmoud asked a few questions, but it sounded like good news. He went to tell his mother, trying to encourage her. He found her in Zahra's room. She was sitting on Zahra's bed, desperately hugging an armful of Zahra's clothes. Ahmed was with her. Since his betting disaster, he had hardly spoken.

"Two more days, mother. Really."

"But what about our bank? They refused to give us anything," she said.

"This is a new account in another bank. It's OK. Al-Muhairi has promised Uncle Saeed that he can get a transfer made tomorrow, if he has the details by 10am."

He felt a ray of hope as he listened to himself. Maybe – just maybe – they could survive this. Poorer but still alive. Inshallah.

41

London

John Tully, the last COO, had his office up on the Executive Floor, next to the CEO. When deVries took over, he had persuaded Property to create a glass box – overnight - on the main trading floor, right between Debt and Equities. It meant that 400 hundred traders and sales people could see him picking his nose. He didn't care. His message to them was clear: "I'm watching you, you little bastards. Yes you."

Right now, his gaze was closer to home. David Trebbiano had just wound up his "Uzgalis for CIO" pitch. John Uzgalis sitting at the other end of the table, trying to look presidential. No diamond studs, no cowboy boots today.

deVries fished for an acid drop from a large glass bowl on his desk. For ten years, he had smoked in his office in defiance of the law, HR and the cleaners. Then one day he gave up, going cold turkey without patches or Nicorettes. But within a week the acid drops had appeared and now he was on twenty a day.

"So if I go with this," he said, looking sourly at Uzgalis, "will it solve our problems with the US regulators? Will it deliver Topeka?"

Uzgalis was a trading floor guy. Knowing Your Client was just paper bullshit that held up the first trade. Anti Money Laundering and checking payment instructions were likewise not in his DNA, and it showed.

"Listen, guys," said deVries, cutting his answer short. "I don't give a shit who runs technology. We need to keep the lights on and solve our problems with the Americans. Nothing else matters. Now scram. Not you, Christopher."

John and David exited, looking brave.

"There is a lot of noise about you, Christopher. EOS keeps falling over. Your new guy in Hong Kong is a disaster. That mad Frenchman – what's he called? – yeah, Philippe – wants me to get rid of you and hire some friend of his from SocGen. Cyrus is defending you, but even he wonders if you were over-promoted.

"But your biggest problem is me. You are not listening. You play detective when you think I am not looking. Listen to me, Christopher. Your job is Equity Technology. Audit says your Disaster Recovery plans are a disaster. You need to fix them. You need to fix EOS. If I don't see dramatic change, your employment here is going to be short."

There was a knock on the door. Tim Hawes was outside, and behind him stood two management consultants. One was the queen bee, rotund and unctuous, the other a worker bee carrying the Powerpoint deck.

DeVries beckoned them in.

"Good morning, Jerome," said the queen bee, "and congratulations on your new role. We think it's a good step for the bank. Not bad for us, too, I hope! Ha-ha! I like your new office."

DeVries introduced them.

"Christopher, this is Praveen Hirani, senior partner at KPC. Praveen, Christopher runs Equity technology."

Their professional smiles were warmer than ever, but the air was suddenly chilly. Management consultants were to the IT department as a mistress to the wife. One was young and sexy, the other burdened by age and family. They competed for favours from the same table and left their wine untouched until their rival had drunk freely and without ill effects.

*

"Olivia wants to have lunch with you," said Holly.

"What? No, I don't have time."

"She says it's important," said Holly heartlessly. "I've booked a table. 12:30 at that new fish restaurant by the Millennium Bridge. And Mackenna phoned. They've identified the man on the website, if that means something to you. And he's having a status update meeting at noon each day. He wants you there."

"Even today?"

"Every day. Saturdays and Sundays included. I've put it in your diary."

"Well, he can forget that. Get me the dial-in number."

"He doesn't do dial-ins. It's in meeting room fourteen on the exec floor."

Chris had never been to meeting room fourteen. From the black walnut and silk wallpaper, he guessed it was Sir Simon's private room.

There were four men in it, three of them sitting at the conference table. One was Mackenna. He introduced the other two as Henry and William. They were younger, his own age maybe. William was thin, with a sharp, beaky nose. His colleague Henry was bulky but carried the weight well.

Chris suspected he played rugby at weekends. They could be young bankers, except their ties let them down. More TieRack than Hermes.

The fourth man was a young, dark Arab in a suit. He was not physically present; he was on a big screen. Chris could see the sea behind him, dotted with yachts and a couple of big ships on the horizon that looked like oil tankers.

"Right," said Mackenna, "bring us up to date please, William."

William touched a key on his laptop and an image appeared on another screen. It was a passport shot of a young man, perhaps thirty. White shirt, no jacket, wearing a tie with the bank's logo on it.

"This is Saleem al-Muhairi. Joined the bank in 2001. Good education, wealthy family. Worked in the Dubai branch, by the airport. Commercial and corporate banking."

"That's what he looked like, until 24th November, 2007. On that morning his body was found on the fifth floor of the carpark of Dubai Banking Centre. It was hanging upside down. The fifth floor was under construction at the time. He kept his car on the second floor. The photos posted on the al-Hamidya website were taken in the carpark. Early on in the process, you might say. This photo was taken later at the Dubai City morgue."

The screen was suddenly filled with an image in bright technicolour.

"Chris, are you OK?"

"Not really," said Chris, trying to control his stomach.

"You can hardly tell he's human, can you? Just a squashy, bloody bag underneath a bigger bag. That's because he was beaten a thousand times with something soft and heavy, like a leather bag filled with sand. Not just his face, his upper body as well. Those white streaks are fragments of ribs sticking through the skin."

"Leather?" asked Chris.

"Traces of leather found embedded in his flesh. Very fine, good quality leather."

"Oh God," said Chris. "Who did it? Do we know?"

"Of course," replied William, "the police chief of Dubai City hates unsolved crimes. Al-Muhairi and his wife employed a Philippino maid and a gardener from Pakistan. His wife felt that her maid and the gardener were becoming too friendly. She appealed to her husband and he sacked both of them. In Dubai, no job means no visa. The gardener was about to be sent back to Pakistan when the police arrested him and charged him with murder."

"Was there any evidence?"

"Some. Forensics identified a rubber mallet from the tool shed as the murder weapon. No-one worried about the leather fragments. The gardener had no alibi. The wife testified that he often collected Al-Muhairi from work and knew the car park. He was found guilty and sentenced to death. Later reduced to twenty-five years. We are trying to track him down."

That was the update. Chris ran down to his lunch with Olivia. He was late, but he was first. He enjoyed watching Olivia arrive in a public place. The sudden attentiveness of the waiters and the covert glances of the other diners. The men envying him and the women wishing they had her looks and her figure.

Today she looked as beautiful as ever, but pale.

"So, Chris, how was your morning? Is Uzgalis your new boss?"

"Nope. There is no new boss. DeVries told us to get back to work. I need to fix our DR plans and make EOS work reliably. Meanwhile a maniac called Mackenna has drafted me into Internal Security. Ha! Talk about conflicting priorities."

Olivia studied the menu for several minutes, in silence. Then she said very quietly, still looking at the menu: "Tell me, Chris, am I a conflicting priority?"

Chris was taken aback.

"What? You? No. I mean, yes. It's hard to balance work and the rest of life. I know I'm not always great at it-"

"That's not what I'm talking about. You brought me chocolates on Monday night. Doesn't happen often. The last time was when you were in Tokyo for our anniversary."

"Well, yes. I mean, I was trying to say sorry-"

"My friend Mandy knows when Tim's been unfaithful because he turns up with chocolate truffles. Just makes you think."

She put down her menu as if she had decided what to order.

"What's happened to that American girl? You know... the one who left Hong Kong just before I arrived? The one you were having an affair with?"

"What? You mean... but that was years ago. Good grief, certainly not, I don't have time- Oh no, that's not what I meant-"

"Oh, you don't have time! You found time for her in those days, didn't you? You were working sixteen hours a day and still found time to get into her knickers. You even missed the Portia go-live party. The pair of you had a private party in her room at the Shangri-La. Everybody knew it, even the business."

"That's a lie. You weren't even there, so how would you know?"

"Dom told me. And you'd be surprised what I know. You haven't answered my question. Are you seeing her? Is she a 'competing priority'?"

"No, certainly not."

"Don't lie to me, Chris. Of course you are. She's working on Topeka with you, you must see her every day."

"No, not every day. And that's work, I'm not having an affair with Annie-"

"Oh, it's Annie, is it? How cosy. Annie Steffens? That's her name, isn't it? So what did you really do on Monday night, Chris? When you had finished kissing and cuddling with Annie at the Pepys? Huh? Did you stop off at the Ibis for a quick bonk on the way home?"

Chris stared at her, aghast. She stood up, holding her handbag in front of her like a shield. A respectful silence enveloped the nearby tables.

"How could you? Especially now, when we're trying to have a baby? No wonder you don't come home, you're shacked up with that cow. Well, don't bother, Chris, screw her all you like, you'll be sorry. Don't bother coming home."

She burst into tears and rushed down to the entrance, trailed by sympathetic waiters.

Scarlet with embarrassment, eyes down, Chris paid for the lime soda and went back hungry to the office. He called Olivia but got voicemail. He left her a long voicemail, apologising for his thoughtlessness but pleading not guilty to adultery.

Then he spent two hours revising frantically for the Topeka drains-up with deVries. It was impossible. He could hardly concentrate and his stomach hurt. Anyway, the project was incomprehensible. You couldn't see the wood for the trees.

At two o'clock, he joined his fellow Topeka victims. They were all nervous, but no deVries. And no Tim Hawes.

"Gawain, is this your meeting?" asked the Ops guy.

"No," said Gawain, "I assume Mr deVries is coming."

At that moment, Anne Steffens walked in, looking cool and calm. And attractive. Chris tried not to look at her.

"Sorry to keep you waiting, everyone. Jerome and Tim are delayed in another meeting. Gawain, why don't we start with the issues log?"

There were eleven pages of issues, fifty issues per page. They started on Page One, Line One.

They gave up four hours later. Neither deVries or Tim Hawes had appeared. They were all exhausted. Chris sat, trying to gather his thoughts while the rest filed out in silence.

"I've got to give Jerome an update. Meet you in the Pepys in half an hour?"

It was Annie, paused in the doorway.

It was only six o'clock but what the hell? His world was in flames.

*

The Pepys was packed. Chris bought the drinks and grabbed two bar stools. Annie took a long time to arrive, and drank most of her bourbon in two gulps.

"Whoa, slow down," said Chris. "Did deVries give you a hard time?"

"I've just been fired."

"Oh my God. What happened?"

"Have you met Praveen Hirani?"

"KPC senior partner. Slippery, talks a lot, doesn't say much? Yes, I met him this morning. In deVries' office."

"Jerome was so pissed off by that meeting that he called them back this afternoon. He gave them an ultimatum. Stop messing about, deliver Topeka by 25th February. Or no more business from us."

"And what happened?"

"They told us to get stuffed. According to Tim Hawes, they just don't think it can be done."

"Sounds like a short meeting."

"No, it lasted an hour. Jerome didn't believe them. He thought they just wanted more money. When he realized they meant it, he went bananas. He called security."

"He what?!"

"He called security. He said 'Show Mr Hirani and his bloodsucker friends to the front door. And make sure they never come back.' I saw them leaving. Hirani is a senior partner in KPC. He's a big swinging dick in his own world and he was not happy."

"Jesus. So what next?"

"So then I arrived, and he calmed down a bit. Finally he said, 'Ok, screw them, we'll do it ourselves.' And then he asked me how the Topeka meeting had gone."

"Oh dear."

"Oh dear indeed. I told him about our meeting. Not a single project on track. Five hundred open issues. That got him going. Who was late? Was it IT? It's everyone, I told him. Everyone's blaming everyone else, every time we figure something out, it throws up more questions. There are more gaps than there were two weeks ago."

"Bold."

"Stupid. He started screaming, literally. We are all incompetent, useless assholes. And worse. As I left, he told me to find another job. By tomorrow."

Annie drained her glass. Her hands were shaking slightly.

"I never wanted this fucking job anyway. I need a cigarette. I'm going outside. Keep my seat. And drink up, I need company."

She appeared later with two more glasses which looked darker than before.

"You'd better call your wife. Tell her you are providing emotional support to a colleague."

"I don't think that would work," replied Chris. "She thinks we're having an affair. She knows we had a drink here on Monday night, God knows how. I told her the truth. She didn't believe me."

"Oh dear," said Annie. "I'm so sorry."

Time passed. People came and went. He went to the bar and bought another round. Was it then? Or the next one? Words flowed between them, effortless. He started to feel happy. Annie's face was suddenly close to his.

"Kiss me, Chris, I need it. Please, kiss me like you used to."

But before he could reply, their lips met and they were lost in a soft, wonderful world where nothing was late and no one was to blame. A tiny voice wondered if there was anyone in the pub tonight who knew him. Probably. Oh well, too late now.

*

They were standing outside her flat in the Barbican, kissing again. Their arms were round each other. From time to time, they drew apart. He caressed her face in wonder, and she did the same.

Their caresses became more direct, insistent. She let him unbutton her blouse while he nibbled at her throat. His hands slipped inside her bra, caressing the soft, warm curves. He felt her nipples swelling under his fingers and her breath was hot and quick in his ear. It was all so new, and yet so familiar. Hardly believing what he was doing, Chris slipped one hand up her skirt, squeezing the silky softness between her thighs.

"Wait, wait," she whispered, "let me open the door."

She fumbled, cursing, for her keys. After an age, the heavy metal door opened into a new world. She pulled him in and shut the door. Her flat was warm and the air was delicately scented. In the lights from the gardens, Chris could see carpets, a sofa, cushions, and a table.

"Are we going to do this? What about-"

"Of course we are, darling," she said, pulling him down onto the carpet, "that's why we're here."

*

Was it his phone ringing? He couldn't remember where it was. He was lying on something hard.

He heard a soft voice next to him. After a while, he remembered. Annie. He was lying on the carpet. In the light from the gardens, he could see discarded clothes. Knickers. Her bra and skirt. His clothes. She was lying naked, turned away from him, talking on her phone.

"Yes, yes," she was saying, "OK, thank you, Jerome. Yes, OK, I will be there."

Silence. She turned to face him.

"I've got my job back. He wants me there at 7am. He's reorganising. What time is it? 2.20am? Heartless bastard, I'm sure that's illegal."

Together they got up and drank a pint or two of water, found the bathroom and then collapsed on her bed. At 6am she brought him a cup of tea and made him get up. At 7.20, horribly hung over and wearing a shirt he just bought from M&S on Moorgate, he walked into Reception. Kevin was on duty and pleased to see him. He found an old box of Nurofen in his office, took 4, and swore never to drink bourbon again. But part of him was happy. Very happy.

42

London

Thursday, 27th September 2012

Not for long. His hangover had the upper hand when Rosemary from HR stopped by, unannounced. She stood by Chris' window and looked out at the rush hour traffic creeping along in the rain.

"You know, Chris, on mornings like this, I hate the City. I wish I could live somewhere sunny, with normal people. How about you?"

It was something that he and Olivia had talked about.

"I'd move to California. I'd get a job coding with a startup – a company that made something cool. Something useful."

"Could you do that? Aren't you – um – specialized in financial markets?"

"No. When I graduated, I worked on missile recognition systems. Then I built games. If I could get a US work permit, I could get a job."

"You're lucky to have options, Chris. Most of us don't. Remember that."

And she left. Weird.

He was going to need another job. His stomach turned to water. He could hardly breathe. Was he imagining it? Shit, hadn't Annie said something about a reorganization?

Holly came in, looking strained.

"Chris, I've just had a call from deVries' office. He wants to see you urgently."

She added quietly, "He's got HR with him."

DeVries was standing in his office, and Rosemary was sitting at the table, her hands folded over the white envelope.

It was a short meeting. Holly looked worried when he got back. She knew, of course. She was in the upper echelon of personal assistants who knew everything and said nothing.

"Give me a minute," he said. His phone rang.

"Gawain? I'm busy."

"Um, Chris, I wanted to give you a heads-up. Nothing bad. I had a long chat with Jerome deVries last night."

Huh? What kind of meeting put Gawain and Jerome deVries in the same room? A club for social misfits? Trainspotters? Classic cars? His imagination failed him.

"It's nothing to do with work," said Gawain, firmly. "Jerome asked me about Topeka. I told him it was a train wreck. He asked what he should do. I told him, put someone in charge. Give them authority. We have to stop all the arguments over scope and who does what.

"Apparently he tried to get Praveen Hirani and his droids to take it on but Praveen had refused. I'm not surprised. Praveen thinks we're a disorganized rabble. So the project would fail and the bank would sue him."

"Gawain, cut to the chase, I'm really not having a good day here."

"Then he said, what about you? I said, yes, you had everything. The business knowledge, the technical knowledge, all the contacts. I said you were brilliant at getting people to work together."

"Thanks, Gawain. Did you wonder how I would run Topeka and do my day job?"

"Er, yes. He said he was going to think about that."

"Well, thanks for the heads-up but you're half an hour too late."

DeVries had been his usual frank self.

"You're a strange guy, Chris. A smart guy. But I never know what you're going to do next. On Saturday I find you in the office, playing detective. I tell you to stop. On Monday, you are still at it, asking Group Property for CCTV pictures of some broom cupboard. Unbelievable. So I decided, that's it, he goes."

He fanned himself with a small square of cardboard. Chris recognized it. It was the beer mat he had given Annie on Monday night. His recipe for fixing Topeka.

"But you have a fan club. People have been queuing up to tell me what a great delivery guy you are. People I respect. I don't see it, personally, but we are in a bloody great hole. So here's the deal."

DeVries helped himself to a pear drop and sniffed elaborately.

"You can take this envelope and go. Now, today. Or you can become my Topeka guy – 100%, 24/7. If you fail, you can fuck off. If you succeed, I will pay you double what you earned last year."

Rosemary intervened, anxious. All this was way, way off-piste for HR.

"Just to be clear, Chris, your existing role has gone. There will be a single head of Trading Technology who will look after Debt Markets and Equities."

"And who will that be?"

"Uzgalis," replied deVries. "John is going to run trading technology, combining debt and equities, while you run Topeka."

"But then who will replace Alexis van Buren?"

"David Trebbiano. I like him. There is maturity there. So, what do you want? Run Topeka for me, or take the envelope?"

"Can I think about it?"

"Why not? I need your answer by eleven o'clock."

*

His hangover crashed like a giant wave inside the shore of his head. Chris put his head in his hands to stop it falling off. It was almost half past ten.

He should talk to Olivia. He got Voicemail. He called her work number. She had gone to see a client. His deskphone was ringing. It was Annie.

"Chris, I know everything, OK? Listen, I read your beer mat. I showed it to Jerome. If anyone can do this, you can. I mean it."

"Annie, it's all so hard. He wants me to work for Tim Hawes."

"Be like us girls. Just say no."

"And then there's all the other departments: Operations, Risk... All the stupid arguments."

"He's desperate, Chris. He won't admit it, but he'll do anything. Remember that. OK, bye!"

He put the phone down slowly. He had lost his job. That thought emerged from his confusion of emotions and perched there, squawking like a flock of rooks, "You've lost your job, you've lost your job."

His Blackberry went *ping*! and a new text appeared.

Please don't leave Chris we make a great team love Holly.

At five to eleven, Chris left his office and walked upstairs. He did not look at Holly as he passed, or anyone else. His gaze was fixed ahead, in the middle distance.

The glass office was full of people but deVries saw him coming and the room was empty by the time he got there.

"So?"

"I will deliver Topeka. Provided that you make it possible."

"I am not bargaining with you. Do you want the job, yes or no?"

Chris said nothing and eventually deVries cracked.

"Well, what do you want? I have a limited appetite for debate."

"One. I decide who works on this project. No exceptions. They work for me. I hire them, I fire them."

"Wrong direction, Chris. Megalomania. This is not what I want to hear."

"Two, whatever budget you had promised Praveen, that is my budget. No bullshit, no committees."

"I see. Unlimited power and the keys to the treasury. Anything else? Let me guess. A title. You want to be President Peters?"

"I don't care about titles. No, just this. I work for you, not Tim Hawes. And you back me wholeheartedly, no matter what. Even if you don't understand it, even if you don't agree, you back me, until the day you decide it won't work."

Chris caught a glimpse of the white envelope, lying on deVries' desk. He could read his name on it. It was top of a big pile. Ten? Fifteen? DeVries was having a real purge.

DeVries finished chewing his pen.

"It is bullshit, but the barefaced cheek of your demands is oddly reassuring."

He scribbled on a yellow pad in front of him.

"You have a deal. You can have the money and the power. You work for me. But you work only on Topeka. If I catch you playing Sherlock Holmes or writing computer games, I will kill you. OK?"

"Yes."

"Angela! Set a meeting for tomorrow, Chris will present his action plan. Where the hell is Annie? I want that announcement out in ten minutes. And shred this envelope. Anything else?"

"Yes. Can I have my beer mat back?"

*

Waves of nausea swept over Chris as he crossed the trading floor. He made it to bathroom just in time and vomited into one of the toilets. The two traders at the urinals smiled sympathetically. While Chris was rinsing his mouth, one of them came over and held out a white crumpled packet covered in Japanese writing.

"Mate, take a couple of these. Fucking A."

"Huh?"

"Shugo Densetsu. Jap wonder pill. Take two. I've got millions. Can't start work without 'em. Superb."

Chris took the pills and headed up to the canteen. He drank a banana smoothie. Then he downed the Japanese pills with a bottle of water. Then he sat at a table for ten minutes until his stomach settled.

Ping! A text from Holly:

New CIO, Uzgalis and your new role now on intranet xx Holly

Jesus. DeVries was a decision machine.

It took him a while to get back to his office. At every corner, there was someone who had just seen the announcement and wanted to talk. Holly was waiting for him.

"Holly, first things first. Cancel my India trip, I'm going to work this weekend. Maybe most weekends. Start looking for another job. I may not be here long."

"Chris, my husband makes enough for both of us. I work here because I like it. I like you."

"Fine, but John Uzgalis likes you. And he's got a role for you."

"Chris, you don't think enough about politics. John Uzgalis thinks of little else. That's not me. Now, why don't we look at your diary?"

And that was it, his first recruit to his new life.

"Gawain was hoping for a word. Alexis used to be his boss. Given your new role, he's wondering if-"

"I get it, Holly. There must be a Topeka cost centre. Get it transferred to me, put all of us in it."

His little band had grown to three. In two minutes. He was on a roll.

"Next Wednesday," said Holly, "there's two hours reserved for the knockouts of the Bot wars. Are you going to that?"

"Oh my God, Holly, I can't. I tried to explain bots to deVries and he threatened me with sudden death if I ever mentioned them again. Which is a pity because Mustard has got some seriously cool attack logic."

"See, that's where you and John Uzgalis are different. As soon as deVries became COO, John had never heard of bots. Why don't you have Mustard adopted?" She saw the confusion on his face.

"Those Indian lads are dead keen. You told them winning the Bot Wars was a way to impress. You could donate Mustard to them. Then he can fight next Wednesday and you can stay out of trouble."

"Brilliant idea, Holly, make it so. Another thing. Get rid of that noon daily nonsense with Mackenna and his gang."

She tried. Forty minutes later, Sir Simon himself sent an email to deVries, copying Chris. It said simply:

Please make Christopher Peters available as required by Bruce Mackenna. SS.

"Well, off you go then," said Holly primly. "It's five to twelve now."

He found Mackenna with Henry and William in Meeting Room Fourteen. They both looked tired. The room smelt of pizza and stale coffee. There was no sign of the Yahoo! investigator on the wall.

"Quick reminder, gentlemen," said Mackenna. "five years ago, one of our bankers, al-Muhairi, was murdered in Dubai. The Dubai police told us he was killed by his gardener. But now we know differently."

"Someone hated al-Muhairi. We don't know who that was, or what he did. But it was so bad that a year later, the Imam Anwar al-Awlaki deemed his death an insufficient redress, and declared a death sentence on SBS, the whole bank. And one of his followers, a man calling himself Anwar al-Parsani, has dedicated himself to carrying it out."

"Who is Anwar al-Parsani? Presumably he is Persian i.e. Iranian. He has pictures of al-Muhairi that only his killers could have taken. Was he there when al-Muhairi was murdered? We don't know."

"What we do know is that he – or they, perhaps – are embedded inside this bank. Inside Global Markets, in fact. On June 15th, a Triple Witching day, he came within a few minutes of destroying Hamilton, our American datacentre. The next Triple Witching, just last week, we were attacked again, using a completely different idea. This man – or his representative – is creative, highly technical and extremely dangerous.

"Our Information Security team under Sheila Collins is investigating these attacks. That is not your job. Your job is to go back in time and find out why this is happening.

"Al-Muhairi was brutally murdered, I would say in anger. I guess this was revenge for something he did, someone he hurt. William, what have you learned?"

"Who had a reason to hate al-Muhairi?" said William. "Whey-hey, he was a banker! We've reviewed the deals that crossed his desk in 2007. We focused on the ones that he turned down. He approved ninety-eight deals that year but turned down hundreds. We've put sixteen into Marple so far."

"Marple?" asked Chris.

"Miss Marple, to be precise," replied Mackenna, "a computer system. A cross between a database and a detective. Marple finds links between events. Henry, how did you select the sixteen?"

"We ignored corporate loans. We focused on individuals wanting money. Plus anything with a political or religious angle. And anything Iranian. Or just ugly."

"Ugly?" said Mackenna.

"Well, like this one. Here's a lady who runs a jewellery business. She and her husband had a three million dollar loan, secured on the jewellery in stock. One day, the husband runs off with a younger woman, taking all their cash and the gems. So, no collateral. Naturally al-Muhairi calls in the loan. It's a criminal offence to go bankrupt in Dubai. You go to jail. Her emails are desperate, then threatening. It's heavy stuff. But no sign of a violent boyfriend."

"OK. Keep going. Henry, you've been looking for bad apples, yes?"

"Yes. I've been looking at the compliance records. Suspicious activity reports. Clients with OFAC violations."

"Remind us about OFAC."

"Office of Foreign Asset Control. A department of the US Treasury. Before we send any money anywhere, we check the recipient is not on the US Treasury bad boys list. If it is, it doesn't go."

"And?"

"There's some interesting stuff. There was a huge client clean up going back in 2007 as a result of a KYC audit. That's a Know Your Client audit. Some of al-Muhairi's clients had their accounts frozen by the KYC team in London. Here's one email from him; 'Twelve of the accounts you have suspended belong to expatriate Iranians. What have they done, apart from being Iranian?'" No reply to that one.

"Okay, so we have twelve pissed off Iranians without bank accounts," said Mackenna. "What happened to their money?"

"Dunno. Just got their names so far."

"Well, get on with it, lad. And put them into Marple."

*

Chris had a handover meeting with John Uzgalis late in the afternoon. John was studiously friendly. And why wouldn't he be? He wasn't the CIO but he had just doubled his empire. And his street value.

"You know what's weird, John? Last Saturday, after we met in my office, deVries wanders in and catches me on the phone, trying to figure out where the attack on the BMS came from. You know what he said? 'I see, it's true'. Why did he say that? Why was he here? He's never set foot on this floor before."

"Man, I have no idea," said Uzgalis, "that man has spies everywhere. Gotta go, lotta things to do."

Chris smiled but he could feel their friendship leaking away into the gutter, like blood from a nasty traffic accident.

He went home early. His head was improving but his mood was dipped lower with every station on the Northern Line. He weighed up the options twenty times and changed his mind twenty times. But he knew in his heart that he had to tell Olivia about Annie, about last night.

He was the first one home. Why? He got more and more nervous. When he finally heard her opening the door, he thought to himself, *in five minutes it will be over*. Of course, his marriage might be over too.

"Got your message," said Olivia cheerfully when she saw him, standing white-faced in the hall, "sorry I didn't get back to you, hell of a day. Let me guess. You didn't get the job."

"Yes but-"

"Well, look, working for John won't be so bad-"

"I won't be working for John. deVries put me on the List. My role had been made redundant. I'm the Topeka program manager."

She was horrified.

"Chris, he's just lining you up as the fall guy. When Topeka fails, you'll get the blame. And it will be much harder to get another job after that. People will say you failed twice."

"But suppose I was successful?"

"Didn't those KPC consultants decide it couldn't work? With all their resources? And an unlimited budget?"

"They did."

"So what are the chances that you can succeed where they can't?"

"About one in a million."

"Exactly. You're better off out of it. Look at Dom, he got a new job in a week."

"Dom has? What? Who with?"

"He's going to be head of Trading Technology at Mitturi Bank, working for Randy Gibbs. And he's going to earn twice what you paid him."

Well, that figured. Mitturi Bank had finally got fed up with John Taylor and project Carbon, the project to build the ultimate mega trading system. They fired one and cancelled the other. Which left them with a huge bill and all their old systems, now three years older. Gibbs had been hired from Credit Suisse to clean up the mess. He cost even more than Taylor. Taylor had gone to a hedge fund, taking his acolytes and – it was said – the Carbon source code with him.

Great. Maybe he should go and see Gibbs himself. Or Taylor.

Olivia came across and flung her arms around him.

"Chris, look, I'm really sorry about yesterday. About that dreadful scene in the restaurant. Please, please, will you forgive me? Someone sent me a picture and it just made me insanely jealous."

"A picture? What picture?"

"Of you and Miss Steffens in a bar together on Monday. I thought you were smooching but when I looked again, I think you were just saying good-bye. It was so silly of me."

She went into the kitchen, still chattering. Holly had called and he wasn't going to India after all so something good had come out of this... it was all so peaceful. He just couldn't do it.

Halfway through supper she said casually

"So where did you stay last night?"

"Oh, in a hotel." *Thump, thump* went his heart.

"Not the Ibis! That would have been funny..."

"Er, no. Not the Ibis." *Help me, help me.*

"Well, go on. Which hotel? I like to keep track of you."

His brain was frozen jelly.

"Er, a small one, near the office. I don't remember the name..."

His voice seemed to echo in the room. He could feel the colour rushing to his face. Olivia looked at him. Then she put her fork down and said, in her quiet voice:

"Never mind the name, Chris, where was it exactly?"

43

London

He couldn't sleep. There were no curtains in the spare room and the walls were lit by the neon of street lights. There was noise from the road as well. Cars, late night drunks. The hours passed slowly. He heard Olivia moving around in the bedroom. He heard a taxi pull up in the street outside.

Suddenly the door opened and Olivia was framed in the doorway, her face yellow-pale from the street lights, dark blue smudges under her eyes. She was dressed. Black leggings, sweater.

"Just listen to me, for once. Do you think this is all about that American bitch? It's not. I'm your wife. I'm not a pet. I don't sit by the front door pining while you're at work and yap when you come up the drive. I'm your wife and I want you to pay attention to me. Not her, not that fucking bank, not your computers. Me."

"Yes, I know, I know," said Chris, "and I know you want a baby, and so do I-"

"Yes I want a baby. Yes. I want a baby made from love. But you treat me like a cow that needs insemination. If you stick your dick in me enough times each month I'll be happy. That's what you think, isn't it?"

She suddenly stopped. She had tears in her eyes.

"It's not just her, or the hours you work. Or the endless boring phone calls in the middle of the night. It's everything, all the choices you make. If you love me, you will make different choices. Don't say anything. I've heard it all before. There is nothing you can say which will save our marriage. Just write this down on your fucking Blackberry. It is only what you do, that can make a difference. No more words. Only. What. You. Do. Otherwise it's over. As quickly as it started, it stops. Understand?

"I can't stay in this house with you. I'm going to stay with my sister and Brian. So you can do what you like, come home when you like. Just don't bring her here, promise me that."

She was gone, down the stairs. He heard a taxi driving off. He rehearsed his defence over and over. The things he wished he had said. And then he realised that all words were pointless. She was right. They were past excuses.

I've lost my job and my wife has left me. He felt like crying.

At 2am, he realised the futility of it all.

I must be strong. Jesus, deVries was expecting his Topeka plan in just a few hours. He found an old notebook and started sketching. He sketched over Olivia. She had gone, for now.

Objectives. Work streams. Organisation. Issues. New ideas came tumbling out of him as if they had been waiting their chance. He wrote short term plans and to-do lists, turning the pages backwards and forwards.

I must be strong. Failure won't get her back.

At 3am, he called Gawain. Then he got dressed and called a cab. On the way in, he felt strength returning. He was committed. There were no conflicting priorities. Gawain was waiting for him in the lobby, looking tired. They went upstairs together.

It was 4.14am. Two or three of his guys were sitting at their desks, silent as night owls, doing some overnight release of new software.

"Gawain, I've understood Topeka. It's not about IT. It's about getting large numbers of people pulling in the same direction, twenty-four hours a day. And I know how we can do that."

He pulled out his old notebook and started talking through it. Slowly, they both got excited. Gawain started drawing on the whiteboard and waving his arms around. Not like him at all.

"OK, let's split it up. I'll do the first three pages, you draft the milestones and risks."

They worked on. The office lights dimmed as the first light of dawn touched the dome of the cathedral. The office cleaners came and went.

At 8am, Chris went down to the trading floor. There was already a queue of people outside the COO's office. Tim Hawes was inside, talking to deVries with a deck in front of him. deVries looked bored. He saw Chris coming and waved him in. He sounded almost pleased to see him.

"Tim, explain your ideas to Chris. Let's see what he thinks."

What Tim Hawes wanted was to split Topeka into three pieces: one run by him, one – an IT stream – run by Chris and one by an unnamed hero from the front office. Chris felt the red mist rising. This was the road to fiddle and fudge, where no-one knew who did what and every department protected its own interests. These ideas were like zombies; you killed them and they came back overnight.

Hawes paused for a moment and Chris leapt in. JFDI.

"That's interesting, Tim, but we are going to be more radical."

He started talking, his thoughts clear from his sleepless meditations. DeVries stopped him, pointing at the queue outside.

"Guys, guys, I don't have time. Can you two get together? Come back with a joint proposal. By c.o.b. today."

"Of course, Jerome," said Hawes.

Chris said nothing. The other two turned and looked at him.

"No," said Chris, "I won't."

"It was not a request," said deVries coldly.

It was fight or die time.

"We had a deal, remember? I decide who works on Topeka. I hire them, I fire them. I don't have time to waste on politics and neither do you, actually."

The pause was longer this time but suddenly deVries laughed.

"Well, well, the cub has become a lion. Who would have thought it? You are right, *belofte maak skuld*, as we say in Afrikaans, we rocks keep our promises. We have a meeting later to hear your plan. So why are you here?"

"Because I don't want to wait until later," said Chris, passing his slim document across. "I need to use the weekend. I need you to light a fire under Property Services. I need a credit card with a lot of credit. I need to steal some smart people from the Commodities Strat Group. And I need two hours of your time on Monday."

DeVries looked down the list, eyebrows raised. Then he wrote 'approved J deV' on the front of the document and gave Chris his black Amex card and his PIN number.

"Tim, don't sulk," he said, turning to Hawes. "He's right, one guy in charge is better. If it doesn't work, we will get rid of him and you can have a go."

Chris left Gawain chasing Property Services around the world, while he went upstairs to talk to the head of Commodities Strat.

In the corner overlooking St Paul's and adjoining the Commodities trading desk, Jerry King and Ravi Narayan ruled over the oddball gang known as the Commodities Strat group. They came from diverse races and backgrounds: there were mathematicians and physicists, economists and computer science majors. There were college drop outs and a guy with a degree in Sanskrit. There were more Russians than Indians, and more

Indians than any other nationality. In theory, King and Narayan reported to John Uzgalis, but in practice they respected no one but their masters on the desk. They were paid better than anyone else in IT and they were an auditor's nightmare.

They were exactly what he needed to turbocharge Topeka.

As an Equities guy, Chris didn't know them well but even with air cover from deVries, this was a high-risk mission behind enemy lines. This was going to piss off John Uzgalis (hooray) and infuriate Sam Tassone and his Commodities traders (extremely dangerous).

"How did that go?" said Gawain nervously, when he got back.

"OK. Jerry King was there, Narayan was out. He didn't scream, you know Jerry. He just stroked his beard in a geeky way and said, 'He's going to raise it with the Business' but I expected that. How's Property Services?"

"Hong Kong was trying to go home for the weekend and New York were grumpy. But deVries' name is like a magic potion, now they're all hard at work."

At 9.30am, his phone rang. It was Mackenna.

"Upstairs, please. Now."

He found Mackenna with William and Henry in Meeting Room Fourteen. The man from *Yahoo!* was back on the wall.

"We've found something," said Henry. "Looks like al-Muhairi upset the drug barons."

"Start at the beginning, lad."

"OK. Well. Um, about midnight, we finished loading Miss Marple with all the dodgy events – that's a technical term – every suspicious deal, default, OFAC failure, etc. relating to al-Muhairi's clients in 2007. And then we ran the cross-checker. Boom! There was one company that just lit up the board."

"Saffron Trading. Also doing business as MSC, Mashad Spice Company. They've had an account with the bank since 1991. Two signatories: Saeed Hashemi and his brother Jafar. We know quite a bit about Saeed. Born in 1968, Iranian citizen. We have a home address in Dubai City and a shop in the Spice Souk in Dubai."

"So?" said Mackenna. "Why did they show up?"

"Loads of reasons. Remember al-Muhairi was upset because the KYC team in London retired the accounts of some Iranian clients? Well, Saffron Trading was one of them."

"What does 'retiring a client' entail?" asked Mackenna.

"It means that we write them a stuffy letter full of vaguely threatening allusions, like this: SBS has legal obligations in relation to prevention of terrorism and money laundering... blah blah... following a recent review of existing clients... it has been determined... with deep regret... you have 90 days to find another home for your money, after which we will freeze your account.

"On November 1st, al-Muhairi emailed a woman called Neeti in London: 'You have retired the account of one of my oldest customers, Saffron Trading. You told me they were PEPs because their father was a Iranian politician-'"

"PEPs?" asked Henry. He was younger and didn't seem to know as much about banking. But sharp. Chris guessed he was ex-Army, like Mackenna.

"Politically Exposed Persons. Politicians or other public figures get extra scrutiny during the Know Your Client process. And so do their relatives. Unless PEPs are ridiculously rich, we don't want to know them nowadays. His email goes on: 'This morning this client Jafar Hashemi came to see me. I explained about PEPs. He became extremely angry. He says that his father was the mayor of Mashed in the 1970s. That is thirty years ago!'

"And Neeti in London replies: 'The bank uses a risk based approach to assess Politically Exposed Persons (see attached FAQ 13). This approach balances seven factors including their domicile and nationality... and possible criminal associations. In the case of your client, several factors may have contributed.'

"Well, al-Muhairi doesn't like that at all. He replies, 'Can I tell my clients they were born in the wrong country?'

"Neeti was not amused. 'Under no circumstances may this document be shared with clients... the approved communication with clients is attached (FAQ16).

"That was on a Thursday. On the Friday, his brother Saeed appeared and tried to take $300,000 out in cash! Wow. He had some cock-and-bull story. Of course the bank said no.

"Al-Muhairi had taken a long weekend, and the young guy covering for him was a bit full of himself. On the basis of the attempt to withdraw so much cash, he filed a Suspicious Activity Report, and he told Compliance. By Monday, Compliance is wondering if Saffron Trading is a front for drug smuggling. It could be true. Spice merchants ship dried plants across borders. The Hashemis come from Mashed, which is close to the Afghan border-"

"I don't care if the Hashemis dealt in stolen babies," said Mackenna furiously. "Gents, stick to the question. Someone hated al-Muhairi so much they spent twelve hours killing him. Why? How did a jihadist like al-Awlaki get involved? Those are the questions."

"Sorry," said William. "Well, when the bank opened on Monday, Saeed turned up and personally pleaded with the tellers to give him cash. They said no. He said he wanted to buy gold and request a letter of credit. A phone call was set up for Tuesday, although al-Muhairi wasn't there. During that call, one of the Hashemi family – called Ahmed, apparently – got so angry that the young account manager put the phone down. The account was instantly frozen and marked for further investigation.

"Al-Muhairi got back from his long weekend and was shocked. He wanted to talk to the Hashemis, but Compliance wouldn't let him: 'to warn a client under investigation could expose the bank to legal and reputational risks.' So he didn't, although they keep emailing him, begging him to tell them what's going on.

"Reading the file, one gets a sense of increasing desperation. Saeed Hashemi has no idea that the bank thinks they are drug smugglers. They clearly need the money desperately and he floats all kinds of wacky ideas. But on the Thursday of that week, al-Muhairi sends them an email. The only way out, he says, is to open an account with another bank. Later that day, he sends a final email: 'Got your message about the new account. Excellent news! Send me account details and I will ensure money is transferred tomorrow.'"

"And?"

"That message went out late Thursday 8th November. After that, nothing. No more emails to them. No more banking. Al-Muhairi himself was murdered on Friday, 23rd November, just a fortnight later. We never heard from them again. The money never left us, it is still there, every cent, in their account."

"That's not right, is it?" said Mackenna. "Something went wrong. Did they not need the money after all? Did we refuse to give it? Keeping digging. We're on the right scent."

Chris returned to the present like a diver returning to the sunlight, leaving behind the ghostly outline of a wreck buried deep beneath the waves.

Except that the present was a sickening mixture of stress and guilt. *Olivia, Olivia, where are you? I'm sorry. Don't leave me. Don't leave me.* He called her. Voicemail. The sound of her recorded voice hurt like a dagger in his guts.

At one o'clock, he and Gawain went down to the Business Continuity site down in East London, taking Tom Hailey and some of his TIS technicians. The main hall was a vast, dark room, the size of a soccer pitch, with further rooms going off it. There were five hundred trading stations and another eight hundred desks for bankers, sales and the back office. Tom Hailey and his crew went into a planning huddle.

He was just leaving when Holly called.

"You had a message from a woman called Martha. Neil Jenkins wants to see you. She left a number. She said it's very urgent."

Chris called Martha. A pleasant Kiwi accent but she sounded stressed.

"You're his brother, aren't you? He wants to see you. Today. At his home."

"In Abbots Close?" Abbots Close outside Chelmsford, in the middle of Essex.

"He's not living at Abbots Close. He lives in the cottage at Scroggins Farm, Nuthatch End. It's about six miles from Chelmsford."

"What's wrong? Where's Sally? His wife?"

"I don't know. Please go, Mr Peters. He wouldn't ask without a good reason. I think he's worried about Harry, his little boy."

"What's happened to Harry?"

"Nothing. He's been with me all week. I mind Harry while Neil's at work. But I'm away this weekend. I'm taking Harry back this evening."

Google Maps knew about Scroggins Farm. A goodly chain of buses, trains and shoe leather would get him there in one hour and fourteen minutes. He took a train from Stratford to Chelmsford and a taxi from the station rank, arriving at half past two and beating Google by twenty-five minutes.

It was better to journey than to arrive. Scroggins Farm looked derelict. There was an ancient cow barn on one side, red brick. The doors were propped open and the roof had collapsed down the far end. On the other side, an empty hay barn. An ancient, rusting tractor sat in the mud. Metal wheels, no tyres. There was no sign of human occupation or anything habitable.

Chris picked his way across the yard. The driveway into the farmyard ran out the other side, through a gate tied open with baler twine. There were tyre marks in the mud leading out of it. On the far side, the drive became a track running through an old orchard. Among the trees, perhaps fifty yards away, was a decrepit caravan, resting on concrete slabs. A child's tricycle lay on its side by the front door. An old Audi was parked behind the caravan. Nothing else in sight. No houses, no cottages, no roofs without holes.

Chris walked over to the caravan and knocked. There was no sign of life. The door was unlocked. He tugged it open. The stench of cigarettes, mould and unwashed clothes was overpowering and he stopped, retching, and backed out into the fresh air.

This couldn't be it. It wasn't a cottage. And Neil couldn't be living here. Neil was a big earner. You had to be, to afford Abbots Close. Abbots Close was a little enclave of prosperous, detached houses, with upmarket 4x4s and BMWs in every driveway. He remembered Sally's pride in her bespoke kitchen and the spotless living room that was hardly used. Maybe this was a hoax.

He got out his phone to call the cab back.

The door trembled slightly. He froze, listening. Was that a noise? Something had moved inside the caravan. He opened the door and called out, steeling himself for a dog or an angry gipsy with a shotgun.

There was a sort of groan, definitely human. He climbed cautiously into the caravan and looked around. And saw Neil.

*

At one end of the caravan was the dining table, under a window. A long seat ran round three sides of the table. Neil was reclining on the far side, legs up on the seat. Dirty white T-shirt, scrawny bare legs.

"Izzat you, Chris?"

Chris took a step closer. Neil had a half bottle in one hand, and a cigarette in the other. The bottle looked empty.

"Yes. Can't you see me?"

"No. Can't see naught. Don't care. Just enjoying... it. S'last one."

"Last what?"

"S'last drink. S'last drink. Las' fag. Las' everything."

His hand dangled the bottle over the floor and let it slip. It landed with a sharp, tinkling sound.

"That's a good pile of bottles, Neil. For a man who doesn't drink."

"S'right. But that's the las' one."

"I've heard that before."

"S'true now. The devil's coming for me. It's over. I'm finished."

"What devil?"

"The devil you know, Chris."

Neil liked this sentence and repeated it several times.

"What's going on, Neil? Where's Sally?"

Neil thought about this question. Finally he said, chewing every syllable, "Number eleven, Abbots Close."

"Don't you mean number five, Neil?"

"I know what I mean! She's gone to number eleven. She's taken the money, and the cars. But, but, and this is really, really important, she lef' the boy behind."

He reached down with his right hand, scrabbling for another bottle on the floor. The first was empty, and he threw it violently across the room. And the next. The third hit the sink and shattered.

"Stop it, Neil, stop it! They're all empty. Stop, for God's sake."

Neil tried to lift himself upright.

"S'one left, I know I have. I got one more, somewhere."

He retrieved a plastic carrier bag on the floor, but it was empty. He fumbled around for another, found nothing, slumped back onto the seat. After a minute he started shouting.

"You fucked me, Chris, you and your friend wassisname. Ushgalis. Jes' trying to do a good job, you know? Jes' trying to do the right thing. Why? Why hate me?"

And then his anger collapsed into self-pity. Sobbing self-pity, fruitless searching for another drink. Chris had never seen Neil like this. He had no idea what to do.

Suddenly Neil stopped and lifted his head.

"Are you standing there? Come here. Don't be scared, little Christopher. Come here. I want to touch you."

Chris moved closer and Neil reached out and grasped his elbow. His grip was strong, digging into his bones and his bloodshot eyes seemed locked on Chris' face. The old Neil was suddenly back.

"Sorry are you? Don' be sorry for me. I don' need sorry. I need help."

"Help? How can I help you?"

"Look after Harry."

"What? Where is Harry?"

"Is safe. Is with wosshername. With Martha. You need a kid, Chris, Harry's gonna be your kid. You and Olivia. 'Cos I'm fucked and the witch don' want him."

Chris said nothing. Harry must be almost three by now. He hardly knew him. Would Olivia like her unfaithful husband to return with a toddler? Something told him, not a lot.

"Why can't he stay with Martha?"

"Good woman. She can't keep him. Going away. Far away, back Monday. But you can take him, you and Olivia, be all right with you."

"Neil, I don't know… this is not a good time. My life is falling apart. I don't think I can. Why can't Sally look after him, she's his mother?"

Neil's grip was painful.

"She won't. Number eleven hates kids. And she don' like him. Never wanted him, see? Now she's free again, she don' want him back. Five o'clock with Martha. Today. Please?"

The more Chris thought about it, the more impossible it was, and he said so.

Neil grabbed one ear and pulled him down so their faces were almost touching.

"I was happy until the day you arrived, Charlie Brown. I remember that day. You with your big head, tiny legs, red all over. You killed my mum. You arrived and my mum departed, both of you yelling. Fuckin' awful bargain that was."

Chris looked at him, trying not to gag with the sour smell of whisky and stale sweat.

"You're going crazy, Neil. I was six months old when our mother died."

"Ha! Six months? Six minutes, more like. Six minutes. White light, bloody water and metal things. Mum screaming and the doctor swearing. I saw it all, Charlie."

Neil studied his shocked face and seemed satisfied.

"Now you know. Now you can visit her grave. Snafell Hospital cemetery. Go on your birthday. It's written on the grave. The day she died."

Chris shook his head. He'd never known there was a grave. His father hadn't wanted him to see it. Obviously.

"And you blame me? All these years, you've blamed me for her death?"

It made sense. It made sense of everything, Neil's anger, his father's lies.

"You fucked up me life, Charlie, and you owe me."

"I can't bring her back, Neil."

"No, Neil, I can't," mocked his brother. "You can never bring her back. You can never take away Dad's pain, or mine. But you can do this one small, tiny thing for Harry. Or die in hell."

It was a strange moment. Chris felt as if the earth had stopped turning. The complex trade-offs that ruled his life disappeared. He felt his brother's anger and sadness washing through him. Suddenly, accepting Harry wasn't a choice, it was the only thing to do.

"Alright, Neil. I will. I will be here at five o'clock. But where are you going?"

"I'm going to hell. Can't take Harry to hell. Look after him, Chris."

There was a sudden noise outside, the low throbbing of an engine. Chris leapt to the window but there was nothing in sight. The noise was moving, going round the caravan. Suddenly there was a loud knocking on the front door.

"Devil's on time," said Neil.

Chris opened the door cautiously. Jerome deVries was standing on the step. Crumpled suit, tie. Behind him, his black limo, engine purring. Chris could see the pale face of George, his driver, inside.

"Peters? What are you doing here? Where is Neil Jenkins?"

DeVries looked past Chris, his gaze taking in the vagrant figure and the pile of bottles.

"Jesus, what a shit hole. Why are you here, Peters? Why aren't you at work?"

"He called me. He's my brother."

"He's half a brother," came Neil's voice. "One mum, two dads."

DeVries looked from one to the other of them, slowly.

"Well, that is a surprise. I would not have guessed."

"My dad was a miner from the valleys. He taught himself to read. His dad is a schoolmaster from Norway. There's the difference."

That was the Disney version, thought Chris. Neil's father was a restless spirit who had left the Welsh valleys and found a job as a clerk in a Newcastle colliery. When he lost it, he turned to drink and with it, beating his wife. When she left him, taking young Neil with her, there was only the drink. Which killed him eventually.

DeVries shrugged, returned to Plan A.

"Right, Neil, come with me. Can you walk?"

"Walk? Fuck, I can't see."

It took both of them and George to get Neil into the car.

"Chris, sit in the back with your brother. We will drop you at the station," said deVries. "If he throws up, stick his head out the window."

Five silent minutes later, the car drew up at the station.

"Where are you taking him?" asked Chris.

"To a place where they can help him."

"Why are you are doing this?"

DeVries pondered his answer, watching a train pulling into the station. Commuters started coming through the barriers, heading for the carpark.

"Look at that," he said in disgust. "These people must work half days. Why? You ask me why? Our industry likes energetic people, Christopher. People who run around a lot. People who talk well; most of them deliver nothing. Your brother is the opposite. He talks badly but he makes things happen. He is a strong man with strong faults. And he is strong in a crisis. Remember that American datacentre?"

"I heard that." This was Neil, suddenly awake and apparently functioning, "I won't live with that lie."

"Neil, it's fine, forget it," said Chris.

"Be quiet, bro. It's my fuckin' story. I think Jerome should hear it before he wastes his shekels on me."

He closed his eyes, going back in time.

"Thursday, June 14th. I was in the caravan. Moved in a week before, with Harry. That night, I put him to bed, then I had some phone calls. A resignation in Sydney. A stink bomb in the Hamilton datacentre. At midnight, I went to bed. My guys woke me at half past five.

"The Laurel hall was out of control already. The temperature going up like a fuckin' rocket. Until you've been through it, you don't know how scary it is. Thousands of machines, frying themselves in their own heat. I'd rather be in a 747 with engine failure, you've got longer to live. I had no idea what to do."

"I was on those calls. I felt hundreds of people waiting for me to save them. Waiting for me and my magic wand. But my head was this empty throbbing space. I heard people saying, 'Where's Neil Jenkins?' and other people saying, 'We don't know, he was on a minute ago.'

"I saw myself in the mirror. I was this naked, sweaty man, sitting on dirty sheets, holding my head in one hand and my Blackberry in the other. I started praying that it would all go away, that someone else would fix it. Then Harry woke up, crying. I put him back to bed. The place stank of fried fish. I thought I was going to be sick. I went over to the sink and it was full of dirty plates.

"I tried. I really did. I went outside and sat in the old Audi. It stank as well. I was still listening to the call, saying nought. Then someone said that the big hall was cooking as well. I threw up on the gravel. But after a couple of minutes I was glad. Because this was going to be really bad. CNN bad, Newsnight bad. So now I could have a drink. I hadn't had a drink, you see, not for three weeks, I was trying to beat it. I promised someone I would try. But I had a bottle stashed away for emergencies and this was an emergency. So I had a little drink and I felt great and I thought, I really must do something. But it was all too fucking complicated and soon the mainframe would go down and, well, that would be that. Finito. My Blackberry kept ringing. Everyone was still panicking, still trying to save the day."

"Then I had a call on my personal phone. It was Chris, my bossy little brother. He said, 'Tell your guys to buy hairdryers.' I thought that was hilarious, I really did. I told him to go fuck himself. Then I sat in the Audi, watching the sun come up and enjoying my bottle.

"And later, you called, Jerome. I hardly knew you. You thanked me for my help. I was that trolleyed, I could hardly speak. Somehow you guessed. You said, 'Neil, isn't it early to be celebrating?' When I realized that you knew, I knew everything was shit. I knew I was finished.

"So that's it. My little brother saved the bank that night. And I began drinking again."

DeVries looked dourly at Chris. "Is this true? And you chose not tell anyone?"

Chris nodded. "Are you taking Neil to a clinic?"

"Yes. A place in Surrey. They know about people like us."

"He's got no money, he told me."

"I'm paying. I have been sober for seventeen years. Once I was like your brother. Worse. And someone helped me. I owe him my life, but he died. Tonight I will repay him. And this evening, being a Friday, I will go to my AA meeting and I will share for your brother. There, does that satisfy your childish curiosity? Now get back to your job, I will see you on Monday."

Chris started to get out but Neil stopped him.

"Wait, wait, something... Christ... where is it?"

He dug through his pockets and came up with a dirty piece of paper, which he pressed into Chris' hands.

"Networks didn' understand your question. I did. It wasn't difficult."

Chris unwrapped the paper.

ldn_dev_1024

What was special about that? *ldn_dev_1024* was Tonto, the dev machine that he and his guys used to access the network.

"It's the answer to your question, get it?"

DeVries turned round in his seat, suspicious. "And Chris – for the last time – concentrate on your job, which is saving the bank from the US regulators. No Mackenna, no detective work, no meetings with Cyrus. Or I will kill you. Now shut the bloody door. George, let's go."

Chris stuffed Neil's mysterious scrap of paper in his pocket and closed the door. As the car moved off, Neil turned and looked at him, his face pressed against the window. His hands were clasped in front of him. Begging him to look after Harry.

It was almost three o'clock on Friday afternoon. He had a couple of hours before Martha delivered Harry to Scroggins Farm. He needed a plan for Harry. A discreet plan. OMG, what would deVries say if he knew about Harry?

He caught the next train into town. It was empty. He called Olivia at work, begging her not to put the phone down. She listened in stony silence, until she realised what he was asking.

"Don't be ridiculous. That child care centre is full, there's a three month waiting list."

"It's an emergency. Just for a few days, surely, they would-"

"Why doesn't Sally look after Harry? She's his mother."

"She doesn't want him."

"She had him. She can have him. Anyway, it's your problem, I'm staying with Brian and Sarah until tomorrow." Something strange in her voice?

"And then?"

"Dom's having a party tomorrow. I'm going." *Click.*

Oh God. No. No. No. Not her and Dom, please. His stomach hurt all the way to Manor Road.

There, he found Gawain and Tom and tried to concentrate.

"Cabs and hotels are done," said Gawain. "We've got twenty rooms reserved at the Holiday Inn round the corner. The screens are due tomorrow. Tom's guys are coming in to fit them."

It all seemed on track. Chris took the next train back to Chelmsford. On the train, he got a bad text from Olivia. The same taxi was waiting outside the station. He sat in the back, brooding over Olivia's text.

I had a good idea. u and Harry can live at Scrogginhall Farm. They have childcare in Essex. Then u can stay at work (or with Annie?) as long as u like. I will pack for you. O

So angry. Damn it. He didn't want to see Annie. He wanted her. Olivia, Olivia, my darling. Oh God, what a mess he had made.

They were passing a little village store. He went in and bought a couple of frozen pizzas and other emergency supplies.

The gloomy yard and buildings of Scroggins Farm matched his mood. The taxi dropped him in the farmyard. As he walked through the gateway, his subconscious noted the fat, perfect marks left by deVries' limo in the mud. Not quite perfect. They were criss-crossed in places by another track. A single track, much narrower, that wiggled.

A tiny alarm went off in his head. The single track vanished into the grass of the orchard, heading for the caravan. He went back and looked more carefully, starting in the farmyard. There was no doubt. Someone had visited the orchard this afternoon – and had left again. On a motorbike.

He entered the caravan cautiously but there was no sign of life or a visitor. The place stank but once upon a time, someone had cared for it. There was a cupboard under the sink with rubber gloves and cleaning stuff. Even some bleach. He started clearing the bottles and emptying the ashtrays. The local off-licence must have loved Neil.

Just gone six o'clock, an old white pickup arrived. Beside the driver, Chris could see the pale, round face of a child looking out. An energetic woman got out and shook his hand. She was thirty something, with long brown hair braided into a thick plait.

"Hi, I'm Martha. Having a spring clean? That's a good idea." She had a refreshing, no nonsense accent from somewhere down under.

She lifted Harry down. He stood, one hand clutching her blue jeans and sucking his thumb with the other. He looked first at Martha, then shyly at Chris.

"Harry, this is your uncle Chris. Do you remember him?"

No reply. The last time Chris had seen him, he was just crawling.

"He's a nice little chap, he doesn't talk much but he takes it all in. Are you looking after him this weekend?"

"Er, yes."

"Well, great. I hope Neil's OK. Here's a bag with Harry's toys."

Martha didn't seem in a hurry to leave and after a while Chris realized why. She hadn't been paid for a month. He emptied his wallet but it didn't quite cover it.

"Don't worry, Chris. I'm sure Neil will sort it out. I must go, we're driving up tonight. I'll be here on Monday morning, half past seven, yes?"

"Yes, fine. By the way, have you ever seen a motorcycle here?"

But she hadn't. He and Harry stood side by side, watching her drive away. Chris wished she wasn't going, and probably Harry did as well.

Chris went inside the caravan, and Harry followed. The light was fading. There was a portable gas lamp on the table and he managed to light it. He toasted a pizza under the grill that he shared with Harry. Then he started washing up the contents of the sink while Harry played with a Duplo tractor. The child had not yet said a word. When he looked round, Harry had disappeared. Chris found him in one of the bunk beds at the other end of the caravan, curled up, fast asleep.

The gas light was running low. He turned it off and lay on the sofa bench just as Neil had done and let his thoughts wander.

DeVries was a reformed alcoholic. He went to AA meetings every Friday evening. That's where he had been when Chris had called from New York. That's where he'd met Gawain, *who didn't drink*. Gawain was a recovering alcoholic as well. It all made sense.

But Neil's parting gift didn't make sense. A scrap of paper with the name of IT's tame computer, *lon_dev_1024*. "It's the answer to your question."

He hadn't asked Neil a question.

But Tom had. Tom had passed on his question to Neil. A computer with the IP address of 174.0.59.119 had shut down the cooling in Hamilton on June 15th. What was its real name? Neil had found the answer and the answer was... Tonto. He had an account on Tonto. So did Dom. So did half of front office IT. But he knew exactly what tools were needed to reprogram the BMS. He knew what to search for, inside Tonto.

His gaze drifted to his laptop, sitting on the floor. In the middle of an orchard in Essex. What the hell, deVries could never know.

He opened the laptop and logged on to Tonto. It was slow going with no broadband, just a 3G dongle. He had two hours of battery when he started. The laptop died, just as he was finishing. But no matter, he had seen enough. He lay on the long seat, under a dirty blanket, his brain sizzling with triumph. It was all true. He had found the secret buried inside Tonto.

He had found the bomb factory. He wished he knew more about the Islamic calendar. One thing was for sure. His quarry was familiar with the Stuxnet story.

Drowsily, he watched the shadow of the window frame flicker across the opposite wall. An old spider's web glistened for a moment in the light. Light? What light?! He was suddenly wide awake, his heart thumping. Oh my God, there was someone outside. With a torch. Chris twisted a little. Now he could see a hand holding the torch, and a face, pressed to the glass, looking through. He froze, shielding his eyes as the beam swept the room. It settled on him for a long moment, half-hidden as he was by the table. Then it went out. He could hear footsteps going round, towards the front door.

Phone? No time to phone. Weapon. He needed something to defend himself. Knife? He slid round the table and felt his way to the sink. He had washed up a kitchen knife and left it there, hadn't he? Too late. He heard the door handle squeak. The torch was switched on and the beam swept round, came back for a moment, blinding him.

"Who are you?" said a woman's voice. Chris lowered his hand from his face.

There was a gasp.

"Chris Peters? What are you doing here?"

"Who are you? Turn that thing off."

"I won't harm you, Chris, it's only me. Anita."

The torch pointed upwards. Chris saw the rounded features and dark hair of the IT recruiter from the pub. The friendly Lebanese who wanted to have lunch with him.

"What are you doing here?"

"I'm looking for Neil," she said, as if that was an explanation.

"Well, come in. Sit down. Oh my God, you gave me a fright."

He found another gas cylinder and got the light going again. His pulse was still racing.

Anita sat down cautiously at one end of the table. She was wearing jeans and a windcheater jacket, and black gloves with pads on the knuckles.

"You came on a bike?"

"My scooter."

"You were here this afternoon."

"Yes. How did you know? There was no one here, so I came back. Where's Neil? I've been so worried about him. Since Monday. He sent me a text. It didn't make much sense. But then he doesn't, you know? Not when…"

"Not when he's been drinking," said Chris, "I know."

"You're his brother, aren't you? He told me that. But I didn't expect to find you here… why are you here? What's happened? Tell me please. I've had such terrible thoughts. When I saw you lying on that couch, I thought I was looking at his body. Please tell me the truth. Is he alive?"

"Yes."

"Is he hurt?"

"No, no, he's fine."

"Oh, thank God for that. He's been so angry and unhappy… I was afraid. I didn't know, I was afraid he'd had an accident."

This was all a bit unexpected and Chris was wondering how much to tell her when another strange thing happened. Harry appeared from the other end of the caravan, snuffling and rubbing his eyes. He stopped in surprise when he saw the new visitor. After a moment, he rushed across and threw his arms around her legs.

"Neeta, Neeta."

"Gosh, well someone knows you," said Chris.

"Yes, Harry and I are old friends, aren't we, darling," said Anita, taking the child into her arms. "There, there, Harry, don't choke me, it's OK. So where is he, Chris? What's happened?"

"I don't know exactly, but I think he's in very good hands."

"Chris, please trust me. Oh God, how can I explain it to you?"

She stroked Harry's hair while she thought about it.

"I love Neil. I never knew what love was until now. I love him more than my own life. I would do anything to help him. Anything. Please tell me what's going on."

So he did.

Anita and Harry slept on the two bunks down the far end. Chris lay down on the dining couch and lay awake, lost in the confusion of his thoughts. He finally fell asleep as the sky was lightening in the east.

44

Scroggins Farm

Saturday, 29th September 2012

He woke up to find Harry and Anita standing by the sink, holding hands. They were looking through the cupboards.

"Morning." The pair turned and looked at him. Harry was looking anxious.

"Morning. I'm sorry we woke you. Harry was hungry."

"That's OK," said Chris, rolling slowly to his feet and stretching. He felt awful.

"They lived on crackers and cereal," said Anita, waving at the empty shelves. "It's not enough. But he wouldn't let me help."

"You've been here before?"

"Oh yes. During the summer, I came here several times. We used to go for walks across the fields. When he wasn't drinking."

Chris wasn't sure what to say. The secret life of his brother was a whole new world.

"What time is it?"

"Almost eight thirty."

Time to call Mackenna and tell him about the secret inside Tonto.

"Vroom, vroom," said Harry suddenly. After a moment, Chris could hear it too. He opened the door cautiously. A white van was coming through the gate, heading for the caravan. A large man in a black T-shirt got out, holding out a piece of paper.

"Excuse me, mate, do you know this place? No one's heard of it. Or this geezer."

Chris looked at the delivery note and got a shock.

"Well, you've arrived. Except it's Scroggins Farm, not Scrogginhall. And C. Peters, that's me."

"Oh, magic. I'll back the van up. It's two parcels, they're quite heavy."

Anita studied his face as Chris opened the suitcases and started taking out his clothes. Sponge bag. Some books. All tidily packed with no note.

"Oh dear, Chris, I'm sorry. We're two lost souls, aren't we? Or four, if you count Neil and Harry." She was pulling on her gloves. "I'm going to the shops. Harry needs food. Won't be long."

Chris decided that Mackenna could wait for his news about the bomb factory. After all, what would he do? Pass the information on Sheila Collins and her useless crew. He would take a look himself, a bit later.

When Anita got back with supplies, he found that he was hungry as well. He and Harry were halfway through their second bowl of cereal when Anita's phone bleeped.

"Excuse me, I have to call someone." She stepped outside and wandered off across the grass. Chris could hear her voice but not the words. It wasn't a language he knew but she seemed to be arguing and pleading in turn. He looked at the time. It was nine thirty already. He needed to get into Manor Rd, to see what was working, what needed a kick or more resources. And what needed escalation. It was Saturday morning, the first weekend of his new job. He mustn't lose momentum.

Anita came back inside, putting her phone away.

"Was that Arabic?"

"Yes. I was brought up in Beirut."

"Well, that's a happy coincidence," said Chris, wondering what drama had brought her to Britain. "Because I have a little mystery to do with Arabic dates."

"A mystery date? Intriguing," said Anita, while she tried to wipe cereal off Harry's chin and dungarees. "Why don't you try me?"

"Well, the year 1428… when's that? Is it in the past or the future?"

"That's not difficult. The Arab year right now is 1434, so 1428 was six Islamic years ago. Say five Western years because the Islamic year is a bit shorter."

"So around 2007?"

The year al-Muhairi died, thought Chris. "Ok, what about 29th of the 10th month?"

"Harry, stay still, darling – the 10th month? That's Shawwal. The month after Ramadan. What day did you say?"

"The 29th. Is there something special about 29th Shawwal, 1428? For example in Iran?"

Anita gave Harry's dungarees one final, despairing scrub. "Harry, I give up. Where are your animals? Mr Cow? Mrs Pig and the piglets? Come on, let's find them."

She and Harry disappeared and after a moment, there was the sound of the farmyard being emptied onto the floor, amid squeals of delight from Harry.

Anita reappeared. "29th Shawwal? What's this about, Chris? Something to do with Topeka?"

"No," said Chris, looking across at his laptop bag. "It's a mystery, nothing to do with Topeka. Not a small mystery, either, it's something quite amazing. I call it the bomb factory. But I'm not supposed to think about it."

"Oh, really? Well, what is this mystery?"

"It's a computer program. I found it last night, before my laptop ran out of juice."

"Where do Arabic dates come in? Is it written in Arabic?"

"No, it's written in English. Well, a computer language called PERL. But before it runs, it checks the date using the Islamic calendar. If today's date is either 29/10/1428 or 10/11/1428, it stops. Just halts."

"Hmm," said Anita. "What's the point of that?"

"No point. It's symbolic. But to people like me, it's a burning beacon. Have you heard of Stuxnet?"

Anita shook her head.

"Well, Stuxnet was a strange, strange thing. It was malware – a malicious computer program – that appeared all over the world in about 2009. Very sophisticated but odd."

"Like how?"

"For a start, the way it travelled. Most viruses and worms travel over the internet. They download themselves from dodgy websites or attach themselves to emails. But not Stuxnet. Stuxnet travelled by memory stick, presumably hidden in briefcases. As soon as the memory stick was plugged into a computer, it would infect it. Invisibly. And then it would spread to any other computer that shared a printer with that one."

"Creepy."

"Creepy is a good word for it. It was slow but it could creep around places where computers are kept off the Internet. Like high security atomic labs."

"Then what did it do? Steal secrets?"

"When it arrived in a new computer, it would check to see if this computer was being used to control a centrifuge. Not just any centrifuge. A particular kind used by the Iranians for enriching uranium. If it found one, it would send the centrifuge instructions to go at speeds it couldn't cope with – so it would blow up."

"Wouldn't someone notice if their centrifuge went bananas?"

"Nope. It also faked the speed readout so it looked normal to the operators. Amazing, eh?"

"Oh my God, that's so sinister. What happened?"

"It was released into the wild in 2009. In 2010, the international observers at Natanz – the Iranian nuclear lab that the Israelis attacked last week – noticed hundreds of centrifuges being taken out and dumped. Maybe Stuxnet blew them up."

"Ugh, that's horrible. So cold blooded. Who did that?"

"No one had ever admitted it, but there's a clue. Investigators who took it apart found this weird little statement. Before it attacked a computer, it checked to see if it had a certain mark in its registry. If it did, it would stop. Do nothing. The mark they used was a date. 1970-something, I forget. On that exact date, a Jewish businessman was executed by the Iranians. They accused him of spying, I think. It's a famous date in Israel. Maybe the mark is a memorial to him."

"The program I found last night – along with a load of other stuff – had the same idea. Check the date, if it's one of these two dates, do nothing."

"And otherwise, what would it do? Blow up the computer?"

"No. It would attack a datacentre by shutting down the cooling until the computers inside have fried themselves. Which takes about an hour."

"Chris, that's dreadful. Would it have worked?"

"It did work."

"Was that- was that what happened in June? There was a terrible disaster in America and Neil wouldn't talk about it but he was angry for weeks afterwards. That night was when he started drinking again."

"Yes, that's what happened in June."

"Do you know who's doing this, Chris?"

"I have some clues. There may be more in the files I found. I ran out of battery last night but I'll take another look when I get into work."

Harry came back with a handful of animals, and he and Anita started arranging them on the floor. It seemed to take a lot of thought and energy. Chris wondered how he was going to cope with being homeless and looking after Harry at the same time.

"Anita? Would you like to look after Harry? I mean, just for a day or two?"

She froze, Mr Giraffe in one hand. She didn't look up.

"Oh, Chris, don't ask that. It's too painful. I'd give anything to have Harry with me. Neil and Harry. But I can't, not right now. I live with someone and he hates children. He'd be so angry, I couldn't do it. It wouldn't work. I'm sorry, I can't help."

"Ok, don't worry. We'll stay here."

"Here? This is no place for a child. Or for you."

"I'll find somewhere. But not today."

"Oh goodness, is that the time?" said Anita, looking at her watch. "I've got to go, he'll be back soon."

Chris and Harry watched her scooter disappear up the road and then went sadly back inside. The place still stank of booze and stale cigarettes, and it was starting to rain. Chris called a reluctant taxi from the station and tried to do some cleaning before it arrived.

With Harry sitting beside him, he decided to take the car all the way to Manor Road. On the way, he called his backstabbing ex-friend, John Uzgalis.

"Just a friendly warning, John. Get out while you can, they're onto you."

"What? Listen, I'm in IKEA with two kids, and a wife with a credit card."

"The machine that attacked Hamilton was Tonto. Our dev machine, right? And the actual script is still there."

"Have you gone crazy, Chris? You've just lost one job."

"Neil Jenkins found it, mate." *A small lie resting on truthful foundations.* "And guess where that script was? In your home directory. Yes, yours, John. Sheila and her forensic team will be in there shortly. I guess they will want to talk to you."

He left John expostulating and called Mackenna.

"deVries says he will kill me if he catches me playing detective. So this is an anonymous tip-off."

"As you wish."

"I have found the bomb factory, including the script that almost destroyed the Hamilton datacentre."

Mackenna listened in silence, until he got to the bit about the dates in the BMS script and how the idea was copied from the Stuxnet worm.

"…which was the date the Iranians executed this Israeli businessman, sometime in the late seventies-"

"It was May 1979," said Mackenna, "and he was not an Israeli, he was an Iranian Jew called Habib Elghanian. His family had lived in Iran for generations. Where is this program?"

"Tonto. It's a Global Markets development server, a lot of us have accounts on it. Dom MacDonald had one, until last Thursday."

"Is there any evidence that points to him?"

"Er, no, not obviously. Actually, the files are in John Uzgalis' disk partition! Someone has a sense of humour."

"Uzgalis? The American with the cowboy boots? I will question him immediately."

"I've just talked to him. He was as surprised as I was."

"You did what?" Mackenna was not pleased. His irritation took several minutes to express.

"OK, OK," said Chris contritely. "By the way there are loads of other files there, I didn't get a chance to look at them properly."

That set Mackenna off afresh. In summary, the evidence was now the property of Information Security and Chris should keep his nose out of it unless he wanted it bitten off.

"Your friend MacDonald," said Mackenna, "what was his father's name?"

"Er. Diarmid, I think. Why?"

"An interesting coincidence," said Mackenna cryptically, and rang off.

Chris stared at his phone, frustrated. They were driving in on the A12, through the grim east end of London. Little Harry was bored with his animals and fretting. Chris tried being Mr Noah. By the time they arrived at Manor Road, he was exhausted. Did Olivia know how tiring it was being a parent, even for an afternoon?

The giant building on Manor Road – an old warehouse from the outside – was a hive of activity. There were TIS and property people running around inside, moving partitions, desks and screens. A lorry load of mattresses and sleeping bags had just arrived. Harry became an instant mascot and got a lot of attention. He played happily all afternoon.

Chris managed a hot shower for both of them. Bathing in the caravan did not appeal to him. There was a shower cubicle, fed by an ancient hose from a plastic water barrel standing outside. The water was freezing cold. He couldn't imagine Neil standing under it. Or Harry. What was he going to do with Harry?

About 3pm, his phone rang. It was Anita. Allelujah! She could look after Harry until Monday morning.

"My flatmate's going out. It's OK."

She turned up in a taxi to collect him.

"And where are you staying tonight?" she asked.

"The caravan. It's OK. It's dry. I've got my clothes there."

"It's a horrid dump in the middle of nowhere. I wish I had never set eyes on it."

With Harry gone, he worked on with Gawain and the TIS technicians. At seven, they went down the road for a curry, washed down with a pint of Cobra. The alcohol was relaxing. He had a second pint and felt almost cheerful. The TIS boys bought a pint for Gawain, but he refused it. So Chris drank that as well. Gawain looked on in silence, sipping his lime soda.

Now he was alone in the back of a taxi, a little drunk. Driving through the darkness towards Chelmsford. It was a crazy world. Every day was new on the trading floor, every day brought surprises, but this was different. His brother, the great Neil Jenkins, was living in a semi-derelict caravan in the middle of Essex. Pursued by a Lebanese siren with a lurid reputation. And yet, it seemed that she loved Neil, loved him to desperation, despite the alcohol and the fiery temper. The predator deVries, was a reformed alcoholic with a heart and a secret debt to pay.

And what about his own life? He'd lost his job and Olivia had thrown him out. Understandably. She was seeing a lot of Dom, he had to face that. Just how far had that gone? Surely she wasn't... she couldn't. The mere thought was like a dagger in his guts. Could she? Did Dom care about her or was he just getting his own back? Angry, bitter Dom. But what did Dom have to do with Islamic jihad and al-Muhairi?

It was after ten o'clock that the taxi dropped him in the farmyard. Lost in his own thoughts, Chris did not pay attention to the tyre marks at the gate, or he would have been better prepared.

The caravan stood dark and empty among the apple trees. The brake lights of the departing taxi reflected like twin red eyes from its windows. He was suddenly uneasy. Anita was right, this was a stupid idea. Tomorrow he would check into one of his Topeka hotel rooms.

At least he had bought a torch. The big bolt across the door of the caravan was unlatched. Hadn't he drawn it when he left? He cursed his absent-mindedness, as he did most days.

Inside, the sweet smell of whisky was back again, mocking his efforts to get rid of it. He stepped forward slowly, looking for the gaslight. There was a bottle on the dining table, where no bottle had been. A square bottle. Bushmills, half empty. Something was terribly wrong.

There was a faint footstep behind him. He twisted round, facing the darkness. With a bang the door closed.

"You took your fucking time."

Chris shone the torch at the door. A man was standing in front of it, staring out at him. He was wearing a tweed cap and a black scarf covered his mouth. He was holding something heavy and metallic in his left hand that gleamed in the torchlight.

"Dom. Oh my God! What are you doing here? What's that?"

Dom raised his left arm. He was holding a golf club. Too short for real play but with the slim shaft and heavy, asymmetric head of a driver.

"Come to settle up with you, we have. Me and Dad's club. Sit down. Over there. Put the torch down."

Chris staggered backwards and bumped into the table. He sat down heavily behind it. His heart was thumping inside his chest like a jackhammer.

"Thirty years of service, this was," said Dom, putting the club on the table and picking up the torch.

Chris tried to think of something to say. His tongue seemed welded with terror. Did Dom mean to kill him? Suddenly he remembered the kitchen knife. By the sink, just two steps away. He shifted in his seat, uncertain, wondering if he could make a dive for it.

"Sit still, or I'll beat your brains out."

Dom was sitting opposite to him.

"What do you want, Dom?" His voice sounded thin and fearful.

"Have a drink," said Dom, pushing the Bushmills over the table.

"No... I can't."

The blow came out of the darkness. It felt like a telegraph pole. Chris collapsed against the window, clutching his ear. He couldn't see for the stars and flashing lights, but he heard Dom's voice.

"Sit up. That was just a wee tap. Drink."

Slowly Chris took the bottle and took a swig. He retched.

"Slow and easy," said Dom. "More."

Dom kept pushing him. Threatening. Until the bottle was almost empty and his throat was burning. On top of the three pints, the world was spinning almost right away. Dom sat, watching, shining the torch in his face.

"Christopher, do you remember your stag night?"

"What? Yesh. You were... best man."

"Really? Best man. And what did I do, after dinner?"

"You made a speech. Very funny."

"Not all of it. One thing I told you never to forget."

"Dunno. Don't remember clearly. Too much drink."

The club exploded against his head. From the other side. Harder. Chris tasted warm blood. His teeth felt funny, there were hard bits in his mouth. Bits of broken teeth. It hurt like hell. And stung from the whisky.

"I said your bride was a lovely lady."

"Yes, I'm sure."

"So treat her right."

"OK. Whatever you say."

"Or I'll be after you... remember now?"

"Yes. Yes. I think so."

"And you all laughed. Big joke."

"Yes, I suppose so."

"It wasn't a joke, Chris. I've been watching you these past four years."

"Wha'?"

Another blow, more blood. More pain. Chris couldn't see, could hear Dom panting like a dog.

Some tiny piece of Chris' brain was trying to stay calm, think this through. Rosemary had warned him, why hadn't he listened? Keep him talking, keep him talking...

"Feeling sick," he sputtered. He got up very slowly and staggered to the sink. Dom didn't move, just sat, watching. Chris put both hands on the sink, feeling for the knife. Must be here somewhere. Somewhere. He felt all over. Nowhere. The knife was gone. Fuck, where was it?

"Looking for this?" said Dom behind him.

Chris turned. Dom pulled something out of his Barbour pocket and put it on the table. It was the kitchen knife.

"I've been waiting hours for you – think I'm that stupid?"

Dom tipped up the Bushmills bottle and drained it. He reached under the table, and produced a new one, glowing amber in the torchlight.

"Someone saw you at JFK, with an American girl. They didn't know who she was, but I knew, right away. I've been watching you ever since. Monday night in the Pepys, there you were, snogging away like teenagers."

"You told Olivia."

"I just sent her the picture. I'm glad I did. She told me about Tuesday night. Your dirty little night on the tiles that you tried to cover up. She cried on my shoulder, half the evening, the poor lass."

Chris felt the red mist rising.

"I bet you liked that, Dom. You've been after her for years, haven't you?"

"Fuck you."

"Fuck you. You're not my friend, not really, are you? Just want- to get in her knickers. Little bastard."

The telegraph pole exploded against his skull and the world went black.

Chris looked up. He was lying on the floor. Dom's face was dark above him, with white spittle on his lips, his eyes staring. The golf club was poised, ready to knock his head off.

"That's why you sacked me, is it? Trying to keep me away from her? What a mistake that was."

"You are wrong. I sacked you- to save your life. You'd be in jail now- I wish I had."

"What did you say?"

"You'd be in jail. Attacking Hamilton. Then Raleigh. You'd be in jail."

Dom lowered the club, slowly.

"Say that again."

"I know it's true, I've seen CCTV of you. Outside Raleigh. Hiding your face, but I knew the car. Mackenna told me, when he catches you, you're going to jail in America. Hunners- hundreds years. So I- put you on Rosebud. I lied, Dom, lied to everyone. To save you."

Dom sat down. Put the torch on the table.

"Are you mad? What the bejesus are you talking about?"

"You sneaked into Raleigh. At midnight. A month ago. Photographs of the fibre ducts. You did, you did."

Dom was silent for a long moment. His shoulders shook in the light, like he was crying.

"Oh, you stupid eejit! Of course I went to Raleigh one dark night. Taking pictures for John Uzgalis. Of Neil Jenkins' wall, the flood defences. John and I were having a beer and he started on about the mystery digger.

'Leave it to me,' I said and off I went. Bit of fun. Weren't you at the meeting? Didn't you see my photos?"

"Yes. I didn't look at them."

"Muppet."

Chris was silent, throbbing with shame, at his single-minded stupidity. It all made sense.

Dom gave a great sigh.

"Oh, Chris, why didn't you just ask me? Have another drink. I will kill you later."

*

The new bottle was half gone.

Dom stood up, swaying slightly and raised it towards the ceiling.

"Let's drink to my father. Stand up, show some respect. Here's to me Dad."

Chris stood up.

"Dadai, I'm thinking of you tonight. There's a black hole in my heart since you've gone. I think of you every hour, every minute. And here's Chris. Remember Chris, my old friend? He's here for you too, Da."

The room spun round him. Dom was handing him the bottle.

"Drink, eejit."

*

Time passed. The caravan was starting to spin horribly. Dom was talking.

"I loved you, Chris. I loved you like me own fockin' bro, I did. I shared everything wit you, all me secrets, 'cept for this one."

"Which one?"

"This one. Not a secret, just a sad truth. I have loved Olivia, Chris, I've loved her since the day … I dunno what day, some fuckin' day long ago with the sun in her hair. And her smile. And this is sad, very sad. Because she don' love me. She will play goff with me, she will sit and talk to me and I want her so badly and she will not- be mine. She is just kindness. I hate that, better if she was angry with me.

"Why? Because she loves *you*, you fucking robot. Why? The English deserve nothing and they have it all. Fuckers. But let me say this again in case you didn' hear it. I have done nothing. I have not harmed one hair on your computers... know what I mean? Hamilton, Triple fucking Day, nothing. And I swear this by Olivia whom I adore."

Had time stopped? No. It was jumping forward in jerks. The caravan was spinning, the table too. Chris staggered to the door and puked outside.

Back inside. Lights flashing. Dom's face spinning.
"Dom, I am an eejit. Forgive me, please, Dom."

45

Scroggins Farm

Sunday, 30th September 2012

It was light and the light hurt. Time passed. Chris slept. The light tried again. He got up and put his mouth under the tap and sucked cold water out of it. Dom was almost invisible, wrapped in a dirty blanket. Chris collapsed again. Noises later, the sound of an engine.

He woke. The sun was high. Almost ten o'clock, Sunday morning. The blanket was empty. Dom was gone. Later he took a taxi to Manor Road and took one of the Topeka rooms in the Holiday Inn Express. He had a hot shower, and then he collapsed onto the bed and lay like a dead man. Perhaps this was all a dream. Or an illusion constructed for him by some alien fantasy director. Perhaps he was himself an alien. This thought – and all the crazy thoughts that followed it – went round and round in his head, he couldn't get rid of them.

His Blackberry reminded him about Mackenna's noon-time meeting, and he got several calls. He slept through them all.

He woke just after four, still dead tired, and listened to his voicemails. Mackenna, terse, asking him where he was. Gawain, sounding anxious. Manor Road and the other locations would be ready for tomorrow. Thank God for Gawain. And Martha. She would be at the caravan 7.30am tomorrow, to pick up Harry. He called her back. Yes, she could pick up Harry from Anita's office instead. The caravan gave her the creeps anyway.

That was a load off his mind. Then he called Mackenna.

"There are seven days in the week, young man. Not five. You missed my meeting."

"I'm sorry, long story… listen, very important. Dom isn't our man. I was wrong. We should be looking for someone else."

"Why this change of heart?"

"He went to Raleigh. He took those photos. John Uzgalis asked him to. To get evidence that Neil Jenkins was secretly building a wall."

"Have you checked this story with Uzgalis?"

"Not yet."

"I see. Hardly conclusive. Perhaps the bomb factory will reveal more, when we find it." *Click.*

When we find it? What was he talking about? A baby could find the bomb factory, in Uzgalis' home directory on Tonto.

Chris went out to the Westfield Centre and felt like a Martian among the crowds of the young and the fashionable. He drifted round. Nothing to do, nothing to eat. Then he went on to Manor Road. It was almost deserted but it looked ready. He sat at a desk in the huge, empty space and logged on.

He should prepare for the Topeka kick-off tomorrow but he couldn't concentrate. He hadn't eaten all day. At six he went down the road, looking for a bite to eat. The girl holding his pasta and black Americano had to wake him up to serve them.

He called Olivia, out of desperation. Her phone rang, and then went to Voicemail. He called again, and this time got Voicemail right away. Bad sign.

Back in his hotel, he lay on the bed for a moment and was instantly unconscious. He woke at 2am. The room was hot and stuffy. His body had slept enough and his anxieties took over. He lay awake, brooding on his life and his failings.

He turned on his side. His head was throbbing. Through the pillow, he could hear his heart beating, "Shawwal, Shawwal." The month after Ramadan. He wondered why that word had stuck in his head.

It took him a long time to get back to sleep, despite his exhaustion.

46

London

The day kicked off with a dawn text from Mackenna: *Call me asap. Bruce.*

He scanned his life. It was Monday morning. Topeka kick-off. No time for Mackenna. This was a long, high-risk day. He stood under the shower, very hot, then cold. He still felt like shit. He dressed quickly and hurried to the train station.

On the DLR he browsed his emails.

There was an announcement on the intranet. Neil Jenkins was taking a leave of absence due to ill health. His interim successor was Tom Hailey, currently head of Networks and Market Data.

Good for Tom. Chris sent him a quick note.

Gawain was waiting for him in his office and they started going through the plan.

Just after 8.30am, his desk phone rang. The caller ID said "Sam Tassone."

Oh shit. The head of Commodities had a hard-core reputation. Chris answered, wincing.

"Peter, this is Sam Tassone. You know what I do?" Tassone's voice was loud in his ear.

"I run Commodities for this bank. That's what I do. Last year we made eight hundred million bucks, biggest business after equities and rates. This year, we're on track for a billion."

"Great."

"It used to be. But not right now. I get in from Asia and what do I find? My top tech guys have been pulled off their work by some asshole. This asshole has put them on an Equities project. So I go to Cyrus and he says, no way, Sam, I wouldn't take your guys without asking. And he gives me your name. I see you're an Equities tech guy but Cyrus knows nothing so what the fuck, eh? Where are my guys?"

"They're working on Topeka."

"Topeka? Topeka is a shitty little town in Kansas."

"Uh-uh. No doubt. I'm talking about the project to save our US banking licence."

"Oh ... yeah. So? Who said you could take my guys?"

"The COO, Jerome deVries. He said he would email you."

There was a pause. Chris could hear Tassone muttering to someone on the desk.

"This place is so fucked up. I can't believe it. Yeah. DeVries. The new COO. Asshole." Another pause, presumably Tassone had found something in his inbox. Then he was back on the line.

"OK, Peter, that's your name, right? OK, Chris, then. You ever ask your parents why they did that? Look, we're all in this together, OK, Chris? But there's a bunch of stuff that needs doing. I need Jeremy and Teresa, like now. And the rest of them back by the end of the week."

"End of the week? Er, Sam, let me talk to the project manager and get back to you, OK?"

Click. Tassone was gone.

"End of the week?" said Gawain. "Ha! End of next year, if he's lucky."

They had just started back on the plan when the door was flung open. It was Mackenna.

"Are you avoiding me?"

"I'm busy and I'm not supposed to talk to you."

"I don't cry wolf, lad. Next time I say call me, just do it. This will take two minutes. If your colleague will excuse us?"

Gawain made a hasty exit.

"Right, log onto your computer and show me this bomb factory. Show me this program that cooks datacentres. With the magic dates."

Huh? Chris sat down and logged on to Tonto. Three minutes later, he was sweating. Mackenna was staring at him, unblinking. It was unnerving.

"I don't understand it. It was here on Friday night."

"Well, we can't find it. Nor can your friend Uzgalis, although he confirms Dominic MacDonald's story about taking photos. He thinks that you have set him up."

"I'm telling you, I saw those files myself. They must have been deleted."

"Those files have been there for months," said Mackenna. "Why would they be deleted this weekend, eh? Well, after your foolish phone call to him, Mr Uzgalis told his whole management team about those files. Now they've gone. It makes you think, doesn't it?"

It might, except that Chris had no time to think. The rest of his day was advancing towards him like a tidal wave hitting the beach.

"I am having that drive restored from the weekend backup," said Mackenna. "I hope for your sake the missing files are there."

Chris didn't like the way Mackenna looked at him. It was almost nine o'clock. He and Gawain hurried downstairs to marshal the new recruits.

47

Down Manor Road

Monday, 1st October 2012

There was a puzzled but excited crowd in Reception. Their excitement grew as the first of the coaches drew up outside and the doors opened.

"Hello stranger."

It was Annie. She leaned forward and whispered, "Good luck today. Knock 'em dead."

He was so grateful, he could have hugged her but he was too stressed. A hundred, a thousand things could go wrong. This was an opening night without rehearsals. He was tired and under-prepared.

DeVries appeared beside him, looking bad tempered.

"I've spoken to Tim Hawes." What did that mean?

"Right, let's go. George is outside with the car," he went on. "Anne, you can come too. We're going to Manor Road, our Business Continuity site. About a mile south of the Raleigh datacentre."

"So," said deVries, as the limo cruised down London Wall, "Anne and I went through your plan yesterday. You want to abolish departments. You have reorganized the project into teams that work round the clock because they have people in every timezone, is that right? While London is sleeping, the team in Chennai is working on a solution and then New York tests it while Chennai gets some rest."

Chris nodded. deVries seemed lost in thought as the car passed Aldgate and headed east, down the Whitechapel Rd. Finally, he smiled. "I like it," he said, "there is only one thing missing."

"What's that?" said Annie.

"Fear," he said. "A little fear. Armies shoot deserters to encourage the others. Don't worry, Chris, I will help you with that."

*

"This is it? What a dump. No wonder the lease was cheap."

"It started life as a warehouse," said Annie. "Mind the puddles, some of them are quite deep."

The security guard in the lobby was struggling with his new popularity. There was a long line, waiting to sign the visitors' book.

"Pielkop! What are you doing?" said deVries to the guard, "there's a bloody turnstile to check their passes."

"Look, I'm just doing my job," said the guard, stung. "John Tully's orders."

"I am the new John Tully," said deVries, "and I say no signing in, OK?"

He marched through the turnstile. The rows of desks and screens stretched away into the gloom.

"Christopher, you did this in one weekend?"

"No," said Chris. "The desks and workstations were here already. We added signs and some furniture. Whiteboards. Meeting tables. A kitchen. The biggest challenge was those wall screens."

Each of the giant LCD screens along the walls showed other meeting rooms: New York, Chennai and Hong Kong. They were all busy as people arrived.

DeVries went over and stood in front of Hong Kong. "Can they see us?"

"We can, Jerome," came a voice from the screen, "and we can hear a sparrow fart in that room, so mind your manners."

It was Peter Elliott who ran Equities in Hong Kong. Hong Kong must be treating this as some kind of global love-in. Chris was happy for the support.

"Those are big screens," said deVries. "Does TIS have them in stock?"

"I bought them on Amazon. £23,000. Using your Amex card."

Even deVries looked shocked.

Chris looked at the sea of questioning faces turned towards him. There was no sign of Tim Hawes, but he could see a gaggle of his cronies exchanging snide smiles. The room listened to Chris' talk in respectful silence.

Someone put up a hand; it was Nigel, one of Tim Hawes' sidekicks.

"Chris, excuse me. Sounds like Technology has its act together. What about the business side? Tim Hawes told us he was going to run the Finance project for Topeka. Where does that fit in?"

"Is there something wrong with your ears, Nigel?" said deVries. "There is no Finance project. There are no departments. Look at the sign above your head. You are a cog in the New Client machine."

"But... Tim told us on Friday that this was just an IT project, that we-"

"As of two hours ago, Tim Hawes is no longer employed by this bank. Or any bank. He did not understand the new world. Let me be clear. Chris Peters is not in IT, you are not in Finance. But he is the boss. If he says jump, you ask, 'How high?' If he says shit, you drop your pants. And if he doesn't want you, you are unemployed like Tim."

He stepped down. Nigel, embarrassed, muttered something to his neighbour, who sniggered.

DeVries stepped back to the podium, his face darkening.

"What did you say, Nigel? Eh? The New Client team does not need you, after all. Go back to the office and see Rosemary. Now. Tell her you are on my Rosebud list. My personal list. You can leave the bank today."

There was a horrified silence among the crowd as Nigel, tight-lipped and scarlet with shame, walked to the door.

"Anyone else? No?"

DeVries glowered around the room, and then looked straight at Chris. His right eyelid flickered. If deVries had a nervous tic, he had not noticed it before.

48

London

It was dark outside. Where was he? In a crummy hotel near the Docklands.

His phone had woken him. It was that bastard Mackenna again.

Bomb factory recovered from tape at midnight. New forensics. Get here asap. Mackenna.

It was 5.34am. The DLR had just started. The carriages were freezing.

Ping! Another text from Mackenna.

Where are you? Get here now.

What the hell? He got in to the office about 7am, keeping his head down and hoping not to bump into deVries. Mackenna and crew were all in Meeting Room Fourteen. From the state of the place, they had been there all night. Even Mackenna looked pale.

"What took you so long? Listen to this. Henry?"

There was no mistaking the excitement in Henry's voice.

"There were two symbolic dates in the program that attacked Hamilton," said Henry. "One was 29th Shawwal, 1428, which is 9th November, 2007. And the other was a couple of weeks later, 21st November, which was just two days before al-Muhairi's death."

"Remember the picture of al-Muhairi hanging upside-down in the carpark, with some dates scrawled in Arabic on the concrete? We thought it was builders' scrawl. We were wrong. They are *the same* dates: 9th November and 21st November, 2007. Written upside down."

"It's obvious, isn't it? The builders didn't write that. Al-Muhairi's killers wrote those dates. They wrote them upside down for him to read while they beat him to a pulp."

"Those dates are memorials," said Mackenna. "Whatever happened on the 9th and 21st November 2007 is the key to what's happening today. That's a huge step forward."

Chris was excited but he was out of time. He turned to go.

"Whoa, whoa," said Mackenna. "Not so fast. There is more. William?"

"I've been in touch with our American Friends," said William, "who track frequent flyers in the Middle East. Jafar Hashemi travelled a lot. Most trips begin and end in Sana'a, Yemen. We think he moved there in 2000. On November 1st, 2007 he arrived in Sana'a from Dubai – and he disappeared. No more travel. Either he died, or he changed his identity, or he just stayed at home."

Perhaps he became al-Parsani, thought Chris.

"On November 19th, his wife Gurjit flew to Dubai from Sana'a, and after that, she disappears as well."

Mackenna was writing on a flipchart.

NOVEMBER 2007:

Thurs 1st Nov Jafar Hashemi arrives home in Sana'a, disappears
Friday 9th Nov this date written at al-Muhairi murder scene
Monday 19th Nov Gurjit Hashemi flies to Dubai from Sana'a
Wed 21st Nov this date written at al-Muhairi murder scene
Fri 23rd Nov al-Muhairi murdered in Dubai City

"So now, folks, I need answers to three questions: one, why didn't the Hashemis collect their money? two, what happened on the 9th November, 2012? three, what happened on 21st November, 2012?"

Chris looked at his watch and got up in a sudden panic.

"I've got to go, I have a Topeka status call in three minutes."

"Wait. Information Security needs help," said Mackenna. "There are hundreds of files in the Bomb Factory and Sheila's people are struggling. Get me some names of some hardcore technical people or I will brand 'Jason Crisp' on your chest with a soldering iron."

Chris gave Mackenna some names. "But remember, they all work for John Uzgalis now." He did not mention anyone from the Commodities Strat team which he had already requisitioned. Good project managers have a selfish gene.

Almost 8am. God, he needed a coffee. By the time he got downstairs, heading for Starbucks, there was a bitchy reply from Uzgalis, copying Cyrus and Tassone: *Sorry. Gave up my best people already. Try the Topeka program.*

Prick.

No time for a coffee, deVries was looking for him. Super urgent. He found the predator in his glass cubicle on the trading floor and in a good mood.

"Ah, Chris, come in. You are going to be a movie star. I need a five minute video of the Topeka war effort. Manor Road, the other centres. New York, especially New York. Huge resources, staff working round the clock. Corporate Events is bringing a film crew this afternoon."

The next shuttle to Manor Rd was in twenty-five minutes. He had a text from Holly. She must be in telepathic communication with deVries' PA.

That was quick. Now you are wanted in the Debt Markets board room. HURRY OR YOU WILL MISS IT!

xx Holly

What now?! The Debt Markets boardroom was a place of ill omen, like Golgotha or Shelob's lair. He opened the black walnut door cautiously.

The room was packed with cheerful, friendly faces. Holly was right by the door, holding an open laptop.

"You're just in time," she said. "Your creation has made it to the finals."

"Huh?"

"The finals of the Bot Wars. Baby Shiva is in the finals. Karthik told me he has Mustard in his genes."

Baby Shiva? Interesting. Had the boys from Chennai managed to combine Mustard's sneaky attack algorithms with the wily defences of Shiva the Destroyer? Surely there wasn't enough memory. His code was pretty tight. Combining Mustard's program with Shiva's was the digital equivalent of fitting a quart into a pint pot.

"Who's he up against?"

"TightSpreads."

"TightSpreads?!"

"A Debt Markets bot."

"Of course."

Baby Shiva had lost the fearsome teeth and eyes of his namesake parent. They took up memory. Hassan & Co must have thrown them out to make way for battlefield intelligence. The bot seemed to halt dangerously between moves, thinking. The first hits came from TightSpreads and there were cheers from Jerry King and a bunch of Commodities guys on the far side of the table.

Chris caught a glimpse of Hassan. He looked in agony as his brainchild was pounded, trapped in the corner. TightSpreads circled slowly, pouring in fire from close range.

And then there was a wave of cheering from the Equities side. Baby Shiva had leapt alongside TightSpreads and was emptying his arsenal into the other bot, point blank. Mustard's genes, thought Chris. His algorithm had guessed where the other bot would go next, and got it right. TightSpreads jumped two spaces forward and returned fire. Chris found himself pounding the table and cheering with the rest. The contest went on for two minutes until a burst of molten fragments announced the destruction of the loser.

"And the winner is..." came Holly's voice from the speakers in the ceiling. "The winner is Baby Shiva, from Equity Technology in Chennai. Sired by Shiva the Destroyer, out of Mustard, or the other way round, who knows?" She looked across to Chris and winked.

Chris went over to congratulate the Chennai grads. Hassan looked unhealthy. His face was pale with fatigue. The dark rings under his eyes could have been painted on. Chris recognized the symptoms. He felt a sudden fellowship with Hassan, as if the young Indian was the younger brother he had never had.

"You haven't slept, have you? How long did it take you to put Shiva and Mustard together?"

"Two nights. It was quite difficult."

Quite difficult. Ha. It was astonishing.

Chris had a sudden inspiration. Information Security needed deep techies to investigate the bomb factory. Hassan didn't know much about forensic work, but he was a real bits and bytes guy and damn smart. And he already worked for Sheila. She could re-assign him from project Vegas to forensic detection with a wave of her magic wand. He called Mackenna from the bus to Manor Road and made the suggestion.

The Corporate Events film crew was waiting for him.

"What is Topeka? How important is it? What do you mean, work will continue night and day?" He gave them ten minutes but what with retakes and adjustments to the sound and the lighting, they consumed a precious hour.

The afternoon flew by. He hardly had time to draw breath between calls and meetings. He had nothing to eat. He drank several cups of black coffee, something he only did during projects.

He found a precious minute to call Martha and check that Harry was OK. Then he sent a text to Olivia:

Please, can we talk? Love Chris

Time passed. He glanced at the screens. The American office was almost empty.

"They've gone home," said someone. He looked at the clock in surprise. It was 1am on Wednesday morning. 8pm in New York. Fair enough. No word from Olivia, not even a text. Nor from deVries. He staggered back to the hotel and crashed.

49

London

The schizophrenic imperatives of his masters were writ large in his inbox when he woke. There was a meeting planner from DeVries: *1.30pm at Manor Road. Review board presentation.* And a text from Mackenna: *There is news. Room 14 at 12 noon. No excuses.*

He worked at Manor Rd for the morning and then sneaked into the office and Meeting Room Fourteen.

Mackenna was pointing at his flipchart:

1.Why didn't the Hashemis collect their money?

2.What happened on Nov 9th?

3.What happened on Nov 21st?

"We have answers to questions one and three. Ugly answers. William?"

"I found someone who was a junior on al-Muhairi's account team back in 2007." said William. "I tracked him down in Sharjah."

"If you remember, al-Muhairi had told the Hashemis their account was frozen but they could get their money out if they opened an account with another bank. And in the end, they did. With the Bank Mellil, an Iranian bank. So Saeed Hashemi arrived at the Dubai branch on Friday morning with the details of his new account, which he passed over to al-Muhairi.

"Apparently al-Muhairi went white when he looked at it. He said absolutely nothing, just stared. Then he poured Saeed a cup of coffee. His hands were shaking so badly he spilt it all over the desk. Then he disappeared, leaving Saeed with our junior. They were both puzzled. The junior thinks he went to talk to the senior banker in the branch. Who was, by the way, one Diarmid MacDonald."

Chris raised an eyebrow and McTaggart nodded, then shrugged.

"Al-Muhairi was away twenty minutes. He came back in, holding a single sheet of paper that he passed over to Saeed. It was a press release from the US Department of the Treasury, dated October 25th, 2007. Just two weeks before. I have it here. The title reads: *Designation of Iranian*

Entities and Individuals for Proliferation Activities and Support for Terrorism.

"Saeed read it and looked puzzled. Al-Muhairi pointed to an innocent little sentence towards the end: *Today's designations also notify the international private sector of the dangers of doing business with three of Iran's largest banks.*

"'See that? We can't do it,' he told Saeed, 'we can't transfer your money to this account. Or to any account with an Iranian bank.' I don't think Saeed believed him at first. He objected, saying that SBS was not an American bank. Makes no difference, said al-Muhairi, we have an American branch. After ten minutes of disbelief, Saeed went absolutely apeshit. He started screaming, 'You must, you must, give me the money,' over and over. Then he went down on his knees and started begging, and weeping, "Oh my brother, Jafar, Jafar …"

"You can't have people screaming in banks. al-Muhairi was embarrassed. He called Security and they hustled Saeed out. Then al-Muhairi said he was ill and he went home. The next day when he came in, Saeed was stretched out on the front steps, begging. Al-Muhairi stepped over him. After that he used the entrance from the carpark. Until Saeed stopped coming. That's it."

"So there's the answer to Question One," said Mackenna, "why didn't the Hashemis collect their money? They were Iranians. Their account was frozen by the US Treasury. Al-Muhairi couldn't unfreeze it."

"Let's move on to Question Three, what happened on November 21st? Henry unearthed this video in the Dubai police archives, filmed by a passing American tourist called Schuster. It happens in front of the SBS building. It's not pretty."

"Fast forward to here… the woman stops at the top of the steps, in front of the bank. She puts down the cans. Then she rubs something on her hands and puts them against the wall. You can see the dark marks on it, there. Like handprints. That figures, it's an old Rajastan tradition, preceding *this*..."

The four of them watched in silence as the woman in the sari doused herself in fuel and frightened away the bank's guards with her cigarette lighter.

"Oh dear God, no," said someone. Perhaps it was Chris himself.

"According to the police report, one of the cans had diesel, and the other petrol. The mixture was like a bomb going off. It set fire to one of the guards as well."

"That's enough," said Mackenna. "Stop there."

Chris could not turn away from the tiny figure frozen on the screen. She looked as though she was dancing, her long hair flowing upwards in the flames, every part of her on fire.

"Who is she?" he asked.

"The police don't know," said Mackenna. "She was burned to a crisp. No fingerprints, no ID. The picture from the mortuary is headed 'Jane Doe - 21/11/07.' But I have no doubt that this is Gurjit Hashemi, the wife of Jafar, who had flown into Dubai just two days before, from Sana'a."

He coughed. "She was a Hindu widow. She burned herself to death on her husband's funeral pyre, or as close as she could get to it. It is called suttee, a powerful tradition."

"So to our second question, what happened on November 9th?" Mackenna drew an imaginary razor across his throat, "I think we can guess, no? No ransom money, no Jafar. I wonder how he died?"

*

1pm. Chris was trying to shake the melancholy which had gripped him since this morning. He decided to grab a sandwich on his way to Manor Road. Tom Hailey, newly promoted head of TIS, and Jane Atwell were coming out of the canteen. Chris congratulated him.

"I dunno, Chris, maybe I'm too nice. Neil did nasty so well."

Well, that was true.

"And Jane, I never thanked you for finding those laptops. Well done."

"It was a fluke," she said, "we only found them because someone complained about the smell."

"The laptops smelled?"

"No. The laptops were hidden under some old sheets and they smelled. Like they'd just come out of Granny's attic. Horrid. But lucky for us, eh?"

Chris hurried up to the little comms room. The lock was still broken. He sniffed, carefully. Yes, there was a faint smell, not unpleasant exactly but with a hint of something rotten underneath. It reminded him of mothballs and old churches.

He felt a tiny bell tinkling in his subconscious. Why? Something he had heard recently. Something about a smell. The smell in the caravan? Yes, but not that... something else. He stood by the broken door and tried to remember. He was suddenly back in deVries' limo, listening to Neil's confession. Neil had got home early, the night that Hamilton was attacked. He'd had some phone calls, things to deal with. A resignation in Asia. *A stink bomb in Hamilton*. That was it. Weird. A stink bomb in a datacentre? What on earth was that about?

Who would know? Paul Carpenter had sacked most of them, but he still had Mannie's number.

Mannie answered on the first ring.

"How are you, Mannie?"

"I'm okay, Chris, thanks. Some good, some bad. You remember Luis? I got some work through him. Still waiting for the big job though. When you make CIO."

"It's a ways off, Mannie, but you'd be first on my list."

"I look forward to it. So, what can I do for you, sir?"

"More history. BaByliss night. I heard there was a stink bomb. Is that right? In the datacentre?"

"Not that night. The day before. Chocolates."

"Chocolates?"

"Yeah. The guys love chocolates. People send them back from vacations, you know? This one arrived in a fancy gold box. Pete opened it, and this stuff leaked all over the table. He got it on his hands. It stuck like dogshit, you couldn't get it off."

"What was it? Any idea?"

"What it was? Chris, you're talking to a Jew. It was camphor. Maybe a little myrrh mixed in."

"Camphor? What's that used for?"

"Mothballs. And my grandmother used to drink it when she had a cold. Not so common nowadays."

It was seven minutes past one. He called Holly.

"Chris, are you on your way to Manor Road? Jerome's expecting you to brief him. There's a board meeting at three."

"Holly, find me a shop that sells camphor. Somewhere round here. Quick."

"But... Jerome?"

"Send Gawain. Anyway, I can still make it. Find me a shop."

He was quick. He was really quick and ran all the way back to the office from Healthy Essence. It was 1.26pm. He ran down to Jane Atwell's lair in the basement, and carefully opened the plastic bag.

"Jane? Smell this. Remind you of anything?"

"Yuck. Revolting, truly pukeworthy. That was the smell in the Comms Room."

"Sure?"

"Of course I'm sure, I spent two hours in that room, dismantling the kit you and your cowboys had stashed there."

Bingo. Two attacks. One attacker.

His phone was ringing. DeVries was getting impatient.

*

Chris charged into Meeting Room Fourteen, clutching his ziplock bag.

"What are you doing here?" said Mackenna, "your boss is on the warpath."

"I'm not here, I'm in a taxi going to Manor Road. Stuck in a jam. Smell this."

Mackenna smelt the smell and listened to the story.

"I've looked up camphor," said Chris, "it's used in all kinds of medicine, like Vicks inhalers. And mothballs. The site of each attack is doused in camphor. It's not a warning, it's late for that. So what is it?"

"It's a symbol," said Mackenna, "he's into symbols. Like the dates in the script. There's some secret here we don't yet know. Camphor is used in Muslim funerals. For perfuming the body. And the funeral shrouds. Now get lost before deVries calls again and makes me a liar."

He found deVries in a meeting room in Manor Road. He was not happy.

"Where the hell have you been? Farting around on some private mission again?"

Mutely, Chris held out the board paper. DeVries threw it across the room.

"I've already been through it, you pielkop. I went through it with Gawain. I like Gawain. He doesn't have your talents but he's reliable. Now there's a thought …"

Chris beat a hasty retreat and went off to find Gawain.

Gawain needed to talk to him about some urgent technical issue. Chris sat down and tried to take it in.

"Chris? Are you listening to me?"

"I'm sorry, Gawain, I can't concentrate. Can't think. Just got a lot on my mind. I gotta go. Keep going, buddy."

50

Manor Road

Thursday, 4th October 2012

The next day, Thursday, the wheels fell off Topeka. Or perhaps it was just the optimism wearing off. Chris arrived at Manor Road early and ran around all day, pushing and pulling, cajoling, demanding.

There was a crop of new mistakes, and old mistakes were coming home to roost. The Americans were getting nowhere on a load of detail they needed from the US regulators. The project plan said this milestone had been nailed two months ago. So now Topeka was going backwards.

Some well-meaning dba had screwed up the test environments overnight. The workflow system was running slow and the vendor was blaming network latency. Which was like blaming the weather, or sunspots.

Around noon, he got a strange call from deVries' PA.

"Jerome wants you in Sir Simon's office at 4pm today. He's sending George to pick you up."

What? If she knew, she wasn't telling.

Sir Simon was in his office, along with deVries and a couple of legal people he didn't really know.

Sir Simon sipped his coffee while he stared suspiciously at Chris.

"Chris Peters? I've heard of you. Can't think where."

"Christopher," said deVries smoothly, "is part of the story we want to tell today. We have taken one of our most talented technologists out of his day job and put him 100% on regulatory remediation. Along with 200 others, who are working day and night to prepare for the US audit."

"Great," said Sir Simon without enthusiasm. "Let's get Chuck on the line."

Chuck Forbes was a tall American who ran SBS in the US. He was New England aristocracy; his parents went to Senator Kennedy's cocktail parties. He had inherited an amazing Rolodex and he had been adding to it since kindergarten.

"Well, Simon, you sure got their attention," said Forbes when he came on screen, "Tomanski's joining from NY Comptroller's Office, Jack Stein from Treasury, we've got Helen Margolis from OFAC..."

He reeled off a long list of names with the easy grace of a banker in his prime.

"Chet Mayhew's the one to watch, the rest of them are along for the ride. As long as they get their share, they'll be happy."

"They're here!" warned one of the lawyers, and they were. A long meeting room appeared on the main screen, filled with men in dark suits and ties, and two women. Chris could see the distinctive piers of Brooklyn Bridge in the distance.

It was not a meeting that Chris understood. There was no agenda. Chuck Forbes made the introductions. There was a lot of discussion about the Letter of the 9th and the Reply of the 12th and the Schedule. Someone hadn't received the Schedule but then they had. Sir Simon said nothing, leaving Forbes to bat. Chris could see Jerome beside him getting twitchy. But eventually the conversation turned to Remediation and Jerome offered an update. The video clip was played, featuring Manor Road and the New York office.

Then Chris was asked to talk about Topeka and the key dates.

Most of his audience thought this was a good time to visit the bathroom, refill their coffee or check their emails. Except for one older guy at the end of the table. Silver hair, tie half done, sleeves rolled up. He watched the video and then Chris' update with the same savage intensity.

Chet Mayhew, wrote Chuck Forbes on a piece of paper.

Mayhew said nothing until the end of the meeting. But when he did, his voice fell like a hammer on a pile of china plates.

"That was a great movie, gentlemen. Maybe young Christopher can build a time machine while he's at it. Because we have emails from 2007 in which your head of Treasury Operations discusses ways to make payments to proscribed parties by overwriting SWIFT payment messages. We have the advice from your own US counsel that these actions were illegal. Your IT department has sent us a file containing 104,000 payment messages totalling $41 billion US, which had been amended. Many of these payments may have facilitated illegal sales of oil, arms dealing, narcotics, money laundering and financing of terrorism."

"Don't be ridiculous," exploded Sir Simon, "we don't deal with terrorists. These are just businesses paying other businesses, who happen to be Iranian and who are you to dictate-"

DeVries and Forbes were making urgent hand signals and Sir Simon stopped in mid-flow, his pale Gaelic features glowing with anger.

There was an edge in his opponent's voice, as well: "You can do what you like with your roubles, Sir Simon, or euros. But when you settle dollars, you do so through your US branch. Which is regulated by New York State and by the Federal agencies round this table. We are considering whether these activities are criminal offences under US law. Perhaps we could discuss these issues on your next visit to the States?"

Sir Simon was visibly shaken but said nothing. Any plans he had for visiting the US had just been cancelled. Chuck Forbes wound up the meeting and restored the thin veneer of politeness over the cracks of mutual contempt.

Sir Simon left the room with a curt nod. Jerome deVries stayed on. So did Chuck Forbes on the other side of the Atlantic. They seemed to know each other.

"That's the last nail, Jerome, right there."

"They've already stuck us $150m for that shit," said deVries.

"Yeah, that was last year. Before Sir Simon upset them by arguing. Now we're gonna get a thousand lashes. In public."

"But," said Chris, "if we can pass the audit, surely-"

"Chris," said Forbes, not unkindly, "you're a good guy and I'm glad you're on the case. But they decided the fine already. They're just arguing over who gets it. Latest I heard, the Californians want a rib or two and that's pissed off the boys from Chicago."

"But the audit? I mean, it can't be that arbitrary."

"Listen, you heard Mayhew, right? The guy who pissed off Sir Simon. Well, the fellow on his right, who was taking notes? That's Joel Feinberg. Senior KPC partner. He's this close with Mayhew and his boys are going to do the audit. Do you think he's gonna bite the hand that feeds?"

"But they won't lie, surely? Can't we convince them?"

"There's no judge, Chris. There is no appeal. This is a straight stick 'em up. The shareholders of this bank are about to lose six billion dollars to a bunch of guys with guns and yellow bandanas on horseback. Half of whom work for the US Treasury."

"Six billion? What?! Where does that go?"

"They divide it between them. Chet Mayhew, for example, he has no budget allocation, he has to kill to eat. When he and the other agencies have all had their fill, the US taxpayer will pay less taxes. Especially residents of New York."

"That's outrageous."

"Welcome to the twenty-first century. Who needs the H bomb? We've got the drones and the US dollar clearing system. I got to go, Jerry. Chris, nice to meet you."

Forbes picked up a remote control and pointed it at the screen, like a weapon.

"Cheer up, Christopher. We're still nicer than the Russkies."

*

Chris went back to Manor Road. Gawain was waiting for him. There was a long list of issues needing escalation and attention.

"Hey, Chris, is something wrong?" asked Gawain after an hour of listless discussion.

Chris gave his best, cheerful smile.

They plodded on through the list. Chris couldn't get Chuck Forbes' words out of his head. *They decided the fine already … they're arguing over who gets it.*

Soon after ten, he went back to Days Inn and crashed. I am a failure, he thought as he lay awake in the stuffy box of his hotel room. What's it all for? I've failed in every department. Even the thing I can do turns out to be a lie.

You're depressed, said an inner voice.

No, I'm just tired. I have no energy.

That's depression, said the inner voice.

Friday was another packed day at Manor Road, full of meetings and conference calls and difficult decisions that rolled in endlessly, like waves on a beach.

But when he looked back later, Chris could only remember two things.

The first was his outburst to Gawain. It was time for a Topeka status call and Gavin kept nagging, "C'mon, Chris, the call has started, they'll be waiting for us." Until finally Chris yelled at him, "What does it matter? It doesn't fucking matter!" and then some other stuff. He couldn't remember what else he said, but Gawain's hurt expression was tattooed in his memory ever after.

And the other was the phone call he got from Peter Elliot in Hong Kong, mid-morning. Chopstix, the equities trading system, was having another bad day, like the one a month ago. Worse, in fact, the system had been down all day. "Chris, hey, listen, I know you moved on, but could you look at this? Jason is running around like a headless chicken and John Uzgalis isn't returning my phone calls."

Chris had sent a friendly email to Uzgalis, asking if he could help. The reply was swift:

Do your own job asshole

What was his job? His own job was meaningless, a fig leaf to cover the bank's past indiscretions and Sir Simon's spats with the American regulators. He worked on doggedly until nine o'clock and went to bed at Day's Inn and lay awake most of the night, mulling it over.

He suddenly remembered that Martha was delivering Harry back for the weekend tomorrow. Saturday morning, 10am at Manor Road. Damn. Another complication. He set a reminder in his phone.

51

London

He must have slept in the end because the sound of his phone was a nasty shock.

"There's been a development," said Mackenna. "Come into the office immediately. Sir Simon's orders."

In the taxi, he scanned his emails dopily, looking for clues. Chopstix in Hong Kong was still misbehaving. Peter Elliott was on a rant to Cyrus, copying the planet, about clients getting each others' confirmations. Raul was talking about restoring from backups, "like last time." It sounded very ugly.

But nothing that sounded like a security alert. No intruders, no viruses, no bombs.

The door into Sir Simon's area had a guard on it. A big guy, unsmiling, in green fatigues, no badge. He had a list of names on a clipboard.

"Sign here, Mr Peters. Please place your phones on the table."

The man had removed his phone and locked it away before Chris understood what was going on.

"You can make calls, sir, but you will need Mr Mackenna's permission. He's in the boardroom, second door on the left."

The boardroom was packed. Mackenna and his guys were at the near end, then John Uzgalis and David Trebbiano. Further down was Tom Hailey, as the new Neil Jenkins, and next to him Sheila Collins with her sidekick Colin. Behind Sheila, at another table were some of Sheila's people including young Hassan Choudhary. On one of the wall screens, Mackenna's Middle Eastern investigator sat in an empty office.

What the hell was going on?

"This meeting is being recorded," said Mackenna, and the room fell silent.

*

"Two IT disasters, one in June and the other a few weeks ago, both on a Triple Witching day. I say disasters, but they could have been much worse.

In June, we came within a few minutes of losing the mainframe computer and all the trading systems in the US. And two weeks ago, we would have lost all trading in London and New York. Headline news, catastrophic damage to our reputation."

"I thought – we all thought – that these events were accidents. Human error. But we were wrong. They were cyber-attacks by person or persons who work for this bank."

"Why do you think the market data meltdown was an attack?" said Uzgalis, "we think Chris and his guys just screwed up."

"Silver paint on a camera. And the smell of mothballs."

"Huh?"

"Some other time," said Mackenna. "Why am I telling you this? Not because I think the bank's secrets are safe with you. I'd rather share them with a flock of parrots. But I have no choice.

"I had hoped that we were safe until the next Triple Witching, in December. Unfortunately not. A new attack is imminent. This weekend, perhaps today. You are the technology leaders of this bank. I need your help.

"There were warning signs before the previous attacks. Although we didn't recognize them."

He turned to the figure on the wall.

"Mohamed, can you show us the latest, please?"

Mohamed hit a key and his image was replaced with the cacophony of red ink, violent images and Arabic script.

"This is the home page of al-Hamidya," said Mohamed. "It's an Islamist website, hosted in Cairo, by people who don't like us.

"Someone called Anwar al-Parsani posted two previous announcements on this website, on the day before Triple Witching. They weren't warnings. He was boasting to the Islamic world that justice was about to be done.

"Well guys, here's the problem. This morning, about 2.20am UK time, Anwar al-Parsani posted a new threat here. This one is more aggressive. It says that justice has caught up with SBS, and that it will be crushed. Crushed. He uses an Arabic word which is rather graphic. It's what you do when you step on an insect. Perhaps annihilated would be a better translation. That's what it says in Arabic, next to the digital clock."

"The clock is counting down. It will reach zero in 58 hours, at 6.30pm on Monday, London time."

"As you said, the next Triple Witching is not until December," said David Trebbiano, "so why now?"

Mackenna nodded.

"A week ago, young Christopher here found a development environment hidden in one of the bank's computers. I think of it as a bomb factory. It contains the script which almost destroyed Hamilton.

"It also contained a lot of other nasty things. Digital weapons. Looking at the forensics, we have learned a lot about them. Highly technical, even brilliant, but not experienced. They were learning as they went along.

"Chris discovered the bomb factory last Friday night. By noon on Sunday, its contents had been erased. Why? For three months, they used it freely. For three months, it was a wee devils' kitchen full of half-baked devilish ideas. And then suddenly – *poof*! It had to go. I can only think of one reason for that. They knew Christopher was onto them."

"Well, how?" asked Trebbiano, "this is all news to me."

"I am pleased to hear it. However, Christopher told John Uzgalis. And John told his management team, and within a few hours, the files were gone. That's how."

"Hey," said Uzgalis, "why blame me? Chris told other people-"

"He told a child minder, a female IT recruitment consultant, and a two year old child. Which of them do you suspect?"

"This is bullshit," said Uzgalis, "why delete anything? It's all backed up, they must have known we would recover it."

"The computer known as Tonto is only backed up once a week. On Sundays, as it happens. What we have recovered are the files as they were on the Sunday, five days *before* Chris found them. Any changes made after that backup are gone. Who knows what we have lost? And it took us twenty-four hours to get the backup restored.

"All because you can't keep your mouths shut. Well, not any more. No one leaves this room. No calls without my permission. Not a word to anyone outside this room, or I will remove your powers of speech with my special pliers. It's bloody but quick. Do you believe me or do you need a demonstration?"

There was a shocked silence, each of them thinking *he's joking* and then again *maybe he's not.*

Mackenna glanced at the clock on the wall. It was 8.23am, Saturday morning.

"Time is ticking. We will move on. Information Security has been analysing what was left behind in the devils' kitchen. Colin, Sheila?"

Colin flashed up a long list onto the screen.

"This is an analysis of the files in the bomb factory. They added anything they could get their hands on. Internal software, loads of open source stuff from the internet. I say 'they' because we cannot believe one person did all this. We've given each effort a RAG status. Red looks really dangerous, Amber has potential, Green, we think it's harmless."

"What are the Reds? They tried to build a virus. In fact, several viruses. There's one that looks like it was meant to run inside our network routers."

"It wouldn't have worked," said Tom Hailey, "but it was a clever idea."

"What's this one?" said Chris, "classified as a Green. It takes up a lot of space and hundreds of files."

"That's a database utility. No obvious threat."

"Really?" said Uzgalis, who had been quietly sulking after Mackenna's reproaches. "That's ShuffleDB. Takes data from production, shuffles it and writes it into our test systems. I think it should be amber at least."

"That's Project Vegas," said Sheila, "what's dangerous about that?"

"Well," said Uzgalis, "imagine someone pointed ShuffleDB at a production system and shuffled that instead?"

"We'd restore from backup," said Colin, "takes about twenty minutes."

The guard – Eamonn – appeared. "Call for Mr Uzgalis from a Mr Raul in Hong Kong."

Mackenna nodded approval. Uzgalis took the phone, heading for the door.

"Excuse me, guys. Got a big issue in Hong Kong. One of my equity legacies from Chris."

"Chris? David?" said Mackenna, "what about this ShuffleDB program? Is it dangerous or not?"

"Well," said Trebbiano, "the beauty of ShuffleDB is that it doesn't scramble, it shuffles. So the test systems still work. A trade with Goldman Sachs Asset Management in a Japanese bond suddenly becomes a trade in Samsung B shares with, er, Pimco. The shuffled system still functions... but in business terms, the data is garbage."

"So to answer your question," said Chris, "if you could shuffle a real live system, the results would be disastrous. Like Polonium B. You're dead, but you don't know it. The system appears to be working but the output makes no sense."

"Is there an unshuffle function?"

"No," said Trebbiano, "once you run a shuffled system even for a minute, you can't go back. You would need a full database restore."

"Colin says that would take twenty minutes." said Mackenna.

"Maybe he hasn't tried it," said Trebbiano. "It's a long, scary process. For some big back office systems, it could take hours."

Uzgalis came back in. He looked venomously at Chris.

"They fucked up the restore. Your man Raul is a complete dick. We're going back two days."

"Well," said Trebbiano, "as you can see, database restores are tricky things."

"So, gentlemen," said Mackenna, "if every database across the bank was shuffled, what would the impact be?"

Chris, John and David looked at each other.

"I can't imagine how we would ever recover," said David.

"Colin, when did ShuffleDB arrive in the bomb factory?" asked Chris.

"Very recently. About ten days ago."

"Oh my God," said Uzgalis, "that's the plan, isn't it? They're going to shuffle us."

*

Whoops! Martha was due to drop Harry off in half an hour, at 10 o'clock. He couldn't cope with a toddler and a terrorist threat simultaneously. He called Martha and begged for an extension. She was on her way but took it in her stride.

"OK, I can keep him until Sunday night, say 6pm? Then I'm going out."

Thank goodness for that. He put a reminder in his phone.

Noon arrived. DeVries appeared, in a T-shirt and leather jacket. And Cyrus, who seemed pleased to see Chris. Then Sir Simon dialled in. He was shooting partridges somewhere in the West Country and the reception was poor. But his contempt floated eerily from the ceiling speakers of the boardroom.

"So, one of our own employees plans to wreck the bank by scrambling our computer systems. We know this, but our IT department is powerless to stop it. Is that right?"

"We're doing everything we can, but the threat is real," said deVries.

"We gave Global Markets a hundred and fifty million quid last year to fix your Disaster Recovery issues. What did you do with the money?"

"Simon, I'm not sure why that's relevant?" came deVries' voice.

"I remember the business case very clearly, Jerome. The promise was that every system in Global Markets would have a backup system. If this maniac can corrupt or shuffle your systems, you can switch to the backup, can't you? Unless the money was spent on something else?"

"Excuse me, Sir Simon, but that's a misunderstanding," said Uzgalis unexpectedly. "Backup systems must have the same data as the live system. Exactly the same data. So if some process shuffles the live system, the data in the backup is faithfully shuffled... that's how it's supposed to work."

"And who are you?"

"That was John Uzgalis, Simon. He runs front office IT in Global Markets."

"Bully for him. It's a pity he didn't consider this situation before you spent the money. So, when this unstoppable evil happens, how long will it take Global Markets to recover?"

"Not just Global Markets, Simon," said deVries, "it's the whole bank. Every major system would be down. Remember RBS and the software upgrade that went wrong? It took them months to straighten out their customers' accounts. This would be a hundred times worse. We wouldn't know who our customers were, even. No customer accounts. No money in or out. No cash machines. No trading, no clearing. Nothing."

"How much could we do manually?"

The IT guys exchanged grim smiles.

"TIS says we could answer the phone. Probably. Or not, because our phone systems are just computers, database controlled. That's if we can get into our buildings. The turnstiles check access against an employee database. And Property says the lifts might not work."

"Too many ifs and buts," said Sir Simon. "Jerome, I want a detailed assessment of the threat and a recovery plan. By tomorrow."

There were noises on the other end. A faint but distinct voice said, "For God's sake, Simon, the drive has started," and then raucous laughter and the sound of gunfire.

"Global Markets brought this Shuffle thing into the bank. Global Markets must fix it. Keep me posted." *Click.*

"While we're all here," said Cyrus, looking across at John and Chris, "what's the deal with Chopstix in Hong Kong, guys? Peter Elliott tells me yesterday's confirms are all fucked up. I've got clients screaming all over the planet. The Hong Kong regulators have been on the phone, wanting to shut us down."

"We're restoring the database again," said Uzgalis. "It seems like there was some problem with the backups from last night and the night before. We're going back two days now, it's going to be ugly."

"Listen, I'm just a simple trader, but this shuffleDB thing? Sounds like Hong Kong: the system works but the data is garbage. Are you sure someone hasn't shuffled Chopstix?"

Chris, John and Tom Hailey looked at each other for a long minute.

"Oh shit. Hardy Hall, Aisle E," said Uzgalis. "I'm having déjà vu all over again."

"It was Aisle F," said Chris, "but yes."

"What are you talking about?" said Tom and Cyrus, in unison.

"One week before the Hamilton meltdown, the cooling for one aisle in the datacentre was shut down. Just for an hour. We think it was a test."

"You think Hong Kong is a test?" said Cyrus. "Let me tell you guys - they must be cracking open the champagne right now. Equities is out of business in Hong Kong. This is a major fucking incident."

DeVries got up to go, and beckoned Chris to follow him.

"I want Sir Simon's threat assessment and recovery plan. By 8am tomorrow. Get cracking."

Shit rolls downhill! thought Chris.

"What about Topeka?"

"I will run Topeka this weekend. It will be good experience for me."

Perhaps it would have been, but fate had other plans.

*

In mid-afternoon, Chris and John Uzgalis were summoned to a conference call with Tom Hailey and Shane Paterson, head dba, to hear what they didn't want to hear.

"Cyrus was right," said Shane, "the Chopstix live database has been shuffled. After the batch on Thursday night. There was a connection into the database from Tonto in London at the time."

"Who was it?"

"No one. It was a generic account, highly privileged."

Generic account. Ha! A generic account was like a car with no number plate. Audit had been whining about them for years but they still existed.

"Is Chopstix working again?" asked Uzgalis.

"No. Thursday's backup was no good. We've had to go back to Wednesday."

"Well, hurry for Chrissake," said Uzgalis, "we're in deep shit."

"Hold on, guys," said Chris, "what was wrong with the Thursday backup?"

"The storage team fucked up. It loaded OK. But the files were mislabelled. It was a backup from two weeks ago."

More bad luck, thought Chris to himself, wondering if it was.

*

Chris went back to the board room and tried to concentrate on his homework, spelling out the business impact if the bank's systems were shuffled. He didn't recognize half the systems that were at risk. He needed to talk to some of the guys in Retail and Commercial. Mackenna let him have his phone back and he started calling around. He was not popular.

Soon after midnight, there was activity down the far end. Hassan and his colleagues had found something, he saw them calling Colin over, and there was a lot of whispering.

At about three, he put his head down on the table and slept. He had strange dreams.

52

Sana'a, Yemen, 2007

Day Ten - Sunday

The cardboard box had mysteriously appeared on the front steps of the house during the night, and little Yousef had found it.

The box was old and battered. It had the words 'Sunlight Soap' on the side, and a picture of a smiling sun with eyes. It was two foot along each side, and one foot deep. The top flaps were folded roughly, interlocking each other but there were cracks between them where the darkness inside leaked out.

It was securely fastened with coarse plastic string, the kind a butcher might use, knotted in the middle.

Little Yousef tried to pick it up, but it was too heavy for him. So he ran up the stairs in great excitement, calling in vain for Mahmoud. Mahmoud had gone out two days ago, looking for his father and sister, and the family had not seen him since. So Yousef's father carried it up the long, winding steps to the family room, grunting as the rough plastic fibres cut into his hand.

"A parcel for your father. It's quite heavy," he said. With a grunt of relief, he dumped it on the low table and left.

And there the box had sat, immobile as a stone god, throughout the day. The horror of its presence transfixed Gurjit and her two remaining sons, Ahmed and Ben. They did not talk. They could not talk, nor could they leave. Nor dared they open the box.

Gurjit had stared at it for so long, she knew every stain, every tiny scratch. But there was one thing she had not noticed when it arrived. The base of the box was darker than the rest. It was faintly discoloured. A thin red brown stain ran along the bottom edge. She looked at it intently – was it there before? Perhaps. Surely it was darker now?

She had to act. But when she tried to move, to get up, her body was frozen.

Please, be gone. Please, vanish. Those thoughts ran around in her head all day long but when she opened her eyes, the box was still there, and the fear was still there, churning in her stomach. Tears came again to her. Ahmed was weeping, his round head buried in his wrestler's arms.

Suddenly Gurjit was on her feet. She went down to the kitchen. She took the little sharp knife, the one they used for skinning rabbits. She approached the box sideways, not wanting to touch it. Or feel the heaviness of it. She held the knife out, point first, as though to stab it. She delicately sawed at the string. The box did not move. She cut harder, pressing the blade down. The string wriggled sideways, and she held it with two fingers, still not touching the cardboard, until with a snap the string parted.

She dared not go further. It was Ahmed who stood up and opened the first flap. It was firmly folded under, and he had to bend it to get it out. Underneath was old newspaper. They were briefly reassured. Newspaper was an ordinary thing, part of the ordinary world.

But this newspaper was covered with a dark reddish stain. At the same time their nostrils picked up the smell, a sickening smell of blood and decay. Ahmed doubled over, retching. It was Ben, clever, innocent Ben, who tugged at the paper until suddenly it came away in his hand.

The box packers had prepared for this moment with special cruelty. They had packed the object in its paper cradle, face up, and opened the eyes. For a few moments, the child boy studied the object, trying to make sense of it. The mouth was frozen in a grimace of pain and the short dark beard matted with blood.

Ben gave a terrible cry of grief and despair and rushed from the room, dropping the bloody newspaper on the stone floor. Gurjit covered her face and wept silently.

"Another box arrived," came the voice of their neighbour from two floors below. "This one's for Mahmoud. It's a bit smaller but just as heavy. Can Ahmed come down for it?"

53

London

Sunday, 7th October 2012

William was shaking him. The clock on the wall said 5am.

"Chris? Wake up, Bruce wants you."

Chris poured himself a stewed cup of black coffee and staggered into Room Fourteen. There was a conference going on. Mohamed was on the screen, talking in a subdued voice.

"OK, well, guys, we know a lot more about the Hashemis. We've got a Yemeni contact in Sana'a and he's been driving around asking questions. Yes, Jafar was a spice merchant, had a stall in the old market. Wife, four children, one called Mahmoud. One daughter. It's not a pretty story.

"It starts with this news item. Not big on the international news, just two lines on AP. Two bodies found in the municipal tip outside Sana'a. No names. More in the local press. alhawyah.com says that the bodies of two foreigners have been found outside the city, and one of them is a missing Iranian, Jafar Hashemi."

"And the other body?"

"That's all we could find in the press. But then we found this."

He held up a photo of a tall, dark townhouse.

"This is the Hashemi house in the Old City, which Jafar bought in 2001. It's a traditional Yemeni tower-house, with stairs and six floors and a mafraj at the top. It's boarded up and for sale. It's been on sale for three years. No one wants it."

"Why?"

"Because bad things happened there. Because it's haunted. One neighbour said she heard voices inside, and sometimes in the dark, she could see lights and figures moving behind the windows of the mafraj. No one wants to live in a haunted house. Especially not in Yemen."

"Do the spirits have a name?"

"Yes. They are the ghosts of Jafar Hashemi and his son, Mahmoud. According to the neighbour, Mahmoud was the second body found in the town dump. Their spirits are still angry, that's the general idea. The local people don't want to talk about it. Even Yemenis find the story difficult."

"What story?"

"I am not sure it is relevant. It's not a story for Westerners."

"Everything is relevant," growled Mackenna.

"Their bodies were brought back to the house. It is said that the mother – Gurjit – was a foreign witch. She – ah – sewed the heads back onto the bodies-"

"You mean-"

"Yes, they were beheaded. Only the bodies were found in the municipal dump. We don't know how the heads got home. The neighbours say that she summoned the spirits of her son and husband, and she tried to bring them back to life. She could not, but their ghosts are still there, trapped and angry.

"We Muslims bury our dead, without delay. These bodies were already four days old when they were found. She refused to bury them while she tried to reattach the heads. She had doused the whole house in camphor. The smell was so bad, you could smell it from the street. You can imagine... after four days. In the end, her neighbours and the police broke in and took the bodies by force and buried them."

"Where were the rest of the family?"

"Her two younger sons were with her. Ahmed the boxer and the youngest, Ben."

"And the daughter?"

"Zahra. Everyone remembers Zahra, she was well liked. She vanished one night soon after her father disappeared. No one saw her again, but our contact heard a strange story from the local police, that she was abducted and enslaved by a man called Abu Malik, whom she later murdered. But the neighbours are sure she's dead."

"That's not the end of it. We searched the ether for Hashemis and we found this picture in the archives of the Yemeni police website."

It showed a young man, muscular, wearing boxing gloves and grinning, with a silver shield held up to the camera.

"Ahmed Hashemi. The neighbours recognized him. He used to fight for the police. William has found a young male with that name in Dubai. He worked as a bouncer for a nightclub. He was killed in a fight in Dubai City two years ago."

Mackenna looked round at the shocked faces in the room.

"Can you feel it? I can feel it."

"Feel what?" said one of the acolytes, after a short silence.

"The anger. The terrible anger. You think Dom MacDonald is angry, Christopher? His anger is nothing. It's a spat. Imagine this family. Your father and brother have their heads cut off and their bodies are dumped on a rubbish heap. God knows what happened to your sister. And why? Because a bank won't give you the ransom. Your own money, for God's sake. Won't give it to you. Won't say why. Throws your mother into the street and shuts the doors in your face. Two weeks later she burns herself to death on the steps of the bank. If it happened to me, I would not rest. I would pursue the people who did this and send them to hell."

The last four words were so loud that they were heard in Reception. There was an embarrassed silence in the room.

"It's a terrible anger," said Mackenna, regaining some self-control, "and it's here. Somewhere inside this bank. It's coming for us. Keep going, we've got less than forty-eight hours."

He got up and stormed out, talking to himself.

"Well, they made a good start on the revenge, didn't they?" said William to the survivors.

"What do you mean?" said someone.

"Al-Muhairi. It's obvious. They got to him. Two weeks later. They hung him up and that young boxer, Ahmed, used him as a punch bag. Pulped his face and chest. No wonder there were leather fragments in the skin. When boxing gloves get wet, after a bit, they start to dissolve. I can imagine it."

They all could.

*

At 11am on Sunday morning, as the bells of a dozen churches summoned the faithful to prayer, Sheila appeared in the doorway of the War Room, accompanied by Colin. She was not looking her best.

"Guys, can you spare me a moment?"

Chris, Mackenna and his two helpers paused their researches with a weary mixture of relief and resentment.

Sheila scanned the litter of coffee cups, pizza boxes and piles of paper records strewn across the table. After a moment's hesitation, she sat down on an empty chair and cleared a space.

"Colin and team have built scripts which look for ShuffleDB activity. In the last 24 hours, we've covered about 98% of the Unix servers, and 50% of the Windows estate. About forty thousand computers in total."

"It's complicated," said Colin, "because of the different builds. And the ones that don't respond. And the ones owned by the business-"

"Shut up, Colin," said Sheila. "The good news – or the bad news – is that in the early hours of this morning, we found this. Set up as a cron job. On a development server in London." She handed round a single sheet of paper.

"I will not excuse my ignorance, young lady, as you do not beg pardon for your presumption. What is a cron job?" That was Mackenna. Two sleepless nights were taking their toll, even on him. He looked ten years older.

Confusion and then relief showed on Sheila's face as she worked it out.

"Cron? Sorry, yes of course. It's a way that you can run a program at a preset time. No human intervention required."

"This particular job was set up on Tonto, the same box that was used to attack Hamilton. When the job gets triggered, it feeds ShuffleDB the database IDs of sixty-three of our critical systems, and gives instructions to shuffle the data inside certain tables. Essentially it tries to anonymise the data as if it was a test system."

"So whoever did this has been working on the ShuffleDB project? Vegas?"

"Yes. But half the AppDev community has worked on Vegas over the summer. We've had training classes, there's loads of examples and sample scripts."

"And when is this thing set to explode?"

"Half past six Monday night, London time. Just as Anwar al-Parsani promised, you might say," replied Sheila. "But that's not the end of the story. As we were walking over here, one of my guys discovered a second version. This time, on a Windows box. This box is in our office in Busan. Different wrapper, same payload, same launch time."

"Busan?" said someone.

"A city in Korea. And no, I didn't know we had an office there either. Let alone servers. Obviously, we have removed these jobs but I thought you should know, Bruce. It's tough to be sure we've caught everything."

At noon, she was back. This time she had Hassan Choudhary as technical backup.

"We've found two more," she said. "One in the US and another on a workstation in London."

*

314

The room got busier during the day, as more people were pulled into the search.

Mackenna arranged a 4pm update for Sir Simon. DeVries came, and brought Annie. Tom brought Sheila. Sheila brought Colin. Colin brought Hassan and two others from his team. These seconds stood or sat against the walls like statues, ready to step in if their principals ran out of detail. Sir Simon dialled in from somewhere else.

"Right," he said, skipping the pleasantries. "Jerome, yesterday I asked you for a realistic assessment of the ShuffleDB threat, and possible responses. Can we have it?"

DeVries didn't sound himself. He rolled his head from side to side and cleared his throat several times. In front of him he had the paper that Chris had worked most of the night to prepare.

"Shuffling data. No data lost. Sounds OK? Well, on Friday somebody gave us a demonstration of what it really means. They shuffled the database of Chopstix in Hong Kong. Chopstix – you may not have heard of it – is a minor trading system in Equity land. It took us thirty-six hours to get it back. The HKMA have suspended our brokerage licence. It will take years, literally years, to recover the trust of our institutional clients in Asia. There will be two inches in the FT on Monday.

"In a minute Sheila and her colleagues will tell us about the target list they have found. This list contains sixty-three systems, most of them a lot more important than Chopstix. It includes all the major trading, operational and risk systems of Global Markets. What a disaster. But that's not the main threat. At the bottom is one little name: CDM. CDM is the bank's client data master. It holds the master customer reference data for all our customers. All divisions."

DeVries looked around the room.

"If the CDM database gets shuffled and nothing else, we are *biltong*. Remember UNITY? We spent years on that program. I have the scars to prove it. After UNITY, every system in this bank takes its customer data from CDM. Scramble CDM, and you scramble everything. Imagine me on Tuesday morning. I go to put my card into a cash machine. But the machine thinks I am someone else! It will take the money out of someone else's account. I am no longer Jerome deVries, I am Richard Smith, a real customer, but I live at an industrial estate in Wales and I have an Argentine phone number and Jane Smith's email. I have the credit limit of a Russian oligarch and he has mine. I get his dividends. He gets my mortgage payments. We have 12 million retail customers across the world. Total chaos. Even for one day. How would we ever straighten it out?"

"Surely," said someone, "we could recover the databases from backups?"

"You are right. Backups. The only way back. We have about fifty dbas, and three of them worked full time on the Chopstix restore. It took us thirty-six hours to recover that system. What happens if sixty-three systems are simultaneously shuffled? How long to recover? Three weeks? Three months? According to IT, the average system receives or sends data to thirty-five other systems. So all that time, the bad systems are feeding garbage into the good systems and the good systems are feeding good data into the bad ones. And that good data is then destroyed when their database is restored and then what? Because you see, we are a bank. We can't stop the treadmill. Every day, we are legally required to partake in millions of transactions - even if our systems can't process them.

"So what will happen? We would never recover. Long before that, we would be shut down. No customer accounts. No P&L, no risk, no management information, no regulatory reporting. All shit. I tell you, the regulators would queue up to shut us down. The Fed, the FSA, the JFSA, probably the Central Bank of Nigeria. Recovery? No, I am telling you, if this program is run, it will destroy this bank as surely as a neutron bomb. There will be no defence and no recovery. This must not happen. That is the end of the story."

"Uddammir. Crushed like an insect," said Uzgalis. "Hardly describes it."

Mackenna gave his audience a few moments to absorb this hellish vision.

"Right, well, let's talk about our efforts to prevent a new attack. Tom? Sheila?"

Sheila took centre stage.

"We have found five rogue jobs hidden in computers around the planet. I suppose you could call them time bombs. As Jerome says, each of them is programmed to shuffle data across sixty-three of our critical applications including CDM. Here is the actual list. I have just emailed it to you, Sir Simon."

"When does this happen?" asked Sir Simon.

"All the jobs we've found so far were set for Monday. Tomorrow night. 6.30pm onwards. Obviously we've deleted them."

"Could there be other jobs still hidden?"

"There are sixty servers we can't reach for various reasons. We're going round them manually."

"What's to stop someone setting up more of these chron things?" asked Sir Simon.

"That's a good question," said Tom Hailey. "We've reprogrammed permissions so that if any instance of ShuffleDB tries to start up, it won't get permission to run. Except the one that's supposed to."

"What do you mean," said deVries, "'the one that's supposed to?'"

"Well, there's a ShuffleDB job in the batch which does what ShuffleDB is supposed to do – extracts production data, shuffles it and writes it back in our test systems. We've checked. That job hasn't changed in two months, and now you can't get to it."

"Why wouldn't we turn that off as well?"

"There's no need. It took months of work to get that job working right. It's in the main batch stream and there are hundreds of dependencies on it. Fooling around with it could cause major problems."

"You're betting the bank on that decision, are you happy with that?" said deVries, who obviously wasn't.

"Yes," said Tom stoutly.

"Has anyone tested these defences?"

"Yes," said Sheila, "we've invited everyone with ShuffleDB expertise to try and run it. People have been trying for the past hour or so. No one has succeeded."

"Excellent," said Sir Simon, "so will we be in business on Tuesday?"

"Yes, absolutely," said Sheila.

"I think so," said Tom.

"Excellent! Good work everyone," said Sir Simon. "Jerome, I want an exec call in the morning. You can brief the Board. Don't make it too scary, or some silly bugger will leak it to the *Daily Mail*. OK?"

He rang off. In the boardroom, people started chatting about sandwiches and fresh coffee. Only Mackenna remained silent, hunched over his notebook, glowering.

Chris met Hassan in the bathroom a few minutes later.

"Hassan, you found these chron jobs, didn't you? Not Colin."

Hassan nodded.

"Tell me the truth. Are you sure there can't be another one?"

Hassan nodded his head gently as he weighed his answer. Then he shook it decisively.

"We are not safe. Too many places to hide it. Too many ways."

There were darker smudges under Hassan's eyes and he kept rubbing his cheeks as if they were numb.

"How long have you been awake?" asked Chris.

"Two days."

"Get thirty minutes sleep, that's all you need. Plus sugar. And caffeine."

They went back into the boardroom together. Most people had gone. Mackenna was still brooding, writing up some notes.

"Hello? Hello?" said a nervous voice from the ceiling speakers. "This is Mohamed with *Yahoo!* in Dubai."

"Go ahead, Mohamed," said Mackenna.

"Well, sounds like you guys have got things under control. I hope so, because something strange has just happened on the al-Hamidya website. The one with the countdown to destruction? That clock just jumped twenty-four hours."

"Another twenty-four hours? To Tuesday?" said someone.

"No, no, I'm sorry. It's jumped down twenty-four hours. Zero hour is now only ninety-one minutes away. 6.30pm London time."

Everyone was talking at once. And then Chris' phone was ringing. He had a sudden premonition that it was Olivia. But it wasn't, it was Sean, the head dba.

He sent Sean to voicemail.

"Be quiet, everyone, be quiet." This was Mackenna. "They're in a panic, that's why they've accelerated the plan. We're getting close, we just need to stay calm."

Chris' phone rang again. Sean again.

"Sean, I don't have time to talk to you right now, we have a crisis."

"No, Chris, I have a crisis. Listen to me, just one second, OK. Remember the Chopstix backup tape in Hong Kong that we thought was corrupt? It wasn't. The catalogue was just pointing to the wrong tape."

"Sean, so what? I really don't care, you got it back right-"

"You're not listening. The backup was there but the catalogue was pointing to the wrong tape. The catalogue of which backups are stored on what tapes is just another database, right? It's been shuffled! We've checked. The whole catalogue. If we had a corrupted database right now, I couldn't recover it. We'd have to search half a million tape records to find it, it would take hours."

"I've got to go, Sean. Fix it, for God's sake. Find an old copy of the catalog."

Sean gave a bitter laugh.

"Oh a backup of the catalog, Chris? And which tape is that on?"

Mackenna was glaring at him, drawing one finger across his throat.

"You think they are in a panic?" said Chris slowly, "that was Sean, the head dba. We should be panicking. Listen…"

He explained his conversation with Sean to an increasingly pale audience. "…So imagine a library with half a million books. That's how many tapes we've got. Then imagine someone destroys the card index. Now the only way to find a book is run up and down the shelves, looking at the titles. That's where we are with the tape catalogue. Until Sean can find a backup of the card index itself, we can't restore anything."

"Why we are worrying?" said someone, "Sheila said we'd shut down ShuffleDB, it couldn't be run."

"Yes," said Chris, "but young Hassan Choudhary over there – who found these toxic chron jobs – says differently."

*

Fear had replaced the brief moment of optimism. A small, desperate group was huddled around Mackenna back in Meeting Room Fourteen, trying to figure it out. Outside, there was a rising hum of traffic, London residents coming back from their weekends in the country. Jerome deVries had appeared from nowhere and was cleaning his nails with a Swiss Army knife.

John Uzgalis had found his way to the al-Hamidya website and put it up on one of the screens. Amid the confusion of Arabic slogans and images of bearded clerics, the digital clock was a beacon of simplicity. 01:03:34 and still counting down. It was difficult to keep your eyes off it. It was difficult not to be dismayed by its robotic confidence. The room stank of fear and the sweat of men wondering if their battleship was about to self-destruct.

His phone was bleeping. A reminder.

Event 18:00 Martha delivering Harry!

Hell's teeth! That was in thirty minutes. How was he going to look after him? Harry would want feeding and entertaining, and what if he started yelling? He just couldn't. He tried Martha. Firm no. Then Anita. No answer. In desperation, he called Olivia.

"Olivia, please listen, just for a minute? You got my text? I was wrong about Dom but this terrorist is real. About twenty of us are here, trying to stop-"

He laid it out, used his last scrap of credibility, begged her.

"Just for tonight. Until we get through this, I swear, I will take him back tomorrow."

"I'm staying at my sister's."

"Brian and Sarah have kids, they'll understand."

In the end, thank God, Olivia agreed to come and collect Harry. In an hour.

"So, who found the body?" said Mackenna, out of the blue. The rest of them looked blank.

"Ask any policeman," said Mackenna, "after the husband, who do you suspect? Whoever found the body. In this case, who found those chron jobs?"

"That would be the shifty guy who smiles too much," said deVries, "Sheila's technical guy."

"Colin?" said Chris, "no way. It was Hassan Choudhary or one of the others."

"Great, let's arrest Hassan Choudhary."

"Sure," said Chris, "but if it wasn't for Hassan, the market data storm would have blown us away. And those five chron jobs were real; why would he plant them and then dig them up again?"

"To establish his credentials," said deVries.

"Who needs credentials? We would never have found them."

Mackenna rubbed his eyes and blinked a couple of times.

"Well, I don't like it. Maybe it's not your young friend, but I'm telling you, this is someone close to us. I can smell him."

"And he can smell us?" said Chris.

"I think he can hear us."

Chris looked at the clock and got up in a hurry.

"Excuse me, I'll be back in a minute. I have to pick up my nephew from Reception."

Martha was waiting by the desk. She was holding Harry, fast asleep over one shoulder and his things in a basket.

The sleeping child was a strange burden as he walked to the elevators. One was just arriving and Hassan Choudhary stepped out.

"Hi," said Chris, softly, "Hassan, could you press eleven for me? Thank you. Are you going to get some sleep?"

Hassan nodded. He suddenly noticed that Chris was holding a sleeping child and seemed politely surprised.

"My nephew," said Chris lamely. "I'm babysitting."

Harry woke up at that moment and found himself in a new place with a tall stranger. He started struggling and trying to get down, babbling.

"Sorry," said Chris, "he's not used to strangers. My wife's coming to pick him up, thank God." Hassan nodded slowly, and walked off, swaying slightly as he crossed the marble floor.

Harry cried and wriggled all the way to the eleventh. Chris took him to Meeting Room Fourteen, found him a biscuit and his bottle of juice and sat him in the corner with his Duplo farm set. DeVries came in and raised an eyebrow.

"Neil's son. Harry," said Chris. "My wife and I are babysitting."

He offered no further explanation and no one seemed to care.

"It's half past five," said deVries, casually, "sixty minutes to go." He put his feet up on the table. On Sir Simon's precious wood but no one seemed to care about that either.

"Tell me, guys," he said, "if he succeeds – and the bank gets shuffled – how would we know?"

"Error code thirty-one," said Trebbiano with conviction, "millions of them."

"What's error code thirty-one?" said deVries.

"It's the error that the risk feed produces when a trading system sends down garbage," said Trebbiano, looking at Chris and John with the air of a long-suffering servant. "Happens every night but with shuffled trades, it explodes."

"How do you know?"

"Because we simulate this in our test systems, remember? Our test systems use shuffled data since Vegas went live."

"And what time would we see this?"

"About 1am."

"Thank you," said DeVries. "At 1am, I will be watching my Blackberry even more carefully than usual."

"No worries, if you miss it, we'll call you," said Trebbiano, smiling. The crisis seemed to have eased the tension between deVries and his new IT lieutenants.

Mackenna appeared, very agitated.

"More news on the Hashemi children. Mahmoud was the eldest, he's the poor chap who was beheaded with his dad. Ahmed was the boxer who died in Dubai a couple of years later. Zahra is next. Apart from the neighbours liking her, we don't know anything about her. No school records, nothing, although bizarrely Yemeni Airways had a flight attendant of that name about three years ago."

"How does that help?" said deVries.

"It doesn't," said Mackenna. "This is what helps."

The document on the screen was in Arabic. Incomprehensible to Western eyes, except for the dates and the logo of the Yemen Interior Ministry.

"This document authorizes one Gurjit Hashemi to leave Yemen with a child aged fifteen. It is dated November 19, 2007. The woman is going to Dubai. The child is called Anwar Hashemi. Aka 'Ben'. And who is posting these threats on al-Hamidya? Anwar al-Parsani, Anwar the Persian. And guess who was active on Facebook until two years ago? Anwar al-Parsani. Here he is."

"My God, he looks-"

"Like a radical? Yes, he does. And he was. The green book, that's the Koran he's holding. Two years ago, he decided this was a mistake. He managed to take off all his Friends, and all the images. But we've got his blog. He is a computer geek. His blog is full of very, very techie things that only you guys will understand. Gentlemen, I think we can put a name to our terrorist: Anwar Hashemi, youngest son of Jafar and Gurjit Hashemi. And he works for us, somewhere in this bank."

David Trebbiano was already searching the bank's email directory.

"Wow, we've got a lot of Anwars. Anwar Singh, Anwar Kulkarni, Anwar Ishmaili, how many fucking Anwars does this bank employ?"

"He may not be called Anwar now," cautioned Mackenna.

At that moment, an extraordinary thing happened. Harry looked up from his toys and started banging his tractor on the floor, shouting as he did so: "Nwa, nwa, nwa."

"That's odd," said Chris, "that's what he was shouting in the lift today."

"When was that?" said Mackenna.

"Just fifteen minutes ago. I got into the lift carrying him and he suddenly started shouting 'nwa, nwa.' Actually I looked round because, you know, I thought he might be shouting at someone. But there was no one there, except the security guy and Hassan Choudhary going for a kip."

"Christopher," said Mackenna after a pause, "would you mind bringing that wee laddie over here?"

Hassan Choudhary's picture on the intranet must have been two years old. He was thinner then, and there was a disconcerting intensity to his gaze. But the effect on Harry was electric.

"Nwa, nwa," he shouted, kicking, and when Chris lifted him close to the screen, his chubby hands slapped the glass right over the dark, sunken eyes. "Nwa, nwa."

"Anwar al-Parsani. Hassan Choudhary. Well I'm damned," said Mackenna, "now where the hell has he gone?"

"Dialling his mobile now," said Henry, "what should I tell him?"

"Just tell him Sheila wants him back here, right away. He'll believe that," said Chris.

"It's switched off."

"Did he hear Harry in the lift? Shouting his name?"

"Yes, probably. Yes, certainly."

"Hells' teeth," said Mackenna, "where does he live? Henry, call the Metropolitan Police and ask for TS3. When they answer, give them my name and his mobile number and ask for a trace. You IT gentlemen, think! Think!"

*

You couldn't make it up, thought Chris, for about the third time that day, *this must be a dream.*

On the far side of the table, Mackenna was grilling an Indian graduate on his phone. It was Karthik, Hassan/Anwar's suave friend.

"What do you mean, he's not there? Where is he? With relatives? Where do they live? I need to talk to him. Now. Who am I? I'm the head of internal security."

He put the phone down and looked at Henry who shook his head.

"Nothing from TS3? Either he's destroyed the phone or he's underground. Damn."

"May I ask a question, folks?" It was deVries, feet still on the table.

"No," said Mackenna, "I'm trying to think."

"This might help you," said deVries. "The question is, 'How do Hassan/Anwar and young Harry know each other?'"

"You're right," said Mackenna, "that is a good question. Chris, where exactly does young Harry fit in?"

"Harry is Neil Jenkins' son," said Christopher, "and until recently they lived together in a caravan in Essex."

"Just the two of them? No visitors? Friends?"

"Not many. His girlfriend. She's called Anita. Harry's in daycare during the week, someone called Martha comes to pick him up and drop him off. I just met her in reception."

"How do you know all this?"

"Neil Jenkins is my brother. Well, half-brother."

"Good God. Well, where is Neil now?"

"I have his number," said deVries. Presumably the rehab clinic, thought Chris.

Mackenna resumed his questioning.

"Where else has Harry been? Say in the last three months? Long enough to get to know someone by sight?"

"To stay with his mother, I imagine. She's moved in with another man. Eleven Friars Close, somewhere near Chelmsford. I don't have a phone number."

"We'll get it from Neil. Chris, anyone else?"

"Last weekend Harry went to stay with Anita."

"Neil's girlfriend? Who doesn't live with Neil? Where does she live?"

"I don't know. Somewhere in London but I doubt she knows Hassan."

"Why?"

"How would they meet? He's is a junior guy, an IT grad. He was only here for the summer. She's a senior recruiter, she spends most nights down the pub, selling contractors to people like me. Hassan doesn't drink, he doesn't go to pubs except... oh my God."

For Chris had remembered something. Tahiti night at the Pepys, the night before Triple Witching. The evening Neil was drunk. Anita had been trying to stop him drinking and then... Anita and Hassan sitting outside, talking. Talking with their heads close together.

"It was a bit strange. I assumed she was trying to poach him, turn him into a contractor. He was desperate to stay in London. But they seemed quite familiar. They weren't even talking, just sitting together."

The digital clock read 00:39:55. Another ten minutes gone.

"She told me something else. She has a flatmate. A man. He was difficult about having Harry. He doesn't like children."

"Bloody hell," said Mackenna, "it's obvious, isn't it?"

No one else thought so.

"Hassan told Karthik he was staying with relatives. I think he was telling the truth. I think we've found the missing sister. When he came to London, he went to stay with her. Of course. Hassan is the flatmate who doesn't like children. Anita is Zahra. Yes, yes, yes. Chris, do you know where she lives?"

"No. I've got her phone number. Email. Office address."

"Guys, do we care?" This was deVries.

"What do you mean?"

"Information Security told us an hour ago that the bank was safe because our defences were secure. It is no longer possible even to run ShuffleDB. So, do we care where he is?"

"We care," replied Chris, "he's super smart and he's worked for weeks inside Information Security. God knows what he's been up to. And his clock is still running. Thirty-seven minutes to go. Hell yes, we care."

"Right," said Mackenna, "let's call his sister. How does she feel about her brother? Is she part of this?"

Chris thought back to the caravan and Anita's confession.

"I don't think she has terrible anger. She loves her brother. But she loves Neil and Harry as well."

*

"Voicemail," said Henry in disgust, hanging up.

"Chris, call her from your phone."

There were five or six agonizing rings and then she answered.

"Chris? Is that you?"

Her voice was uncertain and there was an echo, as if she was in a cave.

"Anita, I need to talk to you. About your brother Anwar. Where are you?"

"I can't help you, Chris. I wish I could, but I can't, I've got to go now. Goodbye. I'm sorry."

Click. He tried again. Instant voicemail.

William came over.

"She's switched the phone off. They say she's within three hundred metres of the transmitter on the Post Office museum."

"The Post Office museum? That's just round the corner, King William Street, next to Merrills."

"There was an echo," said Chris. "It could be a railway station. Or a church? I could hear voices in the background."

"What kind of voices? Talking? Shouting? Next train to arrive at Platform Five?"

"Voices. Not talking, sort of... singing."

"Come on," said Mackenna, "it's six o'clock on a Sunday, it's evensong. She's in St Paul's Cathedral. Chris, bring the little lad with you, we may need him. Henry, stay here."

Chris ran for the lifts, carrying little Harry. He seemed to enjoy the excitement. The others were quicker. Reception was empty by the time he got down. Kevin was on duty but he wasn't behind the desk, he was mopping the floor.

"Kevin. Hassan Choudhary. Tall, young Indian grad. Major security problem. Don't let him in. No matter what."

"I know him, he was here a few minutes ago."

"Don't let him back in. What are you doing? What's that smell?"

Kevin started to explain but he already knew the answer. Camphor. Hassan Choudhary had left the bank for the last time, sprinkling Reception with the same pungent water his mother had used to cover the stench of his father's corpse. Chris was glad to get outside, into the fresh autumn air.

He was given an order of service from an eager verger by the great West door, and Harry grabbed it in his chubby fingers. The others were waiting for him inside. Mackenna, his sidekick William and deVries. Their faces were grim in the dim light from the altar. A verger on the far side was beckoning them forward. The choir had just started singing Psalm 23

The Lord is my Shepherd, I'll not want,

He makes me down to lie

In pastures green, he leadeth me,

The quiet waters by...

Chris looked around. There were perhaps two hundred people scattered across the pews. Mackenna pointed to a lonely, shrouded figure in the back row. Chris walked swiftly forwards and stood, looking down. The woman sensed him and looked up, suspicious, her unkempt grey hair straggling across her forehead.

He shook his head. Behind him Mackenna whispered, "Walk up the aisle. With Harry. Then turn round."

On the way back, Anita and Harry saw each other at the same moment. He wriggled and cried to be put down.

"Neeta, Neeta." He ran shouting down the aisle. Chris ran after and grabbed him. He and Anita stood, six feet apart. She was wearing a black shawl. Her face was puffy and her eyes swollen. She had no makeup. The child wailed louder, reaching out to her.

Chris nodded to the back of the cathedral, where the others were gathered in the gloom. Disapproving stares from the congregation followed him down. After a moment he heard light steps behind him.

"What now?" he said, as he reached Mackenna and the others.

The Scotsman stepped round him, and stood, facing Anita. She stopped, uncertain, ready to run.

"Who are you?"

"My name is Bruce Mackenna, Zahra Hashemi. I wish you no harm."

"Yes, you do. You are after Ben, to take him away."

"If your brother succeeds, others will take him away. They will send him to America and he will stay in jail for the rest of his life."

"He knows that. He will not go to jail. He has chosen martyrdom. I have said good-bye to him."

"You will be locked up as well. In America, if you are lucky. If you are unlucky, they will send you back to Yemen."

"Yemen?" Her voice trembled.

"Yes. Yemen. My people in Sana'a believe that you killed a gangster called Babu Malik. I don't blame you. But his friends will be waiting for you. Have you seen an execution in Yemen? They make you lie down in front of hundreds of people and shoot you through the back. Even women. Perhaps you've seen it? I've seen it."

The short figure facing him shook, like a young tree struck by an axe, and then she sank to her knees and buried her face in her hands, and prayed aloud in a language that Chris did not recognise.

(*Oh mother, mother, where are you? What should I do? Please help me.*)

"If you help me, you can have a life," continued Mackenna. "Even a life with Neil and Harry. But if you do not, I will come after you. These other things will happen. We have twenty-nine minutes to stop it. What is your brother going to do? Tell me quickly or it will be too late."

"I can't trust you. I can't. You are a policeman."

She looked round and saw deVries.

"You are Jerome deVries, aren't you? You came to the caravan to save Neil."

He nodded.

"To repay a debt after sixteen years?"

DeVries nodded.

Anita sat down on the vergers' bench. From the front of the cathedral, came the swelling sound of the choir singing the Magnificat. She seemed to draw strength from it. After a minute, she spoke again.

"Come here. I will speak with you. You will be in my debt. You can repay me tonight. Or burn in hell."

DeVries sat down and she talked softly to him. After a minute, he nodded, the barest nod that sealed a contract. He got up and beckoned Chris over.

"Doesn't mean much to me but listen to her."

Chris listened. Two minutes later he was on the phone to David Trebbiano.

"Is that all?"

"Yes. I don't know what it means. 'They will never find it, because there is nothing to find.'"

"Nothing to find? There can't be nothing to find or-"

"Obviously. But that's what he said. I asked her twice. Get it out on IM. All developers. Call, fuck, I don't know. Call Efraim Hatzoulis and Arshad. Call John, call your best people. It is ShuffleDB, he's going to shuffle the bank. He also boasted that this 'nothing' took him two minutes to set up, after he had the idea."

"How long have we got?"

The service sheet swum in front of him.

"Until the end of the Nunc Dimittis."

"What?"

"Seventeen minutes."

Chris sat, trying to think. Nothing came. Nothing. With thirteen minutes to go, out of desperation or force of habit – he was never sure which – he called Dom. And why would Dom answer? But he did.

Ten minutes later, Chris was shouting down the phone to Tom Hailey.

"Tom, get your guys to kill the ShuffleDB batch. Yes, that one, the one we've been running for weeks. Now! Don't argue, Tom, trust me on this, just fucking kill it. Hurry, it starts in two minutes."

He waited in the darkness for Tom to call back. Some remote part of him was listening to the choir, singing the Song of Simeon.

Lord, now lettest thou thy servant depart in peace, according to thy word ...

Peace. Fuck yes. Peace. Please, no more stress and shame and sleepless nights. The Fates smiled as they wove.

*

Olivia was waiting for him in the lobby when he got back with Harry.

"Where have you been? I've got a taxi on the meter outside-"

"You wouldn't believe what just happened-"

"Chris, I don't need to know. Just give me Harry, I've got to go. Brian and Sarah are waiting for me, OK?"

"Yes but... hang on..."

She was gone, carrying Harry.

Here was deVries, looking for an update.

"She told me Hassan said there was nothing to find! So what did you find?"

"Remember we left one ShuffleDB job running – the one that's been running for a month."

"The one I wanted you to shut down."

"Er, yes. That program reads a file which is a to-do list. It's just a list of our major production systems. It goes through the list, extracting data out of each system, shuffling it, and writing it back into the partner test systems, which it finds in another file. Hassan just swapped the names of those two files. So the list of test systems was now called 'production' and the production systems were called 'test.' The next time ShuffleDB ran, it would extract data from the test systems, scramble it some more and put it into the production systems. All without changing a line of code to the batch. Result: total destruction. Brilliant. Simple."

"Our best brains searched all day and they didn't think of this?"

"Psychology."

"Psychology?"

"He had those ShuffleDB chron jobs around the world, ready to scramble our data. Hidden, but not too hidden. Then he "found" one himself. Tally ho, chaps. Information Security was so busy chasing the decoys, they never looked under their noses."

"Even I was suspicious," said deVries, "but would you listen? No. So which IT genius saw through this?"

Well now, there was a question. The truth would be "Dom MacDonald," but that would lead on to awkward questions like 'and you sacked him because...?'"

"It was a team effort."

Chris went back to the boardroom and sat, drinking black coffee and trying to imagine what other surprises Anwar/Hassan might have devised for him. It was going to be a long, anxious night.

Nothing prepared him for what actually happened.

At 10.30pm his phone rang. Olivia.

"Chris, just checking that Harry arrived safely."

"What are you talking about? You've got Harry."

"No, I haven't. Your man collected him. Nice chap, but a bit odd."

Chris felt a cold hand clutching at his heart.

"Which chap?"

"A young Indian. He rang the doorbell half an hour ago, just after I'd put Harry to bed. He said you'd sent him."

"I haven't sent anyone."

"Well, he showed me his ID. He said his sister was Anita, Neil's girlfriend and she could look after Harry after all. Harry knew him, he went off quite happily holding his hand. I was sorry to see him go, he's a lovely child."

"What was his name?" asked Chris, just to gain time. He already knew the answer. There was only one young Indian who knew Harry, who knew about Neil and Anita, and his name was Hassan Choudhary, otherwise known as Anwar il-Parsani, a digital terrorist and would-be destroyer of banks.

*

Mackenna must have pulled strings at Scotland Yard. Two detectives turned up in half an hour. Their unmarked squad car sat on the pavement outside, flashing blue.

"And where is the sister – er – Anita now?" said the older detective. He was a substantial character, mid-forties with a pockmarked face and fleshy lips. His stomach bulged somewhat over his blue jeans and a leather jacket.

"She's at home in North London," said Mackenna. "She says her brother moved out a week ago. He refused to say where he was going."

"Frank," said the senior detective, "go and check her out. Look for clues, correspondence, estate agent details."

Then he turned to the rest of them.

"So, what brings you gentlemen here on a Sunday evening?"

"Disaster recovery drill," lied deVries smoothly. "It's been running all weekend."

Chris' phone was ringing. Olivia. She was so upset that he could hardly understand her.

"Slowly, slowly... say it again. Hassan phoned you? The man who collected Harry?"

"Yes, yes, that one. He said... he said that he is watching you... he said that if you interfere, Harry will die with him. He will know, he said, he knows everything. He sounded completely insane. I could hear Harry crying in the background. Oh my God, Chris, what's going on? That poor little boy, we have to find him... I'm coming over."

He met her in reception half an hour later, tearful and wearing one of Sarah's old sweaters. As soon as she saw him, she ran over. "Is there any news?"

Chris shook his head.

"I knew it," she said. "I knew it. I knew there was something not right. And I handed that little boy over to that snake... how could I? Why didn't I think? Why didn't I ask more questions?"

"Olivia, it's not your fault, don't blame yourself. He had a cast iron story. Come upstairs."

He took her up to Meeting Room Fourteen and introduced her to Mackenna and the detective, who grilled her for half an hour.

It was eleven o'clock. Chris was in the board room with the police and half the management of the bank. And Olivia, who had invited herself. "He's my nephew," she said, which earned her a respectful place at the table.

There wasn't a lot of good news. Hassan's phone was off the network. The call to Olivia was through Skype, and presently untraceable. The young detective had searched Anita's flat and found nothing.

No one knew whether Harry and Hassan had left in a taxi, private hire car or even public transport.

A picture of Harry and another of Hassan had been circulated to all stations and patrol cars and someone was trawling through the private hire companies. CCTV records from the buses and the Underground were being scanned. The phones of the local council – who had cameras on the streets – were permanently engaged.

"When will he know his plan has failed?" asked deVries.

"If it has failed," said Chris cautiously, "because he may have left other surprises. But if not, he will start to get worried about 1am. He will be expecting a tidal wave of error code thirty-ones from the risk systems. If nothing happens by 2am, he will know he's failed."

"What are our chances of finding him before then?"

"We're trying," said the senior detective, gesturing out the window, "but it's a big haystack. There are five million homes out there. There are almost half a million students renting rooms."

The awful dilemma floated in the ether, in front of them all. Only deVries had the courage to put it into words.

"We could put things back, could we not? Let the shuffling happen."

"What?" said Sir Simon, "and destroy the bank? Hoping this madman will spare the child? That's giving in to blackmail. Absolutely out of the question."

Put like that, no one was going to argue.

Back in Mackenna's lair, Olivia grasped Chris' hands in hers. "Chris, you're so clever with computers, please, please think of something. Find Harry. Stop him." Chris didn't feel clever. His head was one big thumping blank. Just like Neil on BaByliss night.

And then suddenly, magically, he had an idea.

54

Midnight

No one had spoken for almost half an hour. The bells of the City were striking midnight all around them.

"Anything?" asked Sir Simon, looking up. He was looking anxious, sitting in a beaten-up swivel chair. In front of them, messages flowed up the big screens, each bringing some tale of jobs that overran, disks that failed, messages that had no headers and conversations between computers that timed out. If you didn't know what you were looking at, it was a worrying picture.

This was the TIS London Operations Centre. The night shift operators, squeezed into one corner, rolled their eyes and silently prayed that their important visitors would butt out. Technology management would blunder in from time to time, but the visit of the Chief Exec, the COO and all the IT heads – and all in the middle of the night – was unprecedented.

John Uzgalis sat down. "All good in technology. No sign of shuffling. Special backups of the major systems have been taken. Any other news?"

The police were following up on six sightings. Lambeth Council were searching their CCTV. Another forty minutes went by.

"OK, we're starting to process the risk numbers from the trading systems," said Trebbiano. "If he's been successful, the first code thirty-one will show up any second."

Minutes passed. Mackenna caught Chris' eye and raised an eyebrow. Chris shook his head, as though in sorrow.

"What's that?" said someone, pointing at the screen.

"That's two code thirty-ones," replied Trebbiano, "that's OK. They tend to come in spurts. We get about a hundred anyway each night, maybe more after big days in the markets."

"And that?"

"Uh-oh. That's not right," replied Trebbiano, "not right at all. Jesus, five hundred error thirty-ones in a minute, I've never seen that, not in production."

It was 00:51 and all hell broke loose. At 1am there were fifteen thousand exceptions in a single minute. Trebbiano was white faced, talking to his team around the world, trying to understand which systems were producing the errors. It seemed to be most of them.

"Don't ask me again," he shouted at Uzgalis at one point. "I have no fucking idea. Every system we investigate seems fine but the error reports get worse every minute."

Sometime during that hour, TIS set up an incident centre and started sending out category Black incident messages. Sir Simon disappeared to a crisis meeting of the board.

The night flowed by in a chaotic series of calls and updates. Panic spread slowly from London, outwards and upwards. All over the world, incredulous business heads were being briefed by white-faced support staff. Sir Simon called Teddy Feugel, the chairman of the bank, himself. All these conversations went badly because no one could say exactly what the problem was, how widespread the impact or when it would be fixed. Or if it would be fixed.

About 4am, John Uzgalis pulled Chris to one side.

"Chris? There's something weird going on. All these errors, but then the systems fix themselves."

"Huh?" said Chris.

"Yeah. EOS, your favourite system, we get a load of error messages. Bad risk, unmatched settlements, cashflows blowing up. Really bad. But the EOS guys can't figure out which trades are causing it, it's like the system fixed itself."

"Weird."

Jerome deVries was staring at him from across the table. Chris escaped back into Meeting Room Fourteen, where Olivia was sitting, drinking black coffee and hugging herself for comfort. Mackenna's boys were nowhere to be seen, perhaps catching up on sleep.

"Detection runs in the Peters family, I see," said Mackenna. Chris looked blank.

"Your wife has asked herself an interesting question."

"Which was?"

"How did Hassan know where to find Harry?"

"He can't possibly know my sister Sarah," said Olivia, "or know that I was staying there. So he must have followed us. You met him downstairs with Harry, right? You told him that I was coming to pick Harry up. He must have waited outside. When I arrived, I told my taxi to wait. When I came out with Harry, we jumped in and we were gone in five seconds. So how did he follow us?"

"Only one way," said Chris, light dawning, "he was sitting inside a cab... you know what, there was a black cab parked on Bentham Street when I was running out to St Pauls."

"He was probably inside it," said Mackenna, "watching us. Well, finding a cab that spent an hour outside this building, that's really specific. I've got the boys on it."

Tom Hailey called. "How much longer, Chris? We're creating some serious shit here with the business."

"I know," said Chris, keeping his voice down, "and John Uzgalis is starting to get suspicious."

Henry and William reappeared.

"We've found it! A black cab. Hassan flagged it down here. Stopped to pick up a child south of the river. Final destination Swinnerton St. That's in East London, E3."

"Address?"

"No address. The cabbie thought it was all a bit odd so he watched them when they got out. They passed the first houses on the left side of the street and disappeared into a wall. It's very dark, he says."

"Let's go," said deVries. "George can take us."

"What about the police?"

"They will catch us up," said Mackenna, picking up a leather sports bag from the corner. Chris wondered what was in it.

"Well, I'm coming," said Olivia firmly. "I've got Harry's things. Clothes and food."

*

"Let me guess," said Jerome deVries dryly as the limo pulled away from the bank, "this is another Chris Peters surprise. There's nothing wrong with our systems, is there?" He was sitting in the back with Chris and Olivia. Mackenna and George were in front, debating routes.

"No," said Chris, "Tom Hailey and I cooked it up. As long as Hassan thinks he's been successful, he won't harm Harry."

"That's a dangerous game. Many other people are panicking right now, people with a lot to lose. Can you stop it when you want to?"

"Yes. We used the incident system. It creates incidents automatically. Every night the test systems produce thousands – millions – of errors because of the shuffled data being fed into them. Tom just changed the rules. He spoofed the error messages so it looked like the live systems were blowing up."

"But there is nothing wrong with them?"

"No. That's why John Uzgalis and his boys are scratching their heads. The production systems are perfectly healthy and yet there are millions of errors from them. But we don't have much time. Someone will figure it out, and then Hassan will see the chit-chat and then- God knows."

"Get a move on, George," said deVries.

"Steady," growled Mackenna. "Don't get stopped – or caught by a camera."

The big car raced eastwards, through the empty streets. A Number Fifty-Five night bus trundled the other way. It looked warm and ordinary inside. Chris wished he was on it. Olivia shivered suddenly next to him. He found her hand and squeezed it and after a moment she squeezed back.

*

Swinnerton Street was asleep. There were dark red-brick houses and a block of flats, and a few feeble street lights.

"George, halfway down, please. By the wall. Engine off, lights off." That was Mackenna, taking charge.

"Where are the police?" said Olivia, "surely they should be here by now?"

"Not yet," said Mackenna.

"What? You didn't call them?"

"You want the boy alive?" said Mackenna. "This is my job."

He pulled on a pair of thin leather gloves from his bag. Then he took out a torch, and a dark snub-nosed revolver. He slipped a clip of ammunition into it and stowed it inside his jacket. Chris stared in horror.

"Don't worry, lad," said Mackenna. "I've got a licence for it. Stay here. All of you. And be quiet."

He disappeared into the darkness. They waited. Four, maybe five long minutes.

"Listen," said Olivia suddenly. Olivia lowered her window. Over to their left, behind a wall, Chris thought he heard it too, a faint high-pitched nose. A child wailing? Or a cat?

"That's Harry!" said Olivia, and she jumped out. Ten yards down there was an old gate in the wall, standing open. She ran through it, with Chris and deVries in pursuit. They were in an alley with garages on both sides.

Olivia stopped to listen. The faint cry was louder now and she ran on towards it. And stopped in front of a big rolling shutter door sixty yards down. It had a smaller, man-sized door built in. The hinges squeaked and protested as they pushed it open.

All three of them stopped, half-blinded by the lights and stunned by the view.

The back wall was one huge picture, brightly lit. A city on a sunny day. The tall buildings were pure and white against the deep blue of the sky. Right in the middle, the flaming carcass of Flight 175 was emerging from the South Tower of the World Trade Center. An angry slogan in Arabic was daubed across the scene in red paint.

An office chair and a desk overlooked the City, as an air traffic controller might overlook his runways. The desk had an old computer screen and a keyboard on it.

The chair was occupied by a thin, dark figure. He was slumped against the high back, head to one side. His left hand had slipped off the keyboard and dangled by his calves. He was wearing an old leather flying jacket and goggles. A thin line of drool ran from one corner of his mouth.

They walked in like zombies, amazed. Mackenna was bending over the body, perhaps checking for a pulse. There was an empty brown bottle on the floor, with a white label. Curiously, deVries reached down to it.

"Don't touch it, for God's sake," growled Mackenna, "it could kill you, even through the skin."

The screen was still running. Chris recognized the incident reports scrolling down it, reporting meltdown and mayhem across the systems of the bank.

"Where's Harry?" said Olivia. "I heard him."

There were noises from under the desk.

And there was Harry, sitting miserably in a small puddle, surrounded by discarded farm animals. He was clutching one of Hassan's ankles. Chris stepped forward, but Olivia was ahead of him. She scooped the child up in her arms and held him close.

"Wait for me in the car," said Mackenna, "while I tidy up here."

Olivia turned in the doorway. Harry stretched his arms backwards, towards his dead companion.

"Wake up, Nwa! Nwa! Wake up!"

"Don't worry, darling," said Olivia, "he will, soon."

After she had gone, Chris and deVries stood together in silence, watching the fake error messages flowing up the screen. They were seeing what Hassan saw as he died. And what was he thinking? He was Mohamed Atta on 911, flying his plane down the Hudson River into oblivion, driven by the terrible anger. Except his target was not a building, his target was an entire bank.

Mackenna started tearing down the image of Manhattan and stuffing the sheets into a black dustbin bag. He snarled at their incomprehension.

"Suicide we can live with. It doesn't need to be a terrorist attack."

Chris' phone rang. It was Uzgalis. "Chris, I'm here with Dave Trebbiano. The shit is flying here. Where the hell are you? Where's Jerome? What the fuck is going on with these error messages?"

"They aren't real," said Chris. "Those thirty-ones are fakes. Our systems are fine."

"Well, they won't be for long. Sir Simon has pushed the red button. He's going nuclear on disaster recovery, calling the regulators, trying to cover his arse. He has ordered us to swing all critical systems to the backup datacentres. Globally, no excuses."

"What? He's insane. Stop him, for God's sake," cried Chris, scarcely believing it. *Shit.* He called Tom Hailey.

"Tom? It's over. Cut the dummy incident feed. Send the all clear. Make sure no one goes to DR or starts panic recovery from backup. No one."

Within a minute, the error messages stopped coming and the screen was still. Chris breathed a sigh of relief.

Someone coughed. Not loudly, more like a little grunt. Chris and deVries looked at other, puzzled. deVries shook his head.

Another little cough. Chris saw Hassan's body twitch a little.

"He moved. Oh my God, he moved," said deVries.

Mackenna ceased his destruction of the Manhattan skyline and came over.

Hassan's eyes were half open, but unseeing. Now there was the faintest, regular whistling as the air passed in and out of his lips, and little bubbles formed in the vomit that flowed from his mouth. Hassan was still breathing and it seemed to Chris that his breathing was getting stronger. And then his eyes started to roll, up and down.

"He took too much. He threw it up," said Mackenna, "it can happen."

The three of them stared at each other. DeVries was pale, his face drained of blood. He was leaning against the wall for support. Chris remembered that, later.

"We should call an ambulance," said Chris.

"No," said Mackenna, "I'll deal with this. Go back to the car. Hurry. Shut the door behind you. Now!"

Chris followed deVries out into the darkness and pulled the door closed. The latch wouldn't click. As soon as he let it go, it started to drift open.

He tried again.

He heard voices and looked around. But deVries had already disappeared down the alley. The noise was coming from inside. A voice, chatty, like a dentist making conversation. He couldn't make out the words, it was a foreign language.

Had Hassan woken up? As he grabbed the door handle, he caught a glimpse through the gap. At that moment, the Scotsman looked up from his patient in the chair, looked straight at him, his hands still busy. Chris understood and was instantly sick with fear.

He almost ran back to the car. Olivia was in the back seat, holding Harry. DeVries was in the front, next to George. Harry was clutching Olivia as though his life depended on it. Chris could see his eyes, wide open and still tearful. Chris got in.

"Chris, are you alright? You're shaking," said Olivia.

A few minutes later, Mackenna got in, holding his toolkit and the black dustbin liner.

"Home, George," he said calmly.

"But what about Hassan?" said Olivia. "We can't just leave him there."

"When we're away, we'll call the police," said Mackenna, "you look after the bairn. Back to the office, George, and don't get stopped."

DeVries was staring at Chris in the windscreen. *He knows* thought Chris. He didn't see it, but he knows. He didn't look well.

They pulled up outside the office. Mackenna turned to Chris. His face was six inches away, blue and yellow in the glow of the streetlights.

"Are you still with me, Chris? Really?" he said. His eyes were as cold and predatory as a crocodile's. Chris understood and was afraid again. Mackenna was assessing him as a risk.

"Yes," said Chris, as convincingly as he could. Meaning, "your secrets are safe with me."

"And how are you, Jerome?" asked Mackenna. "Are you alright?"

"No," came deVries' voice from the front, "I am unwell. You have destroyed me. George, take me home. You can drop the creature from Loch Ness at the office. Then take the Peters family wherever they want to go."

Dawn was breaking as Chris, Olivia and Harry arrived back at Thurleigh Rd. The smell of his own home was familiar and yet strange. He hadn't been home for a week. Dizzy, almost unconscious, he and Olivia changed the sleepy child and then fell into bed, Harry between them. It was 6am.

55

London

Monday, 8th October 2012

Bang, bang. Bang, bang. Someone at the front door. It went on and on. Chris staggered downstairs.

It was Holly. Behind her was a limo with George at the wheel.

"Holly! What are you doing here?"

"Mackenna sent me. He was worried about you. You have to come with me, now. There's a board meeting at noon. They want you there."

"DeVries is doing that."

"Jerome is in hospital. He's had a heart attack."

He dressed quickly and kissed Olivia on the cheek. She turned sleepily and her lips were soft. Harry was snorting and kicking under the sheets and she drew the child into her arms.

Outside, Holly looked disapprovingly at his jeans and leather jacket but all she said was, "Got your pass?"

It was strange, walking into the board room again. The pizza boxes, the piles of paper and the empty coffee cups were gone. The desks at the end where Hassan and his mates had sat for forty-eight hours were gone. Instead there were acres of polished wood surrounded by silent watchers. Mostly men, all in suits, all with piles of paper. All looking at him as if he had two heads.

"It must be dress down day in Global Markets," said Sir Simon, "this is Chris Peters, one of their top IT people. Jerome deVries should have been here, but he is unwell, sadly. Making a good recovery though. I sent you all a note on Saturday. We had an ugly incident over the weekend. Christopher, are we still in business?"

Chris explained the threat of shuffled data, and confirmed that the threat had passed. He was asked who did it, and ducked the question.

"Not good enough," said someone. "There are already stories on Twitter, connecting this attack with a young man found dead in East London this morning."

"He killed himself?" asked his neighbour.

"Twice. Cyanide and then he hanged himself with his own tie," confided the other, in a whisper that carried around the room.

Chris' lips moved soundlessly. *Mackenna, Mackenna.* His brain was still processing the horror of last night in the cold light of day. *Hanged himself with his own tie.* What he knew, could not be unknown. *Accessory to murder.* The phrase popped into his head, with all its frightening implications.

"The press are calling this an Islamic terror attack," said someone, "on the basis of some posters found in the young man's bedroom."

"Sir Simon, may I?" said Carla Bartoli, the head of HR, "look, this young man was hired as a graduate in our Chennai development centre. He struggled at SBS. There were issues with temperament and discipline. We deeply regret his death and we are looking into his medical history now."

"Yes, thank you, that's the angle," said Sir Simon with relief, "Press Relations will have a statement for all of you shortly. Stick to it. There is no Islamic connection, whatever posters he may have had in his bedroom. Now, can we move on... our problems with the US regulators. I had a successful meeting with six US agencies last Thursday. Christopher, you're up again! Topeka. Do you have an update for us?"

Chris put up a single slide with the project plan.

"What are the red triangles?" asked someone.

"Those are the milestones that are late. No need to count, there are thirty-two of them against fifty green ones and seventeen ambers."

"Well, that doesn't sound very good."

"It isn't," intervened Sir Simon, "but Jerome deVries has re-organised the entire program under Christopher and he is going to get those thirty-two milestones back on track, isn't that right?"

"No," said Chris. There was a shocked silence.

"I'm sorry, I didn't mean to put you on the spot. You are going to deliver the project on time, can we say that?"

"No," said Chris, "I will not waste another day or night or even a minute of my life on Topeka. But don't worry."

Sir Simon looked as if he had just found a worm in his apple. There were sounds of disbelief and amazement around the table.

"Don't worry?" said someone. A man with a neat dark beard. He sounded German. "Why should the passengers not worry when the pilot jumps out of the plane?"

His face was familiar but Chris had only seen him in photos before. It was Teddy Feugel, the chairman of the bank.

"Because the Americans have already decided the fine. They are upset with us for arguing with them. It will be six billion US. Red triangles or no red triangles, it will be six billion. Topeka is just window dressing."

Sir Simon stood up in his chair, his face puce.

"Ridiculous. And if I may say so, way beyond your pay grade."

Chris shrugged. "Ask Chuck Forbes, then. They have already split the fine between the agencies."

"We almost went under four years ago," said Feugel, looking at Chris intently, "and you didn't quit then."

"Then? We were all in it together. The mission was survival. What's the point of us now? We spend our lives ticking boxes for regulators. The public and the politicians hate us. They don't understand what we do but their nose tells them the truth: we're not doing it for them. We're doing it for us. We are corrupted by money."

"Then fuck off," said Sir Simon, "and try life without it. Your resignation is accepted."

He motioned to the door guard.

"Well, just a moment, Simon," said Feugel, "while we are ah – enjoying this moment of Truth to Power, listen to this tweet from *Here is the City*. 'Hassan Choudhary was lauded by IT management. As recently as last week, they awarded him the Golden Bot prize and promoted him.' Doesn't sound like a failure to me. So why did he attack us?"

"Sir Simon was right," said Chris, "he was troubled and angry and he did have problems with discipline."

Sir Simon nodded approval, his face still puce with indignation.

Feugel was still looking at Chris, waiting. One eyebrow raised, not believing.

"Why was he so angry? Do you really want to know? I'm not sure you do."

Feugel nodded, almost imperceptibly.

"Ok. Well then… in 2007, when he was fifteen, his father was kidnapped in Yemen. The family had the money to pay the ransom, but we – SBS – had suspended their account, probably simply because they were Iranian. They begged and pleaded. We then decided they were drug barons. We refused to release the money, we refused even to say why, despite their desperation. Time ran out, and his father was beheaded. His brother also, I don't know how that happened. His sister was raped by the kidnappers, who ran a prostitution business in Sana'a. Two weeks later, his mother burned herself to death on the steps of our branch in Dubai. He hated us. He became radical. He became a follower of Anwar al-Awlaki and he set out to destroy us. Does that answer your question?"

He looked around their shocked faces. No one spoke. Then Feugel said, "And what? You sound sympathetic. You think he was right?"

"No. Of course not. But… I used to think I had the best job in the world. It was fun, it was interesting, it was my whole life. Now I just feel used. And dirty. I don't want to be here and I won't be here."

The man in the dark suit opened the door for him. And he left.

*

Chris walked up the short path to his front door, and rang the bell.

For a minute, it seemed as if no one was at home. But then he heard her steps coming down the stairs, and her voice, "Well, Harry, who can this be?"

She sounded cheerful.

He had no flowers. He had no job. He had no idea what he was going to say. He had brought a toddler into their lives, surplus to requirements. He was armed only with her words from the awful night when she had left him: *it's only what you do, Chris, only what you do.* He was going to let her decide.

56

London: 4 months later

January 2013

The coroner was a small, unimposing man and the courtroom suited him. It reminded Chris of his doctor's surgery. It was too small for today's proceedings. The grey plastic chairs were fully occupied by journalists. The simply curious and the latecomers were standing along the back. He spotted Anita, head covered in a hijab, on the far side. She was sitting next door to a thin, earnest man in a suit and tie. As the coroner announced his verdict, he saw him reach down and squeeze her hand.

Chris and Olivia waited for her outside, although she had covered her face against photographers, and she hugged them both. She and Olivia had become firm friends, united by their affection for little Harry.

"Hello, Anita. This must be your uncle?"

"I am Saeed," said the man courteously, taking Chris' hand and bowing to Olivia.

They sat in Starbucks. Chris wasn't quite sure what to say. Saeed insisted on buying although his wallet looked thin and well worn.

"What do you do, Saeed?"

"I drive a taxi," said Saeed, "for now. I live near Neil and Anita, in Romford."

"Neil is back?" Chris was ashamed that he didn't know that.

"Nearly! Tomorrow. I am going to pick him up."

She was smiling. They watched through the window as the *Evening Standard* seller updated his pitch: "Young Banker Inquest - Verdict."

"Why is everyone who works in a bank called a banker?" asked Saeed.

"It sells newspapers," said Chris, "every industry is corrupt in different ways."

"My God, what's got into you?" said Anita, "you sound bitter."

"No. I have lost my innocence," replied Chris, "but don't worry, I'm still an optimist at heart. How's Harry?"

"He's wonderful. Martha looks after him during the week and I do the weekends. It's easier now that I'm living in the country. We've got a proper cottage, big enough for the three of us."

She suddenly reached over and took one of his hands in hers.

"I feel Ben wants me to tell you something. He talked about you a lot, did you know that? He respected you. And he was afraid of you. He said you were like him, you were always thinking. Always questioning. He wanted to be friends with you. He would be happy to know that you are happy. He didn't have any friends, except perhaps Karthik. The real Indian grads in Chennai were suspicious of him.

"When he was young, he was happy to be alone. His cleverness kept him company. But then, after- after our parents died, he didn't know how to smile, he hated everyone. He was so bitter, he was eaten from the inside… I'm sorry, it's awful to think that he threatened Harry. I will never forgive him for that."

"Anita, he was mad," said Olivia gently, "insane. You heard the coroner, 'the balance of his mind was disturbed.'"

"Do you think so? I don't. That's just an excuse. He was perfectly sane, he was the most sane person I know."

"Please, excuse me, Mr Peters. Let me tell you something." Saeed was speaking, so softly that Chris had to lean forward to hear him. "My brother was killed because your bank wouldn't give us the money, our money, that we had been saving for years. And they wouldn't even tell us why. But in the end, when it was too late, we found out the truth."

"Did you find this out from al-Muhairi?" asked Chris, remembering the terrible images of the banker beaten to a pulp.

"Yes, al-Muhairi. That was his name. He told us that we were on a special list, that we were Politically Exposed Persons and the bank didn't want to deal with us. He swore to us that he had tried to change it. How do you get off the list? You can't. The Americans keep the list. That's when Ahmed went mad."

"You and Ben were there?" asked Chris.

Saeed covered his eyes with both hands, as though to shut off the memory of Ahmed's savagery.

"Later, when Ahmed had finished, Ben said to him, 'you have punished one man. But I will punish the whole bank, even if it takes me the rest of my life. Even if it kills me.'"

"But I think that was wrong. Like al-Muhairi told us, the banks are afraid of the Blind Giant. And so are we. If you destroy this bank, I told him, the giant will be angry and he will make more rules and more fines. Maybe more drones and more bombs – and nothing will get better. So, Mr Peters, it is a good thing that my brother did not succeed. I thank you for that."

"But he wouldn't listen to you?" said Chris.

"'Little people live in the valleys,' he used to say, 'only a few can climb the mountains to the clouds. They can see all of history and they can change it if they are strong. If they are ready to sacrifice themselves. Only the strong die well,' he used to say."

"Who was he talking about?"

"You might think of Jesus Christ. Or Joan of Arc. But his heroes were the pilots: Mohamed Atta and Marwan al-Shehhi, who flew those planes into the World Trade Center. They died unknowing. They changed history but they didn't live to see it. He wanted to be like them. He wanted to die. Actually he thought death was a magic potion. If he died, his plan would succeed."

"I thought that once," said Anita. "I was ready to die, Chris. I was. Did you know that?"

Her uncle reached out and touched her shoulder.

"Don't upset yourself, my niece. You don't have to talk about it."

"I want to talk about it, Saeed. Today. Tomorrow I start a new life. There are things that I never told you, but you should know. I have been living a big lie."

"Don't talk nonsense. Stop it."

"No, no, let me say it. You will hate me, whatever you say now. I was responsible for the death of our poor father. And our brother Mahmoud. What has happened to us, it started with me."

"No, no, don't say that, it's not true!"

"Yes it is. Babu Malik used to drive by the shop every afternoon. I was such a stupid little girl. I liked it. I encouraged him. I used to take my niqab off when I got to work so that he could see my face. To start with, I didn't know who he was but I was pleased that this rich man fancied me.

"His father wanted the shop, and Babu wanted me. So they kidnapped Father. They never intended to kill him, just to take his shop. His money. And his daughter."

"You found out who he was?"

"Yes. Old Abdullah knew him, Old Abdullah told me who was inside the black Mercedes. But I didn't know what he was until he caught me. He supplied girls to the privileged of Sana'a. Rich businessmen. Army people. Foreigners who worked in the embassies. Even tourists – there were still a few in 2007."

"His father owned half the butchers' shops in Sana'a. But as the city got poorer and the foreigners left, those businesses didn't do well. They found a new one. People were coming across the Red Sea from Africa, refugees, desperate people. Babu and his father picked them up on the coast and brought them to Sana'a. And sold them on. Some stayed in Yemen, some went for export."

"I was a virgin when Babu captured me, but not for long. It's so hard to say this. I was his little Indian princess. I was his new attraction to his regular customers. He sold my virginity ten times over. The Indian princess was irresistible to all kinds of cruel men, not just Yemenis.

"But that happened later. The second night, he had a party for his friends, and he got very drunk. He made me wear my sari and some cheap jewellery, and he made me dance. His friends all threw money at me. If they gave enough money, they were allowed to touch me. I can't describe it. It was so disgusting. Only his cousin, the fat policeman, did not take part, I saw him watching from the corner.

"Later that night, I heard shouting outside, and one of his men came in and said that they had found a man climbing over the wall. Bring him here, he said and they did. It was Mahmoud. When he saw me, he started shouting to Babu, 'Let her go, you camel turd,' and 'Where is my father?' Babu said that he had nothing to do with the kidnapping and he was trying to help us. But then his father Khalid arrived. Khalid told them to take Mahmoud down and put him with the African slaves. Babu was a bad man, but his father was a monster. His father used to torture the Africans. Not because it gave him pleasure, just because he was bored.

The next day they locked me in a little room, a storeroom with strong shelves and a thick door. It had a tiny window, I could just see out. It was very hot that day. In the middle of the morning, a man arrived. Later I found out that the man worked for Khalid Malik in his abbatoir. He was a butcher.

"They brought our father and Mahmoud into the courtyard. I heard Mahmoud shouting and my father crying for mercy for his son. Those were the last words I heard. The butcher killed both of them. I heard the men standing around, shouting and encouraging him. That was when I decided that I would kill Babu myself. I would have liked to kill his father as well, but I never saw him again.

"I had no fear. It was as if I was already dead. I started to cut myself with broken glass. All I thought about was how to kill him. But Babu seemed to know. He kept me locked up in that little room. He lost interest in my body, or in selling my body. I began to starve myself, I lost weight. He used to drink a lot, but now he drank twice as much. He used to go out in the evenings, but now he stayed at home. One day he came in to see me and he made me strip in front of him while he played with himself. Then he said, 'Whore, you must brush your hair, you must paint your nails, you whore.' 'How can I?' I said, 'I have no brush and no paint.' That evening, he came back from the souk with a cheap make up box and a hairbrush. In the box was some nail varnish, lipstick, face powder, a nail file and some little brass scissors. Then I knew that Allah was with me."

Anita had stopped weeping. She dried her eyes, and handed back her brother's handkerchief.

"I cut my nails and painted them. I brushed my hair. That evening, he came to see me. He was drunk, but not so drunk. After he had finished with me, he fell asleep on the mattress. That's when I blinded him with the scissors, I twisted them inside his eyes, my fingers hurt, it was harder than I expected.

"He woke up screaming and clutching his eyes and I stabbed him many times in his chest. Someone came and shouted outside the door, but he had locked it on the inside. After a while, Babu collapsed and I banged his head on the floor until he was quiet. I was mad and I knew they would kill me if I didn't kill myself first. But I didn't want to do it. I felt strong."

The others stared at her, wordlessly. She had stopped, as through someone had hit the "off" switch.

Eventually Olivia whispered, "But how... how are you here?"

"The fat policeman, his cousin, came. He told the servants to go away and then he told me to open the door. He said he would not harm me. I didn't believe him, but I opened the door. It wasn't easy because my hands were so slippery. When he was sure Babu Malik was dead, he sat quietly. Then he called in his driver, Tariq, and they removed his body. He made me wash all the blood off. And he took me away. The fat policeman told me that my mother and Ben had left Yemen, that they had gone to Dubai. She was dead already, burned, but we didn't know that. That night, I went back to our house secretly, the same way that I had left it. I hid there for three weeks. Every few days, the young policeman would bring food."

The neighbours say the house is haunted, thought Chris.

"After three weeks, the fat policeman brought me an identity card. He said it belonged to a girl who had been killed by a car bomb. The car bombs were just beginning then. I went to live with him as his cook and housemaid. I was thin, thinner than I am now, and I could speak Arabic, Parsee and some English.

"Eventually he helped me get a job with Yemeni Airlines and I was able to start life again. And one day I stopped in Dubai and I went looking for Saeed and Ahmed and Ben. Saeed told me that Ahmed was dead and Ben had a scholarship to go to Delhi Technical University."

Anita reached across and put her arm round Saeed's shoulder.

"Saeed and I are the last ones left in our family, Chris. We don't want to punish anyone anymore, we're happy to live in the valley with the other little people.

"And how about you? What has changed in your life? I can get you a job, any time."

"Thank you," said Chris, "but we've already got one."

"We?"

"Dom and I. We've found this little software company. Really neat idea, just needs technical help. We start next month, just before Olivia has to stop work."

"Has to stop work? You mean... a baby? Oh Chris, that's wonderful."

"Yes. It is. And thanks to Harry, I think," said Olivia. "Having Harry around made us feel like a Mum and Dad, and suddenly – well – we were."

Acronyms and jargon

AppDev	IT staff who build & maintain software i.e. "programmers"(compare with TIS staff who look after "the hardware")
BMS	Computer system that manages heat, aircon, lighting in buildings
Bot	Computer program that fights (other bots) for fun
Business Continuity	Group tasked with ensuring rapid recovery from disasters
CRAC	Computer Room Air Conditioner – industrial scale aircon
Dba	Database administrator. Looks after computer databases
Dodd-Frank	Major US regulation post 2008 financial crash
DR	Disaster Recovery
EOS	Equity Options System: a major derivatives system in SBS
EPO	Emergency Power Off key for data centres
EWG	Imaginary firm of management consultants
FSA	UK regulators (now split into FCA and PRA)
HKMA	Hong Kong regulators
IR	Incident Report (relates to IT incidents)
KPC	Another imaginary firm of management consultants
KYC	Know Your Customer – hot area for regulation
LCD	Liquid Crystal flat screen display
MDMA	Pure form of the drug also known as Ecstasy
NOC	Network Operations Centre: monitors IT processes
OFAC	Office of Foreign Asset Control; part of US Treasury
PEP	Politically Exposed Person. PEPs get special KYC vetting.
PolyCom	Handsfree phone designed for teleconferencing

Qat	Bush whose leaves are chewed by many Yemenis. A stimulant.
RMDS	Reuters electronic distribution system for market prices and data
SBS	A fictitious but typical large bank
SEC	Securities & Exchange Commission – US regulator
SOX	Sarbanes-Oxley; major US regulation post Enron
SWIFT	Industry utility for moving money around
TIS	Technology Infrastructure Services
Triple Witching	Crazy day in the markets which comes once a quarter
UNIX	A computer operating system

List of players

The Hashemi family

Jafar	Father
Gurjit	Mother
Mahmoud	Their eldest son
Ahmed	2nd son (the boxer)
Zahra	Their only daughter
Ben	Their youngest child
Uncle Saeed	Jafar's brother (based in Dubai)
Old Abdullah	A family retainer and shopkeeper

Other Yemen/Dubai characters

Babu Malik	A crook and libertine
Khalid Malik	Babu's father
Grishigar	A young wrestler
Yousef	A child who is a neighbour of the Hashemis
al-Muhairi	A banker with SBS in Dubai
Anwar al-Awlaki	An Imam of Yemen extraction, born in the US
Tariq	A young Yemeni police driver
al-Omani	An al-Qaeda bomb maker

SBS bank (Group functions)

TeddyFeugel	Chairman of SBS
Sir Simon	CEO of SBS
Chuck Forbes	Head of Americas
Bruce Mackenna	Internal Security
Henry & William	Work for Mackenna in Internal Security
Mike Tucker	Head of Group Property
Murali	Group Property, based in Chenai

Aside from Group functions, the SBS bank has at least 4 divisions: Corporate, Retail, Asset Management and Global Markets (the investment bank). But only Global Markets really features in this book. There is a CEO of GM but he is unnamed.

Global Markets

Cyrus	Head of Equities (a division within Global Markets)
Miyuki	Cyrus' PA
"CK"	Head of Rates
Tassone	Head of Commodities
John Tully	COO (Chief Operating Officer)
Jerome deVries	CFO (Chief Financial Officer) but ambitious
Carla Bartoli	Head of Global Markets HR
Rosemary	Senior HR person who looks after the back office
Hugh Evans	An auditor
Oleg	Another auditor
Dirk Pascalides	Compliance

Working for Cyrus in Equities

Peter Elliot	Head of Equities in Hong Kong
Pierre Reynaud	Head of High Frequency Trading (computer trading)
Chuck Masters	Head of Equity Derivatives
Max	London Portfolio Trading
Hamish	Works for Max on the desk in Portfolio

Global Markets Finance & Risk

Jerome deVries	The CFO
Anne Steffens	A business manager in Finance
Tim Hawes	An acolyte of the CFO
Pandora Stiegel	Head of Credit and Capital Risk
Sarah Kreisel	A project manager in Risk

Global Markets IT

Alexis van Buren	CIO (Chief Information Officer)
Chris Peters	Equities Technology
John Uzgalis	Debt Technology
David Trebbiano	Back Office Technology
Gawain Hughes	Topeka Program Manager

Key players in Equity Technology

Dom Macdonald	Disaster Recovery & other jobs
Holly	Chris' PA
Raul	Asia Equities Technology
Jason Soh	Works for Raul in Asia
Carl	Americas Equities Technology
Dave Carstairs	Production Support guru
P K Ramachandran	India Development Centre head
Arshad Zebediah	Architect of the High Frequency Trading system
Hassan Choudhary	A young Indian grad
Karthik Singh	A young Indian grad
Jason Crisp	Technical team member

Technology Infrastructure Services (TIS)

Neil Jenkins	CTO (boss of TIS)
Mary	His PA
Ashok Kumar	An analyst
Sheila Collins	Head of Information Security
Colin	Sidekick to Sheila Collins in InfoSec
Tom Hailey	Networks and Market Data
Steve Smith	Data Centres
Paul Carpenter	Head of Americas TIS
Mannie Seibowitz	Runs the Americas Network Operations Center (NOC)
NOC shift staff	Frank, Marvin, John and Luis all work for Mannie

Other players

Olivia	A young woman, works for a London PR company
Praveen Hirani	Senior partner at KPC, a management consultancy
Anita	A IT recruitment agent
Harry	Neil Jenkins' toddler son
Martha	Harry's child minder
Diarmid Macdonald	Dom's father

Acknowledgements

This book has been many years in the making, and every year has added a new generation of patient victims. I am sincerely grateful to them all. In particular to Paul Berrey, Neil Boosey, Gary Friar, and Glen Howell for their technical assistance and enthusiastic contributions to the possibilities for digital terror.

Ben Cavanagh, Helen Challis, Lynn Chapman, Hamid Habibi, Greg Hannah, Pat Healey, Rachel Jones, Paul Lewis, Charity Norman, Christopher Mackenzie, Clare Oldridge, Claire Robley, Tony Stennett, Robin Walden, Danny Wicks, and my agent Robin Wade all read the manuscript in various stages. The plot, the action and the characters of Trading Down have benefited enormously from their suggestions. Alas, I have found it easier to add than subtract at their direction. Next time I promise to be more vigorous with the delete key.

Jasmin Kirkbride of Endeavour personally did the final edits. Her eagle eye captured the final wrinkles in a complex plot and helped me to iron them out!

Finally, I am indebted to my long-suffering children: Nick, Bill, Florence and Simon, and to my partner Mary Seymour, not only for all their many insights and suggestions but also unwavering emotional support during many disappointments which are the inevitable lot of an unpublished author.

Thank you all. Really.

ENDEAVOUR PRESS

If you enjoyed *Trading Down* by Stephen Norman, please share your thoughts on Amazon by leaving a review.

You can also follow Endeavour Press on Twitter and Instagram.

For more free and discounted eBooks every week, sign up to our newsletter.